Woe! Woe!
Thou hast it destroyed,
The beautiful world,
With powerful fist:
In ruin 'tis hurled,
By the blow of a demigod shattered!

—Goethe, *Faust*
(Bayard Taylor translation)

The World Asunder

Ian Wallace

DAW BOOKS, INC.

DONALD A. WOLLHEIM, PUBLISHER

1301 Avenue of the Americas
New York, N. Y.   10019

Published by
THE NEW AMERICAN LIBRARY
OF CANADA LIMITED

Novels by Ian Wallace (with dates of eras)

Adventures of Minds-in-Bodies:
   EVERY CRAZY WIND (1948)
   THE WORLD ASUNDER (1952 and other eras)
   PAN SAGITTARIUS (2509 and prior eras)

The Croyd Spacetime Maneuvers:
   CROYD (2496)
   DR. ORPHEUS (2502)
   A VOYAGE TO DARI (2506)

The St. Cyr Interplanetary Detective Mysteries:
   THE PURLOINED PRINCE (2470)
   DEATHSTAR VOYAGE (2475)
   THE SIGN OF THE MUTE MEDUSA (2480)

Dedicated Conjointly
to CARL JUNG, D. H. LAWRENCE,
and ALFRED NORTH WHITEHEAD

First Printing, November 1976

1 2 3 4 5 6 7 8 9

PRINTED IN CANADA
COVER PRINTED IN U.S.A.

Order of Business

Kali. (Hinduism) A goddess personifying creation and destruction . . .

—*The Random House Dictionary of the English Language,* 1966

". . . The deity (Kali) is portrayed . . . by a black figure with gaping mouth and protruding tongue, adorned with snakes and dancing upon a corpse; her earrings are dead men, her necklace is a string of skulls, her face and breasts are smeared with blood. For Kali-Parvati is the goddess of motherhood as well as the bride of destruction and death . . ."

—Will Durant, *Our Oriental Heritage,* page 509

AUTHOR'S FOREWORD

How does the author classify *The World Asunder?*

Perhaps, from several viewpoints it is science fantasy. The partial science called psychology is extrapolated from, there is intertime-play with some time-speculation, and the tale often turns on techniques which are moderately or extravagantly futuristic in their elaboration yet which, for the most part, are budding or beginning to bloom in our time.

Perhaps it is a detective mystery (but without a murder). In the tale, a good deal of attention is given to responsible mental flounderings in search of solution to an enigma which transcends ordinary reason, and one of the two leading men is a detective.

Or, does it have elements of itinerant romance? For sure, the story savors the route as much as it savors the destination, and pleasantries of geographical and intersexual exploration and local color take more space than a late-on space-time foray does.

Could it also be a novel of diplomatic intrigue, in view of the REM Device and RP deftnesses and Kali machinations, with international rivalries a lethally major concern?

Or could it be a meditative morality play, having psychotheological implications, with mental fantasies and time-space-body changes-and-materializations in place of conventional gods and demons and monsters, and with a satanic force obscurely in the background?

Any such classification would be to assign *The World Asunder* to some limited genre. In the author's mind, it is just this novel utilizing this kind of scope; and in the process, the author's main concerns are Dio, Lilith, Rourke, Esther, the RP Fleet, and the soul-nature of Kali.

Two considerations should be made explicit. One is the responses of different kinds of intelligent people confronted

7

by absolutely impossible situations. On page 124, Rourke
Mallory says, "I respect every instance of Man performing at
the highest ability-level that he can possibly evoke." The
other is the degree to which a human mind may be split into
two totally unrelated minds. I have gone quite a distance in
the development of each of these two considerations, ex-
aggerating the latter into an actual materialization.

If some aspects of the story strike some as being male-
chauvinistic, I have no apology: no propaganda is intended
—these are *these* men and *these* women. And nowhere is
any ethnic satire intended, herein or anywhere in my life and
work: my abiding concern is with human universality deliciously enhanced by its individual and cultural variations.

I have never met or known of anybody anywhere any-
when having the name, appearance, personality, or situa-
tional complications of any character in *The World Asunder*.
All are completely author-fictions, as are Pic Dentelé and
Mont Veillac.

The twice-appearing line "Oh, God, no," is out of James
Branch Cabell's *Figures of Earth*. If the word "hell" keeps
creeping in, it is probably appropriate; one notes an equal
frequency of "blessèd."

                                            Ian Wallace

Western North Carolina, 1975

PROLOG

My wife Lilith Vogel Glazer was inadvertently shot dead by a young fanatic in 1975. Twelve years later, kicked upstairs to the status of rabbi emeritus of our temple, I departed American shores for study and travel. My flagging energies in 1992 led me to settle finally in a small apartment in southern Spain, for rest and meditation in the land where Maimonides and Spinoza labored and meditated. Nearby nuns take good care of me.

One outcome of my own meditation was my decision to publish this frank memoir by Lilith. Our children and I have agreed on this, knowing that most of her contemporaries and mine are now either objective enough to read it without malice, or weak enough not to read it, or dead enough not to care; a generation ago, many of them would have been scandalized by its mix of modes: realism and outrageous fantasy and humor and intensely personal candor.

Lil wrote it for my private perusal, after we'd been married about five years and Lil was thirty-six while I was forty-four. I'll get to the circumstances of the writing in a moment; but first I should tell you a bit about Lilith.

Her German Lutheran father, appreciating that his own surname Vogel would belong to his daughter perforce, graciously allowed her German Jewish mother to choose her given name; and her mother, whose humor could be as rich as her tenderness, named her Lilith; so of course she became Lil Vogel except among those who were discerning enough to appreciate Lilith.

She loved her parents as happily-intensely as they loved her and each other, and laughed with them deliciously, and honored their intellectually liberal raising of her. She became a clinical psychologist, which is not unusual for Jews

9

who honor deep study and grasp enough of their heritage to become soul-conscious; but somehow she missed becoming either introspective or paranoid, maybe because her parents so loved each other and were so merry-warm. The parents died together in an Allegheny Mountains plane crash in 1945, he at fifty, she at forty-six. Mourning but all business, Lilith had them *both* embalmed because that would pleasantly shock her Jew-respecting father while amusing her liberal mother, and saw to it that their funeral service was partly Low-Church Lutheran and partly reformed Jewish, and buried both of them together in a reformed Jewish cemetery because her religiously social mother would have preferred it while her resurrection-minded father wouldn't have cared.

The central time-scene of this memoir is seven years later, in 1952, although there are broad sweepings into other eras past and future.

Subsequent to the events of this memoir, and after a decade of psychological practice, at thirty-one Lilith found and married a nice Jewish boy: me. I was thirty-nine and the rabbi of a small reformed temple. Earth's population problems being what they were, we agreed on having just two children; but we had them fast, our ages being what they were, and the first was a girl, whom we named Rebecca, and the second a boy, whom we named David. (Better, we opined as a matter of team-taste, than Sheila and Irving.) Lightly I suggested that, being between us one-quarter Gentile, we should have two more and name them Joseph and Mary; but Lilith *took* it lightly, blessèd be He and she!

We had married mutually open-eyed: each of us knew that the other had known a few other-sex types; so fine; the big thing for both of us was, no serious consequences overhanging, and we loved each other enough to marry and stay that way. Sure, one of hers had been a heartbreak and a more recent one had been a soul-expanding-and-curdling power-house (both appear in the memoir), and a couple of mine had been mighty potent women; okay, great, that makes for maturity going in.

We wouldn't have gotten into intent discussion about any of that, except for a thing. One day when the kids were two and three years old, Lilith was playing with them, and all of a sudden she had a thought and got Jewish-mother panicky although she hid it.

Later that evening, she asked, "Ben—what is Satan?"

I pipe-puffed; then: "Some call him Lucifer and some Sathanas; and there is evidence that the idea may have originated with the Egyptian god Set, who, by the way, was as much Great and Good Friend as he was Adversary—"

"Shut up, I know all that. Tell me what he *is*."

Knowing that she was serious, I laid down my own copy of Gustave Glotz's *The Aegean Civilization* and studied her carefully. "Speaking as a theologian," I remarked, "I don't think I can tell you a thing you haven't theorized yourself. Speaking as a semi-psychologist, I *know* I can't. Now tell me why you ask."

She blurted, "I may have known one of his avatars. And I worry about the kids."

"Why the kids?"

"If I'm right about this, Ben, I think that Satan is a personification of compulsive paranoid wildness when it separates itself from all the balancing soul-ingredients. And some of that is in all of us."

"So?" I wasn't baiting, I was waiting.

"If I'm right, Satan would be potentially universal, wouldn't he? For all people—in all eras?"

I probed, "You said you thought you'd known him once. Want to talk about that?"

She thought about the possibility. She was terrified by one memory-assessment: *his* sense of humor had been sardonic, complicated, cosmic. . . .

Presently she frowned. "It would be awfully complex for talking. I—think I'd better try to write it out. Would you read it?"

"With great care," I assured her; and I meant it. Then I leaned forward in my chair toward her in her facing chair, and I took her wrist. "Go ahead and write it, Lilith. Don't be afraid if you personify Satan. It's fashionable among rationalists to scoff at personified evil—but it just may be that they haven't stated the problem right. Only, Lil—don't hurry the writing, do bits of it when you've nothing better to do. Anything compulsive might—call up Satan, if your analysis is right."

She gazed at me soberly. "Please, Rabbi, pray for our kids. Pray for *all* kids."

Just as soberly, I nodded. Then I grinned: "Assez de Glotz et Sathanas—un peu de gin rummy."

I saw no fragments. Two years later, she brought me the full manuscript. Despite the scrawl (well known to me) and the interlinings (frequent), I skimmed through all of it that night, then reread it twice during a three-week period, before I commented. Never mind our discussions: they were comprehensive, comprehending, and loving.

By mutual agreement, we then forgot it for a decade. By the time the decade was out, I had forgotten it completely, except during an occasional reverie when the memory never quite sparked me to unearth it.

In 1975, when the kids were nineteen and twenty, a paranoid youngster in our big-city temple jumped up while I was reading Scripture and yelled something about "Accursèd myth-huckster for the Establishment!" and aimed a pistol at me. By chance, Lil sat two rows in front of him and in his line of fire; and she leaped to her feet and turned and spread her arms just as he triggered. She took my bullet between her eyes.

Hours later, dying, she uttered, "Ben—publish the memoir."

It has taken me two decades to make up my mind. But I keep brooding over the disasters of this century: two world wars, Nazism and Jew-genocide, cold-core Communism, Korea, Mid-East intra-Semitic confrontation with both sides equally right and wrong, Vietnam, mindless youth-rebellion, dope-pushing, mindless white-black polarization with extremisms hotting-up both sides, rising crime which is often intrafamilial, even the insanity of inflation during economic recession. . . . Having been away from the United States most of the time since 1987, I've somewhat lost track of local developments there; but when I left, it seemed to me that we were still a long way from the settling-in of new order.

What keeps nagging at me is that when you analyze the men and women or the guys and chicks who power and steer all the extremisms local, national, international, interreligious, interwhatever, you keep finding the same personality-dynamic: compulsive-wild paranoid egotism self-separated from all balancing soul-ingredients, regardless how suave and charismatic the operator may be. And that was Lil's formula for Satan.

Lil didn't put the following into her memoir, perhaps because she didn't want to (using her idiom) louse it up with moralizing; so I will say it for her right here, speaking to atheists and agnostics as well as to people of diversified religions. Stay with your god or your dream, whoever he or she or it may be; and helpfully hold hands with people.

My Lilith lived and spoke and wrote with gusto, with intelligence, with deep human feeling disguised by the appearance of a casual toss-off approach. She lived fully, and her 1952 memoir to me was candid about this, and I pass it along to every reader without editing. If Satan is what Lilith thought he is, then Lilith was able to stay clean of him—and yet she knew him, deeply and perceptively; and she knew the often subtle difference between those who have been touched but not captivated by him and those who have allowed him to master them.

My wife chose to write her memoir in straight chronological order, although this necessitated some inter-era alternations. Consequently it thinks and talks and travels and moves through a series of illusions while quest-intensity mounts; but the slowly drawn bowstring doesn't twang until past midstory. A reader who hasn't taken time to comprehend the string-draw won't get full value out of the twang.

Her memoir my personal bias finds to be a good story. Credulity is sometimes strained by time-shifts and materializations and mind-blowing technology; yet, science being still the uncertain science that it is, I have to accept her honest report of her own experience. Meanwhile, my objective judgment is that certain underlying universalities in the memoir require to be exhibited for meditation. If necessarily there are some self-unveilings, the focus of these is never egotistically Lilith herself; rather, she is always being a responsive medium for self-revelation by somebody else. May she bless me for finally publishing.

Benjamin Glazer

Málaga, 1994

Part One

JUNE 1952

America's insistence on fighting a no-win war in Korea is many-ways ironical. I will name three ways. First, it is a limited war because America wishes to avoid involving China, and therefore Russia, which may attack with atomic bombs; but in fact, Russia has only the beginnings of atomic bombs with no massive means of delivering them for several years at least; and meanwhile Russia so fears China that Russia would welcome an American-Chinese imbroglio and would stand passively-gleefully by. Second, though no Amercan even in high places seems to be noticing this, we are on the verge of perfecting a hydrogen bomb which will make mere atom bombs look like containable block-busters. Third, precisely the prolongation of a no-win war is not only multiplying misery for both sides but is even intensifying the world's polarity, so that the ultimate explosion will be all the more terrible.

And this is only 1952, with technology racing ahead so fast that today's ten-year advance equals prior advances during half a thousand years! We need to wipe out this local complication quickly, and start working in a long-range way against infinitely more terrible potentials fifty years from now —if we live so long.

—Neocassandra in *The Progressive Conservative,* 1952

1.

You can carry a torch for a man just about so long, and then you have to face reality and kiss off his image. This I did; and afterward, the doctoral work in psychology proceeded just fine, and temperately I managed enough selective and transient love-life to distract me from that particular man-image and keep my gonads quiet for serious work. Degree-equipped, I eschewed several institutional offers (I'd done time in the very best of all such institutions, and my now-quenched torch had been kindled there) and invaded Manhattan to open a private practice as a personal consultant. With pride, in my semi-seedy corridor, I studied my new gold-leaf door-sign: LILITH VOGEL, Ph.D. But I was realistic enough to forget the sign and start subtly drumming up business.

Ben, you are witnessing the start of a hell of an experience.

Before long, somehow I became involved in police consultation: it was a sustainer, and devilish interesting. That was how I happened to meet Detective-Inspector Diodoro Horse; and before long we were Dio and Lil in private, although strictly on a congenial business-acquaintance basis. Dio was a swarthy little Arizona Indian crowding forty—he'd come up fast on brains, grit, fortitude, and interminable hours; his face was as thin-wiry as his figure, his eyes were a mite too close together, his personality was high-voltage, and his small mouth had buck teeth which he kept sheathing with his thin lips but which broke hard-out of those lips in moments of arousal or amusement. He was married to a religiously unaffiiliated Jew-by-birth named Esther; they lived childless not far from my office in a second-floor apartment; and it was a matter of interest to Dio that Esther and I faintly resembled each other. She was under thirty. Once I

17

pressed him for details of our resemblances and differences, and it interested me that this detective with a photographic memory and trained in facial description was vague about Esther's appearance. He could say that like me she was no taller than he and rather dark and "not bad, not bad at all"; but it seemed that her eyes were a bit closer together than mine (which are a silly little millimeter too far apart), and her mouth a bit smaller and fuller than mine and not quite so easily grinnable but (how would he know?) capable of being more passionate. . . .

As time went on, I beefed up my incomes from private practice and police work by late-afternoon lecturing in undergraduate psychology; my class was located in a nearby high school, but the people were college students and mostly adults, varying in age from eighteen to fiftyish. Along about the sixth week, this being a ranging survey course, I got into police psychology; and it crossed my mind to get Dio to guest-lecture one late afternoon on the realities of police work. Dio bought it—and the story really begins here.

I remember the date well: it was my twenty-eighth birthday, June 16, 1952. Korea was grinding in agony, and the cold war with Russia was gelid; but I was career-drawn-and-driven, and I was conscious only of immediate concerns.

For convenience, I was to meet Dio in front of his apartment building, which was only a few hundred yards from my office with the high school only a half-mile farther on. Approaching his place, I found that I was a bit early: he had wanted to run upstairs first, touch base with his Esther, and then meet me here below. I paused maybe a hundred feet on my side of his building-entrance, saw him approaching from the subway station beyond, waved at him

and jerked my head upward at a chilling woman-scream from above. Flames flared out of a second-story window; and on a balcony in front of the flames a woman crowded her body outward against the iron railing, seared from behind. My paroxysmal sense was: *That woman is ME*. . . . Having run forward a few futile steps, I saw equally agonized Dio running toward me gazing upward

A man materialized between Dio and me just under the flaming balcony. Dio, nearly on him, braked and stared—and froze; I, patterning on a monstrosity, froze also. Inexplicably for a few moments I *was* Dio, gaping at the small flame-haired hero—and he was *my* torch-man; and he was smiling alert, commanding the action. His right hand flicked forward, and out of his jacket-sleeve a tangled skein of slender golden cord tumbled onto the sidewalk; the cord erected itself like a fakir-charmed cobra, snaked goldenly upward-aloft; its head paused undulant in front of the screaming-woman balcony. Leaping for his cord, the redhead hand-caught it a yard above his head and hand-over-hand scurried upward until he clung swaying in front of the balcony, one-hand-clinging, extending the other hand for the woman, who was now silent in everywhere-silence. Now I *was* that woman, back-roasted by flame-roar, high terror hope-diminished, facing the inviting face of my red-haired rescuer: obediently she/I extended a small right hand, clasping *his* wiry wrist while his wiry fingers clasped her/my wrist; she/I made a tiny leap and was elastically swung over the rail against *his* tough small body; her/my legs came up and locked around his hips, his hand in a lightning motion let go her/my hand and clasped her/my waist . . .

I came back into myself, Lil the electrified watcher, as the skyborne man and woman and their rope vanished and the flames died.

Maybe ten seconds I gaped upward at nothing. *Nothing* —except a balcony off a second-floor apartment. No flames. No woman. Nothing.

My eyes came down to Dio: he was rigid in stupefaction, face upward. He cursed a foulness and ran for the door and vanished. I waited below, unwilling to follow uninvited.

He appeared above me on the balcony, staring down but not seeing me, staring up, staring down and around. . . . And certainly I was in no shape to think straight: the woman above had been *me,* and the red-haired man had been a smaller but facially identical version of *my* long-lost man. . . . Aa! how my weak knees yearned for an easy chair on the sidewalk. . . .

Out of the street door stalked Detective-Inspector Diodoro Horse. By now I had my head on fairly straight, and I grieved for him: the woman *had* been his Esther. . . . Abruptly my head came loose again: but the rope-trick and the fire had been hallucination— Me? hallucinating? On the porch six steps above the sidewalk, Dio stared down at me, shook his head once, stumped down toward me. I came toward him. We halted facing each other, mutually awkward with the unprecedented kind of awkwardness that is two common-sense humans who have startlingly hallucinated the same imagery together.

He said, talking to the pavement, "I saw my wife up on that balcony threatened by fire. I saw a little red-headed guy go up a rope and snatch her into the sky. Lil, I'm sick."

I said, not professional, just appalled woman: "I'm sick too, Dio. I saw the same things."

We both stared at the sidewalk.

Our heads came up slowly. We stared at each other—we were equally tall or short, our eyes were level-on. His teeth were sheathed.

I ventured, "How about—up there, in there?"

He wet thin lips. "Nothing wrong, up there. All normal. No sign of fire."

"Was—Esther there?"

He shook his head apathetically. "No, but that doesn't mean anything. She—goes a lot. She should be back in time for supper—"

Pulling control back in gradually, I checked my wrist-watch. It was tough to say, but— "Dio, we're almost late for class. Do you—"

He came up erect, bristlingly erect. I grabbed his arm, and we plodded toward the high school.

After the lecture—he had performed brilliantly for an hour—we met in the corridor; and as soon as we could break away from passing students touching skin with both of us, he said brittle, "Lil, don't comment now, I have this overwhelming urge to call home." Natch. Feeling fire-chill, I took him down the corridor to the deserted office and plumped him down in front of a phone and went out into the corridor.

Out stumped Dio. "No answer."

I swung on him. "Want to go home?"

"No point," he muttered, eyebrows hard down. "I have to tell you, Lil: sometimes she doesn't come home for supper."

It was five-thirty, and he was a good friend in trouble. I grabbed his upper arms. "How early do you start drinking?"

The first drink-round, at a quietly secluded table in a dim small luxurious Fifty-second Street place, conjured up something approaching ease, and it certainly promoted congeniality and unobtrusive candor. At first we carefully avoided the hallucination-subject. I went professional, just a little: to draw him out, I confessed that some adolescent sex hang-ups had led me into psychology (which was a lie, my adolescence having been cheerfully virginal necking-great). "No hang-ups now," quickly I added, "but I remain selective." That drew a wry smile from him; and he ventured to tell me that he was a long way from being a Casanova although he'd known a couple of dames before Esther; but meeting and winning Esther had been sheer luck, he didn't think he deserved her. . . .

I blurted, "That's always bullshit." When that galvanized him erect with culture-shock, I added more delicately, "I mean, man and woman are both humans, aren't they? Don't both of us have to slog at living? don't both of us have sex-itches? Sorry, Dio, but I have no patience with the woman-on-a-pedestal kick."

He looked at me sharply, like back at his office on a case. "Tell me what *your* hallucination was."

It shriveled me. Presently I told what was left of my Tanqueray martini: "I saw your lost love being raped-away on a rope by the guy I've been carrying a torch for since nineteen forty-eight."

Silence. Then Dio: "Oboy." And he signaled for more drinks.

The second one did fine for us. From me he learned that my guy had been named Burk Halloran, that he had looked exactly like the rope-trick guy except that Burk had been more on the tall side, that he had been transiently psychotic, that I had drawn him back into self-confidence, that immediately I had run away hoping that he would cure himself and come looking for me, that he had cured himself but hadn't come looking for me. From Dio I learned that he had met Esther when he was an army major and she was a Wac in World War II France, that at first their married life had been decently happy, that in due course she had had to face the reality of his energetic career-orientation while he had had to cope with her increasing discontentment, that his own unreliability with reference to coming home in time for supper or even before morning had seemed to set Esther equally into unscheduled prowling but not on any sort of duty—and that he had never before laid eyes on the illusion-redhead.

I wanted to know, "Have you ever had it out with Esther?"

Seeing an ambiguity, I grinned and emended, "I mean, have you two ever talked out your problems?"

He nodded at the remnant of his second Beefeater. "Real good conversations. Only, they ended up nowhere."

He looked up, strained. "Dr. Vogel, I have to tell you a thing. I am not happy with myself the way I am. I know that's wild, but I wish I were some other kind of guy."

This intimate confession made me most unhappy, and I gazed at him like a—no, not like a mother, but like the mother of a boy's best boy-friend, which is pretty sympathetic and not at all scary. "Tell me what kind of a guy you'd like to be."

"Like that guy we just hallucinated—only, built like your Burk."

I stared. I swallowed.

He added, making all plain: "Not little, and not buck-toothed, and not an Establishment slave. Tall and handsome and able to create my own responsibilities. Could there be such a thing as an Irish-American Pueblo Indian?"

I grinned into my drink. Conquering this compulsive grin along with my compulsive urge to deny his self-belittlement, I suggested, "We have three choices now, Dio. A third round of drinks, or dinner, or both."

He scared me with his directness: "What time is it?"

"About six-thirty. Why?"

"I want to go home, Lil. Whether she's there or not, I want to check out that apartment like a cop this time."

Having considered him, I tossed off my Tanqueray and stood. "Good luck, pal. Don't worry about me, I find my way home real good—"

"You come with me."

"Why?"

"It's *our* hallucination, Lil. We both together saw your man stealing my wife using the Indian rope-trick. Let's go."

"But if she's there—how will it look—"

"She's been wanting to meet you. Let's go."

He dropped four dollars, which then amply covered four drinks and tip in a plush place, and steered me toward the exit.

Esther wasn't there. But— "Look here," Dio crisped, arming aside a drape and pointing to the floor by the window-doors that opened onto the balcony.

There was a little coil of golden thread-rope, and a note

atop the coil. The note said: "Forgive me, Dio. This note constitutes my consent without contest to your petition for divorce. I love you, but I can't handle you when you are impersonal. I'm going with Kali to my favorite place in all the world. *Esther*."

Having read it twice, I wanted to say harsh, "I suppose it hasn't escaped your trained police mind that this note leaves a few questions, like how the divorce court would view the ambiguity about property and alimony?" I didn't say it, because you don't have to be a psychologist to know that this would be a second- or third-day thing to say. And anyhow, some kind of Horse-action was going on. . . .

Still holding the drape back, Dio was staring at the rope. Good God, the rope's end *ascended* a little!

And fell back inert . . .

So did the drape, hiding the rope. Savagely he swung on me: "Did you see that? *I did* it—"

I nodded, numb. This was beyond science as of now.

He blurted, starting for the kitchen, "*Christ* do I need another drink!" He paused at the threshold and turned, "What's your pleasure?" I shook my head, still gin-warm: "Not yet, but go ahead yourself—and watch out for mixes." He vanished.

I knelt, pushed back the drape, fingered the rope. It was just rope. Not even anymore golden.

I arose and turned to discover that he was in a big easy chair with gin-and-tonic and with shoes off, legs outstretched, head back, eyes closed, teeth sheathed.

Uneasily I perched myself on the edge of a sofa facing him, not sure yet what might be asked of me. What does this kind of a guy do with a not-bad lady psychologist in this kind of wife-crisis? Anything, anything at all: like requiring my professional solace, or demanding my female solace, or needing my friendly human solace, or wanting me to go away and leave him alone. Liking Dio very much, I was prepared to grant two of these possible requirements; as for the other two, I would have to handle either as the situation might seem to be developing.

Eyes closed, head back, he brought the drink faultlessly to his mouth and tilted in another ounce of it; whereafter hand and drink came down and hung over the chair-arm. He said tonelessly, "I could kill myself for not finding the rope when I came up here before—but I guess my mood then was, just to verify that all was really well. All right. Now.

Lilith—what did you see me do with that coil of rope, just now?"

Carefully: "I saw you stare at the coil of rope. I then saw the rope's end rise about one foot, and fall back."

"Good scientific reserve. I *did* it, Lilith."

Still cautious, inwardly frigid: "Bully for you."

"Okay. Well. You shared my hallucination out there, and you saw me just now levitating the rope. So neither was a psychotic episode for either of us. I hate the idea, and so do you, but we have to call both episodes reality."

"I—think I need that drink. One part gin, three parts tonic."

"Please do, but would you mind? The bottles are out on the sink, glasses in the cupboard to the left of the fridge." Still his eyes were closed.

So far, all professional. I went into the kitchen—and realized while pouring that the professionalism was *his;* he was Inspector Horse nosing down a trail, and he'd just given me a courteously soft order to take care of myself while he did it. Well, that I was doing; but I was feeling an increasing urge, undoubtedly professional, to take care of him, too.

When I returned, he was seated straight-up in his chair, eyes open, alert; and his drink wasn't gone. "Please sit down," he urged, waving a hand; I did, leaning toward him. "First, relax, Lil; I'm under control now. Second—can you put a name to what I did to the rope?"

"If in fact you did it, we'd call it psychokinesis."

"PK, yes; I remember. Have you studied that?"

"As a cognate only. Actually, my kick is hysterias."

"You mean like people blowing their tops?"

"No, not that. Let me think of a for-instance. Like a guy whose arm gets paralyzed—"

"Because he thinks his arm is guilty of something?"

"Good, very good. That's a dissociation, see? He gets out from under his own guilt by pushing it off on his arm."

"And that's your kick?"

"Well, I'm interested in the more bizarre hysterias. Like dual and even triple and quadruple personalities."

He sighed. "I'd like to pursue this, it's fascinating, but events are pushing my nose against the psychokinesis. Do you psychology-guys have any good theories for phenomena like these? I don't mean vague hypotheses, I mean hard theories about how the phenomena are caused."

Professionally, Dio was becoming increasingly good to

work with. After a thoughtful sip, I responded: "No hard etiological theories. Very good empirical evidence for telepathy, with good rationale for how it might occur. Equally good empirical evidence for clairvoyance, but lousy rationale for it—unless somebody else is visually seeing what the clairvoyant mentally sees, in which case the clairvoyant may be reading the other guy's mind, so it would simply be telopathy. But psychokinesis—amazingly good empirical evidence, and absolutely no rationale whatsoever."

"You've seen other people make a rope go up?"

"Not that—except professional magicians who admit it's a trick. But making dice come up with the wanted number, and stuff like that—yes."

"But the rope-trick would be an extension of that, if it's real."

"So it would seem."

"And they bring it off regularly in India, according to many reports."

"Right."

"Well—I just did it. No question that I did. *How* did I do it?"

Wasn't this guy *ever* going to mention his gone wife? Well, stay with his lead. A counter-question was indicated: "Tell me what you experienced while you were doing it."

He frowned. "I've thought that out, and some related things. The rope part is easy because it isn't much: I stared at it and—fairly *drove* into it my will for it to rise, filling myself with absolute confidence that it *would* rise. And it did. And then suddenly I lost confidence, and it fell back. Does that help us any?"

I shook my head slowly, thinking. Then the big personal question grew too big for containment; and as gently as I could, I demanded, "Why was rope-levitation your first reaction to the news that your wife had left you?"

"It wasn't. My first reaction was that I should suicide, I'd fouled up the last important thing, there wasn't anything left. Then I took some time to steady myself, remembering what I'd always told myself: that if nothing but suicide seemed possible, I should *pretend* suicide and go off somewhere to start a new anonymous life. All right, I said: but what do I *do* with such a life? That was when it came over me that Esther's weird disappearance was only the last and most personal and otherwise most insignificant of a great many today-questions requiring answers, like the interminable heartbreak of Korea and the growing prevalence of crime and commercialized vice and dope and the meaningless intransigence of the cold war with atom bombs in the picture. So whatever else I would do after pretending suicide and going anonymous, I would be going for those answers; and when and if I would finally get them, then I would decide what to do next. Okay, I said, that should hold me for starters; now, what else is meaningful about the situation here? Let's get on the stick, let's find a way to chase Esther, let's find out face-to-face whether she really *means* it! That was when the rope first came into context with Kali's rope-trick, whoever Kali is; and it crossed my mind to try duplicating the redhead's rope-trick, and I guess maybe I was so passionally involved that it *worked*—"

It was my turn to close my eyes. "Esther says Kali. I say Burk Halloran, only smaller."

We both drank.

Having tongue-dried my lips, I observed in delayed surprise, "That's quite a thought-sequence—during approximately fifteen seconds between your reading of her note and your levitation of the rope!"

He smiled wry. "That long? I guess I am too distraught to think quick."

"I think you are some kind of a nose-to-the-grindstone genius."

He rubbed his eyes. "I'll make a confession. They think I have some unique kind of detective-logic, and that's what pushed me up the promotion-line. In fact, I just have hunches. What the hell kind of a genius is that?"

I gazed. "A hunch is an intuition. An intuition is a subconscious patterning of evidence half-noticed. If you have it, God has blessed you: you're a detective-inspector."

He stared at his nearly done drink. "Right or wrong, my intuition is telling me that I have to try to find Esther. This is a compulsion on me, Lil. I'm about to go, do you mind?"

Some of these crises do open up like umbrellas! Putting down my drink on an end table, I inquired, "Where would you start looking?"

He sipped conservatively on the ice-weak lees of his drink, then told me: "Once I've started driving my car, I'm sure I'll know."

I chanced an admonition: "I will put it to you that this is no time for you to be driving. Let me take you to dinner, then come back here and sleep, or rest anyhow. Start in the morning."

Irritated, teeth-sheathed, he shook his head. "Late lunch, not hungry yet. And I can *not* stay here. Lil—"

"Yes, Dio?"

"I shouldn't be alone, I need pro company. Would you—take me to some motel way out of town?"

Well: it was one of the two possibilities that I hadn't been sure about, and it made me reach for my drink again. Having sipped, toying with it I asked it: "Please carry that idea a step or two further."

When I glanced up from my drink, he was grinning, but then he sobered. "Lilith, I am—well, *God* would I love that! But I am *not* going to cheat on Esther until I know the score. Not even if we have to share a room."

Now I was looking at him frankly. He was a type of man I hadn't previously known in any way at all. He had won my liking and confidence, and without question he was one who could delight me; and if it had gone that way, now I knew that I would have been ready; but since it hadn't gone that way, different values were introduced, and maybe, as between us two, they were better. I smiled broadly, and he answered my smile: the way his teeth broke through those lips was enchanting. I said, "I will cling to the belief that I could have won you if I had worked at it."

"I endorse this belief. But I beg you, don't work: I have this thing about Esther, you see—"

"I am as pure as the driven snow, Inspector Horse. We could even share a bed without—"

"No we couldn't."

I, wholly serious now: "All right, I agree that you need a pro companion. Two communicating rooms, then, or twin beds in a pinch." Most earnest, leaning forward: "Dio, that was maybe my torch-man in that fantasy with your Esther! Look, I'm between cases, I can have any calls switched to the office next door—I *have* to go with you!"

He was practically in consternation. "Look, Lil! I'm not talking about just tonight, and I don't know where in hell I'll be going! Good girl: drop me off at a country motel and take my car and go back to—"

"No." In retrospect, it was at once the nicest and the most soul-dangerous "no" I have ever said.

Slamming his drained glass down on a side table, he came to his feet and joined me on the sofa, pressing both

my hands in his hard hands. "Lil Vogel, I do need you with
me—specifically you. For looks, they'll keep me on edge;
for brains, we'll need to pool them; for psychology because
we're both chasing a mutual fantasy—"

Jumping away from me, he went into the bedroom to pack
a minimum of male things. From there he called, "What
about *your* things?" "No sweat," I answered; "I'll sleep in
panties and bra tonight and buy a couple of changes and a
toothbrush tomorrow." His call: "Got the toothbrush—a new
giveaway from an unopened package of toothpaste. Hey—
would you accept Esther's overnight case and night things?
I swear I don't have *that* kind of fetish—"

I hate phony suspense, even in a memoir. Yes, he would
get me, or I him, whichever; but I require you to accept the
truth that neither of us then intended this.

2.

We took his car, a Ford four-door, but he made me drive:
"I want to think," he explained curt. There was liquor in me,
but I popped a restorative pill from my handbag and then it
didn't go badly. We got out of Manhattan (little tunnel
traffic), and he steered me south along the coast. During the
next hour I drove silently and he sat staring at the road; and
there was little conversation, the exceptions mainly being that as we would approach an occasional route-junc-
tion, he would tell me where to turn. Once I complained, "I
thought I was taking you somewhere, but it seems you are
taking me." Abstractedly he mumbled, "I keep having this
draw, I *know* where to go—" By now I had practically
abandoned psychology: this was a sane man who seemed
truly under the stress of external compulsion, and all my
systematic mind was directed to the problem of trying to
find logic in it. Maybe I wouldn't find any: he had said that

he was mainly intuitive. Me, I was mainly logical—and inwardly I chuckled at *that* reversal of sex-lore.

I knew where I was, though, and so did he; and the smell of salt water began to savor the air. I remarked, "This area is lousy with motels, but they'll all be full; any suggestions?" He, still abstracted: "I'll know; keep driving."

In moon-relieved rural darkness, I pulled up at a stop-sign crossroad; all around were scrub woods, and the salt-smell was enhanced by surf-sound. The sensual combination reminded me that it was nine at night and I was ravenous. "Turn?" I queried. "Straight ahead," he ordered. I crossed the intersection, drove into darkness, and abruptly braked at a dead end with nothing but woods in front of us.

Me: "Now what?"

He: "Cut the engine."

I turned the switch: silence. No, not silence; an outside hissing—and the left side of the car slowly settled. I uttered, "I have the sense of a flat tire."

Not at all disturbed, he opened the glove compartment, got a flashlight, exited, and peered the tires around. At my window he reported, "You're half right. *Two* flat tires. Both on the same side."

Positively I asserted, "Can't happen."

"That," he responded, "is to me the interesting part of it, in view of the evening we're having. And look: there's a motel complex, I think." He pointed to my left: through the trees, several white buildings were moon-illuminated; the nearest wasn't a hundred yards away. . . .

A tow truck clanked to a stop behind us, and a rangy middle-aged driver-mechanic climbed out already explaining that business was bad and they were cruising. I got out of the car while Dio was flash-pointing to the flat tires. The driver said, "Open your trunk, I'll put the spare on the front wheel and tow her in, I'm a mile away." I followed Dio while he went around rear and I handed him the keys, and he put one into the trunk lock.

The trunk lid opened, all right. Also there was a whining noise, and the whole body rose up about three feet on some kind of spring extensors.

Having jumped back when the unexpected action started, I was studying the open trunk when I became aware that Dio and the driver were beside the car looking under it. I came around behind them and followed their eyes.

A broad steel tray sat on the chassis, exposed by the elevated auto-body. On the tray lay naked and erotically supine, arms alluringly extended and legs arousingly open, a dark woman whose deep eyes and lush parted lips called for all three of us. . . .

We stared.

The driver said dead, "Don't go away, I'll have to report this."

The woman vanished and was replaced by an open cubical tin box maybe twenty centimeters on a side, packed with weed. Dio said dead, "You mean because of that marijuana?"

The driver, having coughed, shaky-responded, "I must be nuts, I swear I saw a woman there, but she just—dissolved into a box of pot, like in the movies—"

Straightening, Dio gazed at the driver. "While you decide what you're going to report, why don't you change the front wheel?"

The car-body redescended onto the chassis, concealing the tray and the box; the trunk remained open.

Muttering, the driver shrugged big and went for the trunk. Dio grabbed the two small bags out of the rear seat and steered me into the woods toward the motel. We walked mostly in silence; but at one point he muttered, "That was Esther"; and it came into me that his Esther *did* look rather like me, only maybe softer and more appealing; and then it came into me that Dio and I had shared another illusion, and that this time a third party had shared it.

This motel was called Fishermen's Cove, and it was really a picturesque inn with a big parking lot hidden by shrubs and trees, and it sat ripple-slappingly on one quay of an actual fishermen's cove with good-sized fish-worn cabin-boats tied up: we could see all that in moonlight over ten o'clock dinner by bringing our faces close to the glass to screen off the dim interior lighting. Mostly, though, we attended to shoving in food: for both of us, rare prime ribs and Chateauneuf du Pape. *Faute de mieux,* we'd accepted the best accommodations offered by the inn, although we hadn't seen them yet: communicating chambers, yes, but the large vaulted lower chamber *containing* the upper chamber, which was a penthouse-platform swinging overhead. Who would sleep where we'd decide when we got there.

Still pretty tense, we found that the only possible topics for conversation were our illusions and our past love-lives, both of us understanding that the latter must have bearing on the former. We disposed of the love-questions with rather neat dispatch: each of us dropped a few facts, leaving the other to infer a lot.

His Esther had been young-passionate in 1945; and although Dio deposed that he was a long way from being either physically or psychically deficient in that area, he did have this thing about his careers (first army, then police) with their irregular hours and wearying demands, and during the past year Esther had been relatively aloof and had strayed a lot. How long had they been married? Five years, just over, but they'd cohabited during two prior years. "I'd guess," remarked Dio, "that even before this Kali, she'd found a lover or two. I haven't been jealous, but I've worried, and the uncertainty has been worrisome." He left it there for then, and so did I.

He was looking at me with expectation of reciprocity, and I felt obliged to give about my torch-man; but I kept it concise, not spilling a lot. Burk Halloran in 1948 had been a patient in the plush rest-home where I had worked for a couple of years as a staff psychologist. He was a handsomely, impishly graceful Irish-American in his early thirties, with a sense of humor that was bizarre and devious—"quite capable," I inserted, "of concocting every cockeyed illusion that we've seen tonight, if he'd had the power, just for the sport of it." Burk amazingly blended activeness and profoundly penetrating intellectuality. I had fallen in love with him and had rather intimately helped him through a major crisis; and then I had flown the coop, which might have been dangerous for Halloran except that I had tipped off his psychiatrist before departing. After initial depression, Burk had made steady progress and was discharged half a year later. "Cured?" I had stupidly demanded on the phone. "Vogel, Vogel," the doctor had clucked, "we *never* say that." Whereafter I had rested relatively easy on a working assumption that Burk had risen to the kind of temperate instability which makes for success and even for genius. And some while ago, I had kissed off the crazy romantic hope that he might come hunting for me. . . .

A Dio-hand came across the table to take my hand. His hand and his voice were warm and gentle: "Excuse the egotistical interruption, but I've about decided that Esther *wants* me to come hunting for her. Do you think?"

My other hand went on top of his, and I told him positively, "I am sure of it, and it isn't just a hunch: I saw evidence."

Our hands were together an instant longer, and then he pulled back his hand, and sheathed teeth. "You mean that glaring loophole in her note—she gives me carte blanche to get a divorce but signs no renunciation of property rights or alimony? Just in case you're wondering, Esther is bright enough to know about that—but maybe she left in a hurry, she didn't think—"

"She was thinking clearly enough to leave the note on top of a rope that looked exactly like the one her phantom abductor used in the rope-trick."

His fist began rhythmically and noiselessly pounding the table-top. His hands were small and wiry with long fingers; he used his hands a lot when he was talking. He squeezed out: "You are giving credence to the illusion that some red-head really stole her up out of the apartment into the sky."

I frowned, shaking my head. "I've been thinking a lot about that. Tell me one thing: are you obsessively afraid of fire?"

"My mother was burned to death when our shack caught fire. I was thirteen. She was a widow, or something."

What do you say to a thing like that? Well, it depends on the guy and the situation; this was Dio, and it was right here, and I decided on a few seconds of thoughtful silence, after which I moved on. "Look, this is mere spinning, but it's the best I can do for starters. Esther ran away from you, leaving a note—and I am certain she was hinting that she wanted you to follow if you would. We'll accept her statement that she was leaving with some man named Kali. When you and I neared your apartment just ahead of four o'clock, you had a—now I *have* to bring ESP into it—you had a telepathic sense of this disaster, and it objectified itself as this illusion."

"I get it. The flames were how my fire-haunted subconscious projected the feeling of disaster."

"Right."

"Why the rope-trick in the illusion?"

Me, glib: "Your intuition of the rope that was under her note."

"Then why was there a rope under her note?"

I studied the Hennessey that I was finishing off with.

He added, "And why did you see it all too?"

I looked up, almost smiling. "That I have figured. I think you're one of those guys who broadcast your psychic crises real loud, and I picked it up telepathically. Which may mean electroencephalographically, for all I know—"

"And why did her abductor turn out to be *your* redhead, whom I'd never met or heard about? And why does his name seem to be, not Halloran, but Kali?"

I swallowed air, sipped and swallowed cognac, tried to save it: "When I picked up your illusion, I put my redhead into it, and you—picked it up from me?"

He was totally somber. "I won't dignify that with a comment. I will instead introduce the triple-objective evidence of my misbehaving car and a phantom of my Esther, who instantly was transformed into a box of pot. And I will tell you what I am almost ready to believe, after rejecting all the material common-sense possibilities that I can think of. I am about to think that some guy somewhere, with enormous transpsychic power and a twisted sense of humor, is playing games with us by projecting illusions into both of us and in one case three of us. What do you think of that?"

What I was thinking was ultimately dismal; but with difficulty I forced a twisted smile—he had to be the one to say it. "You are an obviously sane detective-inspector, and I have to listen with respect. Go ahead."

He did, instantly. "I suggest that this guy Kali really resembles your redhead; and in view of your psychic description of Burk Halloran, including his exotic sense of humor, Kali may *be* Halloran."

I bit: "Then he shrank!"

Dio countered: "We saw merely his projected hallucination of himself, and I may have projected my own shortness into the hallucination, and you picked up that ingredient from me. . . . Okay, that's far-fetched; no matter, I'll go on. I am suggesting that Kali seduced and stole my Esther, but first he and she plotted out the method together, which accounts for the coincidence of the rope-trick illusion and the rope under the note; and if Kali is in fact your Halloran, that would account for you being brought in on the illusioning.

"No, wait, there's more. If she wants me to follow her, for some wild reason so does *he,* or he wouldn't have let me see him and he wouldn't have jacked me up just now with the car-acrobatics. And he also wants *you* to follow him, which is why he let *you* see him. Now, here's the next thing: sit tight, Lilith. He wants us *here* tonight: he made sure we'd stop here by flattening not one but two of my tires, unilaterally."

After meditation, I decided that a sip of cognac was in order; I picked up the glass, but my hand was trembling so horribly that I put it down.

Dio gestured for the check, and both of his hands took both of mine. "We'll forget it," he told me, "unless he reminds us again tonight. I had a bottle of Black Label sent up to our room—"

That was when I damn near lost control. Black Label had been Burk's drink.

3.

—————◆—————

We surveyed our room. It was vast and luxurious; and ten feet above us hung on four corner-chains the penthouse-platform, and above that the ceiling beam-vaulted maybe another fourteen feet. Leading from floor to upper platform was a sort of companionway with wrought-iron rails. The two beds on the main floor were both double. Our two bags had been set unopened upright in front of a luggage-counter: the bellman, leading from nothing, had left all decisions to us.

I murmured, "Cost?" Dio throated, "Expense account."

A notion was haunting me: that if *he*, Kali or Halloran or whoever, had used the automobile tricks to make sure that we would stop here, then he planned to strike again here. Looking at Dio, I caught no telepathy, but I intuited that he anticipated the same. No telling how or when, though; so I brushed it away, putting my alertness on low idle.

Exploring, we mounted the companionway, with him behind-below me: if he liked my legs, what the hell, I was pantied. At the top we found a smaller version of the same luxury, including twin single beds. Around the platform's edge there was a waist-high railing; somehow, it seemed inadequate. I giggled suddenly: up here was where they had put the Scotch and glasses and ice, with four ten-ounce bottles of soda and a pewter pitcher of water.

"Your pleasure?" queried Dio.

"Your intuition," I countered, on guard.

"It tells me," he declared, "to bunk up here, I don't know why. And I'll mention again that I really meant it about fidelity: look, I don't *know* that Esther is with a man. So you're welcome up here in the other bed, or you're welcome alone below. Again—your pleasure?"

The question was a tuffie: tonight's hazards were creating a need for a strong man nearby, and I hadn't known any man's strength for months, and none of the three men since Burk had come within miles of the Horse-strength; and then, too, maybe he needed me a little—just for nearby company, I meant. Nevertheless: "I'd better bunk below."

"Very wise. Hey, up here there's no biffy—"

"Call me greetings whenever you come down and go past. Just now, it's your honor—"

Tossing me a soft salute, he descended, and I went down above him. When a few minutes later he emerged, he suggested, "When we're all undressed, how about joining me up there for a nightcap?"

"*All* undressed?"

"I brought me a bathrobe."

"Good. Wear it." I hit the biffy.

Dio had taken his bag up with him; he now opened it on one of the beds and undressed and got into pajamas and bathrobe and slippers. Then he went to the liquor table and iced two glasses and liquored them and added water to his— he wasn't sure about my taste in Scotch mixes. Whereafter he called, "Ready when you are." And he sat on his turned-down bed facing the companionway and cheated a little with his drink. "Soon," he heard me respond; and the lights dimmed, presumably via a rheostat which I was controlling below.

I am about to report what was wholly subjective to Dio; and as we move along, I will be reporting other alien subjectivities. I do so authentically: I did myself co-experience these private experiencings, either at the same time as with Dio now, or later in the course of systematic dreamings. Why or how I can't tell you yet; I am still trying to work out the etiology. . . .

Sipping, Dio became aware that he wanted me, and immediately he made another positive decision not to go for me. This was just good companionship; keep it that way.

His platform quivered a bit: perhaps I was starting to mount.

The entire room-area went dark, oppressively black, sightless.

Alarm-rigidified, by feel he noiselessly set down his drink on the between-beds table and sat action-ready. The quivering continued, and irrationally his heart went into triphammer drive while his hand-palms and foot-soles cold-sweated in the classic autonomics of abject fear, and all this made no sense because regularly on duty in death-peril he was carried through by normal temperature and pulse. Instinct said *freeze;* nevertheless he slipped off the bed and got down on all fours and felt his way in what he thought might be the companionway-direction, intending to help me if it was I

and faced,
over the edge, the same redhead only not smiling but instead soul-grippingly fear-miasmic like phosphorescent death-alive

He hoarsed, "Ultimate good-power, grant me *counter-power—*" Strangle-screaming, he faced the Kali-face, felt the basilisk-blue eyes defeating him, stayed on them, mentally *fought* them

while the platform under him rocketed roof-crashing upward into meaningless night headed for cosmic depths untenanted by stars.

4.

———◆———

Dio had no orientation and couldn't even be sure what orientation *meant* but was thrusting for directions and meanings in desperate tattered ways illogically unsequential and made lurid by his own emotional extravagance, which was a growing meld of hideous anger and draining terror

like he
was driving down a nameless highway alone in an open car
in hot bright sunlight, both hands wheel-gripping, enraged
head jerking from side to side, heedless of zany speed-risk,
charging to get Kali and kill him and rescue Esther.

and smoke-tired
to a halt in front of a spacious-gracious late-medieval French
chateau, and leaped from the car and charged up the green-
lawn while from the Blois-castle with the exterior spiral
staircase toward him floated in a baroque low-cut gown his
Esther. He seized her bare shoulders and rat-shook her,
snarling, "Hate me, Esther, this ravishment is not love, it is
revenge!" He wrestled her to the grass; she hardly resisted,
she looked up at him in wonder as though she comprehended
the justice of this; but she dissolved into nothing, and he lay
on grass gnawing grass and hearing her somewhere whisper,
"At least, you are *trying*—" while he drifted into

total lostness on
an infinite moor that was featureless except for sparse gray
grass and drifting with vague gray haze. He was on his feet,
there was a way to go but he didn't know which way it was.
He cried silently to *something* for help, unable to articulate
a word or a name; the moor was endless, the mist-drift
brokenly continuous. He knew cloudily that he had been
wronged and therefore irrationally had done a wrong, but
there were in his memory no events or faces or names. He
did what he had often done in dreams: closed his eyes and
waited for one of two things—direction-sense, or a change.
Opening eyes, he found no sense; but he started in *a* direction,
indistinguishable from any other direction but defined by the
fact of his moving that way, with the aimless purpose of an
Ouija. His plodding went on and on timelessly, with no sense
of gain and no sense of what there *might be* to gain

gradually,
with the clammy mist insettled and wholly befogging him, it
came into him that walking was more difficult now, each
forward step slower and draining him more. Presently walking
grew so difficult that his urge was to go back; and just for a
few steps he did retreat backward, finding it easier going
backward; and then for further testing he moved a few
sideward steps to the left and then to the right, and found
both lateral directions easier; so he was laboring up some
slope, and the temptation was mighty to yield to gravity and

turn downward. But a question came into him: "What is around and behind me? Nothing but easy directionless meaninglessness." Decision: forward was most difficult—and that made it a kind of *direction*. So he labored forward-upward again—except that from forward-above he was faceblown-chestblown by inchoate chill entailing conviction that if he would keep going forward-upward he would meet Kali the Enemy. So then, of course, there was no way to go except forward-upward

and a time came when he knew that he had passed through the locus of the Kali-miasma, for he was free of it, except that he felt it behind him, cold-breathing him forward. His head emerged above the fog-stratum, and he saw the fog below his eyes like a cloud-top with him emerging out of it and his legs invisible in it. But at last he was all free; and lo, he was moving up a steeply sloping crooked trail rugged with sharp rock-outcrops; and it came into him that if he would persist up the trail, he would come finally to the Blue Flame, and that was good

so he labored up the trail in the clarity of black night, with all about him moon-illumined except that there was no moon nor were there stars. No longer was he driven from below, but only drawn from above; he would keep trying, he was pushing exhaustion but he intended to win

a tall red-haired man plodded upward ahead of him: the stranger was lithe-strong, not small-wiry like Kali. This redhead vanished around an out-crop

Dio had now penetrated snow-heights; he crept-crawled a declivitous glacial ravine, cold-wind-flogged kilometers above the valley; each breath was a pain-crisis, ice particles formed in his nostrils, and still a moonless moon illumined the rockbroken white above and around and below him, and the crest was visible ahead-above and the Blue Flame beyond it. He scrambled upward, bruising knees, bloodying fingers, risking fall-to-jagged-death. He came to a trail-masking rock-jut; precariously balancing, clinging to the vertical rock, he worked around it

and saw the flame

and saw the slender bridge out to the flame—the long spidery rock-thread filamenting outward above kilometers of below-nothing, with the flame flaring cobalt blue at the far tip of it

and saw the tall redhead already one-third out on the filament, bellycreeping toward the flame, arm-and-leg-clinging

and demanded of himself: *If one reaches the flame—what then?*

The redhead did attain to the flame, and he knelt above it and immersed his face in it, deeply inhaling. Then he stood high-erect before the flame—and fissioned into *two* redheads: one soared aloft, the other lost balance and plummeted below.

Crawling to abyss-edge, Dio watched the man-speck as it fell dwindling into below-distance disappearance.

Dio lay prone-shuddering with his forehead hurting on the hard rock-edge. Then he was impelled to pull himself farther forward so that his whole head jutted over the edge, and he conquered dizziness and stared into depths. And there it was. Suction-cupping upward toward him, cupping with bare hands and feet, came the decay-face of naked red-flame-topped Kali. Dio went taut, came up on hands and knees, readied himself to meet Kali here, contend with him, send him surtling into the abyss—or he Dio. . . .

The Horse-eyes turned outward to the Blue Flame. Its allure was incandescent, dangerously distant yet not so terribly distant. It drew Dio as Kali repelled him. Dio therefore stood erect, not teetering at all on the abyss-edge: why shouldn't Dio try *walking* the rock-filament to the flame? Kali the Enemy crawled upward below: Dio would simply ignore him; Dio would walk to the flame and embrace it and then Kali could no longer hurt him, perhaps with the power of the flame Dio could kill Kali. . . .

Erect, cautiously exultant, Dio strode to the base of the filament-gangway

it came into him: "If I can do this better as a biped than as a quadruped, perhaps I can do it best as a monoped—" Eh: hopping on a single leg, it would be like a strong spermatozoon lashing good-desirously forward with his single tail—many were called, but only one was chosen, but none complained who had *tried*.

Praying a blessing on the inspiration, Dio hooked his right foot around his left ankle and monothrustingly kangaroo-leaped in moon-gravity, effortless and soaring. Thus with powerful grace Dio drifted out upon the rock-filament, which had thinned to a tightwire for the single foot that kept slow-high-springing him onward and upward

> only, Kali crouched in front of the flame, balancing easily on the precarious filament: scarlet hair-flare-fire defending blue vitality

Dio tautened for death-combat.

Astonishingly, Kali yelled hoarse, *"Unify me!* For the love of any god, *unify me, and you will win my power!"*

The plea, whatever it meant, was useless-late. Rising off the rock, airborne Dio murderously drove in upon the Enemy Defender

and was thrown

and fell

a cave-mouth snarled at him below, and rushed upward to engulf him; and out of the cavern-maw flowed hundreds of diversified sail-craft

5.

———◆———

He awoke on his back, vision and brain blurred; when they cleared, the figure bending over him was I, anxious. I uttered, "Dio?" He made it out that he was on the floor and that I was kneeling on the floor and that the floating penthouse continued to float up there above us. A couple of excruciating muscle-tests established for him that nothing was broken, and he blinked and demanded, "How did I get down?"

Baldly I stated, "The quick way. You jumped."

He got up on an elbow. I barked, "Dio, no! You might cut your spinal cord!" He shook his head hard, wriggled shoulders, uttered, "No breaks, I'm a black belt." Leaping erect, I helped him to his feet, expertly finger-probed his back, then got one of his arms over my shoulders and started him walking. He shook me off with thanks and did his own walking with experimental care, rather often glancing up at the platform. After a bit of this, he muttered, "Tell me while I exercise."

Sitting on one of the beds, I told him economically what he'd done in physical reality. I'd completed pajamatizing, got on a light robe, and ventured up the companionway. Looking up, I'd seen the Dio-head poking over platform-edge looking down at me; he appeared to be in a seizure of fear. Catching his fear, I had stared back; he had begun to emit strangled screams, and then his head had disappeared. Hastily I had completed the mount up: he was charging around the platform, bumping into furniture; eventually he had bumped me, and had wrestled me down, and had started to rape me. . . .

"Hold!" he commanded, raising a hand, whirling on me wide-eyed. "I thought you just said—I raped you?"

I, deadpan: "Not quite, but you were well around third base and a cinch to slide home—only you chickened out, or something—"

"Lilith—but you didn't *fight* me?"

"It was evident that you were a black belt. . . . No, wait: seriously, Dio, I understood the situation, from you I could take it if necessary, I wanted to let you work it out your own way however it might go."

"You—understood? *Rape?*"

"This is wild, but—I shared every bit of your fantasy with you, even while I was seeing you act it out physically up there."

He gripped my wrists. "Then you know it wasn't you I was raping."

My grin at him was a shade melancholy. "I know, dammit. It was Esther."

"I—apologize, if that isn't too dumb a thing to say."

Soberly: "My pleasure. I don't mean the almost-rape, even from you I couldn't be pleased by *that*—but the meaningful fact that even in the fantasy you made yourself stop short."

"I *didn't* stop myself. She vanished—"

"It was *your* fantasy. If she vanished, you made her vanish."

Silence. Then: "Lilith—in the dream, Esther said, 'At least, you are *trying*.' "

"*I* said that."

He studied space. He snapped at space, "Go on with what I was doing in reality."

Well: Dio had staggered to his feet and had begun aim-

lessly to plod around the platform, presently leaning forward
and laboring his steps as though he were climbing. I was
still on the platform-floor, wanting to get up and grab and
awaken him but deterred by a diabolical kind of fascination
with the unfolding fantasy, which was as clear in my awake
mind as in his entranced mind—only I was watching the
Dio dream-performance quasi-objectively; and toward the
end of it, curiously I had become the sexless Blue Flame. . . .
Then the final almost-catastrophe: Dio had hooked a foot
around an ankle and had hopped hopped *hopped* to the edge
of the platform and had wrestled violently with himself and
lost balance and toppled over the waist-high railing. "My
God, Dio, you just *had* to be dead, I heard you hit! So
then I got up in a hurry and slid down that ladder-thing
and found you on your back, and you were breathing—"

By now he was sitting on the other bed facing me, knees
apart, head down, hands clasping the back of his throbbing
neck. He demanded, rather inconsequentially, "Did the lights
really go out?"

"No. Want a drink?"

"Yes. Got any Bromo?"

"Which first?"

"The Bromo."

When I returned with the fizzbubbles, he was trying to rub
thoughts into his head. I seized the moment to go up the
companionway and bring down the Black Label. Finding his
Bromo gone, I tilted a bit of straight Scotch into the same
glass: no doubts about this, I know drinkers, he was a good
one, his fantasy hadn't been that. I poured myself a little one
too, and resumed my seat on my bed facing him across the
aisle.

He looked at me, troubled. "I'm sorry."

"If you mean about the almost-rape—"

"Not that; even if I'd finished it off, you understood, and
I've apologized. I mean about—my Kali-distortion of your
Burk Halloran."

That hurt deep. My chin lifted itself. "Kali may have been
a Halloran. He wasn't *my* Halloran."

"I know how you feel. But we've just about agreed between us that we are being visited by something hard to explain but having meaning in this world. If it wasn't your
Halloran, I'm afraid you're obligated to try explaining it."

I wet lips, focusing on his feet—which were bare and,
now I noted, male indeed. I told the feet, "It seemed to be my

Halloran kidnapping your Esther, and he would be capable of the rope-whimsy and the automobile-whimsies; but I repeat that in the rope-illusion, his body was smaller, more wiry, more—forgive me, Dio—more like yours. It also seemed to be my Halloran challenging you in the just-now dream, except for that frightfully decaying face—"

My face shivered down: I looked at the rug, not at the feet.

I heard him say hard, "When I was climbing the mountain, there was a tall redhead in front of me. He inhaled the flame and split in two, and one of him rose into sky and vanished while the other fell into the abyss and vanished. Kali was the one who crawled up out of the abyss."

My face came up slowly.

He leaned forward to touch my shoulder. "This is tough duty, but we have to explore this a little while it's fresh, and I do have to control my intuitions with a bit of logic. You'll agree that deciding what to include and what to eliminate is scientifically important. I'd like for you to start by commenting professionally on the following hypothesis: that all these experiences have been purely my own mental fantasizing, not in any way substantial except for what they may tell about my own mind; that insofar as you or even also that driver-mechanic share them in whole or in part, it was merely telepathic reception of my mental broadcasting."

His hand had left my shoulder, but acutely I remembered that it had been there; I didn't know whether this diversion which he had provided was intentionally that or merely his detective-beagling impulse, but either way I was grateful. My head must have gone down again, for his male feet were again in my field. . . .

I tried being hard to the feet. "Look, admittedly I'm hooked on the kinds of hysterias that produce multiple personalities. But I have to confess that I am seeing a bit of this in you, Dio." Now I looked him in the face: "Can you take this?"

He nodded, teeth sheathed. I considered him: he could take it.

"Very early," I reminded him, "you confessed that you weren't entirely satisfied with your own personality, you'd like to be more handsome and graceful. The first fantasy featured fire, which is a standard hysterical symbol. Your Kali was flame-topped; I admit that you must have stolen the Halloran-image from my mind, but you did couple his handsome face with your own body. In the just-now fantasy, you began it with a weirdly fearsome anxiety-figure, and you re-acted into hot driving rage which almost got me raped, but at once you rejected the rape and the rage, whereupon you found yourself directionless on a misty moor. Out of this you settled for hard, slow upward slogging toward a mountain-top blue flame, which had to mean intellect or intelligence or lucid mentality at a nearly unattainable level, calling upon you to risk a fall into an abyss; and closely coupled with this climax was a fissioning into two personalities, one of which became Kali the Enemy. By the way, Kali is the name of a goddess: female."

"I know. Creation-and-destruction. Maybe a coincidence."

"Maybe. All right. It can be hypothesized that you have a personality split, that this Kali-image is your projection of the better self you'd like to be. Perhaps in the fantasies you are subconsciously trying to satisfy yourself that you as Kali, and therefore you alone and nobody else, won your Esther away from you."

I paused, a little breathless, concentrating on the feet. He was silent. My eyes came up to his face. He was studying my face; his teeth were not sheathed, but neither was he smiling.

He said presently, "That is very good, Dr. Vogel. It is also full of holes. Right?"

"Right."

"Like that anxiety and guilt are also ingredients in other types of mental disturbances that I don't seem to have. And a couple of other things that are pretty shaky evidence. And a few little things in the mountain-climbing fantasy which were liquidly slid over by you: for instance, like the red-head up ahead of me whose tall figure seemed more like your Halloran than like Kali, and that he not I was the one who fissioned after attaining to the Blue Flame, and that one of him rose aloft while the other, which was presumably his own rejected ingredients, toppled into the abyss. Or that hav-ing red hair was never one of my self-idealizations, I just wanted to be tall and handsome, probably with black hair, which I have now. Well; and then, don't we have to infer that the Kali who climbed out of the abyss was the reject of Halloran? Only with my dinky body, which I did once re-ject but don't anymore, and which may be a conjoint you-me symbolization of what smallened the Halloran-soul and what smallened mine."

My mouth was open to agree, but he was still going. "Now tell me, Lilith: why would I then *attack* Kali? Have I done *that*—or do I *want* to do that, en route to some blue flame which isn't Esther? And if my self-reconstruction has strengthened me so that I am now stronger than he, how could he throw me? And when I fell toward that cave-mouth, what were all those bubbling-out sail ships?"

And now his silence was definitely awaiting my response. But all I could think of to say was: "Right."

"So we aren't quite ready yet to eliminate the notion of queerly real interference in our lives, not quite ready to scratch it all off as my own mental twistiness."

I inhaled, and exhaled, and told him: "Right."

Studying his quarter-absorbed Scotch, he commented, "Two martinis at that pub, one gin at my apartment, two wines and a cognac with dinner—this makes the seventh round, not counting a little cheating I did up above. What do you think, Doctor?"

"You look practically sober, Inspector. Bedraggled, bruised, maybe oiled a little, but basically sober." (In those days, "basically" wasn't a cliché.)

"If a guy is drunk, Dr. Vogel, how can he tell?"

"Take me. Do I look drunk?"

"To me who may be drunk, you look sober. Fairly sheveled for a near-rapee, and sober."

"Soberly I listen to a reformed almost-rapist."

"I put it to you as a hypothesis that this Kali exists. That he is not your Halloran, but is not unconnected with your Halloran, and is not unconnected with me either. When he stole Esther, he was flaming-high; but if he inspired her to put her note on the allusive rope and leave in the note a cue-omission, maybe he as well as she wants me to follow and find. He played tricks involving an Esther-image with my car: maybe a reminder to follow and find. Just now he threw me off the platform, which suggests intent to murder me; but his face was degenerately deformed, and at the end he pled with me to unify him. Only, look: if he is objectively try-ing to control me, why does he have to deal in fantasy-pro-jected symbols? Why doesn't he come right through and an-nounce to me what he is and what he wants?"

I was biting my lips almost painfully, worrying about *who* this Kali might be with his decaying Burk-face. I managed: "Sometimes a guy or gal has a need for something, and *can't* come right out and announce it, but despite himself he expresses it in symbols—"

Dio frowned down. "You are saying that—somewhere, out there, in there, up there, down there—some guy in deep trouble is trying to tell me, 'I'm drowning, help me.'"

I sat shuddering. Because of course I knew who it had to be.

He tossed off his liquor and set the glass on the carpet. I did likewise. I began to feel a little better, then—well, not better exactly, but readier to sleep. I glanced at my wristwatch and grinned, "Hey man, it's after *two*! And you must be worse pooped than I am—"

He gazed at me. Silence. I did feel generally sober; but perhaps all those drinks were creating a climate or an aura or something. . . .

I looked at the floating platform. "I—don't think you should sleep up there."

"Probably not."

"Want to sleep over there, then?"

"Not really."

Room-darkness was relieved by residual moonlight. Apart in my big double bed, we watched each other sleepily, he on his left side, I on my right. He was a wonderful hard wiry little dark guy, friendly, sympathetic, honest, ultimately incapable of the atrocity called rape even in a fantasy. Seduction of an evidently responsible woman, yes; whore-rental, maybe sometimes; rape, no—it's great sadistic sport for the totally egotistical or maniacal, but dirty pool for a guy who respects other people. Had he completed his rape of me, even though in his mind I was Esther, I respected him enough to have accepted it as necessary self-catharsis; but he hadn't because inwardly he couldn't, with me or with Esther or with any other woman. With that reflection, my peony-garden remembrance of Burk Halloran grew vivid-poignant; and then it receded in favor of Dio, who was here and quiet and battered. . . .

He told me, "I like it in here with you."

I answered, "I like it in here with you."

Some inches away from me, he reached over and put his right hand on my bare upper left arm. Liking this, knowing how it would probably go now, I brought up my right arm from under me and laid the hand on his right hand.

He told me, "I have no intention of using you. I just like you."

"Perhaps you should kiss me good night, and we'll both go to sleep."

He brought his head over and kissed my lips lightly; my lips responded lightly. Then he pillowed his head close beside mine.

For sure the kiss was in quiet light love, mutually. After a moment, my feet were on his feet. And now there was only one way for us. I hoped it would be slow and prolonged and delicious and honest.

It was.

When I returned from the bathroom, he was sitting up in bed, holding two very small glasses of Scotch. "That makes seven and a half," I commented, joining him and taking mine. "Drinks, I mean." Blessèd be He, how comfortable can you get with another human?

He was nosing his. "I know now where I am going. I'd like to have you with me, but you'll have to judge."

It put an edge on the comfort, but the memory of the wholeness lingered whole. I gibed, "Fine time to be thinking! Now I understand how it was with Esther."

He chuckled, "Well, yes—" Then turning seriously to me and claiming my shoulder: "Tonight isn't over, you know."

I sipped, comfort renewed, edge accepted: this was the guy I liked, in his place I would have been doing the same, I wouldn't have him different. I told him, "Believe me, Lilith is all purry. Keep thinking, it's fine; when you finish thinking, that's fine too."

"Good girl. I don't feel at all hurried now, we can sleep late or whatever in the morning, but—what's your thought about Paris, tomorrow?"

My eyes widened. *"Mon*-ey."

"I have an American Express card, the account is CIA. Also a passport. How about *your* passport?"

"I did a theater-quickie in London last year. Nothing that goes into my handbag ever leaves there. Why Paris?"

Releasing my shoulder, he gave worried attention to the liquor. "Again, I don't know. I've been rechecking all the fantasies, and Paris or even France doesn't come out of them anywhere, except one fantasy-reference to Blois—but the conviction is clear, so one of two things is true: either I have subliminally noticed some bit of evidence pointing to Paris, or else Kali is *calling* from Paris."

I gripped his left shoulder with both hands. "You don't suppose the bastard is *watching* us?"

His grin was wicked. "Perhaps he wants a lesson in Kamasutra?"

I, prim: "I have this funny feeling that he may get it."

Part Two

JUNE 2002

REM, as most readers know, means Remote Earth Mobility. This names a device which will blow any selected continental area off the face of the earth, an action generating seismic stresses which could easily break up the planet. Three nations have it operational now: the United States, the U.S.S.R., and China. Smaller nations are known to be in experimental stages with it. The REM Device reduces prior horrors like H-bombs to the relative status of strategic weapons in limited war.

The topic is so grave that understatement is the only sensible kind of language for it. To understate: we urge our Presidency and our Congress to avoid playing diplomatic or local politics with the current REM Talks, which may lead to a REM Treaty. Again to understate: all three REM nations would value such a treaty.

　　　　　—Editorial, *The New York Times-Herald*, 2002

Lovely, lovely RP Fleet-Nation! Delicate-deft, sturdy-romantic concept! What national official, what diplomat, indeed what artist can restrain himself from kissing RP on both cheeks and extending to the fleet every favor? With RP, instead of going luridly down into disaster, our world just might sail chuckling into the peace of permanent understanding and creative delight!

　　　　　—Canard Cassé in *Aux Étoiles*, 1999

To conclude this brief, absolutely nothing about Guru Kali tastes honestly Oriental, and even his rituals and his teachings have an introspectively Western flavor.

Taking this and other grounds for suspicion into account, I enjoin all members of the fleet, officers and crews, to place personal surveillance of Kali somewhere on their several agendas, and to report any observation no matter how trivial it may seem. Many other concerns are momentarily more pressing for all of us; but as a matter of rear-guard attention, watch Kali and report.

　　　　　—Commodore Mallory in a précis to the RP Fleet, 2001

6.

Some of the craft composing the fleet were primarily sail-powered, with auxiliary engines used only in difficult situations. The other craft, still using sail normally, were large enough, and light enough in design, to mount powerful and extremely fast skimmer engines and downjets and stern-jets and maneuvering sidejets; when this type of boat had first become commercially practical a generation earlier, it had been called "hovercraft"; but the combination of sails and skimmers in a single hull was sophisticated because of the keel requirement for sailing; and this difficulty had been conquered by the development of a two-layered sliding keel, which, on activation, rolled upward into the hull walls as separate plies on laminated sections, presenting a fairly flat jet-ported bottom to the surface of the sea. Fleet discipline, founded on a philosophy of leisurely travel for the route's sake, called for sails only and always on open sea and large lakes under Condition Green, except that screws or skimmers could be used for delicate river- or harbor-naviga-tion or when the individual Ship-Condition had to be Amber or Red; otherwise, only when most unusually the Fleet-Commander would call a Fleet-Condition Amber or Red could the auxiliary engines and skimmer-power and (if Red) one other capability be brought into play.

The fleet was known internally and externally as RP, and collectively it enjoyed the status of Free-Floating Indepen-dent Nation under an early act by the World Assembly, which had succeeded the United Nations. The speculations as to the meaning of the initials RP added to the low-key glam-or of this fleet, whose craft were enthusiastically welcomed or serenely hosted or grudgingly semi-accepted in almost any port of call.

Once in a long while, Condition Green was so very green that captains and even the commodore felt free to hit some port for pleasure purposes only. One such occasion in June 2002 brought Rourke and Chloris and Zeno to Fishermen's Cove.

The flagship *Ishtar* and the frigate *Us'ns*, both under sail, made rendezvous in the bay off Fishermen's Cove soon after 1800 hours (ships' bells were still used, but only for aesthetic reasons). Almost instantly after the (rangling) noise of anchor chains ended, dories were simultaneously dropped off both ships.

Aboard the *Ishtar*, Commodore Rourke Mallory paused beside the starboard rail, grinned facing the quarterdeck in semidress navy-blue weskit and powder-blue trousers and cravat and white shirt but capless with his thick white hair awry, tossed the quarterdeck a soft salute, and stepped into the little elevator-kiosk, which dropped him three meters to the seasurface dory-hatch. There he was welcomed aboard, with informality and a fine-toothed smile, by the fulsome blonde dory commander, Lieutenant Cassie Wozniak. The two-person crew (Wozniak and a male senior petty officer) hove to with electric switches, and the dory burbled happily toward the cove dock with quiet merriment in her compressed-air bubble-wake.

Against the dock, Mallory waited quietly in the dory, chatting with Cassie, while the petty officer mounted the dock and went in to check on reservations. He returned to announce that Co-Captains Metropoulos and Doxidoras had already checked in and awaited the commodore in the penthouse room. (The *Us'ns* was the only co-captained ship in the fleet.) "Expected," baritone-chortled the commodore: "less protocol, they move faster." He kissed Wozniak full in the mouth, accepted a hand-up from the petty officer (while Cassie devotedly watched him upward), exchanged this time a sharp salute with the petty officer (both smiling friendship), and loped into the inn.

He found Co-Captains Chloris Doxidoras and Zeno Metropoulos of the frigate *Us'ns* sitting drinking on the door edge of the innermost floor-level double bed in the penthouse room, watching for the commodore. Almost simultaneously: "Hi Rourke. Hi Rourke. Hi Chloris, hi Zeno." Mallory skirted the foot of the outermost bed, sat on its inner side with his left knee touching Zeno's right and his right knee touching Chloris's left, reached to his right for the bourbon and ice and a glass on the between-beds table, sloshed it straight on the rocks, sipped, murmured, "Jesus God. Peace!"

These three had known each other for a quarter-century. Chloris was long, lean, rawboned, precisely and crisply rakish, with chestnut hair and a clipped alto voice; judging age by skin-and-muscle tone and metabolic energy, you'd call her a nifty forty-five. Zeno was longer, more muscularly lean, just as rawboned, sleepily acquiescent until something hit him wrong and then dangerously stubborn-hard, with long fine chestnut hair and a common-baritone drawl; age on the same evidence, maybe forty-five again. You'd call Rourke an energetic sixty and recognize him as being still combatively or sexually dangerous but endlessly trustworthy when trust was won; his figure was hard-lean for his age, his complexion ruddy-fair, his hands flexibly expressive, his middle-blue eyes and his middle-wide mouth equally facile for hardness or for smiling; his voice was middle-baritone but not at all ordinary because of its liquidly expressive resonance, although the voice rarely rose and the diction was easy. When the three were standing together (which was not now), Rourke had to look slightly down at woman-tall Chloris and definitely upward at two-meter Zeno.

Rourke now demanded, "Which beds are whose?"

"Yours," Chloris asserted, pointing upward at the floating penthouse-platform. "It's a cross between—among—an upper berth, a high place, and a hammock. Not for me!"

"Chloris has three phobias," Zeno adjudicated: "bertho-, acro-, and swingo-."

There was more byplay, and another drink around, among these three good companions on total vacation at one of their favorite rendezvous among the most favored port-places the world over. On duty, Mallory was their chief; accepted, fine; but here nobody gave a damn, and this was often true on duty also when the Fleet Condition was Green. In the sharply personal sense of psychic interknitting, Zeno and Chloris were husband and wife with straying privileges, which was entirely within the sexually liberal context of the fleet, while Rourke was their sexually profound friend with visiting privileges. Except, of course, when the Fleet Condition was Amber or Red. . . .

Eight o'clock dinner followed, in the historically famous restaurant overlooking the cove: for the men, prime New York sirloins, medium rare but charred and sizzling, with Burgundy; for Chloris, a delectable two-pound broiled rainbow trout with sauterne (the trout was boned, she was fed up with headed and tailed fish at sea).

The wines during dinner were ample; and afterward, the men brooded over Armagnac while Chloris toyed with crème de menthe. Back in the room, Zeno eliminated himself by collapsing on his bed, smiling, not snoring, but dead: he was a hard drinker, but duty had been tough and he was pooped. Chloris went to the biffy; and when she emerged, Rourke replaced her. Exiting, he found her sitting on the edge of Zeno's bed, one protective hand on a Zeno-shoulder, the other offering Rourke a drink. As the commodore sipped (it was brandyish), she expressed a yielding to RP-established seniority rights: "What do you want about bed partnerships, Rourke?"

The commodore spread hands: "You choose, tonight I can go either companionate or lone. But if you choose me, you'll have to come upstairs."

She studied inert Zeno: "I do have an itch, and he's dead." She looked up at the platform and wrinkled her nose: "But I do hate the idea of that swinging thing up there."

"It won't sway much if we don't get carried away."

"I know, but—"

"I know, you won't even put the *Us'ns* on skimmerdrive without getting drunk first. So get drunk and join me; I've decided that I want that, affirmatively."

"Have to be sober to get up there, and I have a buzz already."

"Pop a restorative and come on up and drink with me."

"To stay up there, I'd need three drinks—and two would put me out. Rourke, what good would I be?"

"Well," Mallory decided, turning to the companionway, "I would like your company, but you decide, I won't hurt."

She bit: "Dammit, I won't sleep alone down here with the body of Zeno! Just give me time to get the two of us undressed and into our nighties—"

Mallory nodded and mounted the companionway to the floating penthouse. Ten minutes later the platform began to tremble slightly; Chloris already?

Only, the room went black-dark; and Mallory reexperienced

seriatim every sequential aspect, in full physical and emotional color, of the Dio-illusion here at Fishermen's Cove five decades earlier—with certain major differences:

The illusion-woman whom Mallory almost raped was named Lilith.

Climbing the mountain, he saw no figure ahead of him; instead, he *was* the tall redhead. But he did sense a climber behind him.

It was Mallory who fissioned, and felt himself gloriously lightened and strengthened by this fissioning, having inhaled the Blue Flame. But thereafter, Mallory was only the one who soared; the one who fell was another.

And aloft, Mallory looked down and saw a small redhead defending the flame and a small dark man challenging; and the redhead was pleading, "Unify me!" But the dark man grappled with Flametop, and was thrown from the rock-finger, and plunged toward a deep-below cave-mouth known to Mallory, out of which flowed hundreds of diversified sailcraft.

7.

The sinking of Venice beneath the ocean had been arrested by massive undersea injections of a heavy-liquid silica compound which quickly hardened into sandstone strata. The process, which had required a dozen years, had begun in 1982: it had been devised and was executed by RP engineers and financed by the Italian government and by worldwide contributions, and it was one of the major visible and invisible achievements which had won from the World Assembly the status of nation for RP.

Captain Giuseppe Volpone was no engineer, but a member of a breed not uncommon in RP: a blend of trader and unofficial diplomat who played it in both capacities close to the line and largely through influential personal relationships. Prowling the doge's palace after hours with multimillionaire Deano Polo and his diamond-cool blonde-Nordic mistress Berta Soren, Volpone had satisfactorily completed his trade of a ceiling fresco by Rubens out of the Louvre for a ceiling fresco by Botticelli out of this palace. It was a complex matter: the transfer-artists would have to do it all in a single night with hyper-electronic equipment, and all the literature would have to be instantly changed. The ethics were borderline, and nowhere would official circles know anything about it before the *fait* was *accompli;* but experts and true amateurs would quickly detect the switch, and the affair would become a cause célèbre with the perpetrators a mystery, but after a while those outraged would be outlaughed by those amused and intrigued; and when inevitably the names of Volpone and Polo would emerge, the stocks of both and the stock of RP would rise, tourist attention to Venice and the doge's palace would be stimulated (this had dropped off during the prolonged sinking and accompanying social desuetude), and both Rubens and Botticelli would be more widely appreciated because of the scrutiny which these transposed works would draw. The idea had been Volpone's, but Mallory had grinned and given it the nod.

Deal completed, the talk de- or re-generated to artistic chitchat as the threesome moved from room to room. Polo was complacent, Berta between them kept privately and alternately squeezing the arms of both men, Volpone kept privately squeezing *her* arm. . . .

There was a tiny sound-sense in the auditory center of Volpone's left cerebral cortex. Mentally he signaled readiness and shifted to inward listening. At the end of it he responded, involuntarily aloud, "Three or four days, right." His companions stared, and Polo blurted, "I beg your pardon?" Volpone shrugged: "I thought you were discussing the time involved to prepare a wall for a fresco—" Berta inserted, precisely sultry, "It all on the wall and the weather depends."

That night, Joe Volpone's twenty-meter sloop weighed anchor, engine-purred out of the Grand Canal into the Adriatic Sea, cut engine, spread full sail ahead of favoring winds, and made southerly course to round the boot of Italy. To Commodore Mallory Volpone cerebrally reported his course and position, adding, "Blois in three or four days confirmed."

Captain Ilya Sarabin was able to receive his surprise call in privacy: he was taking a turn at the helm of his own twenty-four-meter yawl, and his officers, knowing his preferences, were leaving him with it and wouldn't be troubling him unnecessarily. Even alone, Sarabin blurted no replies aloud; he took time to consider the remarkable information, and then he let remote Commodore Mallory taste Sarabin's own semithought-interfolding before he mentated a formed reply: "There have been some possibly pertinent hints at the Kremlin. Want them now?"

"Watch it," Mallory cautioned; "what I told you will suggest that even mindcasts can be less than private here. Where are you?"

"Lazing down the Don, maybe one day above the mouth."

"Volpone can meet us at Blois in three or four days. What's your capability?"

"On sails, Marseilles in three or four. Want me to break discipline and go skimmer-drive, or fly in?"

"Stay green for three days, then check with me and we'll see about the flying. Meanwhile, formulate."

"Acknowledged."

"Out."

"Out."

Dr. Wing Pen—whose weirdly intricate mental counterpoint among several disciplines of science, including electrodynamics and cybernetic theory, had made him an indispensable attendant on one in three meetings of the Chinese cabinet —started awake out of a nightmare to discover that his Eurasian bed-partner Captain Ladyrna Mengrovia was sitting erect in bed, staring at the almost night-invisible far wall of Pen's bedroom. It never took Pen more than three seconds to come awake, a process that he brought off by selecting some visual feature and analyzing it; the feature he instantly chose was Ladyrna's left breast, a succulent semi-elevated long gourd; the analysis was, that as gourds went, the nipple was displaced. . . . He was awake; and he whispered, "Was your nightmare as bad as mine?"

Ladyrna Mengrovia jumped, quivered, quieted, and turned fondly to Pen, who lay on his right side looking up at her;

apart from Pen's more practical values, Ladyrna was a push-over for his round-eyed weak-chinned baby-face and his round shoulders and hollow chest and small, clever inexhaustible phallus. Eye-flooding Pen with amour, Ladyrna mentated to distant Commodore Mallory, "Your story comprehended, I may have a contribution, but the time to Blois would be six weeks by sail or ten days on skimmer-drive; give orders." Meanwhile she was telling Pen aloud, "My nightmare was that you ravished me and I couldn't feel a thing."

While Pen, fingering the misplaced nipple (which obedi-ently erected), advised her, "I dreamed that you were a gi-gantic roc, and with your beak *you* ravished *me*, and I could feel *every*thing," Mallory snapped, "Figure a quick way to get out of there. Stay on sail, but make for a nearby location that has little or no radio coverage. Call me from there in three days."

By now she was on top of Dr. Wing Pen (who worked hard, long hours and had to relax quick and had learned to trust Captain Mengrovia). With her open mouth on Pen's open mouth and her hips elevated to postpone her delicious downward engulfing of his titillating tininess, Mengrovia men-tated, "In view of your news, Commodore, it will take me another few hours to bring off the indirect Wing-pumping that will intersperse direct Pen-pumpings. After that, I'll have to roundup my crew, and we should be embarking on the evening tide. Out, for Chrissakes, *out*—"

Mme. le capitaine Colette Perpignan elbow-leaned, head down, eyes closed, at the head of the ward-room table while her seven officers, male and female, assorted nationalities, young and not so young, watched her respectfully, and the galley crew delayed service. Perpignan was not, however, praying over food; she was listening in her brain to Com-modore Mallory, and her officers knew it. (Only captains and select subordinate officers were fitted with the device.) When the commodore had finished, she mentated, "Pardon while I communicate some of this to my officers—*ça va?*" He re-sponded, "*Cava*—but only some of it." He mind-listened while in her crisp fiftyish contralto she told the ward-room group only that the commodore was calling an emergency session at Blois. Several of them nodded: they knew it was not a time to ask questions, and they knew also that Captain Perpignan would later tell each of them what each needed to know and would entertain private questions or comments then.

Perpignan now informed Mallory, "They accept, pending more information. As you hoped, I can control Blois, being now at Havre. How soon?"

"Three or four days, indefinitely. We can count so far on only yourself and Volpone physically present, along with Metropoulos and Doxidoras and me; but set up tri-d visuals at Blois—this is a full conclave and I am contacting all the others."

Her brows flattened; she said aloud, "That important!" Volpone was noted for impulsively responding aloud, and noted equally for his quick wit in covering; contrariwise, Perpignan *never* responded aloud impulsively, but in this case she wanted her officers to hear, and of course they heard and went on alert. Mallory had no serious complaint with either captain.

RP had no voting delegate to the World Assembly, nor did it have an accredited ambassador to the court or government of any other nation; the former uniqueness was part of the agreement whereby RP had been declared an independent floating nation, the latter was a unilateral RP decision. The peculiar world role which RP played excluded the former; the entrée which RP had built and was consistently building obviated the latter.

However, practically all delegates to the World Assembly and practically all national diplomats of any stature knew Esther d'Illyria, and those who were competently attentive to the RP lines (there was never any one clearly distinguishable RP line) had a strong sense that she espoused them, and those who were properly attentive to pertinent private intrigue knew that Esther d'Illyria and Commodore Rourke Mallory were close friends although both had other close friends. Just a few were almost dead certain that Esther was an RP; but this never stopped them, indeed it often stimulated them, with respect to serious consideration of the positions she espoused or with respect to confidential information when she hinted interest.

Esther was one who was touched by the Mallory mentation-round: she carried the cerebral device. In her case, prior knowledge of her history caused Mallory to avoid reference to his Fishermen's Cove fantasy. After greeting-exchange, he said merely, "I'm calling an emergency conclave at Blois, and

I think the point of reference may be Guru Kali. What can you tell me that could be pertinent?"

Esther, promptly: "He is lobbying for the REM Treaty."

Silence for a bit, while she awaited his double-take. Then Mallory: "I heard you say that he is lobbying *for* the REM Treaty."

"That's right, just as you are doing. Problem?"

Pause; then: "Nothing that I understand yet, so keep on doing what you're doing. Meanwhile, where *is* the treaty?"

"United States: President for it, forty-seven senators for it, forty-one against it, fourteen uncommitted. Russia: Chairman for it, Praesidium divided with count indeterminate. China: inscrutable. United Kingdom: Prime Minister for it, Parliament seething. France: President for it, Assembly seething. I can keep going—how long do you have for this?"

Mallory considered. He and Chloris and Zeno had tentatively agreed that his fantasy had been a threat or even a murder-attempt by Guru Kali; and the news from Esther that Kali was *for* the REM Treaty was—not upsetting, but confusing.

The REM Device—meaning Remote Earth Mobility—had been developed almost simultaneously by scientists in the United States and Russia, and China had rapidly followed; and each of these nations had fed it to some of its friends and satellites in the course of political dealing. This device made H-bombs a toy by comparison; and its general knowledge had blurred out all efforts at nuclear disarmament. Any nation possessing it could activate the REM Device to explode off the earth, from inside the earth, any small or large area of the earth's surface-and-crust which the activator might designate. The maximum area now known to be blastable was seven million square kilometers—e.g., all of the continental United States, or all of western Russia along with the western part of Siberia—and there was no possibility of a Distant Early Warning System.

Any use of the device, however—apart from humanitarian and economic considerations—would wreak seismic, oceanic, and atmospheric havoc on the planet. Some scientists were calculating that the imbalances might rupture the globe or wobble it out of orbit.

Consequently the international pressures were multiplying to forge a REM Treaty quarantining use of the device. Such a treaty, entailing adequate inspectional safeguards, had been drafted and was in process of international debate; but the conservative and isolationist counterpressures against its adoption were formidable.

RP, quite naturally, wanted the treaty and was working for it. RP was trying to do even more, but so far its scientists had been unable to find a way of neutralizing REM. And Guru Kali had been potently preaching *against* RP as the enemy of all morals and religions.

Yet the guru was working *for* a REM Treaty?

Esther had waited patiently. She was alone tonight. Mallory said, "Good girl. Keep at it. Love you."

Esther said, and he felt her smile, "Love you. Out."

8.

Mallory aboard the *Ishtar* and Chloris and Zeno aboard the *Us'ns* were unsurprised to find two-thirds of their crews still aboard: Draft Boards had been activated, naturally, so that afloat for most of them was as good as ashore in this godforsaken Jersey area distinguished only by the archaic Fishermen's Cove. Activating their watch-people, they got back full crews within two hours, and weighed anchors immediately. Both yachts went on skimmer-drive, by special authority of the commodore, who wanted to be at Blois real quick and wanted Chloris and Zeno with him.

The unusual action made an officers' call imperative, and Mallory called them right after lunch. A few had to be duty-absent, but most were there including American black Captain Clarice Vanderkilt and her French white executive officer Commander Jean Duval. As the flagship, the *Ishtar* was naturally the biggest yacht in the fleet: forty-one meters in length, nine in beam, and carrying a crew of ten officers, twelve petty officers, and twenty-seven others—all neatly balanced racially, ethnically, and sexually. The flagship had to set the RP pattern. (Religious balance had been ignored, it was whatever it happened to be: three balance-factors are more than enough for any purpose that is practical.)

To his officers, Mallory crisped the gist of his reific dream. He then told them candidly: "This could be a big pfoof, in which case I'll report to the fleet psychiatrists and you can elect a temporary commodore. But I have an excessively strong feeling that Guru Kali is involved, that it is *not* a pfoof, that trouble is threatening all of us and maybe more than all of us. Beyond that I haven't the foggiest, and hence the conclave at Blois. Some of you will be there, of course, and I want to encourage you now to be talkative with anything pertinent; but I also want to approach Blois with any advance prepping I can get, and I now welcome random brainstorming."

When that elicited nothing except a few lambencies from even the best of them (and they were all good), Mallory told them: "Okay, don't feel bad, I can't do any better yet. Backburner it, and hit me individually if a thought-bubble blubs up in your subconscious mud. Be as ready as you can for Blois; churn up all your background about anything.

"One other point. The fact that we are on skimmer-drive has already told you that our Ship-Condition is Amber: not the fleet yet, but the *Ishtar*, and also the *Us'ns*. Now hear this: in *all* respects of discipline, we are Amber until further notice; and further notice may well be Red."

"Shit," remarked a male voice.

Blonde Lieutenant Wozniak raised her hand: she'd commanded the dory which had ferried Mallory into Fishermen's Cove last night. "Commodore," she crisped, "I'm disinterested, being biologically Condition Red for a few days, but on behalf of the others I'd like to suggest dispassionately that in all respects except skimmer-drive, Condition Amber begin at 0800 hours tomorrow."

Mallory grinned: why not? "Point understood," he acknowledged; "request granted. Nevertheless, Ms. Wozniak, I take it you won't be on the Draft Board tonight?"

"Definitely not," asserted Cassie. "It's always appealing, but I hurt."

"Hit sick-bay," Mallory advised. "Try dyswomennhoresic, they tell me it's great for that. All right, humans: Condition Amber starting at 0800 hours tomorrow and continuing until further notice." Then he frowned down: "As you well know,

at my age I don't join you regularly—but tonight, don't wait
to find out: I want to be alone for thinking."

Cassie Wozniak told the floor, "I guess it's too late for me
to say shit. But if dyswomennhoresic works, I'll want to.".

Nobody, except possibly founder Rourke Mallory, knew
what if anything RP stood for. "Rendezvous Paris" was a
prime contender, since that was where many of them often
were; on the otherhand, their shore base was at Blois—the
chateau had been declared part of the RP nation by the
World Assembly, with arm-twisted French consent involving
historical guarantees and tourism concessions. "River Pirates" had numerous whimsical adherents, and the ambiguities
of Commodore Mallory seemed often to point toward this
one. For certain sour outsiders who saw an RP career as a
lifelong vacation, the suggestion was "Requiescat in Pace."
But nobody actually knew—except Mallory, if he did.

Here and there some esoterically inclined philosopher or
statesman or diplomat would drop a hint that RP was all that
was holding the world together for the moment. Everything
else that meant to bind—treaties, the World Assembly, secret agreements, the works—was mainly restrictive; and every
schoolboy and his mother knows that restrictions work just so
long, whereafter they intensify the blowoff. RP, however, was
glamorously and alluringly concerned with all the world as
community-in-variety.

Let a major nation or an insignificant jungle village assert
its individuality, and RP would hear about it and sing its
praises, would go there for study and absorption, would challenge, would stimulate—and would not fail to endow that
nation or village with a new cognitive-connative sense of its
dependence on the welfare of everybody else for precisely the
preservation and stimulation of its own individuality. Meanwhile everybody everywhere imagined the city-state-yachts
which composed RP sailing seas and nosing up rivers; and
often and often, into some sea- or river-port sailed an RP ship
with trade and with fun and with human glamor, often to depart with a young recruit or two.

RP had arrested the sinking of Venice; RP also published
the good works of a thousand obscure literati and musicians
and artists who did their own things intensely with insufficient
market-eye to be published elsewhere. There was sly deviltry
in RP, like Volpone's art deal between the Louvre and the

doge's palace. As for religion, RP worshipped everywhere, reverently.

The World Assembly supported RP, not with funds (for RP was self-supporting and frankly commercial in many of its dealings), but with endorsement by almost three-quarters of its delegates and guarded tolerance by most others; hence, when RP would ask the Assembly for some concession or privilege or cooperation, usually the yes was swift. But RP normally spared the Assembly the worry of a problem: instead, RP went to national or individual sources and elicited interdealing where none previously had been possible. The World Assembly valued RP as a conspicuous and voluntary ally with no Assembly obligations; and the RP endorsement in the Assembly remained stable despite dark rumors that eventually RP might replace the Assembly as arbiter of world problems.

If I, Lilith Vogel vintage 1952, seem to be exceeding myself in these 2002 reportings, bear with me: they are personally authentic.

Established in this trans- or supra-establishment security, with an intra-social morality which many considered scandalous but which most secretly envied, why now would Commodore Mallory study with grave concern an apprehension which had arisen in him purely out of individual intuition involving an illusion? And why would he direct his precautionary attention toward a religious charlatan named Guru Kali?

This guru's recorded history as a guru dated back only to 1981; but by 1986, precocious youth Kali had become sufficiently world-visible to engage Mallory's interested attention. Precisely a decade ago, in 1992, Kali—then still a very young man—had preached to fifteen thousand rapt listeners in Detroit's New Olympia a sermon which had singled out RP as being conjointly the Antichrist and the Antibuddha. The sermon, internationally reported, had helped RP by focusing new attention upon it; and Mallory, respecting both Christ and Buddha, nevertheless had been forced to admit a rightness in the sermon insofar as both the reported Christ and the reported Buddha had advocated passivity and renunciation of all worldly aspiration. Nevertheless, the sermon had announced a sustained undermining drive against RP by Kali; and while this quasi-Oriental adversary had made no visible inroads into RP prestige, assuredly he had been piling up Brownie points.

With age, Mallory had long since overcome a modest tendency to discount the world value of RP. He knew, subjectively and objectively, that his RP was world-essential. That was no immodesty, as long as he didn't start imagining that his RP was great. Hence the onslaught by Kali struck him, and with years the impression settled in, as being an onslaught on Mallory's concept of what the world needed for peace and stimulative growth; and except on one point, personal pique was not in question.

The single point of personal pique was the personal appearance of Guru Kali. Was he East Indian in appearance, as his name and title and discipline implied? He was not! Instead, he looked like a lean-graceful Irishman with sea-blue eyes and flaming red hair and (when occasionally it broke through his prevailing serenity) a grin that was positively impish.

In sum, Kali looked like a young version of Rourke Mallory. When he first saw a color-picture of the guru, Mallory was so totally discombobulated that he barged out of distinguished company to go back to his ship and check out a few early pictures of himself. They checked out. Guru Kali *was* in physical appearance the young Rourke Mallory—with one exception: Mallory was respectably tall, whereas Kali was slender-short, indeed (as men go) a wiry runt.

Currently, Kali numbered his worldwide flock at a hundred million, its wealth (whose purse strings he controlled) at a billion world dollars, and the longevity of his religion at a hundred thousand years—whereafter he would come again with a new revelation for those who would have kept the faith and so would be ready for a further advance. He possessed a personal jetliner which would have roomily accommodated five hundred people commercially, a worldwide fleet of expensive skimmer-cars, and a hundred costly tabernacles worldwide with attached voluptuous manses.

Was Kali a flamboyant ruthless tycoon? Well: tycoon he was; but despite his personal appearance (which Malloy grudgingly had to admit was a bit on the flamboyant side), Kali appeared serenely-intensely devoted to his Gospel of the Inner Light. Of ruthlessness there was no indication whatsoever, except legitimately when he leveled off those whom he considered Enemies of the Inner Light, including and eventually featuring RP. Malloy couldn't criticize the guru for his jets and wheels, which could be taken as merely replacing the sails and skimmers of RP. And since RP encouraged self-searching and philosophy and conscience and even temperate religion, tolerating an extremely broad spectrum of sincerity provided that it *was* sincerity, Kali earned only Mallory's applause for directing his followers toward some inward light which encouraged them to be moderately conservative; and if they in return wanted to make the guru rich, why, it is only gracious to accept and use love-gifts as long as they don't set up unacceptable conflicts of interest.

Nevertheless, Guru Kali had made himself for RP "The Adversary." And some others who tolerated or endorsed RP had set themselves against the guru. For instance, back in 1987, influential old evangelist Denny McIntosh, who was uncompromising about the orthodox Christ but willing to listen respectfully to a wide spectrum of honest non-Christians, had expressed interest in the work of RP but had flatly branded Kali an instrument of the devil. And in 1997, the Pope had released a more guarded statement which expressed and recommended favorable attention to RP but distrustful watchfulness of Kali; and the Pope or his Vatican prelate-writers had been learned enough to mention that Kali was a name originally associated with a sinister pagan goddess. Every rabbi whom Mallory had ever met liked RP; but when the topic of Kali was broached, each rabbi deftly changed the subject.

During recent years a particularly puzzling aspect of Guru Kali had come to the forefront. There were numerous convincing testimonials about ways in which Kali had mystically helped people to make their impossible dreams come true. Long prior to the Fishermen's Cove illusion, Mallory had engaged several of his most philosophical captains and commanders and lieutenants in an attempt to analyze these frequently substantiated reports. The tentative conclusion had been, either that Kali had power to project the illusion of wish-satisfaction, or that he possessed other powers not understood by science.

This was the background against which Mallory now meditated his Fishermen's Cove illusion—in which, for Mallory, the Enemy with his symbolically decaying face was nobody other than Kali (whose actual face was vital-young). And it looked almost unmistakably as though the guru, with established powers of illusion-projection, had used this method precisely to strike at the soul of Mallory, hoping to drive him insane and thus cripple RP; and when the persistent self-containment and drive of Mallory in the dream could not be beaten down by the guru, Kali had used his illusion-wiles to drive Mallory off the platform in the hope of killing him.

Crisis for Mallory and therefore crisis for RP was indicated; hence the conclave-call for Blois. And the word from Esther that Kali was lobbying *in favor* of the REM Treaty which RP considered survival-essential was so totally uncharacteristic of the guru that it did nothing but heighten Mallory's apprehension.

And it didn't help one little bit that Kali in the illusion had looked so much like a decaying version of Mallory himself when young.

There was one tiny irony entailed; but as Mallory whimsically inspected this irony, his small smile was twisted. If Kali had used the illusion as a murder attempt on Mallory, the effort had been a waste, even if it had succeeded, unless half a year mattered to Kali.

Now the smile disappeared, and the mouth-twist reflected inward anguish. Probably because of Mallory's too-complete and too-charismatic leadership, not a soul in RP—*not a single soul*—was evidently ready to replace him in command.

Softly he beat his desk with his fist a few times, then arose and went for the Black Label. Not one of his captains or commanders, was what he had really meant. Somewhere down in the ranks there *had* to be . . .

He sipped it straight, handling it like fine brandy; and going to the stern picture-window of his cabin, he considered the wake created by the skimmer-jets. Six months to find that one guy or chick way down somewhere in the officer or petty officer ranks. No, worse than that: no more than three months—because, once found, the command-successor would have to be readied *somewhat* before this diabolical and unstoppable mosaic virus would

9.

There wasn't any ceremony at Blois; merely, Captain Perpignan was at the dock to welcome her commodore. He was
the first to arrive, the power of the *Ishtar* having left the
Us'ns a day behind. Perpignan had got the chateau closed off
and readied; the red-velour-warm Valois or Medici wing with
the low ceilings and the (François Premier) spiral staircase
were enough for top-officer assemblies and side-committees;
all three period-units had been modernized for comfortable
quarters and offices, and crew members not involved could
either sleep aboard ship or shack out in Blois-town.

Assembly opened at 1400 hours next day, which was Day
4. Twenty-eight bodies, including Chloris and Zeno and Volpone and Sarabin, were physically present; Mallory had decided to authorize flying in for the last two; and there were
three more captains and six executive officers and a sprinkling
of junior officers having special talents. Additionally, all other
yachts in the fleet were represented by tri-d electromagnetic
cubes: each of these was primarily occupied by the image of
the ship's captain, but invisible behind the captain were always
one or two or three chosen officers who could hear and
could be heard and might even enter the cube. They were all
in a big circle with bodies seated at floor level and cubes
overhead. They didn't worry about protocol: the commodore
sprawled in no special location, and also random-localized
(but not sprawling) was Captain Colette Perpignan, whom
he'd asked to chair the thing.

Perpignan gaveled (*still*, in 2002!) on her chair arm and
stood lean-erect, slapping a hand palm with her gavel head.
Uniform was semidress, like Mallory's at Fishermen's Cove;
but there was no visible way to distinguish a captain from a
commodore or a lieutenant—an officer would merely mention

his rank at a first meeting, and after that you were supposed to remember. You might, however, sometimes be able to discriminate sex by two aspects of uniform: all men wore long pants and, when appropriate, slouchy visored caps; women could wear the same, but they had option to wear miniskirts if they were by God unshaven bare-legged, and another option for unvisored caps if the hairdo seemed to require this. Perpignan wore primly a miniskirt above long thin bare legs lightly furred; but just now she was bareheaded like everybody.

The chairman (RP shemen had long ago voted down the term "chairperson" on the ground that "man" was a category generic rather than sexual) began with her normal crisp, reminding them that Commodore Mallory had summoned this assembly for reasons on which Mallory had already briefed them in individual telementations and on which he would soon enlarge. (This conclave was oral: mentation had its drawback of psychic strain.) It was all she needed to say, and Mallory made ready to start talking at her signal; but Perpignan, one-sheman battleground between the prim Huguenot and the florid Catholic traditions, thought it worthwhile now to perorate a concise history of the RP fleet-republic and a commentary on its world significance and dedication: an independent multiple-mobile nation whose fractionated territories were comprised of all its floating hulls and which by World Assembly action and international consensus would forever have sanctuary on the high seas, while its hulls were privileged to penetrate the rivers of all other nations except in an unheard-of case of exclusion. . . . Others were fidgeting, and presently Mallory looked hard at the chairman and raised an eyebrow. She had an eye-corner on him, she stopped in mid-word, she coughed once; she stated, wittily enough, "Assez de gaz; un peu de Mallory," and sat.

Keeping his seat, Mallory unemotionally and without excision of image-detail or connative experience gave them the whole of the Fishermen's Cove fantasy, including the on-his-back awakening and the report by Chloris of what he had been physically doing up there (rape and all) as the fantasy unfolded. A couple of times he saw Zeno smile sleepily while Chloris, beside him, frowned down in annoyance. Whereafter Mallory sketched a good deal of his subsequent rumination, omitting however reference to thoughts related to his mosaic virus, which was a secret between him and a coterie of Paris physicians.

"All right," Mallory ended. "Sorry that took so long, but you had to have everything pertinent or possibly pertinent. This session is being taped; any of you is at liberty to listen to the tape whenever you think it may help you pin down an idea.

"I am convinced that in some way Kali is involved in all this monkey business, and that his involvement may be grave for us. I don't know whether he deliberately threw me into that fantasy or whether I was having some goofy insight. Maybe one or more of you was at the time having some experience with a subliminal Kali influence, and your spillover mentated me and tossed me into the fantasy. Maybe anything.

"I called this emergency convocation because something far transcending reason assures me without question that Kali is involved in some way that is sinister for RP and consequently for the world's immediate future. He has been whittling at us for years: my dream says that he is ready to strike. And this conviction has an important ramification. *Why* does he want to hurt us? What is he up to that we obstruct? How big and what sort of big would that something be?

"All right, I'm shutting up now. Any or all of you fire at will. Chairman, please don't interfere unless at least four people want to speak all at once—any three of us can settle the order among ourselves."

He waited. Nothing. Well, perhaps they were concentrating too tightly on Kali as a guru. To widen the scope, he gave them his information from Esther d'Illyria: that quite surprisingly, Kali was currently lobbying hard for the proposed REM Treaty. And he waited again.

Soon the sultry voice of Ladyrna Mengrovia filled the room without special amplitude: on trivideo from mid-Pacific, and uniformed, she was cool and all business but involuntarily luscious even so. "I was with Wing Pen the other night," she began. . . . Zeno murmured, "Ah so." A few snickers, some on trivideo. Urbane fortyish Mengrovia smiled hard: "You hemen should have his good fortune, and you shemen mine." Ilya Sarabin scowled: "Ah so." Mengrovia sobered: "Wing was worried all evening, until I talked him out of it, about the mutual Chinese-American-Russian confrontation with the REM Device. I kept reassuring him that the REM Talks would surely produce a stabilizing treaty; but Wing was in a black mood, his doubts persisted until I—found means to divert him. Sorry, but I can't connect Kali." She subsided, brooding.

Sarabin injected a contribution. "Here's a possibly related thing from St. Petersburg, and it's sexless. There's currently a lot of Dostoevsky-type guilt among Russian physical scientists, I got a strong dirty taste of it in a saloon-bull with Rostov and his top assistant Mischkin—"

Chloris interjected, "Is Rostov the guy who supervised development of the Russian version of REM?"

"Precisely. Well: Rostov was well into self-spoliation by his third drink, with Mischkin glooming and moaning, when Sonya Rostova—that's his sister—joined us. After listening a bit, Sonya said 'Fiddlesticks!'—that's a free translation—and iced her brother and colleague with the truism that they had only been conscientious scientists, they'd followed and developed their scientific leads, they had no responsibility for consequent political choices."

From above, Mengrovia bit: "Great, Ilya, but pertinent how? Of *course* REM tortures the scientific conscience; how is that related to the proposed treaty, or to Kali?"

Ilya gazed up at her. "Thanks, Ladyrna: I was counting on it that you'd ask that question; it sets a focus while I go on and tell what Mischkin then said." Looking across the circle at the commodore: "Mischkin then said, 'That might be true if it weren't for the fact that Guru Kali is operating warm on one stratum and cold on another. Tell me, Meteorologist Sonya Rostova—what happens when warm winds and cold winds intersect in contiguous strata?' Sonya got her mouth open to reply 'tornado'—but her brother snarled, 'Shut up, both of you'; and looking at me, I swear he seemed fearful, he bellowed for another round of drinks. That's all."

Silence.

Mallory shifted it. "This has been: China on the REM Device—and Russia on the REM Device with a vague suggestion of double-dealing by Kali. Anything from the United States?"

The response was nil, except for a few headshakes. This meant that the United States, which possessed complete REM potency but also was pushing for a REM Treaty, had thus far dropped no Kali-pertinent hints which these captains or their officers had overheard or noticed. Mallory frowned: he recalled Esther's information—Kali lobbying, President for it, forty-seven senators for it, forty-one against it, fourteen un-committed—and recalled also his own concern that no captain or commander was ready to succeed him.

"All right," he snapped, redirecting it. "Zero in on Kali, then, in any connection at all. What do you *currently* have on him?"

A lot of them started to volunteer something, then held back and looked around. They had a lot of current stuff on Kali, but each of them thought his information might be trivial and decided to wait for something important to come out.

One of those who had got her mouth open, then shut it, was Chloris. Mallory decided to hit her. "Somebody has to start. Chloris, you start."

She glanced uncertain at Zeno; solemnly he nodded. She turned to the commodore and blurted, "About a month ago I spent a night with Kali. I will summarize it obliquely by saying that he gets his kicks with devices other than phallic penetration. And this is because he has no phallus. He is in every respect male—except that his genitals are female, and they aren't functional." She looked down, pursing lips, tapping fingernails on chair arms: "Pump me not, Commodore—but the way he gets his charge is, to arouse a woman with his mind, then reveal himself and enjoy her letdown. If "he" is the pronoun to use."

Shocked silence. Shock, not at the sexual attitude, but at the new-revealed anomaly. . . .

Mallory found words to break it. "Bravo, Chloris: it may be insignificant, but every detail is pertinent now. Was there anything that he *said*—"

She finger-rubbed her forehead, which flamed. "I don't think so. I may get back to you."

"Good, Chloris, do that. Now, the rest of you notice two things: first, that Chloris was willing to be intimately candid before all of us in the interests of RP; second, that I have listened with attention to this item, which may be trivial and may be major. May each of you be both ways guided. Tell me what *you* have."

Zeno asserted soberly, "I hate to say what I'm going to say."

"Sex, my friend?"

"Not sex, Commodore. I got into a bull session with him in Bangkok two months ago—I'll keep on saying 'he,' Chloris—and he asked me if there was anything I'd always wanted. Knowing his reputation, I asked him if it was true that he could reify the impossible for me. He answered with his usual formula: if I would follow his prescription for finding my own inner light, and concentrate on my wish in that light, then after long hours of concentration excluding all except my need in the light of my inner light and in a mood of absolute faith, why then I would discover within myself new powers inherent in every human, and the impossible *could* come true for me. I expressed polite skepticism, and our evening broke up courteously on that note."

Mallory thought rather heavily. He queried, "Any sequel?" Zeno negated, smiling down, big hands clasped between high-racked knees, remarking: "Anything possible for me that I ever got, I got on the up-and-up; and anything impossible on the up-and-up I don't want; and besides, I have no time to concentrate long hours on some inner light."

"But I have taken such time," low said Ilya Sarabin.

The story that Sarabin told merits verbatim repetition: "This I must now confess, it has been on my conscience.

"I have not talked with the guru, but I have listened to him at one of his great meetings. He told us generally what he tells all his listeners, exactly what in private he told Zeno. I resolved to test the guru's teaching, having long ago found independently what I considered to be my inner light.

"I fabricated an impossible test-wish and recorded it as a dated entry in my personal log. The wish depended on the fact, a matter of public record, that my father and mother were publicly executed by a Nazi firing squad near Stalingrad in nineteen forty-four as spies for the Russian government; I was then an infant. My wish was that my father and mother would return alive to me, and that they would be healthy, reasonably prosperous, and unscarred by the firing squad; all these conditions were made essential in the structure of my wish.

"That same night I secreted myself aboard ship, found my inward light in a way that I have learned, engendered a fullness of undoubting faith, and during many hours leaned emotionally hot against the dream until soon after dawn I lost consciousness. At that time I lay at anchor off Baklava, which is as you know a Georgian port on the Black Sea.

"Well: at about ten thirty-five that same morning, I was awakened in my cabin by a peremptory knocking: it was my steward with word that two who claimed to be my father and mother awaited me aboard. You can conceive my confusion. I had them brought to me; they were accompanied by the town's vigorously nonogenarian Greek Orthodox bishop-emeritus. He came to identify my parents of his own knowledge. My parents were old, but they looked hardy; my mother was profoundly emotional about the reunion with me her baby although she forebore to touch me until their identification had been satisfactorily completed with photographs and documents and the bishop's testimony; my father was gnarled and stolid—at one point a tear oozed from one eye corner, but that was all.

"When authenticity had been established and all four of us had embraced and my mother and I had laughed and cried and clung and cried and laughed and my father and I had embraced, at last it came into me that this had been an impossible test of Guru Kali's teaching, and I remembered my essential conditions.

" 'Are you healthy?' I demanded. At that, the bishop and my mother laughed, and even my father smiled. My parents worked their own fields; they were as strong as oxen.

" 'Are you prosperous?' My father spread hands: every year during the past ten years he had been decorated by the government for being the most efficient manager of any collective farm in the district.

"I hesitated, then blurted, 'Are you bullet-scarred by the firing squad?' Inexplicably my parents turned pale and the bishop grew somber. I waited, anxious.

"My father said dead, 'We never faced the firing squad. Two of our cell mates in the POW concentration camp, a male and a female, insisted that our value to Russia was greater than theirs, we exchanged identity documents and bracelets, they were executed for us. We merely continued as prisoners until the Russians retook the area and freed us.'

"Chilled, I studied my father while stolidly he eyed my feet and continued: 'Months earlier, we had used our associations in Germany to leave you with a family we knew in Bavaria. Subsequently we tried all official channels to communicate with your foster parents, but the Soviet government silenced us; the identity-substitution must never be known, it must die with us. They shipped us to Georgia with private honors and good credentials under assumed names; we had strict orders on pain of death never to break our incognito in any way direct or indirect. However, under Church Sanctuary, eventually we confessed to the bishop, here, and gave him for safekeeping the documents and snapshots which you have seen; these as an experienced spy I had found means to bring out with me. In the photos you saw us holding you as an infant—if you have independent child-photos of yourself, you can compare; in the photos you saw our faces, and you see those young faces true now in our old faces only distorted by age and sorrow. Our one delight began seventeen years ago when I did find secret means to contact your Bavarian foster mother—already a widow, and dead now—and to learn about your own fortunes, my son. Until she died two years ago, your foster mother kept me advised of your letters to her and of your upward mobility in RP; when she died, through the bishop I established an RP contact and kept track of you further. When yesterday I learned that your yacht lay off Baklava, I consulted with your mother and with the bishop, and we resolved to make ourselves known to you.

" 'Now, that is a long story, my son Ilya, but what it comes to is this. No, we are not bullet-scarred or otherwise wounded, because our friends bought our lives with their lives. And we joy in finding you alive and doing so well, and in embracing you again. But never in our lives will we cease to lacerate ourselves for letting our friends die for us. They were young, and she was two months pregnant with their first child; we too were young, but we had a child born and safe with friends. We should not have let them do it—'

"My father broke down; my mother comforted him uselessly. The bishop took me apart and told me, 'This visit is risky for all of us. We must depart immediately, already it is noon; do not try to seek us.' I knew better than to stop them. We embraced once more, and they departed.

"Commodore, colleagues—"

Here Ilya Sarabin lost courage: his head went down on his arms on his knees, and all his body began to shake. Mallory raised a hand, warning the conclave-comrades to hold a silent posture of respectful self-containment.

After several minutes Ilya's head came slowly up, and he looked around, and licked lips, and uttered, "I have done a great deal of brooding over this. I can show you the dated entries in my personal log. My wish came as close to being impossible of fulfillment as one can well imagine; and yet, on the very morning after the night when I faithfully followed the guru's prescription, my wish was fulfilled in every specification.

"I said that the matter has been on my conscience. You may wonder why I feel guilty. Let me try to explain, although I may break at any moment.

"The wish was fulfilled in all its specifications: my parents came alive to me, they are healthy, they are prosperous, they are unscarred by bullets, in miraculous refutation of what had been officially and historically established. But there is a damnable thorn in my mind, that somehow this was brought about by *changing the actualities of the past.*

"In the first actuality, it seems that my parents were in fact slain by the firing squad; in the second actuality, substitutes were slain for them, and they escaped. Commodore, I keep asking my inner light: Was the first actuality truly actual? And did my impossible wish—call it a prayer, if you will—did that wish go back into time and exchange the second actuality for the first?"

Ilya now seemed about to break again, and Mallory opened his mouth to thank him warmly and let him off; but Ilya waved a hand and struggled with himself and brought out one summary thought:

"I had chosen my specifications most carefully, colleagues: healthy, prosperous, unscarred by bullets. . . .

"Only, I forgot one essential specification: they must be *happy!* And perhaps another, that no unhappiness should be created anew anywhere by the fulfillment of my wish.

"Well: and the substitution of Actuality Two for Actuality One became—shall I say *possible,* inanely, because my specifications omitted the exclusion of unhappiness. And I—"

He did break finally, then.

The commodore stood. "We meet here again at two thousand hours tonight. Relax or caucus as you may until then. Adjourned."

As they all arose—except Ilya Sarabin, around whom clustered several good RP comrades—Captain Colette Perpignan, still seated, glared around at Mallory. The commodore bowed slightly to her: "Your pardon, Madame Chairman, for preempting you. Under the circumstances, I trust that some day you will find it in your heart to forgive me this breach of protocol."

Part Three

JUNE 1952

10.

Aboard the Super-Constellation, before dinner:

Stewardess: "Drink orders?"

I (in the window seat): "Granddad if you have it, with a modest shot of water."

Dio (in the adjacent aisle seat): "Grapefruit juice."

Stewardess (hitting her ear with her right hand): "Pardon me, sir, a touch of prop-noise deafness, it's occupational—I thought you said grapefruit juice."

Dio (nodding): "That's right."

Stewardess: "With *bourbon*?"

Dio: "Just grapefruit juice. I take it straight."

Stewardess: "Yes sir." She departed.

I: "In-*spec*-tor *Horse*!"

Dio (wry): "I don't like it, but I have this sobriety sense."

I: "No dinner, either?"

Dio: "Big dinner. No booze."

I: "If you are staying sober, it's a good thing I have the window seat."

Dio: "As soon as we begin the Paris approach, I'll take over the window seat."

I: "To see the Eiffel Tower from above?"

Dio: "To watch the ground coming up to hit us."

I: "Not most people's idea of good fun—"

Dio: "When I die, I want to experience it happening. When after all I don't die, that's even better."

I (checking wristwatch): "Let's see, now. We took off at twelve fifty-five EST afternoon; scheduled Paris touch-down one thirty-nine A.M. EST. But by then it will be seven thirty-nine A.M. in Paris. Yes, you can watch the ground come up—barring fog."

Dio: "Hey, that means we're coming up on dinner late—midnight Paris time!"

"I: "Venerable Moses, I *knew* I was too hungry—"

Aboard the Super-Constellation, after dinner, long after dark:

I: "Damn few people aboard. How come?"

Dio: "All the people whose numbers were up stayed home. We're secure."

I: "Also, we can sleep across two seats each. Sleepy, Dio?"

He: "Not much time before touch-down—but I suppose I should."

I: "The situation is unconducive to dual stretch-out, even without any action."

He: "I have the outside seat, so I'm the one to head for the tail."

I (laying a hand on his thigh): "You're sweet. I'll hate to see you go."

He (laying a hand on my hand and speaking so low that I almost lost it in prop noise): "I was afraid maybe I blew it last night. I mean, it was great, for hours—but maybe you—"

I (leaning back and closing eyes): "I like you, Dio. For a lot more than that. But I am not jealous of your Esther, and I will not be sticky."

Silence like that, except for the omnipresent bone-vibrating prop-snarl. I was by now resenting the snarl and recalling with envy reports from some of the Korea fly-boys that jet planes would seem practically silent if you could be seated ahead of the engines. The thought momentarily diverted me from my emotional tangle, but only for a moment. . . .

Dio's voice (while his hand squeezed my hand on his hard thigh): "I like you, and I want you, but I love Esther. That's how it has to be, and I credit you with knowing it and agreeing."

I (eyes still closed): "Instead of you heading for the tail, why don't we just nap together here?"

He: "Great idea, I buy it. 'Night, Lil."

I: "Dio—"

He (drowsy): "Beautiful?"

I: "Why Paris?"

He: "Dunno. Takeoff point. I'll know."

I (wistful): "I'd enjoy taking time to do Paris—"

He: "That would take at least a year. No chance, I'll be pulled out immediately."

I: "I meant to ask where we're staying."

He: "Esther's favorite place in all the world: Paris, Hôtel Odéon. Remember her note? One block from the Luxembourg Palace. She liked that little hotel—"

It was interesting, how detached I felt from Dio and from Esther, yet how sympathetic with both and how ready for companionship and physical pleasure with him, yet meanwhile how intensely curious and indeed emotionally *drawn* with respect to the cockeyed Burk Halloran angle of this partner-quest. I inquired, with respect to the Odéon, "How long?"

Dio: "Twenty-eight hours."

I (opening eyes wide): "Why that?"

He: "After hotel-arrival, six hours sleep or whatever to recover from time change. Then five hours foot-cruising the Left Bank. Then three hours dinner at some place good, with wines natch. Two hours recovering from dinner. Eight hours in bed. Three hours to pull ourselves together and make a few phone calls and have *déjeuner*, which for us will be brunch. One hour to get to some depot in Paris traffic. That makes twenty-eight, with an assumption about train schedules—"

I (removing my hand from his thigh and folding it with my other hand): "Where will we go?"

He: "Dunno. I'll know. 'Night, Lil."

Landing outside Paris at Le Bourget: clear early morning, virginal summer having begun after the six or eight weeks of miserableness that always follow the two-week April Island in Paris. Taxi from Le Bourget on surface roads (no freeway yet) to the Hôtel des Invalides, then left on St. Germain to Place de l'Odéon. Female cabbie, hard but quite nice; Dio impressed her and me with his precise rapid-fire French. (To me he commented, "Five times in Paris in 1944 and 1945, and four times since, with or without Esther; this is like coming home.") Middle-aged clerk, heavy-mustached, in tiny Odéon lobby; sleepy but polite, throating French with pursed lips, interspersing it with purse-lipped English; carried the two light bags himself up the short stair-flight to the self-serve elevator, shoved in the bags, handed Dio the key to Numéro 21, stepped back, was saying "À votre service, m'sieu'-'dame" as Dio pushed the button and closed him out. The second-floor room (not counting the *rez-de-chaussée* as a floor) was typical Odéon, conservatively clean provincial French with a plain double bed and ordinary furniture; by leaning out the window and looking left, one could see in gray dawn the Senate building behind the Luxembourg Palace. I said, "I like it, and I'm time-confused and pooped"; and we undressed like a veteran married couple. This aspect of our brand-new relationship privately interested me; its comfortableness (despite Dio's dynamism) was unlike any man-association I'd ever known.

In bed, we lay on our backs staring at the undistinguished ceiling. Dio murmured, "Tu n'as que vingt-huit ans, ma'm'selle—ton plaisir?" Lazily I responded, "You have thirty-nine, and you won't hurt my weary ego if you want to sleep now—or not, but I'd be lethargic." Turning to me with a sleepy smile, he patted my cheek: "Tu es gentille, chérie. Et j'espère bien pour ce soir." I patted his cheek, sleepily smiling: " 'Night in the morning, kid."

We slept, but not dreamlessly. And we were vitally together in the mutual dream, but my sense was that his dreaming was primary. . . .

The first part of our dream was a swift and almost purely cognitive review of Dio's career-past since 1942: one of those oddball dreams in which there is no feeling and very little imagery and yet a sense of images. Dio the red-hot psychopath flaming brilliantly and murderously in 1944 European combat, battlefield-promoted up to major. Then Major Diodoro Horse in 1945, ludicrously reassigned to command a station complement in a backwater French town many miles from any combat, gnawing his frustrated soul at the breech-end of a broom. Consequently Dio, to relieve his suicidal boredom, getting himself involved with the local Communist underground in a brilliantly maniacal attempt to take it over and turn it to the service of his own long-range plan for personal conquest of the world. Dio caught red-handed, court-martialed—and, utilizing his own legal talents (he'd been a lawyer) and schizoid logic, completely stalemating the trial judge advocate with a defense plea that he had embarked on this role solely for the patriotic purpose of exposing the Communist underground. Dio therefore found guilty only on a charge of conduct unbecoming an officer, and discharged "for the convenience of the service" but not dishonorably, and re-

taining his rank of major. Dio afterward privately contacted
by a military intelligence officer who expressed the admiration of Army Intelligence for Dio's undercover and court-
room adroitness and, working subsequently and confidentially
with the New York Commissioner of Police, got Dio placed
as a detective-lieutenant on the New York Police Force, provided that Dio would be available on call to the intelligence
services. Dio going through a profound and agonizing self-
reappraisal and reorientation which was more effective than
what any psychiatrist I know could have done for him. Dio
then honestly, ambitiously, aggressively nerve-driving himself
sixty, seventy, eighty, ninety hours a week in police work that
frequently made headlines, rocketing himself upward to inspector's rank in a cool half-dozen years, and bewhiles taking
leave for Army Intelligence and then for the CIA in this or
that sort of cloak-and-dagger assignment in several parts of
Europe but frequently with a French involvement. . . .

That was the swift dream-review. Most of it Dio had never
told me about, I would simply have to check it—but that
was a later awake-reflection: just now I was still in the dream,
which had flowed me or us into a swift meaningful nearly
unintelligible reprise at an almost purely connative level.
Dio's emotionality, experienced pure: vibrant, anxiety-ridden,
driving, murderous-raging, yawing with cosmic frustration,
rapiering into a crack in the blockage wall, irradiated with
glory-ambition, cynical, wicked-grinning, involved with Esther in lustful-domineering-contemptuous self-gratification—
then involved with a Frenchwoman in desire and frustration
and unexpected victory and keening passion and high triumph *capped by bitter tragedy.* . . . And the long grind of
lacerating self-reappraisal, and the mothering fidelity of Esther, and the marriage with Esther, and the self-surrender to
Army Intelligence and Esther and the New York Police
Force and the CIA, and the realignment of his Promethean
fire on civic dedication in his new career sustained by the
home-warmth of Esther

　　　　　　and then the rope-running of Esther

　　　　　　　　　　　　　　　　　and then
abruptly the dream opening out into the full imagery of us
lying together here on a bed in the Odéon . . . But neither of
us awoke, this actuality was part of the dream, and here we
lay and here we lay

　　　　　　　　　and without transition were rocketing

across France alone together in a train compartment, with the window-flashing scenery growing rugged and rugged as we approached the Alps, with altitude-cold progressively permeating our compartment

We disembarked in Switzerland at Alpine Pic Dentelé; and now the dreaming was three-dimensionally multisensorily realistic and sequential minute-by-minute. We stood forlorn in the tiny old depot at Pic Dentelé, listening to the departing train as it mourned our destination. Pic Dentelé was snow-wintry, in a small flat valley with snowpeaks jagging all around us. In 1952, the moon-mountains were thought to be toothed like that, although snowless.

I clutched his hand, delightedly gazing around and upward. He clutched mine, warily sniffing around and upward. . . .

A big black voluptuous airport-type limousine pulled up in front of us with snow creaking under the tires. The uniformed bareheaded driver shot out, ran around in front, and saluted Dio: "M'sieu' le directeur Horse?" This driver was a redheaded Kali. Dio, sheathing teeth, nodded. The driver seized our bags and led us to the limousine and opened a door and shoved in bags and us before we had time to protest; then instantaneously reclaiming his own seat behind the wheel, he called back, "Your reservations are ready at the hotel, m'sieu'-'dame." And the limousine top dissolved, exposing us to the radiantly bestarred sky of lofty winter night.

Alone in this vast limousine, we crunched off in brittle snow between close-together-packed chalet-buildings, mainly conscious of snow-creak and frost-nose-nip and hard black starspecked sky and congealing breath-steam, until on a broad street we approached and passed through a high city-arch gate and stopped before a classic Swiss hotel. The Kali-driver swished around to get our bags and lead us in. All alone, we descended from the topless tonneau and snowtreaded into a cavernously fireplaced and massively beam-raftered lobby which could easily have housed a hundred weary skiers but just now was empty

except for the desk clerk, who was a flame-topped Kali. Our bags stood in front of the desk; the driver was gone.

Dio gave his name. They had a two-person reservation for him (now why? he hadn't made one). He and I were turned over to a bellman who was a flame-topped Kali. The bellman took us up a short flight of stairs and on the landing (right-angled left turn and more stairs) pointed above and said approximately, "Votre chambre, c'est Numéro 7 en haut. Pour uriner, toute la distance à droit ou à gauche, n'importe rien; pour l'autre, au fond, naturellement; même pour tous deux." He vanished, leaving the bags there: no chance to tip, no desire to tip.

I murmured, "I'm about ready to traverse *toute la distance à droit ou à gauche—*"

By the inward bite in his belly, Dio knew that he was on the track of something big. Seizing our bags, he clumped upward to Numéro 7 with me wife-obediently following. In the room (which was nice enough, with twin beds and a washstand), he dumped the bags on one of the beds and closed the door and dropped into the only chair, glowering straight ahead.

I sat on the edge of the unbagged bed, studying him.

He kept glowering at something on the far wall. I turned and looked: it was some kind of place-photo, and under it was some kind of script. I swung back to him; alert, gripping the bed edge with both hands and leaning forward, I suggested, "Ready to talk about what it is?"

He began beating on the chair arm. "No," he said.

"I'll unpack," I told him, rising and beginning it. . . .

He barked, "No!"

I dropped the bag lid, sighed, grinned, resat, and waited.

"We don't stay here," he told me bitterly. "I'm being had. There's a message here—I'm getting a goddamned sense of a fox-and-hounds game. Did you notice all those redheaded Kali-guys?"

"How could I help—"

"There's a message there on the wall—and *he* left it there *for us!* Go read it!"

Up close without transition, I considered the photo and the legend beneath. The photo showed a cave-mouth, and unquestionably it was the same cave-mouth which had gaped at Dio as his Fishermen's Cove illusion had ended. The verses beneath said: "Quand tu penses à la sagesse de l'homme moderne, souvenez-vous de l'homme de Mont Veillac."

I muttered aloud a halting translation: "When you are thinking about the wisdom of modern man, remember the man of Mont Veillac—"

As though my words had opened Pandora's box, out of

the cave-mouth flowed hundreds of diversified sail-craft, champagne-bubbling our space. . . .

We awakened on that, in the Paris Odéon; and each of us was impelled to sit up in bed and punch up his pillow and lean back against it staring straight ahead. All of the dream was hard before both of us: Dio's cognitive past, Dio's emotional past, the train trip, Pic Dentelé, the cave. . . .

My watch said 1:09; window-light said early afternoon. I took his hand; he gripped mine. I said, "Pic Dentelé?" He nodded. I said, "Why there? I never heard of it." He shook his head slowly. All right: note-comparing was not for now, it was presumably for later. I left him with it and went to the bathroom down a short corridor. Here in the Odéon in Paris (the dream was hard on me, I had to keep reminding myself that we weren't in Pic Dentelé), quite naturally at this hour I caught the bathroom unoccupied—there were only five rooms on this floor. Returning, I got dressed while he made the same visit; then he dressed in silence, and we went out on the street and walked three blocks and found a little restaurant for lunch on the Boulevard St. Germain.

With coffee gone and refilled, and ham and eggs partially stowed away, Dio told a tattered egg; "You and I dreamed the same dream again, right?"

"I think so."

"Then you know all about my pertinent past. And Esther."

"I know some. The dream didn't tell me all."

"Of course. Why Esther never got bitter, I'll never know."

"Some women don't—depending on the man."

"What does that mean?"

"It isn't bad. Go on."

"Lilith, you and I seem to be having conscious experiences of an amazing sort. Tell me what consciousness is—and don't give me some damn verbal runaround like 'Consciousness is attention.' "

I laughed my delight. "But it *is!*"

"Now why isn't that just a nonexplanatory synonym?"

"For this reason, Dio." I was grinning, but I laid it out. "I'll give you that we can't say what consciousness *is*— but we *can* say how it *works*. See, your mind is able to pay attention to only a small number of things at the same time, right? But your brain knows a lot and absorbs a lot that you aren't noticing at any given moment, right?" He was nodding at each "right." "But any time you want to or have to or are led to do so, you can divert your attention from something you *were* noticing, in order to dredge up and study something that was stored there *beneath* your notice —right?"

"Computer retrieval?"

"Right—except that every computer including a brain is mind-directed. Now. To say that at a given moment you are conscious of X, just means that at the moment you are noticing X, you are paying attention to it."

"Provisionally okay. Now—as Lo the Poor Indian once inquired about electricity, after they'd told him all about how it worked—what *is* consciousness, Dr. Vogel?"

I looked at him solemnly: my own ignorance after years of specialized study and practice never ceased to challenge and appall me. "Dio, I do think I've given you just about the best short sweeping summary that scientific psychology can responsibly offer. But now, if you want to move out several energy-orbits into the metaphysics of *experience*—"

He shook his head hard, waving his hand up and down palm-toward-me in the cease-fire signal. "I want it, but not at this minute. Stay scientific. Here's my hot question: Why can't I pay attention to something that I probably know but can't think of? That's a thorn-bush in any investigation, and right now on the Esther/Kali trail it is driving me absolutely batty!"

I was on an elbow with chin palmed, my right hand fork-toying with a ham-remnant, looking at him; he was gazing earnestly back. "Dio, if you were psychoneurotic, which you aren't now although I suspect you were once, you would have inward fears which would keep your computer from being *able* to retrieve a lot of stuff—exactly the kind of stuff which would help you cure yourself if your neurosis would only let you at it. Well: even if you aren't psychoneurotic, some things that your brain has stored are elusive; you just can't bring them into clear notice. And that's all there is, in my opinion, to Freud's famous *unconscious:* it is the whole body of brain-knowings and attitudes that the mind either *hasn't* gotten at or *can't* get at. I like the word *subconscious* better, myself: that which is below the level of conscious attention at some given moment; all of it is potentially available, but some of it may be tough to dig."

He assimilated that. I let him.

He, slowly: "Is any psychoneurosis ever completely cured?"

With him I should be honest. "Maybe not really. It just comes under better control."

"When you shared my dream this morning—your sharing included the first part, about my past?"

I nodded.

"What was the diagnosis?"

"Off the cuff, aggressive-type paranoid-schizoid."

"I was a legitimate bastard. That means a legitimate child who is a self-made bastard. And I'm not even sure about the legitimacy."

"Good boy."

"I—think maybe remnants of that old neurosis are keeping what I want to find suppressed. How would I melt through that block?"

"Old remedy. Figure out what you feel most guilty about, then face the facts of that guilt, including everything—your real guilt, your phony breast-beating guilt-overlay, and all your stupid inadvertencies. Then—verbalize it, to somebody you trust."

His gaze was shrivelingly direct: "Didn't I *do* all that—in my dream this morning?"

I brooded over him, really loving him. "Your self-serving wildness during your last months in the army. Your callous using of Esther. Your partially self-serving career-drive with the police and the CIA. Your consequent neglect of Esther—"

He leaned toward me, pleading, "Lilith, God damn it, she *didn't* want to *absorb* me, she only wanted to share my life! And I *denied* her that—"

I, coldly direct: "You tell me why you denied her that."

He, looking down, fists clenched: "Because I was afraid to love her, I was afraid of getting sucked into her."

"And now?"

Hard: "She's gone, and God bless you, Lil, I've shot my anxiety into you; I hope it doesn't trouble you. And I know now that Esther *wasn't about* to suck me into herself. And that is *not* a phony guilt-overlay, it is *guilt*!"

I, lightly: "Because you have rethought and confessed, *absolvo te,* psychiatrically speaking. And now there shouldn't remain any neurotic barrier to your brain-dredging."

Following an afternoon of Left-Bank cruising, an exqui-
site dinner at the Restaurant Méditerrané, on Place de
l'Odéon just across the street from our hotel. The Méditerrané had caught my fancy as we had walked past it; Dio
had wanted to blow me to Maxim's, but I had counter-ap-
pealed to the equal rights concept: "Look, chum, you've
chosen all the places and paid all the bills—this one is on
me, and I pick the place—and I do the actual paying and
tipping, none of this bull about slipping you the lettuce under the table—" He'd shrugged and hadn't fought it; and after my first gratification at this mark of his fellow-to-fellow
respect, I'd passed to forebodings about whether he might
begin expecting me to do this all the time—until it penetrated my stupidity that he had merely been too preoccupied to pay much attention. I reminded him while we were
at the hotel cleaning up for dinner; his eyebrows hit the ceiling,
but he grinned and acquiesced, and I had a pleased feeling
that he was pleased.

It was at the Méditerrané that he butterfly-pinned some of
the pertinent elusiveness in his subconscious. His announce-
ment of it was casual, except that his teeth were exposed
while a forkful of pike quenelles Lyonnaises midair-hovered.
He said, "It is like this, Lil. You and I have got to go, not to
Pic Dentelé—we've already *been* there—but instead, to
Mont Veillac."

It caught me with a mouthful of fish; and I stayed ladylike
until I got most of it down, whereafter I queried around the
rest of it, "Where in hell is *that?*"

He laid down his fork, sheathed his teeth, and reached for
the wine bottle in the nearby icebucket stand; the alacri-
tous wine-waiter, who had been halfway across the room,
easily beat Dio's hand to the bottle, filled both our glasses,
bobbed, grinned, and vanished. Dio remarked, "You're supposed to tip them separately." Preoccupied, I muttered, "The
hell with that, I'll leave one healthy tip, they can split it their
own way. . . . Mont Veillac: that would be the cave in your
Pic Dentelé dream?"

"In two dreams," he reminded me. "Remember the legend
under the photo? 'When you are thinking about the wisdom
of modern man, remember the man of Mont Veillac.' That
man was Cro-Magnon man, vintage twenty to fifty thousand
years ago; and in caverns in Spain like Altamira and in
France like Lascaux and Mont Veillac—and maybe too in

Switzerland, possibly even near Pic Dentelé—they did frescoes with skill and sophistication rivaling the Italian Renaissance—"

Maybe I was staring: he cut himself off with a grin and apologized for lecturing. I said intently, "Keep going in detail, it's fascinating me. And eat your fish, it's costing me." He nodded, took up his fork, and began to stuff in while he was putting out, talking intelligibly around his food because of his army training. . . .

He reminded me that his dream this morning had linked in a single continuity a review of his pertinent past, with special reference to Esther, whom he was seeking. Then the Pic Dentelé portion of the dream had taken us into mountain country, mountains on a grander scale than those around Mont Veillac but not dissimilar in winter. Three successive men who received us at Pic Dentelé had been Kali-guys. (Personally, jolting consideration!) The third Kali had told us that our room was *"en haut"* (rather than *"au dessous"*), in retrospect associatively suggesting the Mont Veillac highlands. In the room, his attention had first of all and last of all been drawn to the photo of Mont Veillac— "And as a small thing," he added, "the third Kali had told us to go either left or right, *'n'importe rien,'* to urinate—i.e., if you'll forgive me, go anywhere we like for pissing-types of business, but for serious business, *'au fond,'* into the depths—the cavern, Lilith."

Under my ant-prodding, he gave milk like an aphid. His dream-impression that Kali or somebody was playing him for a pawn-hound in a fox-and-hounds game. The identification between Kali and what he now recognized as the Mont Veillac cave in the Fishermen's Cove illusion, and Kali and Mont Veillac at Pic Dentelé. Then he sketched multiplied allusiveness in the historical perspective of the Cro-Magnon art in the Mont Veillac cave, hinted at by the dream-injunction to guard any gloating over modern achievements in the deep light of the prehistoric achievement at Mont Veillac. This animal art was not merely head and shoulders above anything before or since until the Italian Renaissance, it was up in a higher plane of mind: Minoan fresco-art had touched it, with more elaboration and less feeling, but neither Egyptian nor Greek nor Roman two-dimensional art had touched it. Mont Veillac, like Altamira and Lascaux, represented an authentic artistic *naissance,* relative to which what happened in Italy in the fifteenth and sixteenth centuries had been merely a *renaissance*. . . .

"I am tentatively proposing," he said low, "that this Kali, or Halloran, or whoever, is leading me—*us*—through Mont Veillac as an allusive jumping-off place to—maybe some kind of a new human renaissance in this world that needs it so hideously."

I queried, "The bizarre fleet of sailing-ships emitted by the cave-mouth in both illusions?"

His hands were flat on the white tablecloth; he was gazing at his messy platter with all the pike gone. "Maybe so. But I have to confess that my own silly subconscious may have put that aspect into both dreams. Many years ago, I had a vision about an independent nation of sailing ships which would sail up the world's rivers and unify Earth. But that went away with my reformation. . . . Hey, remember? Kali was pleading for me to unify *him*—"

His voice trailed off. The food-waiter had been waiting, and now respectfully he inquired of Dio about dessert, while nearby the wine-waiter eagerly awaited a new wine-order. I gave both orders, while Dio inattentively mused; they bowed uncertainly to me and then to Dio and went away to meet our wishes. These wishes were met in approximately two minutes, and my estimate of the tip went up to 20 or 25 percent depending on the check. (Francs we'd picked up at Le Bourget.) Meanwhile I was watching Dio.

He said presently: "Kali stole Esther with an Indian rope-trick which is magic. Presumably it was Kali who hit us with the auto-body levitation and the erotic Esther changing ridiculously to a box of pot: magic. The entire Fishermen's Cove illusion was whole-cloth magic; the emergence of fantastic sail-ships from the cave-mouth in both dreams was magic. Well: and the original purpose of the cave drawings at Mont Veillac was—magic, having either or both of two purposes: to assure hunting-prosperity, and to remind both men and animals of the brotherhood between Man and animals. Lilith, magic has been the quality of the entire fox-and-hounds trail; and my training simply does not prepare me to deal with magic that isn't mere trickery."

Warmly I commented, "But your *self*-training *has* prepared you to talk about the meanings of Mont Veillac man, and to suggest a dual magical meaning for their animal frescoes—"

His face came slowly up from the monumental sugar-cream peach Melba, which he was ignoring along with a sparkling glass of Piper-Hiedseck *douce.* "Lilith—what *is* magic—I mean, not modern illusion-craft, but the the *real* magic that primitive and ancient peoples were continually trying to use?"

I bent to the problem, not however ignoring the palatal goodies. "You don't want categories, like imitative and—"

"I know the categories. What *is* it?"

"Well, they didn't have science, and I think magic was their primitive approach to—"

"Could it have been *more* than that?"

Slowly I shook my head, not in negation. "There is so much in human experience that science can't handle. Religion: we can study the mental states, but the reality of their reference eludes us. Or the opposed powers of light and darkness that have meant so much throughout history and prehistory, which meant so much even to a dynamic twentieth-century psychologist like Carl Jung. Or Jung's collective unconscious. Or, for that matter, the universality of symbols in dreaming. Or the mechanics of ESP—" I cut it off, smiling: "Eat and drink your goodies. When do we leave for Mont Veillac?"

He stared, nodded, scooped desert, savored it, slugged champagne, repressed a burp, and blurted, "Remember this afternoon when we spent a couple of hours browsing bookstands along the Seine?"

"Separately from you, I had a ball—"

"Separately from you, I found a two-year-old timetable for trains out of the Gare de Lyons."

Sharp again! "Okay: the train for Mont Veillac?"

"At seven A.M. daily a train departs for Bordeaux. Next day, we pick up a train out of Bordeaux to Sore and points southeast. The seventh stop is at Mont Veillac. Just incidentally, in our Pic Dentelé dream our room was Numéro 7."

Weakened, I gulped champagne, and it rallied me—and rallied also the wine-waiter, who came to refill. I hurled my little dart: "Right after you checked that timetable, that must have been when you excused yourself and went into a bistro to make a couple of phone calls."

"One was to the Gare de Lyons; we entrain tomorrow morning at seven, I have reservations to Bordeaux, and from there we take our chances. The other was to the Vicomte

de Mont Veillac; I should have added that I also found a
beat-up old pamphlet about Cro-Magnon caves which mentioned Mont Veillac and identified the vicomte as proprietor
—" And he told me about *that* conversation.

Re-weakened, all I could do was finish my refilled champagne; he managed his and one more glass. Then he looked
a question at me; and I signaled for the check, which was in
front of Dio in forty-seven seconds, and Dio passed it to me,
and I was just able to bring off a rapid calculation and leave
a tip of high generosity.

When we departed the Méditerrané, with the wine-waiter
eagerly in attendance, I explained to the wine-waiter that I
had left at the table a gratuity for both waiters to divide
between them. The crestfallen expression on the wine-waiter's face would come back through years to haunt me.

During the short walk back to the Odéon—just across the
street, really—I pondered all this with more swiftness than
I usually manage; but my mind kept focusing on one un-
answered question—why was the locale of the dream at a
place in the Swiss Alps called Pic Dentelé? I am perfectly
aware that in a significant dream, the totality of the dream
with respect to the significant essence is as the environment to the pertinent happening, as soda to whiskey, as bread
mold to penicillin: in other words, the psychic significance is
bedded in a context of random dream-work contributed from
many irrelevant associative sources. The trick is to separate
out what is significant, and this means elimination of what
is mere dream-work. Yet Dio seemed to have wrung all the
juice out of the orange with only a suppositious reference to
this Pic Dentelé context which made no clear sense for his
interpretation; and I resolved to question him about it in
our room. . . .

My resolve died a quick death in the Odéon lobby, where
I waited, attention drifting, while at the desk Dio settled the
bill and requested a 5:00 A.M. call. (Here, they called you
with door-rapping.) Half a dozen scenic photographs hung
in this lobby. One near the desk was a photo, shot downward from an overhanging mountain, of a Swiss village in
winter. It was labeled "Pic Dentelé."

Oh, well: one travels with a detective-inspector, one
should expect a photographic mind.

11.

Entrained for Mont Veillac, Dio: "Want to tell me more about Burk Halloran?" Clearly he was the detective-inspector looking for Kali-related evidence, but so sympathetically was the question put that I surrendered instantly. What the hell, hadn't he confessed to me?

I told it to my lap, sitting across from Dio, considerably expanding what I had let out at Fishermen's Cove. "He came to our rest home as a mixed psychotic, but my God, he was so graceful-brilliant and apparently so objective about his own impulses and so-called delusions that none of us on the staff could figure out for a month whether he was nuts or faking. Look, he heard leprechauns, he had to obey them, they lured him into climbing flagpoles! Well: I was his psychologist, and I was young but a virgin saving myself for my unknown husband; I was liberal, but I endorsed the old double standard—which means, if you've forgotten, that a man's nature is to philander while a woman's nature is to be one-man-true, and both sexes should honor their natures—"

Passionately now, gazing at Dio: "Dammit, he *got* me! Let me tell you in a simplified way *how* he got me. He seemed to be an American-Irish rogue, he had every nurse in the rest home lathering for him, but somehow he never seemed to score; and meanwhile he and I became *marvelous* friends, he somehow understood me entirely, I *almost* understood him, and I mean understanding in all the personality-ways, motives and philosophies and beauty-appreciation and laughter and all the rest of it. He savored the ultra-antiquity of my name Lilith; he enjoyed comparing me with Ishtar the horned-and-bearded star-moon goddess of fertility-and-mind. . . .

"Well: one evening I was in his room as psychologist-friend with patient-friend, and what the hell, we got necking, by then I was almost sure he was faking the psychosis and I wasn't going to let him score anyway; but then all of a sudden, blast him, he froze away from me. And afterward, analyzing it, I realized on certain negative memory-evidence that he must be impotent—and a whole lot of neurotic interweavings came clear in the structure of their web, one being that his phallic impotency was not merely a symptom any longer but had turned around on itself and him to become a keystone cause. So I—"

Pausing, I reddened. Dio dryly finished for me: "—hardened and softened the keystone."

My chin hit my chest, I could feel my hot flush coolingpaling. I told my together-clenched hands: "*He* was perceptive like that. So next day I departed the rest home for collitch without seeing him again, and I spent many weeks alternately asking myself had I done him good or harm and if good would he try to follow me or not and was I pregnant and did it matter. If you followed those four thoughts, the answers turned out to be, respectively: good, no, no, yes. As to the last, about pregnancy, since he *didn't* chase me, I am —not like the wartime French girls I heard about who begged their American paramours, 'Donnez-moi un GI souvenir.' I want no souvenirs, friend: Halloran or nothing. And since it has so far been definitely nothing, I've decided that I like the free life of the intellect with a rare selective topple-over—" Swift remorse: "*No*, Dio, it is *not* like that! When rarely I bed with a guy, he is a *friend* and I want to know him that way among the other ways, and I've *loved* all the ways I've known *you*—"

Both his hands came out to grasp both of mine, and he told me, "This has been very good for me. All my hope for the future is that Esther and I will see you often."

I leaned toward him, uncertain: "Will you tell her?"

"Would I put her at a disadvantage by introducing you when I hadn't told her?"

The way he had put it was almost Jewish. Clasping his hands, I gazed at him a long instant; then releasing his hands, I leaned back in my seat and sort of collapsed, eyes closed, smiling. "You are good in all the ways that there are."

"Exclude marriage," came his gloomy reply. After a moment, he added, "Besides, you haven't really answered the thrust of my question."

Abruptly wide-eyed: "I—haven't?"

His little grin was very slightly dirty. "The thrust was—more substance about Halloran *himself*, apart from Lilith Vogel."

"And I—" But my protest aborted into laughter, and he joined in, and as we came out of it I managed a giggling apology for my own arrant egotism, and then we got sober and I studied his question hard.

I saw what he really wanted, and I told him so and tried to lay it in front of him clearly. Burk Halloran had really been two people all scrambled into a one that dwelt uneasily with itself but with an external appearance of total ease. The externality, and much of the genuine internalness, had been eager, buoyant, self-confident, highly gregarious, energetically zestful, sexually hearty and compelling but with sympathy and concern and grace. The other side, what Jung would call the chthonic dark as opposed to the shining side, was metaphysical to the point of being able to develop competent cosmic theory, introspective to the point where it sometimes seemed as though he could watch his own thoughts and feelings developing, analytical of others to the degree that as a pro he would have burned up psychology and psychiatry, and so detached from the world that he liked the sylvan rest home far better than outside and practically made a career of it during the month I'd known him. The psychotic outcome of the uneasy mix had been beautiful to watch and to talk with and play with and to know on the surface—and underneath, impotent limbo. If this paragraph has been hard to read, my extrusion of it for Dio's attentive comprehension was excruciatingly difficult to bring off; and I ended breathing rather hard, physically fatigued.

There was quiet for a while. He opened a brown bag that we'd brought and offered me (gratefully accepted) wine and a bit of cheese. After munching and sipping, I was thoroughly ready to go on—and that in itself interested me: seemingly I had gone quite a healthy way in my objectification of Burk.

Dio's hands were between his knees, his fingers were restlessly interlacing, he was watching them as he observed with care: "I too was an uneasy mix, a wild nutty mix, although different from your Halloran analysis. I got myself largely straightened out, I think. When that happened was about nineteen forty-eight. When did Halloran get straightened out?"

I was alert. "1948—basically, anyhow. Probably he is still having to work on himself—"

He looked up, his hands now still. "So am I. Can you tell me what he straightened out _as?_"

Frowning, I tried to remember exactly what I'd learned. "This is competent hearsay. He embraced the bright extroverted energetic side of his personality, tempering the extravagance with certain useful infusions from his dark side while turning away from certain other dark aspects. I suppose you know that you must never totally reject your dark side, it is where you get your depth; well, he knew that."

"Which dark things did he reject? Which did he turn away from?"

"I—understand that he kept his tendency to philosophize but turned away from compulsively intricate systems; kept his tendency to analyze himself and others for purposes of growing and understanding, but turned away from morbid self-scrutiny and from morbid in-scrutiny of others; kept his liking for special worlds, but required that they always be dynamically related to the whole world; got his free-floating anxiety tamed by learning to laugh at it in the perspective of cosmic time—"

"That's a pretty large observation for your institutional psychiatrist-colleague after dismissing a patient and without ever seeing him again."

My little smile wasn't happy. "To tell the truth, I'm drawing on more than his report. I've had a spy on him. He seems to be holding it nicely."

Almost angrily, Dio clutched the neck of the wine bottle and grated, _"Now_ you tell me!"

Understanding, contrite, I leaned forward to lay a hand on his arm. "There was no point in my telling you, friend, because I don't know enough to help us find him. I don't know where he is now or for several months back—"

Dio shook off my hand, swigged wine, replaced cork and hand-heeled it home, brown-bagged the bottle. "Okay, forget that, I was unfair, it's just that I _am_ a bird dog—"

I nodded slowly. "And you think maybe he stole your girl."

He stared out the window: the scenery was becoming as rugged as during our dream-approach to the Alps. "Let me tell you about my own inward split and my nineteen forty-eight reformation. My bright side was—zest for life, eager but not compelling sexuality although I did all right in that quarter, and—forgive me—a luminously photographic and almost infallibly logical mind. And I guess another trait counts as bright side: determination to move upward and onward no matter what, along with a lot of dreamings about what would be upward and onward. Now, dark side: hideous and continually present anxiety, bitter inferiority feelings about my Pueblo Indian social status and my runty ugliness, and a hell-hot feeling inside all the time that I would let myself be damned by God or the gods before I would surrender to all that or do anything except use it as fuel for my drive. Well: the dynamism of that mix was crushed in nineteen forty-five by its own extravagance; you got a whiff of that when you shared my dream at the Odéon. And between nineteen forty-eight and now—I *think* —I have kept all the bright and flatly rejected all the dark, except that a certain amount of the old anxiety and inferiority has kept seeping up to keep Sammy running. If your Halloran's self-adjustment was as beautifully balanced as you say, then he did a hell of a lot better than I have done; but at least, I think I'm a constructive citizen now and won't ever be anything else, and I like it this way."

He snapped a grinning face toward me: "Especially when I can use a Police Department vacation and CIA credit for a personal chase like this one!"

As bemused I gazed at him, he went sober again. "You said your favorite specialty was the sorts of hysterias that can produce dual or multiple personalities. In your opinion —was Halloran's illness such a hysteria? Was mine?"

I meditated, then told him: "In my opinion, there is rarely if ever a neurosis or psychosis so simple that it can be flatly classified by any standard category. There were *elements* of hysterical personality split in Burk: certainly the phallic impotency was hysterical; it was a subsconscious rejection of a part of himself deeply involved in interpersonal relationships. Maybe your psychoneurosis also had a hysterical underlay, I really don't know enough about you—"

"Okay, you've gone far enough. Now: what happens to a light when it goes out?"

"Dio—"

"Sorry: bad analogy. I'll say it directly. When there is a dual personality, and the—ego resolves to embrace one personality while turning away from the other— *What happens to the other?*"

Closing my eyes, I rubbed them. Fingers over eyes, I essayed, "I don't think you want a Freudian lecture. I think you are trying to get at something."

Then I let my eyes come open. He was frowning heavily out the window; and he said: "I think so too, but I don't know what. I think maybe it has something to do with the fact that you seemed to perceive Halloran as The Adversary in my Kali-illusions—but that doesn't at all correspond with the Halloran you knew or with the final self-adjustment that you report about him. And I think there is a way for me to use this intuition, but I am a very long distance from knowing what that way may be."

12.

After more than two days from Paris to Bordeaux and then to Sore and on southward, in late afternoon we train-wheezed into the village of Mont Veillac. Apart from pervasive irrational gut-feelings that here we might be nearing trail's end, we greeted the arrival with charmed and multifaceted anticipation: the mountainous wild of the countryside, the unforeseeable ways of the locals, the antiquity-weird of the cave, the medieval glamor of the vicomte's tall-blunt rough-stone castle, where we were to be housed—and the hearty hospitality of the stranger-vicomte, who, phoned by Dio from Paris without warning or introduction, had welcomed this American detective-inspector because Major Horse had helped liberate France from the Boches. Dio, who as a detective had made a subtle private study of age as reflected by voice, believed that the vicomte was probably in his vigorous late forties or early fifties; and from the impulsive staccato throaty-hearty manner of the vicomte as he talked with Unseen Stranger Horse, Dio expected (with amusement, knowing how wrong such expectations could prove out) to find that our host was a bluff affable realistic sociable countryfellow who probably kept a good house without putting on any airs at all.

We were met at the tiny station by a slender, dark young male driver who identified himself as Raoul; being a southerner, he pronounced his own name more like *Rrrrrrowlll* (reed-vibrating his tongue tip) than like the uvula-quivering Parisian bobcat-threat *Grrrah-ool*. He was abjectly apologetic: "Monsieur-'dame, the vicomte is desolate, but a sickness came suddenly upon him yesterday, and there is no way he can receive you at Château Mont Veillac. We have provided for you at the hotel here in town, you will have every comfort at the vicomte's expense, pray phone me instantly any wish that you may have, stay as long as you like, tell me when you wish to enter the cave and I will take you there—"

The hotel was three-story white frame, cubical, clean, and quiet. We had separate but communicating rooms: Dio, I was interested to learn, had been sensitive to the possibility that the vicomte might be a stickler for appearances if not a prude, and on the phone had identified me as his female police aide. Between our rooms was a private bath with an old-fashioned king-and-queen-size bathtub and an overhead pull-chain tank for a commode whose seat was perfectly and (Dio's phrase) arse-embarrassingly circular; the robinets on tub and washstand were gold-simulating polished brass. Raoul laid open our bags on racks, checked the rooms meticulously, hovered anxiously. Dio reached into his pants pocket; Raoul, demurring with upraised hand and pained expression, assured Dio that a gratuity for Raoul would be unnecessary although "as touching the hotel help, you know how it is, monsieur." (He never said "m'sieu' "; he always said "mongsioorrrr".) Having secured from Dio a schedule of 10:00 A.M. for pick-up to visit the cave, Raoul started away, paused, turned, added that we would be guests of the vicomte in the hotel dining room for all meals during our stay and any wines or liquors we might wish, and departed.

We stared after him. We looked at each other. Dio's brows were down; I had one eyebrow up.

Dio bitterly asserted, "It's happened to me before. The vicomte had second thoughts about letting the American upstart into his chateau."

Gently I counter-proposed, "The vicomte is genuinely hospitable and embarrassed, he is really ill, his apology is sumptuous and his man Raoul is a dear."

Slowly Dio's brows eased. "Do you think so?"

"Dio, there's a simple difference between our personalities. You distrust people until you know better; I trust them until I know better."

"My way has made me a goddam good cop. With your way, how can you be a goddam good psychologist?"

"My psychologist-way is your way; my human way is my way. I'm not here to psychologize the vicomte, and I don't think you're investigating him." I tried adding a pointed funny: "At least, Raoul is not a Kali."

Unsheathing his teeth, Dio checked his watch. "Would the dining room be open already at six-thirty?"

"The tavern would be open since morning."

We went down—there was no elevator, but we had to descend only one stair-flight from our rooms on the first story above the rez-de-chaussée. No specialization here as between tavern and dining room: one room having ten tables offered five on one side with tablecloths and five on the barside without; seven people, all French, were wining or beering at three of the bare tables, and all other tables were untenanted. We ventured toward an empty bare table but were intercepted by the single garçon, who demanded, "C'est M'sieu' Horse?" and at Dio's assent, delight: "Poor m'sieu'-'dame, une table spéciale, compliments du vicomte—" He ushered us to a most generous white-cloth-covered table in the bay, seated us, handed Dio a handwritten wine list, announced: "All these bottles have been provided for m'sieu'-'dame by the vicomte from his own cellar, nobody else sees this list; but also you should know that for your American pleasure he has provided Old Granddad, Chivas Regal, and Tanqueray, and for mix options, Schweppes tonic or soda and Stock Vermouth both sweet and dry—and the house has lemons, limes, cherries, and olives."

Faintly I preempted, "Now before dinner, I think Chivas Regal on the rocks with side water; wines later. Do you mind?"

The waiter enthused, *"Épatant!* The wonderful American palate!"

Dio remained somber and incommunicative through two drinks and dinner; and afterward he led me prowling the Mont Veillac twilight and night; and when finally we bedded down in his room, for the first time he was rough with me, almost frantic in his self-catharsis upon me and into me. Very early into it I knew how it would go, and I shook myself down into total and loose acquiescence: I *can* be a masochist when I let my soul-body drift into that mood, and it was clear to me that he terribly needed this, and before it had gone far it was equally clear to me that *I* terribly needed this. And it went far, with me shaken and semi-tortured and semi-outraged, and I flung myself deeply into it and suffered it and suffered it. . . . And when it was done, and he had collapsed into slumber, and I lay quiveringly pulling myself together and slowing my heart-pound into the heart-serenity that I need for sleep, I comprehended that while he had hurt me some he had always stopped himself short of hurting me importantly.

When in the morning he sheathed teeth and bumbled out an abject apology, I knew finally that I was in love with him. What sort of thing that might mean with respect to me and Burk Halloran remained to be seen, and my moment-mood was to cross off Burk: hell, what had he done for me since what I'd done for him? No; but the problem area was going to be, Dio and Esther. I resolved that I was *not* going to be a predatory home-breaker: Dio and I were good companions for now, and that was all of substance no matter what my hormones might be screaming.

Besides, I was *not* writing off Burk until I could verify a new dream.

Dio, I learned, had not shared this dream: it was mine privately, and it could only have symbolized a fearsome new intuition about the nature of Kali and his relationship to Dio and to Burk. I was not a dream-participant, but only the witness of the action. . . .

Out of a greening park, a broad many-storied high rise erected itself. Successively two figures emerged from the ground-foliage and began to scale the high-rise exterior, working their separate ways upward from story to windowed story. I was granted two brief close-ups: the first climber was Burk, the second Dio; they were mounting well distant from each other, Burk above, inattentive to each other.

Burk climbed much more rapidly; he reached the top when Dio was only a third of the way up. From this point on, my perspectives grew interconfused, as though I were simultaneously seeing close-ups and distant views from several angles; and now the growing analogy to the Fishermen's Cove illusion seemed to be reinforcing whatever had been intuited there.

From roof's edge now appeared two aerial stairways, one leading skyward and the other groundward, the angle between stairways being sixty degrees. These stairways had no solidity—they were mere abstract linear profiles. Atop the roof, Burk now lost human form, becoming a red circular blob; and the Burk-blob mitoted into *two* red circular blobs, and one started to bounce up the up stairway while the other began to bounce down the down, always vertically even with each other but increasingly divergent in periodic steps. At each step a linear printout between stairways expressed the growing distance between them: "TWO WILL NOT BE CROWNED UNTIL FOUR"; "THREE WILL NOT BE CROWNED UNTIL NINE"; "FOUR CROWNS TWO BUT WILL NOT BE CROWNED UNTIL SIXTEEN" . . . Spread it on down! Spread it on down like that! *Spread* . . .

At the fifteith upward or downward stair—the printout said "FIFTY WILL NOT BE CROWNED UNTIL TWO THOUSAND FIVE HUNDRED"—both red blobs paused, the high one nearly invisible, the low one now down on a level with Dio, who had progressed halfway up the high rise. Now Dio lost human form, becoming a circular black blob; the Dio-blob mitoted; one Dio-blob shot horizontally outward to fuse red with the lower Burk-blob, the other Dio-blob shot sharp-angle-upward to fuse black with the upper Burk-blob

At the instant of the two fusions, the stairways disappeared; and the lower red blob, now smaller, shot upward while the upper black blob plunged toward it; and just before they collided. I awoke with my mind screaming DON'T! DON'T! DON'T . . .

During most of an hour, with Dio snoring beside me, I was held awake, belaboring and belabored by the aweful sense of intuitive meaning. What it seemed to mean was physically impossible. Wasn't it?

Later, I would chill at a related aspect of Dio's morning apology. "I swear to you, Lilith," solemnly he told me, "that whatever caused last night's fiendishness has been excised from me forever."

Part Four

JUNE 2002

13.

By the end of the Blois discussions, a lot had come out about Kali and his lieutenants and their recent activities, and for Commodore Mallory a distinct pattern was beginning to emerge linking Kali with the diversified interests of three mutually competitive governments—Russia, China, and the United States—in process of arriving at mutual accommodations. The prime factor of linkage was now almost certainly the proposed REM Treaty. Consequently it was a devilishly dangerous fishing-expedition that Kali was on, whatever he might be fishing for; and the world-hazard made it all the more urgent that RP's private fact-finding investigation be pursued delicately.

All the RP officers physically or trivisually present departed the conclave with specific shadow-assignments either volunteered or handed out and accepted. And the Fleet Condition was declared Amber—which meant, among other things, that transportation discipline was broken: dispatch was more important than boating leisure, semi-emergency had overcome for the moment the superior value of aesthetics. A drawback was that Guru Kali would not fail to notice RP's Condition Amber; but he couldn't be sure that he was RP's quarry; and as a smoke screen, the commodore arranged nineteen worldwide leaks that the World Assembly had RP checking attitudes about the REM Treaty. Drawback: if Kali could actually intercept private thoughts, he would quickly pierce the screen and see the truth. Shrug: if he could do this, he would certainly be beaming his telepathic intercepts at RP anyway. And it wasn't *known* that he possessed such power.

The commodore wasn't supposed to give himself a specific assignment, nor did his flagship-crew have any assignments other than to coordinate incoming reports and respond to the commodore. Mallory, though, had something foggily in mind for himself—nothing sharp-definite, but something cloudily nucleating.

He began by touching base again with Esther d'Illyria, this time in person in Paris. Esther's biography was as intriguing as her svelte high-Jewish personality. She had married and divorced an American army officer, and had subsequently married a rich old bastard, the Vicomte d'Illyria. Her new husband had humored her whim of becoming an international cosmetician; he'd thereafter died on medical schedule at eighty-three, fully testate (as to his will, that is), permitting wealthy Esther to capitalize Cosmétiques d'Illyria unbeatably. She had a worldwide stranglehold on everything from economy stuff at twenty-five dollars an ounce on up indefinitely; her best and most expensive stuff was labeled, not simply "d'Illyria," but "Esther d'Illyria," so that she could personally claim an élite (and this élite could claim *her*). A necessary consequence was her potential of entrée into select social groups, and a few of them tested her, and her cool interpersonal deftness won them: the word spread, and there were no more testings, merely more invitations than she could accept, so that securing her presence became a hostess-coup. Among other talents, Esther owned and practiced the graces of sympathetic listening, known total confidentiality, and practical selectiveness as to occasional paramours. A few perceptive people suspected that she might sometimes pass a confidence or two to Commodore Rourke Mallory—but because Mallory enjoyed an equal reputation for discretion, nobody really minded, not even a couple of prime ministers. When in fact Esther *did* pass a confidence on to Mallory, she allowed herself to do so knowing that Mallory was totally confidential even as to his RP colleagues. Mallory might, she knew, *use* her information to put RP on to things; but never would Mallory *divulge* her information when it was confidential.

On the day after adjournment of the Blois conclave, Esther and Rourke perambulated pleasantly in the Parc de Vincennes. (Down Loire to Atlantic, up Atlantic to Seine, and up Seine to Paris is fast on skimmer-drive.) Dark slender Esther (who walnutted her hair) and silver slender Rourke had embraced the new senility-arrest technique coincidentally

at about the same time, in 1979, when those in the know
and the bucks could be sure that it was reliable; it wasn't of
course perfect, there would be subsequent aging at the slowed
rate of one year in ten. As a result, eighty-seven-year-old
Rourke Mallory was a physical late-sixtyish, looking and
feeling somewhat younger because of drive and physical
conditioning; while seventy-nine-year-old Esther d'Illyria was
a physical late-fiftyish, looking and feeling much younger because of drive and physical conditioning and her own cos-
metic techniques. Thus both of them were still reasonably
vital, but their old sexualitiy and their always-availability was
an accustomed thing which was comfortably there if wanted
but not intrusive on more valuable things

                                like eating peanuts
and trading reminiscences and high political gossip and stroll-
ing five miles or so in the parc and tossing peanuts to
bears here and swans there and very often just being silently
together as infinitely deep friends.

Of course they bedded together that night, using assumed
names (both of them had all kinds of identification cards
for concierges) in a small friendly Vincennes hotel that she
knew—it would be three ways better, they agreed, than bed-
ding in her house, although she apologized for failing to entertain Rourke at home. Although Amber and Red Conditions precluded sexual activity among RP members, each
RP had dispensation outside RP if he or she could inwardly
justify that it was desirable for RP purposes and not merely
for pleasure. Being Esther's *friend*, Rourke reminded her of
this regulation before they registered; and she observed with
a contented smile, "To be free with you, my old friend, I will
satisfy even your self-justification."

After the mutual climax (each of them was good for about
one per night, on occasional nights, although of course they
knew how to stretch pleasure before and beyond that), for a
good share of the remaining night before ultimate sleep they
talked with intimate seriousness, their arms about each other
in bed, or across a room-table from each other over cheese
and wine. When regretfully Rourke departed in the morning
(she preferred to use her own means of making public appearance in Paris just ahead of noon), it was with a quiet
regret that they parted, each with a profound personal value-
sense that leaving the other meant having been with the
other. But when Rourke Mallory left Esther d'Illyria, he took

with him more information and more disturbance than all his RP had been able to afford him.

It was not that Esther had given him any really *new* information about Kali or about the REM-Talks. It was rather that Esther had confirmed all that she had told Mallory by telementation before the Blois conference, and had contributed a great deal more evidential support along with a strong sense of Kali-progress. Kali *was in fact* about to swing the opposition-minorities in Russia, China, and the United States toward concurrence in a REM Treaty. And while Mallory and his RP also supported a REM Treaty, Mallory's feeling of confused dismay on learning that Kali was working in the same direction perhaps resembled the feeling that John Calvin might have confronted on learning that the devil supported his doctrine of predestination-and-grace.

Mallory, leaving Esther, was new-armed with the names of four American cabinet officers, eighteen American senators, six members of the Soviet Praesidium, and three Chinese ministers who had confided to Esther, or whose spouses had confided to Esther, that they were profoundly under the religious influence of Guru Kali and therefore spent much of their own private time seeking their inner lights and pressing mentally for success of the REM Talks. And this was because they were convinced that if the REM Talks should fail, beyond question one of the three powers would sooner or later use REM against one or both of the other two. Esther had quoted one minister, who happened to be a world-respected physical scientist, as asserting, "Those who have been looking for the end of the world through an Armageddon have overcomplicated the formula; the simple method is REM."

Then Kali was *benign*? Yet Mallory, in common with Denny McIntosh and the Pope, had kept thinking of Kali as a Mankind-Enemy, or at the very least a supernally dangerous self-interested Mankind-Predator. But, logic, logic: RP was benign, and RP supported the REM Treaty—and Kali supported the REM Treaty!

And yet, there was no question that Kali was RP's enemy.

Mallory was more confused than he had been at any time during the past fifty-four years. (The "fifty-four" span was clear in his mind: he could peg the date and occasion of his prior deeper confusion.) What bugged him most painfully was a conviction that somehow he wasn't asking himself the right questions; that a *right* question, like the right fly, would lure to the surface the elusive trout of a right *clue*. . . .

Back on his flagship *Ishtar*, he got out an APB mentation to RP: "Those of you who can best check on (he read off Esther's name list), check on them with reference to the target and report when ready."

And he sat on deck stewing while the *Ishtar* purred northwestward down the serpentine Seine toward the ocean. He knew where he was going—it was a shrine that he had long ago discovered, most productive for devotionals and resulting inspiration; during an early pilgrimage there, he had hit on the idea of the RP Fleet. It wouldn't do to fly there; shrines you don't hastily visit.

14.

Debouching from the Seine at Le Havre, the *Ishtar* dolphined north of west around Cherbourg, then south of west around Brest, then doubled into the long southeastward thrust down Biscay Bay past Bordeaux into the little Bassin d'Arcachon. Skimmer lift-and-drive brought it all off from Paris in twenty hours.

They anchored in the basin, the *Ishtar* even with skimmers being too much for the River Leyre; and the commodore pushed upriver in his longboat, skimmer-airprop, whose small task-force crew was commanded by Lieutenant Cassie Wozniak. Blonde Cassie and the commodore were good friends. He'd preempted her several times on the Draft Board and they'd both enjoyed it despite her less than perfect catharsis in view of Mallory's age; each time, afterward they'd talked a lot and liked each other. (That's what loving or friendly Eros is *for*, he reflected, after the passional aesthetics of mutually crafted psychic-neuronic blow-off.)

During this upriver push toward his sanctuary, however, she and he didn't talk much: she knew where he was going and how to get him there, and she respected his brood while he respected her competency, and so they congenially left each other alone. It's a good formula for certain kinds of friendship, rare to achieve; in this circumstance, Esther and Mallory would have been like that.

They put in at Sore; and there the commodore disembarked, to move alone overland to Mont Veillac, where his sanctuary was. (He would use a light skimmer-harness, following the roads.) On the fisher-dock at Sore, he and Cassie shook hands (RP didn't salute unless they chose to do so). She asserted, "Sir, I understand that I am to wait here for five days, and on the sixth, if you haven't rejoined me, I am to alert the ship." He responded, "Right, well done, I'm off," and turned to leave.

"Sir—" It was her voice behind his back.

He turned: "Ms. Wozniak?"

Her blonde eyebrows were flat over steady blue eyes. "When you do return to the ship, I respectfully suggest one night of the Draft Board; and I further respectfully suggest that you select me."

Half-smiling, he considered her with favor. "Is this request aesthetic or practical?"

"Sir, it is not without its aesthetic aspects. But primarily, in view of the current situation, it is practical."

"Is there something you perhaps could tell me now?"

"Sir, I need time to think about it, and the Draft Board situation is best for it."

He was divided between interest in the proposition and faint irritation at Wozniak for the Tantalus-trick; but he concluded to trust in her sincerity; assuming that she really needed meditation-time, what he might now strangle out of her wouldn't be worth having. He grinned: "Thank you, Ms.; I will take it under consideration." And he departed.

It was still true that damned few people lived in Mont Veillac. He paused in the hotel long enough to phone the vicomte; he got old Raoul, who knew him well, and advised him of intentions and probable timing, after first making sure that the health of the very ancient vicomte was sufficiently borderline for old-friend-guest reception. As for the cave, the steward knew that no directions were needed:

the commodore was practically a habitué. Before disconnect, there was an understanding: Mallory's call for pick-up would be instantly responded to, either the next day or the next after; but if by the third day there had been no call, Raoul would bring a few experienced cave-men to investigate.

Having checked his ground-heavy skimmer-harness at the hotel, Mallory with leisure hiked the difficult two-hour trail upridge and then deeply downridge to his sanctuary: the practically unknown cave of Mont Veillac.

Its entry was generous enough: he could penetrate erect. He entered the fifty-two-degree dank, already feeling like a prehistoric pre-priest. When darkness was dangerously total, he touched a known wall-switch: the oozy labyrinth ahead was dim-blue-illumined; vividly he re-imaged the Blue Flame. Was Kali lurking here, embodied or enghosted, to do him hideously in? A merry smile irradiated Mallory's unseen face: bodies you fought, ghosts you outscared. He moved on inward.

Perhaps twenty minutes later, the blue-lit sanctuary flared wide for Mallory. He found his favorite seat, a natural rock-bench toward room-center, and sat there, and began his customary deliberate panoramic scansion of the art on the cave walls, magically frescoed with magical creativity for magical purposes in this deep hiding place, intended to be forever invisible to all but the spirits and the tribal élite.

Drive your fancy maybe fifty thousand years into your own past. These angrily defensive humped bison, these eagerly crouching carnivores, these spear-armed men magically disguised by tiger-heads and bear-heads, charcoal-drawn or torch-char-drawn by cave-creeping priest-artists presumably less able than we in their intelligence (although this is debatable) and immeasurably more improverished in their culture-heritage (or better, immeasurably less wealthy in it, less embarrassed by it) leaped soul-mightily upon each other in the faintly flickering blue; they were drawn better than we draw, they lived as vitally as we live, *we* had drawn them. I know at first hand: fifty years earlier, I had been there with Dio.

Forget the cave-cold. Rourke Mallory worshipped whatever God is.

And meditated.

He had been known to stay here for many days. He resolved to remember to fingertap-stimulate his old-fashioned

tuning-fork-movement watch every time it said twenty-four
(since he wouldn't be moving about much) and to keep an
eye on its date indications: three days were the maximum
he allowed himself, this time. Three days, though, constituted
a leisurely span: he could meditate and dream as the dreams
might take him. He wouldn't be fasting, entirely: in a
shoulderstrap-purse were cheese and wine.

Concentrating on a bison hump, Mallory reviewed what he
had learned about Kali. It was neither formulative nor reassuring; indeed, in view of Kali's physical resemblance to a
younger Mallory, it was soul-troubling. For system, Mallory
numbered off points, guardedly reminding himself that the
points were not number-discrete—they interflowed.

One: Kali, having established himself as RP's mortal
enemy, had mortally threatened Mallory in the Fishermen's
Cove illusion and perhaps had tried to murder Mallory. *Two*
(and this was a complex point): Kali was using his religio-
magic spell to penetrate international politics at the highest
levels in order to influence a game for national power and
territorial survival—and the direction of his influence was
on the same side as RP's. Three (a point that kept haunting
Mallory): at the end of the Fishermen's Cove illusion, the
Kali-phantom had begged for self-unification. *Four*: if Ilya
could be believed—and Mallory did believe him—Ilya's intense application of the Kali prescription had worked, as
millions of others were testifying; but it had worked by
changing the unchangeable past—and in a distressing way
which argued that whoever had answered Ilya's prayer, Kali,
or someone greater, had with satirical callousness clung to
the letter of the prayer, disregarding essentials of its spirit
that Ilya had not thought to formulate.

Now, Point Four troubled Mallory excessively. He could
think of only two ways of changing immutable past: a raw
natural triumph of mind over temporal extension and indeed
over any intelligible time-logic; or, intervention of a deity in
response to Ilya's deep intercessive prayer.

(Of course Mallory understood the concept of continually
changing past as advanced by pragmatism's creativity-wing;
but this he had long ago discarded as metaphysical sophistry
having only perceptual truth.)

There was, of course, the appealing possibility that the
past had not been changed, that everything had always been

that way, only Ilya couldn't know it, even that Ilya's test had
been *precipitated* by his proximity to his parents which subliminally he had apprehended through the telepathic influence
of *their* intentions about *him*. Eh, but wouldn't it be easy to
explain *all* the countless Kali-influenced wishes-come-true as
wish-impulses inspired by subliminal apprehension that
they were about to come true anyway? But that possibility
was controverted by the improbability of every impossible
wish intensively prayed for being a priori something about to
happen anyway; Kali would never pin his reputation on *that*
sort of gamble—he must *know* something! Mallory decided to
call this the a priori theory and to push it far back in the
oven while he concentrated up front on the two ways in
which the past might conceivably be changed.

That it could be a raw natural triumph of a mind, such
as Ilya's or some little guy's, communing with his inner light
and intensively wishing—simply, this went by the board when
one thought of the enormous complications of past-changing.
Ilya or another would actually have to *know how* to change
past, would have to build the methodology into his prayer.
And Ilya's report had made it clear to RP that he had not
known how, nor had he even thought of needing to know
how; instead, naively he had pressed for fulfillment of a wish
that he deemed impossible to fulfill. When Illya's parents and
the bishop had revealed the complications of Actuality Two,
these complications had involved changing actions and memories of countless people in 1944 and in all the intervening
time right up to the present. It might even have been necessary for the cosmos, in this changing of itself, to have pur-
posely manufactured the two sacrificial friends and even the
bishop. The ramifications rippled out until the bison hump
told Mallory to drop the hypothesis.

Consideration of this hypothesis had, however, taught
Mallory something of what a deity would have had to bring
off, did the deity exist (the alternate hypothesis) and had he
responded to Ilya's prayer. For a while, then, Mallory de-
liberated, in the light of this new problem, the perfectly possible concept that a deity did exist who was interested in
Man, or whose influence could be enlisted, and who knew how
to do anything he wished to do ("he" here meaning he or she
or he/she or it, immaterially).

Had such a deity responded to Ilya? *Objection:* it sure took
a lot of doing, then, to get the deity's attention. *Answer:*

maybe the deity, like a human consciousness controlling a whole human body, was usually interested only in his own purposes through or with his body (which would be Man, or maybe, more generally, Life), and responded to a single part of his body (such a Ilya) only when through deep intercessive prayer (— neutral pain-impulse) oriented toward the deity (= inner light), the part expressed acute and self-injurious pain. *Objection:* a deity interested in Man or more largely in Life could scarcely take time for such complex therapy for a single replaceable cell such as Ilya. *Answers:* this might be fun or dedication for the deity, considered by him worth his while; much of our time might be little of his time; and Ilya might not be replaceable. *Objection:* Ilya had thoughtlessly left happiness out of his prescription, and so the deity had in the process created unhappiness, and this did not add up for a deity conceived as omnipotent, omniscient, and good. *Answers* proliferated: the deity might have his own interpretations of *good,* or he might not even *be* good but only cold-interested in this case or that case; and he might not be actually omniscient-omnipotent but only potentially so, meaning that he could figure out how to do anything he might happen to think of or be directed to. Eh, Mallory considered: there might be a lot to say for the deity-hypothesis, if one were allowed enough latitude in his concept of deity.

It struck Mallory that he was going far afield indeed; and he concluded that he should now back-burner this metaphysical Point Four and return to hard thought about hard-human Points One and Two. His attention began to flit between One and Two uncontrollably, as though he were watching a ping-pong game in action; for each point's meaning depended on prior point-meanings, and the ball's action was the outcome of their counterpoint. After a while he stopped this and focused on dead center, imagining that the bison hump was the ping-pong net, and required himself to think nothing at all. . . .

And that was when it hit him. For *deity,* maybe substitute *Kali?*

The notion almost blew his mind. For it brought back all the old God-Satan opposition concepts which he had long ago discarded; and it cast Kali in the diabolical role at a supernatural level.

But—all right, God damn it, let's fly it and see who salutes!

He got past the front of it quite easily. Start by assuming that Kali is a deity, presumably diabolical, who *knows how* to change the past in order to grant otherwise impossible wishes, thus realizing the wishes while making it all seem entirely natural.

Mallory had already gone through the generalities of what Kali would have to do in this process. He now faced down a key question: how had Kali *known* what Ilya was wishing? More complexly, how could he know what *all* his inspired followers were wishing? If Kali intercepted inner-light prayer, could even a Satan-deity be expected, in the time between the decision to pray and the start of the prayer, to intercept, and identify as his own, *all* the Kali-inspired intensive prayers that were going on in the world all at once, mingled with all the other non-Kali praying which was going on and which Kali would wish to ignore? And if Kali as a deity could do this and still do all the other things which Kali was doing, could the guru also simultaneously be bringing off the intricate maze of necessary manipulations for *all* the millions of his own who were claiming success for his method?

Mallory tried a few eliminations, starting from the assumption that Kali did hear all the prayers but had to be selective about answering them. *Elimination One:* a lot of his past-changing for some people might cancel the past-changing needs of others, reducing the number of actions necessary. *Elimination Two:* a lot of the "impossible" wishes might in fact be possible wishes, and the wishing might stimulate the necessary human action; and if Kali could identify such wishes, he could refrain from action and still these followers would claim success through his method. These two eliminations were somewhat simplifying, but there was no telling how much. The hypothesis remained plenty difficult.

The commodore then turned to a more direct question: was there a possibility that Kali had recognized Ilya in his audience physically monitoring the guru, and thereafter Kali had been telepathically monitoring Ilya? After some thought, this came through to Mallory as a nonproductive possibility. Ilya had simply, unannounced and unregistered, dropped in on a very large assembly, listened to Kali, and drifted away. No: occult as it seemed, it was better, given the assumption that Kali intercepted Kali-prayers, to imagine that there was something distinctive about Ilya's prayer which had attracted the guru's favorable attention. . . .

And Mallory had it! Ilya had deliberately designed this intercessive prayer as a *test* of Kali's method! How many others would do *that*? And if *this* ingredient had telepathically stung Kali while countless other prayers were drifting through him and being screened, perhaps it had galvanized Kali's attention, bringing him quickly to recognize that Ilya was high in RP, a final fact driving him to bring the thing off for Ilya—satirically twisted by the dirty little irony.

This quasi-logical imagining made Mallory faintly dizzy; his bison kicked and snorted a bit. A watch check told him that it was 3:00 A.M. of his second day here; a knapsack check added that he'd been involuntarily munching and nipping—half the wine and cheese were gone. It was time for sleep; he could do this in the cave without blankets, he'd learned long ago to control his body temperature somewhat under unfavorable conditions. Only . . .

No, this he had to pursue just a bit further, before sleep. For he had come dangerously close to convincing himself that the deity hypothesis was the right one, except that Kali was the probably diabolical deity. Where was the goof in Mallory's reasoning?

Eh—not a goof-identification, but a *supporting* consideration. Hadn't Kali presumably driven Mallory into near-suicide using a *projected* dream-fantasy? Well: if Kali could *project* all this at a distance into a living mind—then, what *couldn't* he do?

For that matter, if Kali could receive and screen telepathies, was he now receiving and screening in Mallory?

"Guru," Mallory mentally muttered, "whatever you are hearing of all this, do what you can with it; I dare hope that my underground depth is muffling. Besides, now belatedly I think about it, maybe I have an inbuilt scrambler—" Whereupon he activated peculiarly the in-brain device which he used for mentations to RP; thereafter his thinking stayed intelligible to himself, but perhaps it was scrambled for any other receiver.

Ridiculously, a great deal of constructive thinking had gone on before the scrambling; and now that the scrambling was achieved, he was ready for sleep. Heigh ho: at least, his dreaming would be scrambled. . . .

Curling up on the rock-bench, he activated an almost-

always effective method of sleep induction. Drowsily and
faintly, he was troubled by the reflection that he hadn't met
Point Three head-on: the Kali-phantom's plea for self-unification, which now seemed vaguely linked with Kali's resemblance to Mallory. But this troubling was not sufficiently
strong to interfere with success of the sleep-induction method.

Cave interiors ignore sun and stars and temperature
changes. A night passed, and a forenoon; Mallory was often
in darkness, extinguishing the blue glow while he slept or
napped or meditated; sometimes, omitting the blue illumina-
tion, he used a powerful pocket lamp whose beam resembled
daylight, or another which emitted ultraviolet light, while he
prowled studying the long-familiar art in *endroit* after weird
endroit. The ultraviolet was new for him in here, and it il-
luminated marvelous new truths. . . .

He came at last to a narrow tubular crawl-space, and he
worked his way in and along it—with multi-plied inward
disturbance. Two of the plies were related to a rockfall here
in 1952, reported to Mallory some years ago by Raoul: one
dimension was, naturally, to make Mallory queasy about a
rockfall upon himself; the other was weird—a man and a
woman who were in the inner chamber had been trapped by
the rockfall, but when Raoul and his party of strong young
locals had cleared the rock-blocked crawl-space and gone in,
the man and woman had vanished, nor to the vicomte's
knowledge had they ever been seen again. The third ply for
Mallory was the remarkable fresco, radiating some kind of
meaning, which he knew he would find here. The deepest
ply was an irrational sense, neuronically signaled by an almost sexual groin-thrill, that this time he *would* grasp the
meaning—and it would be related to Kali.

Emerging from the tube, he stood erect in the inward
grotto-darkness, stretched out his muscles and joints, and
used his daylight pocket lamp to floodlight the far wall three
meters ahead. The fresco, which had often haunted his
dreams, represented a giant predatory bird talon-and-
hooked-beak hurtling down upon a huddled people-group.
(The people, as in Cro-Magnon art generally, were clumsy
slash-faced crudities, by contrast with the hyper-realism of
the animals: maybe some kind of people-image tabu? Or
maybe animal-totem people, seeking to regain some kind of

lost unity with other animals, didn't want to emphasize their human difference?)

Until now, this artwork had always meant for Mallory a kind of primitive concrescent abstraction of raw power. Now, quivering with anticipation of new meaning, for the first time he hit it with the ultraviolet. . . .

New meaning began to come when, for the first time in repetitious viewings, he saw under ultraviolet a thing about the skydiving aggressor-bird. In this light, its plumage was purple.

He advanced upon it, studying the arousal-erected feathers. Adjusting his ultraviolet lamp to small-focus intensity, he scrutinized the purple head and the violet eyes.

Faded now by tens of millennia of cave-damp, the crested head-feathers had originally been flame-red, and the eyes murderous blue.

Kali! Ultrasophisticated power!

Fifty thousand years ago?

Soul-shaken, he backed away and cut his lamp for darkness-brooding. He was remembering Point Four: that at the end of the Fishermen's Cove illusion, Kali had pled with his small dark challenger: "Unify me, *and you will win my power*—"

His daylight lamp came on, almost of itself; in *this* light, the bird feathers did maybe seem to have a suggestion of vestigial ruddiness which he hadn't heretofore noticed. Substituting ultraviolet again, he saw the red-betraying purple unmistakably again; and immediately new meaning leaped from another element of the fresco, one which he had always dismissed as merely a balancing element in the concept of the artist. The predatory bird screamed down from above toward below-leftward where cowered the people; but still farther below to the right, clinging to an escarpment with his observing head just above the cliff edge, a skin-clad spear-armed man was watching the attack. Now for the first time, in ultraviolet, Mallory saw head-hair on this man-figure: the purplish hair must originally have been painted red; and the man's eyes, glowing violet, must originally have been blue.

Almost ill, Mallory switched off the lamp and squatted in darkness on the cave floor. After meditation, he deactivated his brain-scrambler, and he sought and found his own inward light. Then he murmured with deliberate intent to communicate, "Listen, Kali, I have a counter-deal. First, you

give me your powers; *then* I can find a way to unify us. . . .
But listen, Kali: in this unification, *I will* be on top, *you
will* be subordinate—"

Presently, feeling no difference, he opened eyes to darkness and chuckled awkwardly, embarrassed in darkness, embarrassing the cave-silence with his noises. And he departed
the inner chamber, crawling in darkness back through the irregular tube. Once erect in the main chamber, with the blue
lighting on, he tossed a soft goodbye-salute to his bison;
whereafter he headed for the telephone near the entrance.

Mallory had progressed as far as he could in this cave,
this visit. It was time for him to depart, accept the hospitality
of his revered old friend the Vicomte de Mont Veillac for a
night, and then return to Sore. What he would do after that
he didn't know yet; but maybe, returning to the *Ishtar*, he
would find some helpful dispatches from colleagues.

15.

Antoine Rochereau, Vicomte de Mont Veillac, was maybe
about a hundred years old, now in this (for both men) regrettably late year 2002. When Mallory entered his parlor,
Rochereau swayed afoot in centerfloor, then tottered toward
the commodore with arms outstretched; Mallory embraced
him with affectionate caution for his fragile skeletal frame,
wishing that conservatism had not prevented Rochereau
from embracing Senility Arrest, grateful nevertheless that the
vicomte's own heart and resolve had arrested senility for
his mindbrain. The ancient man's hands quavered on the
moderately younger man's shoulder blades, and his mouth
reached up to kiss Mallory's cheeks (thirty years ago he had
been several inches taller than Mallory). Rochereau squealed
for Raoul, who was already there, ordered brandies, which
were already there, clawed Mallory's arm, led Mallory to the

vicomte's own favorite easy chair, sat precariously in a secondary chair nearby. Mallory held respectfully silent during the following three minutes while helpless Rochereau sought and found his breath again.

Looking up at the commodore, the vicomte groped for his brandy and found it and raised it. Mallory found his and raised it: he'd forborne until the vicomte was ready. Rochereau inhaled; Mallory inhaled; they both had sloshed first, of course, but the vicomte's slosh merely followed from his hand-palsy. Having pretended to sip, Rochereau set his down; Mallory did sip, but sparingly; and while critically Rochereau watched, Mallory once again earned the vicomte's approval by not swallowing but mouth-holding the sip until rather quickly it soaked into the membranes. Then, hand-warming the brandy, Mallory adjudged, "Armagnac Capuchon, 1991. An excellent year."

"So," nodded the vicomte, dodderingly studying his guest. Mallory mused: *Why do I keep noticing his dodder? Equalize our ages at thirty, and he could at least equal me with my own choice of weapons. I don't think I am pitying extreme old age, just because in my eighties I'm stabilized in my sixties; I think I am admiring insistent longevity in despite of the* merde *of senility—the more so because my own longevity is done no matter how hard I may insist. I salute Mont Veillac: if our relative times had been different, he might have been competing with me for command of RP.*

Rochereau said presently (we'll elide his breath-pauses), "So you have been in the cave?"

"It is my sanctuary."

"I know; and it was mine once; and mentally, still it is. I have not been in there for five decades."

"It is the same Cro-Magnon sanctuary; except for some lighting improvements, it has not changed; disrespectfully it ignores a mere five decades."

"I am glad. Often I repeat my orders to keep it so. I was even reluctant about the dim blue lighting, but perhaps the Cro-Magnon would regard this as magic and therefore appropriate. I marvel, though, that such a cave should be the sanctuary of an American."

The truth of the national-origin label, and indeed of the culture-nativity, hit Mallory as being whimsical: his tastes had been international as long as he could remember, and for consistency (but with explicit regret) he had renounced American citizenship soon after his RP had been declared a nation. But he merely said, "I respect every instance of Man performing at the highest ability-level that he can possibly evoke."

"So: we understand each other, Rourke; we always have, since your first visit here in nineteen fifty-one when in my cave you conceived the idea for your fleet. And both of us have spoken of a five-decade lapse. For some reason I am remembering, not the last time I entered the cave, but the last time I *intended* to enter—only there was a small stroke which canceled all future entries for me."

"Perhaps, Antoine, you would finally want to tell me about that."

"Not about the stroke, but about the intent. Two other Americans were involved. Today is—what date? Oh yes, it was fifty years ago, only a few days off the exact date. An American detective-inspector named Horse, and his aide named Vogel—"

Both names *pinged* for Mallory: Horse distantly, Vogel poignantly. Bypassing Vogel, he pressed, "You said Horse?"

"Cheval, yes: Horse. Do you know him?"

"First name Diodoro?"

"Curious name. Yes, I think so."

"He was once known by a friend of mine in Paris, Mme. Esther d'Illyria."

"I know Esther. She knew Horse?"

"Yes—but what about him here?"

"It was simple but rather embarrassing. He had phoned ahead from Paris, and of course I offered the hospitality of my house. He would arrive in two days, and I planned on the following day to conduct him personally into the cave, which was his reason for coming. But my stroke contravened, and I had Raoul put him up at the hotel—as my guest, of course. But I never met him—and never since have I entered the cave."

"C'est grand dommage."

"Oh well, I know the cave by heart anyway. Perhaps the greater pity is that I never met Horse or his lady aide, because they vanished in the cave."

Mallory's heart accelerated. "*They* were the ones—"

"You heard about them?"

"Raoul told me, years ago; he mentioned no names, it never crossed my mind to discuss it with you."

"Assez mystérieux, cet évanouissement."

"And—this lady-aide, she was named Vogel?"

"*Oiseau*, yes: Vogel. The discretion of Monsieur Horse with respect to Mademoiselle or Madame Vogel was monumental: he called her his psychologist-aide, and he asked for separate rooms—but adjacent, for police convenience—"

In the midst of his restrained amusement, Rochereau seemed abruptly to weaken, putting a hand to his emaciated forehead. Quickly Mallory leaned toward him: "My friend, you must not exhaust yourself."

The ancient smiled thin: "I am sorry. We dine at eight, that is three hours; my talking-strength will be good then. I eat sparingly, you will have a feast; you can mumble at me juicily around your joints while abstemiously and avidly I listen fingertips-to-fingertips—"

He had touched a bell button on his chair arm (the single chime was charming), and the venerable Raoul was here, and Mallory was standing. Raoul said, "Monsieur le Commodore, be so good as to wait a bit, and I will show you to your rooms." The steward then bowed before the vicomte, allowed the ancient to clutch his arm, put his own arm under the shoulders of his patron, helped him erect, paused facing the vicomte toward the commodore.

Rochereau murmured, "Monsieur, you command my chateau. Pray command." He nodded and was helped from the room.

Having subsided into the vicomte's easy chair, Mallory meditatively nursed Armagnac, considering the old salon well known to him: heavily tapestried and carpeted and furnished in a worn seventeenth-century mode, large and square but not vast, high-ceiled but not lofty-ceiled in a simple sort of baroque, with a generous but sedately plastered fireplace that was dead now in June. The dining room, Mallory knew, was vaulted and timbered; but as to this salon, which was where *he* lived, the vicomte was elegant-plain, accepting the design of his ancestors, who had eyes for the practicalities of warmth in winter. Even here in southern France, that was a noteworthy consideration. . . .

Raoul reentered and stood silently with an eyebrow up. He looked a middle-class distinguished sixty; Mallory knew that he crowded seventy. Since the age of ten he had served the master as a kitchen-boy, as a driver, as adviser, as steward; either before or after Rochereau, he would die for Rochereau.

Mallory raised his chin to meet Raoul's eyes. "Confidentially, how is your master?"

The steward raised his big chin, looking down at the commodore's eyes. "Sir, I know that you love him. Perhaps he has one year remaining, perhaps five."

"So I surmised. What will you do then, Raoul?"

"Is the commodore ready to be shown his rooms?"

Shut off. Okay. Grinning, Mallory told him, "Pray fill my brandy glass about half full, and give me an hour here; then come back."

Raoul nodded slightly, disappeared, returned quickly with a half-gone gallon jug, bent with it over Mallory's glass, brought the liquor level just a bit higher than half, stood erect, nodded, departed. During the process, Mallory had been reading the jug label's irregular handwriting: "C'est l'Armagnac des Capuchons 1991, mis en bouteille pour le vicomte de Mont Veillac." Mallory wondered how many of these jugs there might be; he might be pulling on the last. . . . No matter, he was going to stretch this admirably.

The hour alone Mallory spent brooding on everything without really trying for solutions, knowing that the brain fire-lessly cooks what isn't being directly noticed. Fifty-four years ago, he could not have meditated like this. Now for many decades he had been able to meditate like this, and it never proved to be time lost.

When Raoul then returned, his eyes were on Mallory's brandy glass, and he allowed his face to express fleeting pleasure when he saw that the level was down only just below half. Mallory arose: "I am ready now." The steward led him up the decaying staircase and around the precarious balcony of the dining salon; he opened a door, stood just outside, bowed slightly, and emitted, "Pardon." Mallory entered; Raoul closed the door from outside, having asked absolutely no questions about the commodore's lack of baggage other than the shoulder purse containing flimsy pajamas, one pair of undershorts, one pair of socks, one handkerchief, an empty wine bottle (which Mallory would *not* leave in the cave), and no cheese—along with two small devices resembling radio headphones.

Mallory's rooms were: a tiny salon with an easy chair and table and sofa, a decent-sized bedroom, a commode (which contained a w.c.), and a lavatory (where you *really* washed your hands). He had brought up his brandy-remnant. For the sake of using what he was given, he sat for half an hour in the easy chair bird-sipping Armagnac; setting it aside, then, he went into the bedroom and lay in his clothes on his back on the four-poster bed, contemplating the brocaded red canopy, expecting sleep to come—which it did. In due course, Raoul would be knocking.

It was a formal dinner for two at a heavy mahogany table three meters long and two wide and stretchable, with lighted candelabra and with the vicomte at one end and the commodore at the other. Mallory brought with him what was left of his brandy, but set it to one side because of course there were wines: first sparkling Burgundy, then rosé with the soup, then Chablis with the fish, then still Burgundy with the meat. After the sparkling Burgundy, Raoul whispered into Mallory's ear, and for the remaining wines and food the commodore moved down to a place immediately at the vicomte's left, Rochereau's right ear not being very good and neither of his ears nor his voice good enough for a three-meter separation: ends-of-table ceremony had been satisfied, now let's eat and talk closely. . . .

Having solid respect for the vicomte's continuing mentality and attention span, around food and wine Mallory crisped all the story. During this feast, the ancient merely nibbled at a wafer of cold roast duck; and the only wine he touched after the sparkling Burgundy was the rosé, stretching the single half-glass for the whole time.

Mallory talked without interruption, he was glad of the chance, he reviewed what he told as he talked; but he made no comment, he offered no hypotheses, he merely reported the experiences. When the narration was done, the feast was done; Mallory had tucked away a rich dessert, an amazing sugar-cream right out of Chantilly, and thoughtfully Raoul brought him his brandy glass, which Mallory had left at table-end. An ounce remained in the bottom; it ought to be enough for now.

Silence, while Raoul cleared the table without so much as a clink or a footpad.

The vicomte said: "I have paid no mind to this Kali or indeed to the REM Device, having felt that political and social events went entirely out of control sometime during the *deuxième guerre mondiale*. I attend only to those things which I can control or which are decorative. Nevertheless, perhaps I can bring you an old man's assurance with respect to the internal coherency of what you tell me. Even the parts which thus far remain incoherent have for me a feeling of coherency-potential. In my view, Rourke, you are on the right track—for whatever that view may be worth to you."

Suddenly Mallory tossed off the remaining half-ounce of Armagnac; in his brain and belly it glowed; Raoul, as though sensing the destruction *à distance*, appeared at the door, facially inquiring; Mallory nodded, measuring two centimeters with thumb and forefinger; Raoul disappeared, reappeared with the jug, poured just two centimeters, departed.

Mallory said low, "All of a sudden, my thoughts have gone back fifty years—to Horse and Vogel."

"Ah," delicately invited the vicomte.

"Do you know about time-flutter?"

"I have heard of the theory, but the details—"

"Briefly, Antoine, it is a derivative of Henri Bergson's theory that subjective duration does not proceed at the same rate as objective sidereal time. The theory has now been tested somewhat—"

"Difficult enough to devise a test!"

"Exactly; and of course, the tests have been indirect and inferential, but speculative measurements have been applied. Well: it appears that the exact second of a subject's event-apprehension may not be the same as the second inferred by a later observer—it may be an earlier or a later second. And when a way was found to measure this at intervals as much later as two days or three days, there could be more than one second variation one way or another; and the progressive widening of the error margin seems to be geometrical."

"*Bien; entendu.* And the present application?"

"It is that this particular date in June 2002 is not necessarily the precise anniversary of the same calendar date in June 1952: the anniversary may vary one way or another by as much error as several days. Conversely, a given event in 1952 may find its subjective anniversary in 2002 several days off the sidereal calendar. What I am saying is: this calendar date in 2002, *right now,* could be the *subjective* anniversary of the two-people burial in the cave in 1952, even though that calendar date was several days earlier than today."

"Épatant!"

"And—they or their bodies were not found, when you searched?"

"There were no people, there were no bodies; Raoul personally sifted the rubble, which entirely choked off the crawl-passage so that they could not possibly have escaped that way. And from that chamber there is absolutely no other egress. Nor have Horse or Vogel been seen again to my knowledge."

Mallory meditated, studying his brandy. He then asked, in a transparent attempt to seem offhand, "This Miss Vogel—was her first name possibly Lilith?"

"Horse did not give her Christian name. . . . If she *was* Christian . . . But, my friend, you are ill?"

Mallory forced a ghastly grin. "Guère une maladie, mon ami. Un peu de gaz—à l'estomac." He eyed his friend: of *course* Antoine knew that Rourke was concerned about some long-ago lady-friend; hadn't Rourke picked a specific rare name for the question?

But the vicomte only smiled wan. "I am relieved—but also, I am being visited by fatigue. I must leave you to discharge your temporary infirmity while I cater to my permanent one. Rourke, my friend, if you depart tomorrow morning, I probably won't see you. I wish you success, and you have my friendship always."

"And you mine, my dear." Mallory said *"mon cher"*: it escaped from Mallory, it won a smile from Rochereau.

The Lord of Mont Veillac told what was left of his rosé: "I have just this word of counsel. You tell me that Kali represents his special powers as being inherent in every intelligent human. It follows that with or without some mystical and possibly evil Kali-unification, these powers are inherent in Rourke Mallory. *Find and use those powers."*

"And how would I find them?"

Rochereau inhaled as deeply as he could, and exhaled raspingly, and cocked his head so that his eyes engaged Mallory's, and told his guest straight: "Listen, Rourke. There will be something impossible that you want to come to you, something impossible that you want to do. All right: marshal total confidence, and inwardly *demand* that impossibility! If it works, you have the power. If it doesn't work, then either you don't have the power or you don't know how to use it."

"But that," Mallory expostulated, "seems little different from the promises of Kali! I am *not* going to play into *his* hands—"

The vicomte was now breathing with labor; Mallory forbore, and Raoul was at his master's elbow helping him to his feet. Once up, though—and Mallory had stood—the vicomte halted Raoul with a gesture and fixed his guest with a glittering eye:

"Kali," he reminded Mallory, "requires intense confrontation with your inner light. Well, you don't bother with that: just be yourself and call for what you want and see what happens—"

He went into a fit of coughing. Raoul, nodding to the commodore, got Rochereau out of the room on the way to bed.

Mallory sat, and drummed on the big table, and nursed brandy.

When Raoul returned, Mallory demanded, "How is the master?"

"Easy now. He will sleep well. And you, monsieur le commodore?"

"Raoul, the hell with noble protocol. How are you fixed for beer?"

"Sir, reflect that I know you. In your private salon there are eight bottles of Heineken, iced. You'll find the bottle opener on the wall of the closet where you *really* wash your hands."

"Why eight bottles, Raoul?"

"You, sir, will want four or five. The other three are for some contingency. There is also, if needed, a half-bottle of Hennessey: four-star, naturally."

16.

Had the Vogel woman been Lilith?

Undressed, pajamaed and dressing-gowned and slippered by grace of his host, Mallory stood by a window clutching a Heineken bottle and frowning at a new-risen three-quarter moon fuzzed by trees high on eastern hills. Fifty-four years ago, she had come to be all his meaning; fifty years ago, for his own soul-salvation and hopefully also for hers, he had required himself to forget her; a few months later, finding that he *could not* forget her, angrily he had consigned her to happiness with the parts of the Halloran-self which he had rejected; thereafter, miraculously as now he realized, Rourke Mallory during half a century had never, or hardly ever, allowed himself to slip into even brief reverie about the Lilith who had redeemed Burk Halloran.

The temptation was potent to think about her now. *Dare* he think about her now? Why should that sort of yesterday-thinking compulsively possess him, when what he *needed* to think about was the Kali problem in relationship to RP and REM and some species of occult power which conceivably Mallory himself might possess?

He glugged Heineken and grinned: a grin was a potency for chasing away morbidity. A frown raped the grin: maybe Lilith had *died,* in the cave with some guy named Horse. (He was pleased to notice that he felt no irrational jealousy-twinge.) He went grim: that would have been soon after Esther had left Horse; and Mallory, who loved Esther as a dear friend, contemplated with distaste the notion that his own Lilith had been the other woman. . . .

His own Lilith!

Eh, yes, he *could* think about her, he *had* to think about her!

Maybe an hour later, he was interested to notice that he was sitting in an easy chair beside the dead fireplace gazing stupidly at his half-gone second beer. He didn't remember going for another bottle.

He shook himself. *Boy* had he revivified Lilith Vogel! At one point in the remembering, he had erected—and that had a most special meaning, not at all mere animal sexuality; for by this means she had reevoked his human self-confidence, giving him her virginity in the process.

He smiled small: there was a little irony. He began to formulate it. . . . Frowning, he shook it off, it was unworthy: let what she had done for him mean for Lilith what it had meant for Lilith, as now it meant for him what it meant for him. Because otherwise his defeated soul would have

what *would* it have done? Gone to Hell? Shrunk into Limbo? *Split in two?*

He had come to identify her with the goddess Ishtar, after whom he had named his flagship: a blend of horned eroticism and bearded intellect, walking on clouds above the earth, deigning occasionally to descend to Burk Halloran and fence with him wit-for-wit, then ascending again to smile ambiguously down upon him while nocturnally her luminous pallor irradiated a garden of peonies. And yet, during her brief descents when they were not fencing, she was warm, warm. And at the climax which had led to his self-freeing, by night under a full moon beside a pond in a peony garden, she had whispered up to him, "I am Ishtar. I have shining horns tonight, I have no beard at all. . . ."

He broke it off and glugged beer and fisted the bottle and stared at it. Consider this a long-ago life-interlude with a mind-mature woman who had loved him a little and who subsequently had gone her own ways in (God grant it) self-fulfillment, as he had gone his own ways in self-fulfillment. If she had died in the cave with Horse, there she had died; if not, not; no way to know; hope for the best, believe in the best, go on.

This meditation had been nice, indeed it had been blessèd. Leave it there. Mallory was convinced that he had done the right thing when in 1952 he had rejected the name Burk Halloran, linking the name to the dark extremisms in his psychosis, and had adopted legally the name Rourke Mallory, and had determined finally not to look for Lilith, and had gone on from there. But he hurt that he hadn't found a way to notify Lilith. "To Lilith, with love and rejection . . ."

He finished the beer and went for a third: what the hell, there were eight. Tonight, there were two major projects: to arrive at some conclusion about this Kali (who allowing for stature-difference so much resembled the earlier Halloran, whose occult accomplishments so much resembled certain dark-delicious dreaming by the earlier Halloran); and then, perhaps, to grapple intellectually with Antoine's concept that if Kali meant literally what he said, the powers of Kali were potentially the powers of Mallory.

Part Five

INTERTIME

My responsible kind of muckraking often has led me to soul-distressing facts which my journalist's conscience had to disclose. But this is the first time in my life when I have been forced into the position of forecasting the imminent end of the world; and I mean, physically and literally. We'll keep hoping it won't happen; but the diplomatic work necessary to avoid it will have to be titanic.

From a high-ranking source in Washington: "Of course we are working for a REM Treaty; but even if it happens, we simply can't rule out the possibility that distrust of our allies will precipitate a preventive button-push."

From a high-ranking source in Moscow: "The unreliability of treaty signatures by Washington and by Peking is historical. We will sign; but nevertheless, we may have to be first with the buttons."

From a high-ranking official in Peking: "We honor the concept of a REM Treaty, and we will sign enthusiastically, assuming that we and the other signatories will still be available for signatures. Every political philosopher must eventually balance the question, whether a world haunted by subterranean time-bombs controlled by fallible humans is better than no world at all. We are walking the tightrope that Lao-Tse mentioned, strung between Heaven and Hell."

I cannot go far enough in emphasizing the knowledgeability of these sources . . .

—Zack Manderson for the
Washington Journal Syndicate, June 2002

Keep up the good work; we are nearly there.
—Guru Kali, in a private communiqué
to seven lieutenants, June 2002

17.

2002:

In Paris, Esther was not quite abed, but she was alto-
gether ready for bed—alone, after a tough day at the
office. She sat before her dressing-table mirror dutifully
brushing her long hair before braiding it for the night. She
wore blue pajamas, quite plain, almost mannish: with Esther,
slinky stuff was for manning, and this she chose to do less
and less often.

In the psyche of Esther through more than seven decades
of life, there had been an alternation like the vowels and
consonants in *banana:* childhood exuberance, early-adolescent
cynicism, late-adolescent exuberance, wartime cynicism, ear-
ly-Horse exuberance, later-Horse cynicism, early marriage-
to-Horse exuberance, later marriage-to-Horse cynicism—and
then a probably psychotic fantasy involving a rope-climb into
nowhere with a flame-haired stranger named Kali—followed
by institutionalized cynicism (in l'Hôpital de Villejuif
whither she had mysteriously arrived and where she had recovered consciousness) which persisted through her subsequent marriage-of-convenience to the Vicomte d'Illyria,
then early-cosmetician exuberance, then later-cosmetician
cynicism, then the early exuberance of becoming a De-
siderated Hostess . . . Now, thanks partly to her final dismis-
sal of illusions and partly to her warmly rewarding friendship with Rourke Mallory, Esther had kissed off attitudinal
fluctuations and had settled into something approaching
serenity.

The brushing had ceased, she was curiously examining her
own face in the mirror—neither with vanity nor in the mood
of criticism which must precede planned reconstruction, but
with a (fey) sense (do all of us sometimes have that sense,
mirror-gazing?) that the face might or might not be her*self*,
that both the identification of face with self and the some-

times-awareness of deeper and different *self* were cosmically amazing matters worthy of meditative exploitation. Allowing this meditation to persist and lead where it might, she found herself quite objectively evaluating the effect of many long-ago years with Diodoro Horse upon her face and upon her deeper psyche.

Objectivity wavered, and her eyes dropped. *Still* she missed Dio. He should have followed her, but he hadn't. After her post-escape coming-to-consciousness at Villejuif and another year of waiting for Dio-action, her desolation at having to accept his *non*-action had been succeeded, for a while, by total astonishment at this totally un-Horsemanlike failure; and that was when, despairing, she had divorced him unilaterally in a small European principality and had surrendered to the kindness-and-wealth blandishments of lonely old d'Il-lyria; but still she had been puzzled, and still she was. The Dio whom she had known might or might not have valued her enough to pursue her merely for the sake of getting her back—but the Dio she had known psotively *could not have stopped himself* from pursuing her with the threefold purpose of solving the enigma and learning *why* and buttressing his own ego by success in the search. In perspective now, her disappointment in Dio and *for* Dio (whom she *had* loved) seemed a more important ingredient in her psyche than the personal chagrin of not having been pursued.

Again, as often before, she asked herself why as Madame d'Illyria she hadn't discreetly checked on Dio, why she didn't do so now. He could easily be long-dead now; but at least, she'd like to know whether he had prospered, whether his own agitated soul had found serenity with another woman or in his work or both. Well: during a number of years she hadn't dared touch the question of Dio's present reality, it had been an exposed hot wire; and during more recent years, when she had grasped that Commodore Mallory was perfectly capable of getting the information for her, she had somehow not brought herself to reveal that much of herself to Rourke, not even in bed, not even when all they were doing in bed was pillow-talking.

Dio. Rourke. Kali. *Kali* . . . What out of Hell had *that* been? Five decades later, still Esther was subject to nipple-pucker when Kali's name came up. Back then, Kali could *not* have been today's all-important guru, whom she knew slightly and who still looked and acted early middle-thirtyish and who on first presentation to Esther at a soirée had given no sign of prior acquaintance; but good God, or bad Satan, wasn't the guru the veritable twin brother of *that* Kali? Trying to slow her heartbeat, Esther faced down once again that 1952 Kali whom she had comprehended as a man-dressed woman: petite, breastless, slender-agile, face disturbingly like Rourke's, with flaming red hair where Rourke's had been silver as long as she had known him. And with charm, charm! Instantly total captivation . . .

Well, look, Esther told herself for the thousandth time, it had all come about like *this*. Dio was due to drop in on her one afternoon, just to check in before leaving with that nice lady-psychologist for a late-afternoon university lecture; he'd phoned ahead, and he expected to be back for six-thirty supper. Well: their relationship had been difficult for a long time, Esther had been quite candidly stepping out on him with a couple of younger men although she was sure he had not been reciprocating, his phone call and check-in concern had activated conscience-twinge while reactivating love; Esther had therefore been sprucing up for Dio, she had been sitting in her slip brushing her hair before her mirror just as now she sat before her mirror. . . . Warm female-feeling hands had grasped her bare upper arms from behind; turning her head, unaccountably with pleasure and without shock, she had looked up into the face of Kali. And hitherto and subsequently heterosexual Esther had been instantly ready to die for Kali. But Kali had not attempted love; instead, holding toward Esther a coil of rope, Kali had told Esther what to do, and had vanished; by hindsight, Esther recalled that there had been no mirror image, or at least she remembered none. And now there had been nothing at all in her mind or heart except to do the bidding of Kali. Esther had written the note, and placed it on top of the rope coil, and finished dressing, and waited by the balcony doors. When the flames had come, unafraid Esther had gone out on the balcony and stretched out her arms, ecstasy-suffused, possibly screaming: *imminent total fulfillment*. . . . She had seen Dio staring down there, and some woman staring on the other side, while Kali erected magically a groin-quivering golden cord and slid up it and seized her (*gladly* she had surrendered) and took her on upward

and she had come to consciousness at Villejuif. . . .

Aa! no dice: reviews and reviews produced nothing more, no meaning, no clue about the time which must have intervened between the rope-rape and Villejuif. And even her memories of l'Asyle de Villejuif were fragmentary, and interestingly untouched by strong emotion. She remembered being aesthetically ravished by rhapsodic flower-woman murals on high in the dining hall, done by some long-gone schizophrenic artist-inmate. And she remembered being mystically pleased by a romantic Rodin-type sculpture in the courtyard of one of the wards: Mercury rescuing Eurydice, naked holy Mercury clasping flowing-gowned bare-breasted languishing Eurydice's waist and flying her aloft out of Hell with caduceus rampant. (Before she had departed Villejuif, an imp had led Esther to take two snapshots of the statue, noble bow and butt-muscular stern, and to label them *Mercury Coming* and *Mercury Going*.) And psychiatrists with owl-spectacles patiently questioning and questioning, pronouncing her finally "a victim of some transient amnesia resulting from marital strains, during which apparently she traveled here; but apparently recovered in totality, giving no present evidence of severe mental disturbance . . ." And, on a tour for patients, the first meeting (chance) with amiable old d'Illyria in the Egyptian wing of the Louvre . . .

She stood, impatient with herself: decidedly she must call a final halt to this fruitlessness. Abandoning her mirror image, Esther attended commode and killed lights and went to bed, musing by choice about Rourke because meditation about Rourke was so tranquilizing. His psyche, alone among all the souls she'd known, blended realistic serenity and fantastic enterprise in a blend so perfectly organic that it might have been a harmonious rainbow.

He'd hard-won the blend, too. At thirty-three he'd graduated from an American rest home for the mentally disturbed: that he'd told Esther, dismissing his prior life and the nature of his illness as "stuff that sublime and evil dreams are made of—forget it." He'd had money in the millions at his command, but during a couple of years he hadn't touched it, pursuing instead the traditional Grand Tour of the world at poverty level, subsisting on lucky earnings and handouts. A chance meeting with a bitter young scion named Randolph, who had sailed his own yawl into a harbor at Corfu, had produced between these two men the grand idea and the mutual eleven-million-dollar foundation of the present RP fleet which Rourke commanded: this RP which was increasingly constituting itself as a charismatic ambassador-at-large for Earth-consciousness as a replacement for nation-con-

sciousness, for regional cultural variety as a magnificent substitute for international jealousy . . .

Commodore Rourke, though, was in his eighties now; and
despite his physical sixtyishness, advanced age meant uncertain mortality. And Rourke was fretting because no prom-
ising successor was visible. "It isn't because I am sitting on
them," he had told her believably. "Everything about the RP
structure prevents me from sitting on them and encourages
their upward mobility. I—am beginning to suspect that
my reputation may be sitting on them. Maybe if I were to
vanish—"

Esther had leaned over to kiss his naked chest in the
night; and she had told him: "Never do that until you are
sure you are no longer competent. Until then, RP needs you;
all of us do. Who knows? It may even be in the cards that
Mallory and RP are synonymous and will run their full time
together, whereafter RP will no longer be needed in the
world."

Having counter-kissed her naked belly in the night, he had
responded, "I will die, but RP never can; it is too beautiful."

"Then," she had told the invisible ceiling, touching his hair
with her fingers, "worry not, my friend; your successor will
come."

Now, with a new kind of foreboding, she noticed for the
first time what he had then muttered, "It better be soon—"
His next light comment had come so immediately that she
had missed the dark note, or missed its possibly grave import. Was Rourke maybe concealing something about his
own health? What was still incurable? Not cancer any longer,
but. . . .

Mosaic virus? You don't know it's there until your doctor
tells you; it does not sap your vitality until nearly the end,
which is swift; there is no pain; it is almost like a merciful
god telling you that your time has come and easing you out.
And it is just as implacable. . . .

She bit her lower lip. If *that* had been the fatal import of
his muttered response, how enormously like Rourke to blow
it away immediately with a light quip! "Who knows? it might
even be Kali."

1952:

Led by Raoul, who carried a portable floodlamp (no lighting had been installed in the cave), Dio and I penetrated the

prehistoric sanctuary at Mont Veillac, he prowling intently, I highly aroused by a meld of fascination with remote past and cavern-weird and a sharing of his sentiment that this would be *it*.

Awed, we looked while Raoul crisp-lectured: he was felicitously phlegmatic about it; he would make some necessary five- or ten-word statement and then shut up until a question or the next thing.

We took more than an hour to review synoptically the paintings in the main cavern; Raoul was patient, I felt that he was pleased at our leisurely inspection. Then he suggested, "There are a few minor cells that you will want to experience—"

Turning to me, Dio growled low, "Nothing yet, Lil; so far, a blank draw. Let's follow him for the whole view, and then come back here for a few hours."

When, after about five smaller deeper chambers of inspiring nonproductivity, Raoul directed his lamp into the just-above-floor-level opening of the little crawl-space, Dio looked at me with his teeth sheathed. Terrified, I managed to utter, "What the hell! I'm dressed for it—" Raoul nodded and went in first; Dio gave me the honor at Raoul's heels (sepulchrally the lamp beam focused ahead back-illumined the tube); hearing Dio scraping along behind me, I hissed at him, "Don't take advantage, you legitimate bastard!" and was heartened by his counter-hiss: "Just imagine if I did: Raoul popping out of the tube like a blown cork." It was hard to giggle without butt-butting the tube roof; I repressed it and crept on. . . .

We three then stood stupidly in the end cell, gazing at the prey-bird descending on the terrified people.

"Oh, *say*, now!" low ejaculated Dio in French. "This is the best of all; this I shall have to study for a while—"

Raoul responded, "Then, monsieur-madame, perhaps I should go get the cheese and wine; I left them in the main room."

"Do that," Dio murmured; "do that." A moment later I heard the tube-scraping of Raoul; but I didn't turn to look—Dio's preoccupation with the fresco was too engrossing.

"Look here, Lil!" he exclaimed after some minutes; he was using Raul's floodlamp, Raoul had departed with a little flashlight. "I'm not yet ready to say what this means, but—"

His voice was buried in the cell-filling tube-roar.

Panic-paralyzed, of course I didn't think to time-out the

reverberations. Maybe a couple of minutes were enough to complete the rockfall and seal us in; but even after the catastrophic part was done, I kept hearing scattered rock shards pinging on rock.

At some time during the noise, I must have faced around toward the tube-end. When I came into self-collection, the first thing I saw was Dio's bottom: he was on his knees using his lamp to peer into the tube. He cursed and funneled himself into it. Then his lamp went out. Abruptly I was done, and terrified by solitude and darkness, and beginning for the first time in my life to experience oppressive claustrophobia. . . .

Dio backed into view carrying blessèd light, emerged, stood, turned. Keeping lips well over teeth: "It's plugged, Lilith, maybe ten feet inward or outward, no telling how thick the plug is. I couldn't see any light through it when I turned out my lamp; if Raoul is using his flashlight in or near the cave, it isn't visible through the plug. I couldn't budge it with hard pushing, I couldn't get my fingers into any helpful crannies. Any useful conclusions, Doctor?"

At that I giggled, and he rewarded me by unsheathing teeth. And the giggle helped me, too; as it died, I swore that I was *not* going to be a silly ass, that I was going to concentrate on thinking. . . .

I made a wry funny: "Great spot for smooching."

He sobered: "The greatest, except for the aspect of accelerated air-use. What do you say we smell around our cell a little?"

Having lamp-surveyed the cell to eliminate rock- or hole-hazards, he killed the beam to save the battery and to sharpen the one sense we needed right now: our smellers, to detect any fresh-air intake. He took the waist-up high road, I the low on hands and knees, moving with deliberation in opposite directions around the walls so we would contact on meeting, sniffing every cranny. When we did meet, he said "Nothing," and I echoed "Nothing." Pause—and then I giggled again: "Logic, Dio, logic! Did you think we'd gone all around?" He said, very low, "Oh, shit." I exploded laughter, which died quickly; it was like laughing inside a kettle drum, there might be danger of stimulating a new rockfall. He said, "Okay, we've met, that means we've done half of it; let's go." We switched sectors—I high now, he low—and up-and-down dog-sniffed until we met again. Long silence; then: "Nothing." "Nothing." He demanded, "How are you at standing on a man's shoulders and smelling *very* high?" To control that, we turned on the lamp long enough to start at the tube, and I got balanced on his shoulders with him gripping my thighs and me bent because the ceiling averaged only nine feet high, and he killed the light, and we went all around once more with me doing all the sniffing, until he touch-found the tube again. Still nothing.

I dismounted. Long silence.

He: "We may be getting a minim of fresh air through the rock-block in the tube. But it will come in only at the rate we suck it in. And the faster we suck, the faster we'll build up carbon dioxide. So breathe very easy, sister, very easy—and not much talk."

I: "Agreed, but we will have to say some necessary things."

He, talking most low: "Right, but minimal words; leave color to be inferred."

I: "Okay. Raoul has probably gone for help."

He: "Unless he was trapped in the fall."

I, resolutely: "Assume otherwise. How long?"

He: "Two hours to get help. Don't know how long to dig through."

I, teeth clenched: "Okay. How long breathable air?"

He: "Don't know. With care, a few hours."

Very long silence; I was carefully composing myself into practically a state of torpor to minimize my oxygen requirement, he was probably doing the same. I did exercise myself enough to reach out and grope for his hand; he responded, and we held hands almost all the rest of our time in there.

I: "It is necessary for you to finish telling me what you saw on the wall."

The lamp went on, flooding the prey-bird fresco. Silently he let me survey it for several seconds. Then: "I'm sure that bird was originally redheaded and blue-eyed. Ultraviolet would show it. Flaming power devouring people. Kali. He brought us here. And he *got* us here."

The lamp stayed on. I studied. My gaze drifted to the right, and I contemplated the man watching from the downward escarpment.

My grip on Dio's hand tightened. "Man to the right. Original color of hair and eyes?"

"Wait, let me analyze. I think—red hair, blue eyes."

"That's Burk Halloran."

Silence. Then: "Oh? That duck-faced caricature?"

"If you see those colors, I see Burk."
The lamp went out.

2002:

In a decent little hotel at Sore, Lieutenant Cassie Wozniak lay on her back with her bountiful bosom heaving. She wanted Mallory; she *wanted* Mallory, and her desire would *not* let her sleep. She fought with the desire, insistently reminding herself that he was an old man; the image of his age kept flickering into vague insignificance, distorted by her acute tactile imagery of his skill and her exciting psychic imagery of his charisma and her warming emotive imagery of his human sympathy. Distraught, she resorted to religious tradition in the context of Freudian materialism: *Cassie, you kook, this father-desire, this is moral incest, it is childish, forget it, hit sleep, dream it off. . . .* The recognition only fired her higher, and she turned over and buried her face in the pillow and slowly beat feet against the mattress. . . .

She became aware that her right hand had slipped into her nightgown to stroke her left breast, and that the nipple was hardening. That did it: she whirled to her back again, and stretched her arms out taut, and gave herself over to a vivid serial imagining in the hope that the very consecutiveness of it would put her to sleep before anticlimax.

Forget the commodore, she ordered herself. *Concentrate on that young hard Commander Duval; he's only in his late thirties, that's young, he tears me apart, this I need. . . .*

She set herself to imagining that she was back aboard ship and a Draft Board had been ordered for tonight, to be activated just about now. Cassie had registered *green* (available), which meant that hopefully she would be drafted, necessarily by some officer who ranked her. The commodore —scratch that! The next officer in seniority to make a selection would be Captain Vanderkilt, who being a heterosexual woman would not be selecting Cassie. And the next to draft would be Commander Duval. Of course, he might pass or choose somebody else; and the other five male officers above Cassie might likewise pass or choose somebody else or might have been chosen by women above them; in which case it would be unchosen Cassie's turn to make a draft from among the males below her rank (two ensigns, and several petty officers, and sailors). Now which one would she choose? No, wait, this was a *happy* fantasy, she must not imagine any miserable contingency. Not that the lower-ranking males

were miserable; for instance, she could easily think of . . .
Hold! keep the fantasy under control! She *had* been drafted
by *Duval!*

Well: by the rules of RP, to which Cassie had happily sub-
scribed on recruitment, she would have no choice, having
registered green. And so she would arise and thread the
ship's corridors and pass through her drafter's door and stand
before her beloved for tonight, saying the ritual: "Here I am,
yours to do with as you wish as long as we do not injure
each other. I love you tonight, Commodore—"

No! *No!* Correction: "I love you tonight, *Commander*—"
Oh, fudge! *This* is a means for *sleep?*

18.

2002:

Resolutely, in his Mount Veillac suite, Mallory suppressed
the material which he *wanted* to inspect: the possibility
that Lilith Vogel had been here (whatever may have happened to her in the cave) precisely fifty years ago tonight
allowing for the probable error of time-flutter. That had been
mere yesterday; and by any measure, it had been four years
later than his last prior knowledge of her. That she had
been with another guy, probably as his permanent or
transient mistress, shook Mallory not at all: either a guy and
a chick are *for* each other, or they are not. If they are, but
far apart without hope of seeing each other, doesn't the love
of each hope for the other's happiness? And if they are
not, what's the difference? Lilith would have been nearly
thirty, either that or marriage would be a natural necessity;
and apparently she had been discriminating, Horse having
been a detective-inspector and all. . . .

Lilith, if alive, would be into her late seventies now.
About the same age as Esther; maybe even looking and
feeling as relatively young as Esther, if Lilith also had found

access to Senility Arrest. Heights about the same; and if
Mallory had any ability to extrapolate from an aging woman's present appearance to her earlier appearance, figures
about the same (only Esther would never show Mallory an
earlier picture of herself). Psyches, though, very largely different . . .

Diodoro Horse! That *had* to have been Esther's first husband; he had been a detective-inspector, the identity was
unmistakable. And from her scattered references to his
mind and his heart—hey, would *he* have been a fleet captain! But with another woman already—and that woman may
have been Lilith Vogel! The dating would have been almost
immediately after Esther's departure with someone impossibly named Kali who looked impossibly like the guru; but
if Guru Kali had been mature fifty years ago, he'd have
been in his fifties before Senility Arrest became a possibility
—yet a generation after the Esther-snatching Kali had been
a mere youth!

Anyhow—Horse and Vogel! Esther still carried the torch
a little for Horse; and Mallory supposed that *he*, way down
deep, still smoldered for Lilith. The coincidence was wild—
if, with the guru just possibly involved, it *was* coincidence.
What it did prove was, that Horse may indeed have been on
Esther's trail immediately, even if he did have a woman
along; and he had been prevented from pursuing it all the
way to Villejuif only by the cave disaster. In a melancholy
way, Esther would be glad to know this.

But why with Lilith? He was working to recall Esther's
account of her departure with this Kali-apparition: Esther
had been on her apartment balcony, and down below to the
left Horse had been staring up, and down below to the right
some woman had been staring up. . . .

He stood, weird-chilled. If the apparition-man *had indeed*
been Guru Kali, and if the woman below had been Lilith
Vogel, and if both Horse and Vogel had seen Kali—who was
a runt-twin of Rourke-when-young . . . Eh, wait: maybe Lilith
had been that psychologist who was meeting Horse to take
him guest-lecturing; then if she had thought that she was
seeing Esther rope-raped by Burk Halloran—hey, now, would
Lilith have joined the Horse-pursuit of Esther in a private
Halloran-pursuit of her own?

Bah! chase that away! More pertinent concerns were facing him.

The apparent powers of Kali! To change the past—to be selective in telepathic interception at a distance—to project illusions at a very great distance—to win allegiance among the greatest of the great—and *what else*?

And if Mallory truly had those same powers latent within himself, he could use them to beat the guru at his own game, whatever that game might be. If, that is, Mallory could evoke those powers. Perhaps *that* had been the meaning of the Blue Flame. If so, it was Kali who had led Mallory to the flame; did this mean that for some reason Kali *wanted* Mallory to find and use the powers?

Unify me. . . . A plea addressed, not only to the little dark challenger, but also to Mallory aloft . . .

There weren't any clear logical roads for determining what those powers might be. Eliminate all the powers that one could deploy anyway, and the special ones would be some other powers.

He grinned, recalling the report by Chloris: special powers the guru might have, but whether he was in fact male or female, seemingly he lacked a quite ordinary power of either sex. Was that a price which the guru had paid for his powers? Must Mallory pay a similar price in order to realize the guru's powers? His grin went diabolical: at his age and with his memories, what the hell!

Well: the powers. Dissolving his grin, Mallory beetle-browed an interesting question: how would he test the powers if he should have them? What subjects were immediately available other than Antoine and Raoul? Fantasy-projection? The vicomte was too frail for such tampering, and Raoul was too vicomte-indispensable for such tampering. Telepathic reception? This the guru seemed to bring off only when the thoughts emanated from somebody engaged in high-energy mentation focused on some inner light, and the telepathic blank which Mallory now drew told him that either Mallory was unreceptive or neither Antoine nor Raoul was thinking energetically at the moment. And he already had their allegiance, won through years quite normally—the very best kind. And as for past-changing, that one Mallory proposed to leave cautiously alone until he had some sense of how to go about doing it—and doing it without crossing wires and shorting something dangerously.

All right: he couldn't actively start with any of these powers tonight, although two or three of them he might fiddle with tomorrow aboard the *Ishtar;* but a direction had been suggested, and that was something of a breakthrough.

Breakthrough . . . O-ho! Assume that Lilith Vogel *had* been down there beneath Esther's balcony, that she *had* seen what Horse had seen—Kali, alias early Halloran, skinning up a sky-hung rope with Esther and vanishing into nothing. Well: if both Vogel and Horse had seen it, then maybe it had somehow *happened!* And then: if Kali could also cross time into the past—and if his *real* method of stealing Esther, beneath the illusion, had been teleportation . . .

Two more powers—teleportation and time-travel?

Oh, b'Jesus! Those powers too? And they're maybe mine? Then theoretically I could go back now to be again with young Lilith-Ishtar in the peony garden

only, I would be old. Wouldn't I.

1952:

We'd been mostly silent in the refrigerating cave-darkness during most of two hours, sitting relaxed with our backs against a cave wall, holding hands limply now because tight hand-gripping requires energy and therefore accelerates breathing, concentrating on balancing our breathing at the minimum threshold of depth and frequency required to stay minimally oxygenated without depriving ourselves to the point where compensatory deep breathing would be stimulated. Although I felt that I was about to freeze, I knew that fifty-two degrees is way above that point; I was wearing sensible underwear and wool hose and sturdy tan denim pants and shirt, my collar and long sleeves were buttoned, probably my body temp was still in the early nineties; I should be grateful for cave-chill, it was lowering my metabolism. To my smeller, the air seemed now to have a staleness; but I refused to think about carbon dioxide for fear that my stupid autonomics might get apprehensive and heighten my breathing. Several times it crossed my mind that if Dio and I would cling together we could warm and hearten each other; this notion too I flatly dismissed, at least for a while, suspecting that even in this extremity we couldn't embrace without speeding our metabolisms.

We talked only when necessary; but under the circumstances, this became necessary every so often just for its own sake. Since we had settled into precautionary quiet after the rockfall, there had been only a few such occasions, and usually a few meaningless words had done the job. I said, "Think Raoul will get us out in time?" and he said, "I wouldn't be foolish enough to doubt it." Or, much later, he said, "Have you read any good books lately?" and I said, "What's a book?" Like that.

When I began to notice the air staleness, naturally I began to have a thought or two about death by suffocation; it alarmed me a little, so I tried a semantic correction and considered death by indiscernible seepage of vitality, coupled with the traditional Hebrew notion of blessèd eternal sleep (the resurrection idea was too exciting for this survival-situation, and I figured I'd be resurrected if I'd be resurrected, and if not, not). Finding the death-tranquillity idea rather serene and even tranquillizing, I allowed myself to muse on it for a while, until I caught myself drowsing off; that was too tranquil, and I roused myself a little by asking, "Dio—if we die here, how's that for you?"

He, after a pause: "I would feel frustrated."

I allowed myself a brief blurt-giggle. After a moment, he said solemnly, "Ha."

It crossed my mind that maybe we should exchange dying sentiments, we might not have another chance. I composed mine and stated them: "I want you to know that I find you likable and exciting and a very, very good friend."

After several seconds, he responded in an odd voice, "No shit?"

I giggled again, quite content. His hand gripped mine hard for the first time in maybe two hours, and he lifted my hand to his lips and kissed the palm of it.

"Cut it out," I told him taut, "before I climb you and murder both of us."

His response was to kiss the *back* of my hand with surprising tenderness. I brought his to my lips and kissed the back. We gripped hands hard a moment longer. Then his grip relaxed: "Ease off, pipe down, save breath."

Our hands, limply clasping, went down to the cave floor. I closed eyes and made myself relax, and did almost relax —except that I felt a sneeze coming on. "Have to blow nose," I whispered, and let go of him, and reached for my shoulder bag. . . .

He said terse: "Blow quick and listen—this may be important."

I blew, arrested sneeze, put away handkerchief, grabbed his hand. "Talk."

"Remember the rope coil in my apartment after Kali stole Esther?"

"Yes—"

"Remember that you saw me make the end go up? Remember that Kali promised me his powers if I would unify him?"

Careless of energy expenditure, I gripped his hand. "Shoot."

"Maybe that was an easy promise—or my own intuition. Maybe I have his powers already. Maybe you do, too. Maybe everybody does, latently."

My thrill was occult. "Not known to be impossible. What?"

"Let's try."

"Okay. Why not, in here? How?"

"Dunno, maybe just intense concentration will do it. Look —what if you concentrated on being with Burk while I concentrated on being with Esther?"

I warned, "One minute of that kind of concentration would blow an hour of oxygen!"

He said tight, "I'm willing to shoot the moon. Are you?"

And I was, by God! I said low, "Let's do."

He said, agitated, "If it works, we part here, Lilith. Maybe now it's each of us on his own."

That time comes for everybody, it had come for me when my parents died and had come repeatedly since. I murmured, "Bless you, Dio. I guess we'll have to let go hands."

He said, "Bless you, Lilith." He let go my hand.

I let go his. I prayed.

2002:

Back in his chair with his fourth beer, Mallory got Lilith backburnered by indulging in whimsical meditation about the diversified compulsions of sex in its romantic and sentimental secondaries and tertiaries, the flower-petals and more generally the landscapes and natural beauties which aesthetically cloaked the stamens and pistils of primacy.

And this caused him to remember that what starts as primary romantic or frankly erotic arousal may, with fidelity and devoted mutual steering, become secondary to lifelong mutual friendship and indispensability—a sort of relationship which Mallory respected although he hadn't found it and didn't feel any particular need for it although sometimes he desperately wanted it.

And that made him think of Lilith. He banished her again by reflecting upon the magnificent sublimations through which genius ignores and potently rechannels sexuality into mighty new horizons for art and science and civilization and humanity. Only, this Freudian interpretation could be shortsighted wrong; maybe sexual drive and genial sublimation both emerged from the same primordial fire—which would explain why so many geniuses had kinky sexual hang-ups: the power that flooded the creativity was overflowing and side-flooding the brain centers of sexual activation. . . .

Inevitably this line of thought brought him back to Guru Kali. No doubt about it, Kali was a genius, to the degree that his genius drained his or her sexual potency. . . .

On the other hand, others deliciously embraced the stamen-pistil primacy as a value above all other values! For instance, how about that Lieutenant Cassie Wozniak suggesting that she'd appreciate being selected by the commodore on an early Draft Board?

For diversion, he mused that idea. He had a sometimes self-annoying habit of imagining things in the form of little stories: thus, if he wanted to imagine a seduction, he had first to imagine the build-up with all the two-person give-and-take; and if something wouldn't work out in his build-up, he could never quite get to the seduction. (Of course, in the context of planning command-action, the habit had proved invaluable.) Luckily, the Draft Board situation was easy; he had nearly no problems with it because it was so comfortably regularized: that was its true beauty when RP needed release but was so intensely concerned with other action that its members couldn't fool around with the intricacies of woo. And yet it didn't entirely cut out the intrigue elements of surprise or disconcertment: for each green awaiting, which higher-ranking he or she would draft him or her? For each unchosen chooser, why had the one person he or she really desired tonight decided to go dark tonight? And even when a draft was consummated, the process of consummation was infinitely various and unpredictable. And meanwhile, all were good companions co-working a ship. . . .

Mallory now went mentally through the routine of announcing a Draft Board to be activated (in this case) immediately; and mentally he drafted Cassie. And now he found himself eagerly stimulated by the concept of Lilith—*Cassie*—willingly coming to his quarters. He closed his eyes tight, imagining all the corridors she would thread en route to his quarters.

Caught up in the fantasy, he found himself almost praying: "Let there be total happiness in all this draft. Let every-

one who wants someone get that one; let everyone who is got
want to be got by that one. Let it be so, it is right."

He opened his eyes.

*Some*body was here—only, not a she! The man sat on the
floor with his back against a wall, he was dressed in mid-
twentieth-century hiking-style, his eyes were closed, he appeared to be in suspended animation. . . .

Only, now his eyes were opening. They were beady-black
eyes, and the shape of the small man's face suggested that
he might have buck teeth behind those sheathing lips, and
his face was coppery-swarthy. Really, the man was astonishingly ugly! Having surveyed the room, those eyes were
looking speculatively at Mallory now; and after the eyes had
inspected Mallory during perhaps five seconds, the lips moved
to pronounce the following careful words in a harsh baritone
which struck Mallory as a lethargic version of something
potentially electric:

"Whoever you are, thanks for getting me out of that cave.
I take it you got out Miss Vogel also?"

2002:

In his little cabin aboard the *Ishtar,* lean thirty-fivish Commander Jean Duval, at his diminutive desk-board, which
folded down from the wall when needed, completed his
radio summation to the person at the other end: "—so at
this point, it seems that Mallory is just as mystified as anyone
else; and I think you can continue to operate in confidence
around him."

"Good," radio-answered immediately a clear light almost-
contralto baritone. "How is his mosaic virus progressing?"

"I don't know. He won't mention it. He seems perfect."

"Don't be downhearted, it will come; the timing is not
exact. Do not forget what I keep telling you, Duval: keep
in close touch with your inner light, and everything will
come out as you and I both wish. Where is he now?"

"I don't know that either. But he let drop that he was
going to a private sanctuary not very distant from here;
Lieutenant Wozniak will be reporting in."

Pause; then: "Good again. I feel strongly that my private
confrontation arrangements are rushing toward confirmation."

"Guru, I don't quite understand—"

Here Duval developed an extremely potent sense that
someone was staring at the back of his neck; and prudently

he inserted, "See you soon, chérie. Out." Disconnecting, he reflected: either he was alone or he was not alone; in the second instance, whirling would be appropriate; in the first instance, who could know that he had whirled? He whirled in his swivel chair. Lieutenant Cassie Wozniak stood there, distinctively out of uniform in ordinary medium-blue pajamas and bare feet. The pajamas were male-type whirlon and not really ordinary on blonde blue-eyed semi-tall full-breasted medium-waisted full-hipped full-thighed Cassie.

After half a minute of mutual paralysis, during which the commander decided that either she had heard or she had not heard and he must assume the latter for working purposes, he came to his feet in a combination of courtesy and electrification. And Cassie was just as electrified. He said carefully, "Lieutenant, I see that we are both surprised. May I have your evaluation?"

She didn't have much by way of eyebrows, and their blonde made them almost invisible, but they both went up a trifle, and her medium-small mouth went almost into a puzzled pout. "I was reading in bed, Commander, and evidently I dropped off, because here I am dreaming of you." Her brows came down in a frown: "Only, my man-dreamings aren't always this consecutive. And why am I standing, since I was in bed?"

Duval, whose prior draftings of Cassie had been sadistically rewarding, was seeing a rare chance to combine pleasure and inquiry: *had* she heard part of his conversation with the guru? Had it *meant* anything to her? After he had primed her, she could be pumped. His voice went soft: "In fact, I wasn't working very well, I kept thinking of *you*. I was imagining that I had called you on a Draft Board and you were coming to me. . . . And here you are. *How?*"

No blonde Pole can hide a blush, and Cassie didn't try: it started in her throat, which was exposed by the unbuttoned top two buttons, and suffused her face. But she held up her big chin and asserted, "I was imagining a Draft Board too— and dammit, I was feeling green—" That was too much even for a liberated woman of 2002; she stopped herself from adding "for you," and her head went down, but a little smile was tugging at her lips.

No experienced Frenchman can allow such a situation to grow awkward. "Sit down, *ma belle*," said Duval, "while I provide us with cognac." He was thinking pretty hard as he turned his back on her and knelt to open his miniature liquor cabinet; the consecutive action and tiny tensions of selecting two glasses and uncorking the partly used Bisquit bottle (vintage 1989, an excellent year) assured him that if this was a dream it was *magnifique* and he should treat it as no dream and assume the probability that she had come to him through the corridors and found his door unlocked . . .

When he stood and turned, holding open bottle in one hand and empty glasses in the other, Cassie sat on the edge of his bunk, leaning back, head far back, eyes closed, pajama shirt off, breasts up, nipples erect. Smitten with an acute case of satyriasis, Duval discarded one glass, tilted some brandy into the other, set down the bottle, and touched the glass to her lips. Obediently she sipped and immediately swallowed—Cassie was no *connaisseuse*. "Oh, boy!" she breathed, "is *that* a gas! Hit me again, Commander—you only need one hand for the cognac, do what you like with the other."

Between the personal arousal that she was experiencing and the Kali-information that she planned to pick up between bouts of arousal, she was seeing no conflict whatsoever. The same commodore who needed the Kali-information had originated the Draft Board.

19.

—◆—

2002:

Commodore Mallory was on his feet, and so was Detective-Inspector Horse. Mallory said evenly, although his excitement was high, "Now that we've exchanged names and incredulities, I think from what I know of you that you can handle a pumping in of some pretty hard stuff."

Horse answered cold, intent, "Skip what you know about me, that's for later. Make it swift and pertinent, we have a damsel to rescue."

Mallory made it crisp: "You are now in the Château de Mont Veillac in the year 2002. That's right, 2002. I brought you here, but I really don't know how or from where or from when, and it wasn't you I wanted to bring here. Got that?"

Horse: "All right, it's wild, but in a cockeyed way it fits. You and I together teletemported me here—by accident."

Mallory: "How's that again?"

Horse: "You brought me here from the Mont Veillac cave in 1952; I was trapped in there with Lilith Vogel. Right now—get her out the same way you got me out."

Mallory: "Oh, my God."

He dropped into his chair, while Dio stared down upon him. Mallory muttered, "I don't know how, but Christ, I'll *try*—" He closed eyes and hand-covered them; Dio fiercely let him. Mallory wished with all his heart that Lilith would be here with him. Nothing. Abruptly his hand dropped away from his flared-open eyes: "Horse, I assure you—she *isn't there!*"

"She—*isn't?*"

Mallory, earnestly: "Believe me, I *know* this: she *isn't*. And I don't know *how* I know, and I don't know where or when—"

Suddenly Dio's arms went limp and he exhaled a long rasping sigh. He told the ceiling: "Mallory, you know what I think? I think that you and I have been playing around with powers that we don't understand. And I think they worked, by accident and in the wrong way, which may turn out to be right. So here I am, out of the cave, fifty years out; and apparently she's out, you telepathed that, but God knows where or when you sent her. I see you have beer: got anything stronger?"

"Sit down," weakly invited Mallory, "and I'll bring you some Hennessey."

Staying with the Heineken, Mallory watched Horse viciously slug off an ounce of cognac, swallowing it immediately, sitting then with head down and eyes closed while he savored the heat in his belly rather than the flavor in his mouth; he opened eyes, sloshed the cognac, slugged off the other ounce, brooded shut-eyed over *that* glug; then open-eyed Horse jerk-outthrust the glass, asserting, "That was to bring me back to life; may I have another for gracious living?"

Blinking, Mallory finished his beer and arose to take the Horse glass and refresh it, pouring one for himself also:

what the devil, he had restorative tablets. His mental lethargy troubled him, he wondered whether the virus had moved higher than he knew.

Then they sat contemplating each other. This time, Horse was handling the cognac exactly as Mallory did, seeming used to this membrane-absorption approach. And Horse abruptly broke ice: "Call me Dio and I'll call you Rourke; I can screw a man by his first name just as easily as I can formally."

The Mallory smile broke open; and he decided that his brain wasn't dead yet, only nonplussed. He said direct, "Dio, the convincing sense of my telepathy was that Lilith is in no trouble. I am sure that we have time to come to an understanding."

"That's good, that's very good. Tell me, Rourke—was your hair ever red?"

Rourke froze: "It was."

"*Flaming* red?"

"It was."

"I put it to you that a few days ago you backtimed into the year 1952, pulled off an Indian rope-trick, and snatched my wife Esther out of the 1952 world into your own."

Rourke started to deny it, but he saw something to say first. "Dio, I know about you as a logical man, and I am amazed at your easy acceptance of my claim that I have pulled you into the year 2002."

Dio, flat: "Call it a working assumption. On that assumption, did you or didn't you?"

Rourke, flat: "I did not."

Silence, while Dio studied his brandy.

Rourke couldn't resist it: "But I do know your Esther."

Having bead-eyed him a moment, Dio snapped, "The way you said it says she's alive fifty years later, so fine: we'll backburner that and stay with the main line. Provisionally I trust you that you weren't Esther's seducer, although I'll give it to you that you look like one who could have done it; but my intuition says that you are not an enemy. And I think now it's your turn to lead the discussion until I want to change that."

He sat staring fiercely at Rourke—who reflected with awkward amusement that he hadn't during half a century been so badgered without flattening or fatally undermining the badger. In Dio he felt strength, probably hard-won strength; and a certain amount of balance was indicated by Dio's handling of the upsetting time-transition and the ambiguity about the situation of Lilith, although how much balance remained to be seen; and the same evidence equally argued perceptiveness, although how much remained to be seen. It was even faintly and remotely possible that—Fisherman's Cove—no, don't rush *that* idea. . . .

Rourke leaned forward, softly challenging. "You have just been referring to a rope-trick fantasy involving a man who looked like me. Is it maybe crossing your mind that I may have some identity other than Commodore Rourke Mallory?"

"It is. You concealed it, but you were gravely and personally concerned when I told you that Lilith Vogel was in cave-trouble, and your relief when you were assured of her inscrutable safety was visible. And you handled her name Lilith with an ease that was familiar and almost affectionate. All this, despite the fact that she was lost in a cave fifty years ago and apparently you haven't seen her since. You look to me like a much-older version of the guy in my rope-trick fantasy, only taller—and you tell me you once had red hair—while the guy in my rope-trick fantasy, which Lilith shared, looked to her like a red-haired guy she'd known. To be that guy, you'd have to be well into your eighties. You strike me as being merely a vigorous middle-sixty—voice and all; I'm an expert on judging age by voice—but I would anticipate that age-retarding medications would have been discovered during the late twentieth century. On the working assumption that this is really the year two thousand two, I am assuming for working purposes that you were once named Burk Halloran."

Rourke studied Dio. Dio bead-eyed Rourke. Rourke whistled low.

"Two things," Rourke said.

"Go ahead."

"One: you are right—but I legally changed the name so long ago that I'd almost forgotten it. To avoid confusing the issue for other people, except maybe Lilith, please call me only Rourke Mallory; it's my name, I like it better anyhow, I never much liked any of my Halloran kin."

Dio was repressing a smile. "Okay. Second thing?"

"Here you are in two thousand two. What if you're stuck here?"

The teeth were sheathed, the eyes were glittering beads. Dio's voice had a new low timbre: "If I should stay here, would I find any kind of challenge other than getting adjusted?"

Rourke leaned back, many ways stimulated: his brain was still in liquid-smooth high gear, he'd regained advantage over a new and enormously potent temporary-adversary, and the faint remote little possibility was beginning to . . . Scratch that! Stay with immediacy!

"We have parsecs to go before we sleep," he reflected aloud, sloshing cognac. "Shall I continue to lead, Dio?"

"I think so, yes—for a bit."

"This is delicate. I raise the question whether you, no older than forty, can handle the presence of your Esther, who presumably was in her late twenties when you last saw her but who now, a week later for you, looks fifty and is actually in her late seventies."

Dio frowned down and held breath during seconds; laboriously and noisily then he filled his lungs with air, held it a second or two, exhaled with his mouth wide open. After which he slumped.

Concerned, Rourke watched and waited.

Dio demanded, "Can you find out what *she* thinks?"

Holding up a hand, Rourke bowed his head and went into concentration: telepathy wasn't needed here, he and Esther could mentate directly with their brain devices. Presently his mouth took on a droll shape, and it was Dio's turn to lean forward. Rourke looked up: "Lilith is with her. *Boy* did I mess up that teletemportation!"

"We cooperated," grinning Dio confessed. "In the cave, she concentrated on going to you, I on going to Esther; I won't question your own desires, but—we got mixed up, didn't we? Tell me—are the girls friendly?"

Wryly, Rourke: "Both of us have been disassembled."

Dio's teeth gleamed. "Imagine all four of us together! Battle royal! How much cognac have you got?"

"If I can bring them here," Rourke declared, "I can also bring up a couple of bottles from the Mont Veillac cellar." Then he went serious: "I mean, Dio—if *we* can bring them here. Good lord, horizons, *horizons*—"

When we women arrived, however, there was no heat at all. The men were courteously standing. Negligéed Esther, as the senior woman, raised a hand to silence them while she specified: "We must all four be good old friends and otherwise impersonal while we get all this unraveled—agreed?" Beside her, I nodded vigorously, still cave-dressed. Smiling at me, Rourke spread hands-and-arms; gaping at Esther, Dio spread hands; promptly we women found chairs and sat uneasy while Dio dropped into his chair and Rourke busied himself with cognacs around. Some double reunion! And I guessed it was probably the best kind, for starters. . . .

Seating himself, Rourke suggested, "I think we should first take sixty seconds to gaze at each other." It was a wise idea: when Rourke broke the gazing-séance, he and I for our part, and Dio and Esther for theirs, had somehow tacitly satisfied each other that no personal injury was felt and that still there was some sort of love between us and them although what form that love should take remained to be settled eventually.

"Good," then said Rourke, taking control. "We love, we are friends, we work it out later. Now. Lilith—*Doctor* Vogel, now?" I nodded. "Fine, just fine," he said, meaning it. "Well: I take it that Esther has briefed you on our situation now in two thousand two?" I nodded. "And I have briefed Dio," he added, "so we will assume this common knowledge."

He turned to Dio: "Inspector, correct me if you disagree. All of us share some kind of colossal problem involving this Kali, and the four of us together have a better chance of solving the problem than any one of us alone—but we can't solve the problem until we can formulate it, and in order to formulate the problem each of us has to know everything pertinent that all the others know. Your comment, Inspector?"

Dio, somber: "Agreed, Commodore; but that pooling of information is going to require many hours of talking."

"Not necessarily," responded Rourke, rising and exiting into his bedroom. His voice emerged from there: "Esther and I have inbuilt brain-devices for transmitting direct mentation; and I always carry a couple of portable devices in my knapsack. I call them headphones—you simply clip them over your temples." He emerged with the compact contraptions, handing one to me and one to Dio; clipping mine on immediately, I told Dio, "Some advanced adaptation of electroencephalography"; he nodded and instantly donned his. . . .

Rourke's *mind* came into mine, and (I assumed) equally into those of Dio and of Esther; and it was the old Burk Halloran mind that I had known, vital, kind, concerned; I seemed to be getting also a background of his connation, and in it there was no hint of the old yawing conflict. His mind said: "Dio, I give you the honor: start remembering chronologically and synoptically all your experiences with respect to Kali, raw and without interpretation, and see if you can bring it all off in about two minutes."

Dio's brilliance flooded me: he did it, my God, in *less* than two minutes—*all* of it; I *swear* there was nothing missing, except (bless him) the very personal things between him and me, which really were unrelated to Kali.

"Burk—no, Rourke, I must sell myself on this new name, better for him because he had chosen it and had known himself as Rourke during five decades—physically nodded and turned to me. "Lilith, tell us mentally how much of this you confirm of your own experience, and whether you have anything to correct or add."

I tried to be mentally as concise as Dio; in general, I confirmed most of it and commented that I had nothing to add.

Tension was building, we felt it as connately mutual; but Rourke merely nodded again and cued Esther. She, taut, mentally crisped out her pertinent history, even the parts that Rourke already knew, including Villejuif and all. But I kept feeling a screening off in her mentation; and eventually I was sure that she was repressing something about her original Kali-feeling. . . .

Physical and cognitive silence, then—but an interfused blending of (connative) disturbance.

Dio, snatching off his headset, barked, "That's a great technique for fast review—but now let's get human-talking while we probe!"

"Agreed," said Rourke instantly, while I removed my headset with a good deal of emotive relief. "Now please listen. Inspector Horse has described a series of fantasies which were shared by Dr. Vogel; the first of these fantasies was shared also by Mme. d'Illyria, and the second by a random driver-mechanic. This multiple sharing makes them projected fantasies and ties them convincingly to Kali. I will now toss the bombshell. Just one of the Horse-fantasies was reexperienced by me only a week ago; and it was the Blue Flame fantasy, at Fisherman's Cove for me as well as for Horse. By hindsight, Dio, I was the guy in front of you, and you were the guy behind me. Now, I have been assuming that this fantasy was mine alone for me alone; but now I am beginning to wonder whether it was directed at me at all. Dr. Vogel, you're the psychologist here—"

I demurred: "Holy Moses, Commodore—in two thousand two? I'm vintage nineteen fifty-two—"

He grinned: "Quiet, you have a discipline that is partly scientific and partly occult; in fifty years there hasn't been that much advance. Just tell me this: do you think that a sleeping mind could intercept experiences or thoughts of other minds?"

I was appreciating him: even back then, his probing had been unconventional. "I have thought of this possibility. But I can't theorize it."

"Here is the basis of a theory. Suppose that every thought chain of every human, having a physical basis in the brain, is somehow perpetuated in space as a sort of trace-filament. Suppose that—by chance, maybe—another sleeping person, as the earth whirls, is physically taken through the locus of these filaments; they pass through his brain, and his mind distortedly recreates the thought chain in his dream. Well?"

"Rourke, you're beyond the scope of nineteen fifty-two psychology. Go on."

"This recreation would involve a time lapse between the original thought chain and the interceptive dreaming: fifty seconds, or fifty years, or anything, depending when by chance the filaments of old thought would hit the new-sleeping brain. So my dream recreated the Horse-dream—just by chance—"

Dio injected: "*Not* just by chance! *One,* this re-creation of yours happened at Fishermen's Cove, the same place and indeed the same room and platform where I originally dreamed it. *Two,* this twice-dreamed dream was central in two contorted series of events, fifty years apart, which have converged simultaneously on Mont Veillac and have culminated in our absurd togetherness. *Three,* you *know* Kali, *you* are concerned about him somehow; you have *that* to tell us about—"

"As an extension of your *two,*" Rourke mused, "whither the illusion-series brought you was here to Mont Veillac. And as a logically untraceable outcome of my own Fishermen's Cove illusion, I was impelled to visit that cave on about the anniversary date of your visit; it has long been a sanctuary of mine, and in fact my idea for my RP Fleet was spawned there in nineteen fifty-one—"

Dio, low: "Is that maybe the phantom fleet of diversified

sail-craft which came bubbling out of the cave-mouth in two of my fantasies?"

Rourke: "Precisely, I am sure. But continuing: the place where the rockfall trapped you—I know from the vicomte and his man Raoul that this is so—was a deep cell-room; you'll be time-amused to learn that rescuers got in there the same afternoon, but you and Lilith had vanished. And in that same cell-room today I was aroused by a new meaning that I perceived in a fresco—"

Dio, low: "A flame-crested blue-eyed bird driving down from the sky upon people. A symbol of sheer power. Watched by a nearby red-haired blue-eyed Cro-Magnon who could have been you, Rourke Mallory."

Rourke, wry: "For me, it took ultraviolet light to reveal the colors. For you, Inspector, apparently stray pigment-traces were enough."

Abruptly Rourke raised a hand. "In this roundup of my happily inept teleportation, I've had a feeling that a precinct was missing, and I've just remembered what. Without asking for details, please put on your headsets; I want to try contacting the other precinct—"

I felt him mentally calling for some Lieutenant Cassie Wozniak.

I felt her response: "Mmf?" The sense was that he had caught her male-involved. My somehow-sense of her was voluptuous nude blonde.

Rourke: "Untangle yourself for a moment, Lieutenant; this is the commodore."

"Mallory?"

"Right. Just for a couple of minutes—"

"Oh." Then a sense of verbal hissing to someone: "It's Mallory." Then sweet: "Commodore, I can't *begin* to tell you how much I miss you—"

"Drop the stuff, Cassie. This mentation is privately person-to-person, your partner couldn't pick it up even if he had the device. Tell me where you are, and with whom."

"Aboard the *Ishtar*. With Duval. And boy, do I have a lot to *tell* you—"

"Tell me first how you got there. Tell me what went on in your mind just before you got there."

What he got back was a blend of mystification and erotic richness. But she interrupted herself: "Look, Commodore, I have a lot to *tell* you—"

"Okay, tell."

Her mentation went low, as though her voice had gone low. "Duval is in regular contact with Kali. Kali has arranged for you to be infected with mosaic virus. As soon as you die, Kali will arrange for Duval to take command of the fleet. Is this worth knowing, Commodore?"

I went cold: I knew about mosiac virus in tobacco, but this human version involing *this man*. . . .

And I felt Rourke's responsive chill, backed up by the responsive chills of Dio and of Esther. But with a build of admiration I grasped that Rourke had already known about the virus, but had kept it quiet and hadn't known about the Kali connection. He now mentated with tranquility: "The virus is top secret, Cassie; don't tell anybody, and if you can find a way, be sure that Duval won't. Is that why you wanted me to draft you?" That I didn't get: *draft*?

"No, it was something else. How come I'm with Duval, do you know?"

"We'll talk soon, Cassie, and I'll tell you. What was the something else?"

"It starts with I've been cheating on RP."

"Cassie!"

"Well, you know how it is, a handsome young Russian diplomat and all; and the upshot was, an upshot. Well, after about the third upshot and his fourth vodka—*his* fourth, I had only two because I was technically on duty—he got all rheumy-eyed and confessional, and I felt tender about him so I saw no reason why my ear shouldn't be sympathetic. Well, I'll boil it down to essentials, Commodore, no point in going through the maudlin totality. What he let on to me was, that he had conceived a soul-worship of Guru Kali because the guru had helped him find the soul of his deceased young wife and to learn that she forgave him everything and gave him a green light for anything. And so he had promised the guru any favor that the guru might desire. And the guru asked . . . Commodore?"

"If you tell me that the guru asked him for bodily favors, you will make liars out of Chloris and Zeno."

"No, Commodore, nothing like that. The guru asked this young diplomat to—wait, let me get this straight, it's not my bag—to get him the—the series-progression—is that right? yes—the series-progression of—of—" She halted in midthought, mentally pawing air.

Rourke waited, knowing better than to puncture her search-and-retrieval.

Haltingly she said, "The series-progression of *extabule contabulary*. Yes. Extabule contabulary, that's what he said."

Long meditation by Rourke. I was lost, and so was Esther; but the laboring lips and eyebrows and fingers of Dio told me that whatever it meant was only just out of his reach. . . .

Cassie anxiously interjected, "It seemed maybe important to me because it was so zany. Commodore, does it help any?"

Rourke had grown extremely somber. "The taste if it tells me that it means something important; and I am coupling this with what you've told me about Duval. In return, I'll explain roughly how you got to be with Duval in the first place. I tried to teleport you to me, and I missed."

"*OOoo*—"

"Gratitudes, Cassie. Out."

My headset stayed on, and so did Dio's. Esther and I were alertly watching the men; we're both egalitarians, but series-progressions aren't our field. Both men were slumped, appearing torpid although we knew they weren't.

Without looking up, Dio said, "Series-progression of extabule contabulary. Ten to one it's some mathematical thing. Rourke, what's going on that might lead Kali to pump a diplomat about some mathematical series?"

"REM," promptly responded Rourke; and mentating, swiftly he made us acquainted with this futuristically continent-lethal weapon, the associated REM Talks, the world-wide influence and top-level entrées of Guru Kali, the strange apparent powers of Kali, and the peculiar REM-associated behavior of the guru.

"All right," Dio acknowledged aloud. "Then, bypassing a lot of other Kali-concerns, the series-progression which interests Kali, for which he was reaching through a sub rosa diplomatic channel, must be REM-related. And that may relate the progression either to thermal activity in Earth's mantle or to electromagnetic or nuclear stimulation or control of same. Extabule contabulary. Ex-tabule—"

"*Ex tabula?*" I ventured.

"Out of the tables—or notebooks," Rourke translated. "Possibly. Then maybe Contabulary could be the name of a mathematician whose notes contain the series-progression. Contabulary. Substitute *i* for *y*, and it sounds vaguely Italian—"

Esther advised, "Wake up Joe Volpone and hit him with it."

Rourke began mentating. When a sleepy male mind responded, the intertransmission went Italian; it was highly verbal thinking, which I couldn't follow. After disconnect, Rourke turned to us, and his face had hardened.

"Contabularius," he told us, "was a late-nineteenth-century mathematician at Florence. *Ex tabula Contabulari*, 'from the notes of Contabularius,' is a term conventionally applied by mathmematicians to his classical series-progression quantifying the relationships among four variables related to the molten magma of Earth: electromagnetic input, increase of thermal energy, unitary expansion, and time."

Dio quivered alert. "Then if the REM Device operates by —wait, let me say it slower. The REM Device, you tell me, can blow a continent-sized land mass off the surface of Earth. Suppose it does this by suddenly expanding the upper depths of mantle under that land mass; converting the mantle to a continent-sized volcano of gas and molten magma, using a method of increasing thermal energy by means of electromagnetic input. Well: wouldn't the pertinent series-progression be—ex tabula Contabulari?"

"I'm with you."

"And—Guru Kali wanted *that* smuggled to him?"

"He wanted it, and he got it—hold, something's coming in—"

The transmission was from Captain Ilya Sarabin (I'd get to know many of these guys), and the highly (verbal) mentation seemed to be in rapid Russian (of which I know precisely two words, *da* and *nyet*—a girl has to know these in any language, if you don't mind a plagiary from an old Doug Fairbanks film). Rourke listened with growing tension; and at a pause he interjected, "Do it all again, but try to think English." It slowed Sarabin, and then his new mentation came through in English pure, with a few odd idioms but free of the sound distortions which tongue and lips impose.

The sense was utterly clear, and its imminent-threat meaning was unmistakable, and Ilya's informant today had been no less an executive scientist than Dr. Rostov, who had developed the Russian REM. Russia had been maintaining a main headquarters and two widely dispersed alternate headquarters for REM activation, and another alternate headquarters was in the works. For the alternate headquarters, a multiselective switchboard-console, a power unit, a power-booster unit, and a directional transmission unit had been in storage awaiting assembly; the total weight of these units was about two tons. A month ago—with all storage-security locks in order, and without any discoverable complicity on the part of any worker—all four of these units had vanished. . . .

"Wait, Ilya," Rourke interrupted, "there's another signal; stand by—"

Dio was on his feet, action-ready; Esther and I in our chairs were almost in foetal positions. Co-Captain Zeno Metropoulos laconically told Rourke: "Commodore, I thought you'd like to know something about yesterday's minor earthquake on or in Alaska. It just came through that no seismologist so far questioned has been able to allocate any source of the disturbance except in the mantle directly underneath Alaska—and they all assert that this localized thermal expansion of the mantle is unexplainable by any present theory."

Caught up in the mentation, Dio's brain almost screamed: "Commodore, f'gossakes, emergency—don't you agree? Kali swiped the formula, Kali teleported out the activation units, Kali was testing in Alaska—he's ready to blow Alaska and stimulate an international exchange of REM-strikes! Have you forgotten his sardonic sense of humor? It's like tossing a cork into the array of corked mousetraps—"

Mental silence. Then Zeno's thought: "Who in hell was *that*?"

The physical Mallory-posture was catatonic. And then his brain yelled, while his silently moving lips mimed the yell: "ALL CAPTAINS! *ALL CAPTAINS!* CONDITION RED! CONDITION RED! CUT FOR SPACE, CONTINGENCY RENDEZVOUS Y!"

I was nausea-gripped as all external physical reality vanished. They and everything around me were gone. I was awash in evanished nothing.

When something like reality came clear again, it was a cosmic fantasy. All my visual field was a wide-screen cinema of star-studded black; and centered in the field was the seeming of a blue-white sphere made of agate. . . .

The voice in my brain said, "That's Earth." Confused, I from 1952 pre-Apollo Earth protested, "I thought it would be blue-and-green—" The voice insisted, "That is Earth. *Watch it!*"

A mighty chunk flew off the sphere. The agate wobbled. Another chunk departed another quartile; then a third.

The agate entered into tremulous agitation

and disintegrated, leaving black void in the center where Earth had been.

Part Six

SPACE

20.

The *Ishtar* and all other small and large ships in the RP Fleet had, as it turned out, a hidden capability. With foresight, Rourke in 1986, backed by a preponderant majority of his captains and in behind-scenes consultation with key leaders in the World Assembly, had ordered installation of this capability. Some of the newer larger ships like the *Ishtar* had been adaptable to it; but for most ships, total ship-replacement had been required. The replacement of the last and smallest boat had been completed a few months earlier: sixteen years at enormous cost of money and energy had brought off the fleet-conversion on a maximum secrecy level and with so few ships out of action at any given time that the public had not missed them.

What Rourke had just activated in emergency, with his general command RED ALERT, was precisely this hidden capability. All ships had pulled in sail, telescoped masts, closed over their decks with transparent shells rolling up in halves or quarters or hexagonal sections from the hull walls to lock hermetically overhead, activated nuclear rocket-drive, and departed Earth for space, to meet here at prearranged and rehearsed Rendezvous Y orbiting 50,000 kilometers out. And Rourke had succeeded in teleporting us four to the *Ishtar* just ahead of thrust-off.

Here on the bridge we had been watching, I came slowly to understand, not an actual disintegration of Earth, but an animated simulation on a large trivideo screen which now rolled up to reveal beyond us through the transparent hull-shell—dead ahead it seemed, *dead* ahead—the *real* blue-white agate, perfectly intact *as of now*. . . .

I was hearing the commodore's dry radio-commentary and comprehending that watchers on every bridge or in every chart room in the fleet had been witnessing that same disin-

170

tegration on their own screens. Rourke was emergency-briefing all of them:

"You recognize this animation as Contingency Omega, the worst possibility if the REM Device should be activated. Our high-probability information and inferences now indicate that Contingency Omega is imminent. It appears that Guru Kali may intend to REM Alaska or some equivalent area; and this will certainly be misinterpreted by the United States as a testing by either Russia or China, whereas both Russia and China will instantly anticipate this reaction by the United States. Almost inevitable result: mutual activation of Contingency Omega.

"In case personal survival means anything to any of you as reinforcement of your Earth-dedication, I remind you that destruction of our Earth base will leave us out here in space self-sufficient for no more than sixty to ninety days. There would have been no point in bringing you out here for that kind of limited survival. Rather, I brought you here for two reasons: to let us plan and then operate in a free-from-Earth environment, and to guard all of us against the possibility that only a single continent with some of us on it would be destroyed by a REM-action less than Omega.

"You are all enjoined now to concentrate on methods of preventing any REM-action whatsoever and bringing off this prevention with all dispatch: tomorrow may be too late, or we may have some few days beyond tomorrow. Our fleet-ethic prevents us from making any direct attack on Guru Kali in the absence of preponderant court-supportable indictment-evidence and a consequent World Assembly warrant, and we are far short of that level of evidence. Nevertheless, Kali and his bootleg REM-capability have got to be quarantined almost instantly. Your assignment is to figure how, and to reach trial recommendations immediately.

"I will be back with all of you in two hours for the purpose of arriving at courses of action. This is the commodore. Out."

Listening to his transmission, I had been musing space beyond Earth's albedo and halo. The stars, of course, were electrifying; but here and there, this side of the stars, I could see pinpoints of glow which were presumably sun-reflections off the other listening ships. . . .

Toward the end of the transmission, though, I concentrated on the figure of Rourke seated erect in the screwed-down swivel chair of the commodore. And as his transmission terminated, Rourke slumped; and my still-clinging headset told me that his brain was going into lethargy. Something about the situation reminded me poignantly of Burk Halloran in 1948, and I hurried to him and grasped his shoulders from behind; one of his hands came up to close shakily on my hand.

I became aware that four pairs of eyes were on us: the others on the bridge were Dio, Esther, Captain Clarice Vanderkilt, and Commander Jean Duval. I released Rourke and stood erect, staring at Duval. . . .

Rourke muttered at his own lap, "Now hear this, Captain Vanderkilt, Commander Duval. I am ill, but I continue in fleet command, being mentally competent. Captain, please call the roll of the fleet."

Vanderkilt, grim: "Sir, roll call is in progress."

Rourke: "Very good, Captain. Tell me, Commander Duval —did you expect this dismal result out of your flirtation with Guru Kali?"

Duval, icy: "Sir, I do not understand the reference—"

Rourke: "You are under arrest, Commander. Wait, don't go to your quarters until I dismiss you, I want you to hear this. Captain Vanderkilt, I think you know Mme. d'Illyria; and I want now to present Detective-Inspector Horse and Dr. Vogel, who have been invaluable in helping me pinpoint the high probability of Contingency Omega. Captain, you remain in full command of the *Ishtar;* but you are to understand, and you are directed to instruct the fleet, that Inspector Horse speaks for me as to fleet command, and that both Dr. Vogel and Mme. d'Illyria are to be accepted and responded to as top aides on the command staff. Any questions, Captain?"

While the captain with prim decisiveness responded, "None, Commodore, for now; understood and to be activated," bewildered I looked around me at the people: Esther was meditative, Dio paralyzed, Duval impotently evil.

A lieutenant mounted the bridge: "Commodore, Captain, I am pleased to report that all captains answer roll call, have heard the commodore's transmission, are activating discussions, are nearby here at rendezvous."

"Good," said Rourke. "Lieutenant, I regret to inform you that Commander Duval has been placed under arrest; pray accompany him to his quarters, and deactivate his radio, and lock him in. Duval, I will send for you later."

My sense of Rourke's brain was that of restored self-confidence, although he was broadcasting no intelligible message. "Inspector Horse, do you accept this responsibility?"

Dio was rigid: "It's too big, but if you say so, I guess I should. Yes."

Rourke, gentle, almost wondering: "You know, Dio, every human responsibility is really too big for any human—" Then he clipped: "Good, I am glad. I beg that you will accompany Captain Vanderkilt to the visiradio room while she presents you visually to the fleet captains and asserts your deputy command; but Inspector, don't say anything, merely nod acknowledgment and maybe let them have a restrained smile and let them recognize you during a few seconds, and then the captain will disconnect and you are to come to my quarters. *Winning* the captains will be your problem later. Mme. d'Illyria, pray accompany the captain and inspector and be recognized. Dr. Vogel, I will need you with me. Please activate, Captain."

Vanderkilt nodded and led grim Horse and thoughtful d'Illyria off the bridge. Rourke and I were alone there, except for a watch officer, who seemed to be paying no mind.

Rourke said wearily, "Maybe I need you to help me physically, Lilith."

With my help, he got to his feet. Hanging his arm over my shoulders while I armed his waist, heavily he showed me how to guide him to his quarters.

It was soon after 8:00 A.M. I'd had no supper or sleep or breakfast. It didn't matter. World's end was what mattered.

I got Burk—*Rourke*—into his easy chair; and I sat on its arm and contemplated his face, trying to shake off my pervasive impression that this was Burk's father, having many of the finest Burk-characteristics but otherwise a stranger. At first his eyes were closed while he slowly brought heavy breathing into tranquility; then his eyes flickered open and regarded me while I regarded him.

The old relationship was a remote memory. A new relationship was waiting to be born.

He meditated aloud: "Our past was immeasurably good for me, and I hope that it had some good ingredients for you. I have never let myself believe that you gave yourself to me just as objective therapy. I wanted to seek you, but it wouldn't have done because I had come to depend on you too much. I was totally sure that you could manage beautifully well without me, and I had to be able to manage well without you. Perhaps I should have sent you word about this, but I didn't dare contact you even indirectly in any way at all. Do you understand?"

I smiled openly, finger-touching his cheek. "If I had been prescribing for you, that would have been the prescription. To see that such a prescription would have been right, this is an ego-booster—and a personally pleasing thing, because I did love you."

He smiled back: "If this reunion were in nineteen forty-nine for both of us, I think we would be in bed together now as rhapsodic lovers vowing total fidelity forever. Agree, Ishtar?"

"Agree, Rourke, Burk."

"I bless that vision. Often I have fantasized that vision."

"I too, my friend."

"Perhaps, as an as-of-then possibility, it is real."

"I say that it is." My heart was most full.

Long intergazing silence. No embrace, no thought of one.

He, then: "But for you it is four years later, and there have been some intervening men; and for me it is fifty-four years later, and there have been countless intervening women; and apart from our sexualities, there have been ambitions and ideals and drives. Maybe it is somewhat as though the father of Burk Halloran were meeting the twin sister of Lilith Vogel, both well-briefed by son and by sister about that old love, both curious about each other, both very ready for trust and even eventually for affection."

I frowned down, hurting. He was formulating what I was feeling; and my headphones assured me that his brain-mind meant it. . . . Abruptly I snatched off the hateful-lovable headphones and threw them on the carpeted floor of his cabin; and I grabbed his neck and hugged him with closed eyes, trying to stifle my sobbing, while he held me tightly and rubbed and patted my back. . . .

Pushing away from him, I gazed with my blurring eyes into his wet eyes and strove to make my mouth smile. I articulated: "I'm an ass."

He was smiling quite easily, although his eyes *were* wet. "I know. Thank God. And I'm equally an ass. Thank God."

We interstudied.

I sat up on the chair arm and finger-dried eyes and worked with my hair, while I observed with a voice that was nearly normal: "All right, I'm glad that happened, we two won't forget it. Now. Rourke Mallory. *Commodore* Mallory, with allegiance to no woman and with colossal responsibilities and concerns and with a great deal of bothersome mystification involving an evil semi-double. I am Dr. Lilith Vogel, a psychologist out of a time primitive for you, probably unable to pass a today-exam for whatever your equivalent of *doctor* may be, but nevertheless, that is what I am. If the time and the situation confuse me, I shall try to approach them as though they were a patient new to me: it is merely that I have a lot of learning to do before I can act, and that's part of my professional discipline. Please guide me, Commodore."

He said: "During your time with Horse, have you come to respect him?"

"Endlessly."

"Thank you, I hoped it would be like that. Well: he'll be here shortly, and so will Esther, and I think we four should continue working it out together. Meanwhile I feel more rested now—I guess this virus periodically attacks and then allows remissions. But you've had a murderous time in a cave, and three traumatic teleportations with a vicious time-change, and no sleep at all during most of twenty-four hours. Do you want to nap?"

"No."

"Then are you up to a fast game of pingpong?"

Dio sat zombielike before the transmitting visicamera while Captain Vanderkilt introduced him to the fleet captains. His photographic eyes darted among numerous tri-d images in front of him and above him: Chloris, Zeno, Ilya, Giuseppe, Ladyrna, Colette, many others. He heard Vanderkilt asserting duty-crisp: "Inspector Horse for the time being is the commodore's deputy for fleet command; you will accept his word as the commodore's word." Then, either forgetting or contravening the commodore's injunction on Dio to be silent for now, the captain invited unrefusably, "Inspector, I'm sure you must have a few opening remarks for the fleet."

It threw Dio, but not visibly; he knew he *had* to say something. For some reason, his eyes fixated themselves on the image of Captain Colette Perpignan—who immediately knew this, and so did the others. He licked lips and sheathed teeth and cleared throat and uttered: "I guess it has to turn out that I'm a lot older than I look or feel. When I was an army major in World War Two, I had a bright dream of a

fleet precisely like this one and having the same purposes.
But I didn't follow through on the idea. Rourke Mallory did,
and I'm thrilled to the soul to be impossibly associated with
all of you. I'm a raw newcomer, not only to this fleet but
even to this era. My last memories are from the year nineteen fifty-two, which is ancient history to all of you, and
I don't know how the hell I got here or why, and I don't
have the foggiest why the commodore gave me this assignment. But he gave it to me, and I respect him, and I have
to accept it—*with enthusiasm*—until I goof it up. I will
intend not to goof it up. I hope I can count on your help
and guidance"—his teeth abruptly flashed—"even if some of
you would like to murder me!"

He waited, holding the grin with difficulty, while Esther
(off camera now) admired and loved and prayed for him. . . .

Colette's answering grin came and went so fast that strobe
light would have been needed to photograph it, but Dio
had caught it and so had most of the others; and as now aus-
terely she frowned at him, the lips of Chloris and Zeno and
Joe were twitching, while Ilya and Ladyrna gazed at Dio
with introverted eyes. Perhaps all of them deep-compre-
hended what Rourke knew: that none of them was really
ready for fleet-command succession, that new extra-sharp
blood was needed, that *just maybe* this Horse might prove to
be the one. . . .

Captain Colette clipped, "Acknowledge, Inspector; ready
on." "Acknowledged," instantly intoned Zeno; "Acknowledged," echoed disparately all the others. And Chloris
added, "Welcome aboard."

The grin on Dio faded, but he didn't sheathe his teeth.
Looking about him in something like wonder, he blurted,
"Jesus Christ, why didn't *I* ever have a crew like this?"

Perceptively, Vanderkilt cut communication. That was the
note; let's not louse it up with some lame aftermath.

21.

Dio and Esther went together to the commodore's quarters. So far they hadn't interchanged any personal things, but they held hands going there.

They found Mallory semicollapsed in his chair, sweat-bathed; I was applying moist cloths to his forehead. Seeing them enter and hesitate, Rourke waved a fatigued hand and gestured them to seats. He took hold of my right wrist: "I'm coming around now, thanks, Ishtar; one game too many, that's all. Now we all have to talk. There'll be an Officers' Call in about one hour, to discuss tentative recommendations; and I want to go into it with a tentative plan of my own, holding it back until I've heard all the others, maybe modifying it by the time I let it out—"

While I left him and found a chair, he got himself seated upright and his breathing under control, and a smile came onto his mouth. "First, RP. Never mind what the initials mean—"

Dio spat, "Rendezvous Paris? River Pirates?"

Grinning, Rourke acknowledged, "Those are current guesses; since you mention them out of a pre-fleet time, I have to imagine that you thought of them yourself for your own fleet-idea. You'll know eventually, Dio; be sure that RP does *not* stand for *Requiescat in Pace*, although the *Pace* part has plenty of relevancy—"

He grew serious. "This will be a brief summary. I met this man Randolph in nineteen fifty-one and bought into his yacht, and we founded RP in nineteen fifty-two and went on from there with a snowballing recruitment rate. By nineteen eighty-one, with Randolph regrettably long dead, RP had become an international power; and we had succeeded in doing this in such a way that almost no nation was seriously annoyed at us. Right now some call us the power behind the World Assembly holding the world together—"

Dio mused, "I used to think of my fleet as a soothing suture."

"I like that way of saying it. But that's enough about RP for now, time is short. The point is, that except for RP and the World Assembly, the nations of Earth would blow apart violently even without a REM Device. But our soothing suturing has somehow held them together and decreased strain and heightened international interest, until recently there was beginning to be some hope that after five decades the chill alternately called Cold War or Détente might gradually become at least Lukewarm Peace. Only, Guru Kali got into the act—"

He was talking into space. "From his first emergence into my view in nineteen ninety-one, I distrusted this Kali as a charlatan, and irrationally as an abortive twin of myself. By hindsight, I now grasp that his religion of Inner Light was world-devisive except as it recruited a faithful world-crew for Kali. No wonder he declared war on RP—"

I objected: "How can emphasis on an Inner Light be world-divisive? Don't both Christianity and Judaism preach Inner Lights? And don't they seek to be world-universal?"

"Ducking cynical sophistry," said Rourke, "I will agree with you as to the intents and meanings of these religions. But there's quite a difference from Kali. For the enlightened believer in Christianity or Judaism, his Inner Light is the personal immanence of an all-transcendent God who loves all people everywhere even when they don't embrace Christianity or Judaism. I'll add that for an enlightened *and honest* believer in any one of several Indic faiths, his Inner Light is the All, and it is impersonal and grants no special favors to any individual but is identified with all existence; this too is a binding idea. For Kali, though, your Inner Light turns out to be Kali, who grants your every wish no matter how selfish or trivial; and if he doesn't happen to like your wish, he can always duck it by contending that you must have not really attained to your Inner Light. The effect is to split an individual off from the world and enslave him to his own private interests and to Kali. . . . Hold it, though, we really don't have time for metaphysics; we're much less than an hour short of Officers' Call. Pertinent *immediate* question: how do we quarantine Kali's command of a REM-detonation device before he sets all Hell in motion by blowing up Alaska—or some place else, for that matter?"

Dio: "I have to ask this ridiculous question: is there no known defense against REM?"

Rourke: "Not ridiculous, but the answer is, yes there is not. You have to find and smash the triggers."

Esther: "Have you tried using your newfound ESP to do a sweeping reconnaissance of the world in the hope of clairvoyantly finding all the triggers including Kali's?"

Rourke: "I have. Lilith, during my physical poop on the bridge and en route here with you, and again when I wilted after pingpong, I was doing precisely that sort of mental radar-sweep, and I rang in the moon and the manmade satellite-belt. And I did locate nine triggers, but all of them belong to the United States or Russia or China. Concerning Trigger Ten, nothing. Kali must have it anti-ESP screened so exquisitely that my scan didn't even notice an anomalous blank."

Heavy silence. On the wall, the commodore's crystal-vibration chronometer indicated twenty-one minutes before Officers' Call—and our own minds comprehended the possibility that Earth might disintegrate even before that. I reflected that we might as well take time to think effectively, because a botched attack might speed disaster, and we didn't know how much time we had.

Dio's comment, when it came, was incisive and deeply thought through. "It seems that unless we get unexpected new information, we have no hope of locating Kali's trigger, not at least *where it is now.* I have a silly idea, which again depends on your ESP but in a probably impossible way. It would require that past events be retroactively changed, and I see no theoretical possibility of *that,* but let me float the idea for what it may stimulate. If your Captain Ilya Sarabin could talk his Russian contact Rostov into revealing confidentially *where the trigger was stolen from,* and if at that place you and I could backtrack in time to the theft-moment, maybe we could—"

"—head it off," Rourke snapped. "Beautiful. That sort of time-backtracking may in fact be a power that we can deploy; and as for changing the past, my God, Ilya has potent evidence that Kali can bring this off somehow, but he may well be wrong and I'd have to figure out how. Dio, that's great, but the insuperable problem is somewhere else. Never by appeal or allure or dupery or torture would Rostov

or any other knowledgeable Russian give that location even
to RP on a confidential basis even under threat of world
destruction. And this bullheadedness would not be irrational;
there would be two good reasons—"

"One," Dio picked up, "they may plan to build another
trigger there. Two, if not there, they certainly intend one
some place else; and if we knew where they weren't going
to put it, that would narrow our search range for the new
site."

Esther and I were head-flicking back-and-forth between
them: it was almost one mind divided between two special-
ists each with his own brain. "Right," Rourke acknowledged,
"but you may have deflected me into a new line of thought.
Wait: sixteen minutes to Officers' Call—I can delay it, but I
don't want to. Well. We've shot all the common-sense possibilities, unless one or two of my captains has something else,
but I doubt it—what else would there be? Except maybe
some new information . . . Well: assume no new information.
Then we have to play with offbeat possibilities. We just did
play with one and dismissed it, not because it was offbeat,
but because of diplomatic reality. Now I am beginning to
think that we should go for the guru himself. But notice the
restriction: it would do no good just to seize and immobilize
the guru, because undoubtedly his crew has dead-or-missing
go-ahead contingency instructions. And so I am starting
to wonder how in hell we could go about *changing the guru's
mind*—and not by a death or blackmail threat, he'd laugh at
either."

Silence. Dio was nodding slowly, but he had no immediate
comment.

Rourke turned to me. "Ishtar—any contribution here?"

Was he going for a psychology-inspiration, or was he just
courteously trying to include me in? I assumed the former
and gave what I could. "To get at this question, we'd have
to understand Kali as a person pretty thoroughly. Between
our illusions and your contemporary knowledge, we may
have a lot to go on, but there's also a lot of cryptology. For
instance, when his name first came up in Esther's note to
Dio, I recall wondering why a man would be named Kali
when that is the name of an Indic goddess of creation-and-
fertility-and-destruction. I dismissed it as a coincidence; but
now that I learn he is Guru Kali—there must be a reason—"

Esther said, closing her eyes and flushing, "Dio, forgive

me, have to tell you this. When Kali seduced me, I comprehended Kali not as a man but as a woman. The seduction was Lesbian."

Stunned silence. *That* was what her mentation had been screening! Dio was looking hard-soberly at Esther, and he told her with deliberation: "I wouldn't hold that against any woman, particularly you. But with you particlarly, knowing you as intimately as I do, it is my studied belief that you never seriously felt anything like that before and wouldn't ever again. I think my own behavior with you made you slightly vulnerable, and that vulnerability was exploited for sardonical purposes by the subtlest charismatic who ever hit Earth. I love you, Esther."

After that, it was hard to talk. Minutes crystal-vibrated away: nine minutes to Officers' Call. . . .

Rourke inserted, cutting a prolonged inter-eye engagement between Esther and Dio: "Excuse me if I stay insistently businesslike. On eyewitness evidence of two of my trusted captains, Kali is male physically in all ways except as to the genitals, and they are female but nonfunctional. And Kali never physically philanders, but takes perverse delight in a little business of mentally inducing orgasms in select women."

Probably he understood that if I now closed my eyes and dropped my head, it was because I was trying to arrive at some psychophysical reconciliation of this new anomaly. That a sexual incompetent having charisma and illusion-projection ability would utilize both for perverse amusement, this didn't throw me at all. The physical part of my concern was that a hermaphrodite would be so sharply male in face and figure, including even hips, and so specifically female in the single aspect of genitalia. But the griping psychic aspect was, the—no, impossible!—wait, weren't illusion-projection and even teletemportation experienced facts? all right: the *just barely possible,* God forbid, coherency of this weird instance of hermaphroditism with all the other ingredients of my rejected-but-growing hypothesis about the origin-identity of Kali.

Six minutes to Officers' Call. Dio had been staring at me; and, as I began to feel, he had been partially comprehending. Now he broke in, "Commodore, we're getting mentally fuzzed, let's chop this for now and reconvene after your fleet go-around."

As Rourke assented with a grin, Dio jumped up and muttered " 'Scuse me" and departed the cabin. Esther and I got up too, I smiling, Esther grave; I made ladies-room excuses for us, and he told us where it was, and we promised to be back in five minutes and departed.

Both of us immediately flanked Dio, who was leaning on the rail: this was a lot more important than our not-very-itchy bladders. Esther said blunt, "Lilith, you talk." And she listened attentively while Dio and I in a very small number of minutes crisped out the specificness and agreed on a tentative course of action.

I would love to devote many pages to a practically verbatim report of this Officers' Call, seeking to convey its marvelous fruitfulness. These numerous captains—I know there were more than eighty—ship-penetrated all the rivers of Earth, keeping intercommunication and mutual allure alive among people of all nations. They had, each of them personally and all of them collectively, unprecedented entrée to the highest and the lowest circles everywhere. The little people of the world conveyed their feelings to them; the great leaders of the world confidentially unloaded their secrets upon them. Every captain had a sharp deep intrigue-sensitive mind, and no subtlety escaped any of them. A detailed account of this conclave among these able and sensitive men and women would be a desideratum. . . .

. . . Except that in fact it was fruitless. All of them, and all their crews, had found themselves up against an opaque wall with respect to Kali. Oh, they had suggestions, every one of them, but every suggestion was one or another rehash of the common-sense possibilities that we four had already rehearsed. ESP didn't come into it, they didn't know that the commodore had it; had they known, they mightn't have been ready to propose any use of it—except, perhaps, for Ilya Sarabin.

Most of what I got out of it was liking and admiration for the people. This was a high coterie that Rourke had assembled—wonderful, wonderful men and women. They simply were stopped dead by their first encounter with something supernal. Even we four hadn't yet explicitly recognized that this was what it was.

Actually, the call was all over in less than an hour. Rourke smiled wearily and wound it up: "Stay at it, guys and chicks, but take safety-valve breaks. I guess I'd recommend that as an individual decision by each captain a Draft Board be called on each ship: there's nothing like it for diversion, and sometimes a bright idea can irrelevantly pop up in the middle of God knows what. . . . Anything else, captains? Okay for now. Dismissed."

Vanderkilt waited. Rourke told her candidly, "Clarice, please forgive me, these are *very* old intimate friends——" She smiled restrainedly: "Of course, Commodore," and turned to leave. Dio whipped over to her, took her arm, accompanied her to the door whispering to her, earned from her a delighted laugh at the door, stood watching her depart. Then he turned, stern: "Okay. Let's get it done." Rourke, from having with pleasure watched Dio's diplomacy, raised an eyebrow and turned to me.

I said level, "How's your vitality at the moment, Commodore?"

He answered level, "Good enough to handle a trouble-shot, Doctor."

I'd made up my mind, feeling that once again I knew him well enough to hazard a risky one. "Subject: Guru Kali. Looks like the twin of a certain Burk Halloran. My friend, Dio has to stay for this, but——if you wish, Esther would be perfectly willing to leave."

He said steady, "Maybe I've been trying not to face what I think is coming. Excuse me, Lilith, but I've known Esther a lot longer than I've known you, time being the screwball thing that it is. Please stay, Esther. Lilith, say anything."

I was leading in. "Dr. Jekyll, did you ever meet Mr. Hyde?"

He blinked but held steady. "I've met and talked with Kali, I've entertained endless reports about Kali. He is my twin as to face, and I have to admit that he exhibits all the personality attributes that I rejected decades ago. Now you are suggesting an idea which has often worried me: that I am a dual personality, that I have lapses and foxily vanish and turn up as my own worst enemy and don't remember any of it afterward. If that were the case, my own Mr. Hyde would be on the verge of annihilating Earth. Please notice that I pay you the respect of anticipating your idea and taking it seriously. But it won't wash, Lilith. I have met me face to face, and witnesses including Esther can attest to this. And Kali is many inches shorter than I, and dammit, Rourke Mallory has male genitals and uses them decently well! Look, I know, Stevenson's Dr. Jekyll underwent physical change when he became Mr. Hyde——but in real life, this would be ridiculous!" He was leaning forward and being passionate about it: "Nevertheless it worried me so much that over a period of several years I have kept a time log on my own locations during waking hours and have had every entry witnessed. Kali has *repeatedly* turned up in one place while I was witnessed awake in some other place! No, it can't *be* that—"

I waited, possessed of my double-Burk double-Dio dream-intuition at Mont Veillac and brooded in agitation.

Rourke burst out: "Excuse my arousal, I'll pull it in pretty quick, but this is a *thing* with me, I *can't* be defeating my own purposes like *that*! And yet, Jesus, he's an illusion-projector, isn't he? And good lord, I'm uncovering his powers in myself!" He went cold-white: "Lilith, when I'm one place, could I be projecting an illusion of my presence into witnesses in another place? In my persona as Kali, could I be projecting an illusion into millions of people that I am short? Could I even perversely be going so far as to project an illusion into selected people that I have female genitalia which are powerless?"

I was crucifying a sick man undeservedly, but I kept it up a bit longer without mercy: every doubt that was in him had to come out, and it had to hurt him, there was no other way. Esther sat extremely pale, Dio stood rigid. I reminded Rourke, "Burk Halloran was an impotent male. That kind of perversion in Rourke Mallory's alternate personality would not be illogical—"

He gripped his chair arms, half seated, half erect, terrible. He absolutely rasped at me, "Lilith, I honor you, stay at it! You are on the track of something—*but I swear it is not exactly that!*"

Our eyes were steady-on—and then my stare faltered, and I closed eyes and leaned back in my chair. I told him softly, "God damn it, Rourke, I believe you. And that seems to leave only the other thing, which is whole-cloth occult."

My eyes flickered open. He had dropped back into his chair, licking lips, breathing hard, glancing swiftly among the three of us. His eyes fastened on Dio, and he said almost evenly, "Horse, she's a scientist, she doesn't want to say it. You're a bit of a daredevil; *you* say it."

Dio said curt: "She's done enough lead-up, I'll slap you with it. In nineteen forty-eight, you sharply rejected some of your own personal ingredients, while I about the same time sharply rejected some of my personal ingredients. But both of us kept finding that those rejected ingredients kept sneaking in to haunt us. When Esther deserted me in nineteen fifty-two, I consigned those ingredients totally to Hell; and I suspect that along about the same time, *you* drove out your corresponding ingredients once and for all. This is weird-wild, but the coherency makes sense in the light of all the other weirdnesses. Lilith and I are agreed that your rejects and my rejects together constituted a coherently evil personality, and they took psychophysical form as Guru Kali."

The prolonged silence palpitated. Then, his voice-note almost one of relief, Rourke queried of Dio, "You are saying that Kali *is* different from me?"

"I am hypothesizing this."

"Seriously?"

"Honestly."

Quizzical query: "Which of us is the father, do you think?"

It sent Esther into the kind of laughter which is called hysterical, and I was plenty happy-shook myself; but I was able to see Dio unsheathing teeth in a flashing grin.

I don't think I ever again saw Dio sheathe his teeth.

When we all quieted, Dio volunteered to serve coffees around; we had a long way to go yet. Four seated and mugs in hand, Dio said soberly (but teeth *not* sheathed, please note): "It's worse than that, maybe, Rourke. I think our purpose is to get at the nature of Kali so we can figure how to get at the person of Kali?"

"Right," answered Rourke—all business; edgy but basically tranquil again.

"Here it is," Dio said. "All these phenomena could of course be explained away in terms of Kali's known powers. But in nineteen fifty-two, when theoretically he was an infant or just being born, he was able to use those powers to appear for Esther and Lilith and me as a mature adult, and to project other shared illusions. And in the Mont Veillac cave, you and I independently recogized his power symbolized as of maybe twenty-five thousand B.C. or earlier in a flame-haired predatory bird, with you watching the bird; I suppose he might have changed the past to create *that* fresco retroactively—but even if he did, the allusion is meaningful. Well: what I am hesitating to propose—"

"—is a sort of negative diabolism," Rourke interjected.

"Go ahead," said Dio.

Dreamily Rourke meditated aloud: "It all sounds a little bit like old Satan in whom I've always refused to believe. On the other hand, I've always believed in God, as a matter of decision about my intellect—but I've concluded that God's knowledge and powers are limited to what he comes to notice, what he finds that he can deploy: unlimited potentially, but at any given time, so limited. So if I believe in God, why not in Satan? Perhaps God has rejected certain potentialities in himself, and this is the meaning of the Fall tradition, and they have taken potent form in Satan to haunt God. And Satan is perverse. He is a fiery creator; but once he has created a stable situation, he is bored by the stability, and he reacts perversely into a destroyer of that situation. Dio, you and I are comrades indeed: our rejected ingredients not only have united to form a coherent perverse personality, but that personality has combined with the perversity of ages, or maybe appears as the current avatar of the perversity of ages. And now it is about to destroy its own Earth. And we are up against *that*?"

Esther gentled: "But if you are right, then it *wants* you to somehow defeat it. Didn't it steal me to draw Dio here, and didn't it do so in such a way as to draw Lilith also, and didn't it make sure that we four would be united here? And didn't it cry out in dispair, 'Unify me'?"

The commodore said hard, "I conclude that all four of us are taking this weirdity to be a *working* hypothesis."

Dio nodded; Esther nodded. I don't know what inwardly it cost them to make this affirmation; I know that it cost me a lot. "Yes," I said.

Rourke leaned forward, all business. "Okay, it's a working hypothesis, let's work on it. Dio, here is a suggestion. In late June nineteen fifty-two—I remember this dating clearly—Randolph and I were docked at Blois in our yacht the *Star of Boston*. Lately I had been wrestling bitterly with precisely those old rejected personality-ingredients, and off Blois I had some kind of a crisis that I don't remember very well. Adjacent to my cabin I had an inner room where I used to go privately when I felt inward trouble in order to work it out with myself; nobody else was allowed in there. On this particular morning—I don't remember the exact date but it was late June—I felt this old trouble coming on, and I went into privacy there. Somewhere along the line I lost consciousness, I guess; and when I awoke, I felt marvelously free and clear. This was climactic: it was when I became wholly sane, if I am wholly sane—me, myself, knowing where I was going, no inward conflicts since that have been worth shaking a stick at. All right, Dio, what do you think? Is there anything fruitful for us *there-then*?"

Dio answered promptly, "He's been inviting us, and rather urgently. But if his appointed rendezvous is Blois in nineteen fifty-two, why didn't he suck me there instead of to Mont Veillac? Especially since you were already there, and he could have pulled you back to nineteen fifty-two—" Then he held up a hand and bitterly amended, "No, I see, it's his sense of humor, it's the fox-and-hound game, we had to get the idea ourselves, and we had to figure out ourselves how to get to that rendezvous. Rourke, do you think you and I can teleport you and me there-then?"

"And me?" "And me?" urged Esther and I almost simultaneously. I added, "If everybody has it potentially, guys have no monopoly—"

"New as we are at this," Rourke grinned, rubbing his nose, "the more the sorrier, maybe. Look, ladies, I hate to be discourteous and top secret and all, but why don't you go freshen up for lunch while Dio and I get a couple of damn urgent man-to-man things said, and we'll meet you in half an hour in the ward room?"

"Come on, Esther," I said, rising. "This time, let's *really* find the ladies' head."

Underneath, it nettled me to be excluded from the man-talk; but when I made a wry crack about this to Esther, she commented that she was used to it with both men. "Besides," she added thoughtfully, "I suspect there's some big stuff going on there, with maybe some highly personal overtones; those two are really taken with each other, that sudden arbitrary action by Rourke in making Dio his deputy over the fleet was unprecedented in Rourke."

For a moment I wondered what about all this made me feel so melancholy-alone—and then I knew, and my comprehension remotely amused me at myself. Burk had been *my* patient, confiding intimately personal things to *me*; contrariwise, the older Burk whose name was Rourke was his own man, choosing another man whom he considered his peer as repository of his most intimate concerns, which for sure had nothing to do with romantic or erotic interests; and I was out. Again: I had known Burk for a month and Dio for a week; Esther had known Dio for years and Rourke for decades and me not at all; again, I was out, lonely-awash in space and time. I had found my lost love, but so very much too late that he and I had nothing in common other than an extremely remote romantic-interlude memory: I was to him maybe like the aging Lotte returning to the aging Goethe in Thomas Mann's imaginative novel, both remembering young hot blood, but she now mainly basking in the status of being the great man's sometime lover, while he accorded her every courtesy but failed to get his love rekindled because his mind kept flying away to higher altitudes. . . .

Esther said gently, "Forgive me, but—can the self-pity, Doctor; each of us has her own problems, and they are smaller than theirs."

I said deliberately, as to a restorative slap in the face, "Thanks, I needed that."

We were on deck again, gazing through transparency at space-black star-punctuated, with Earth not visible at this rail. Esther said low, "Then he *did* try to find me." I gazed on her, pulled out of myself, comprehending all that she was thinking-feeling.

I laid a hand on her hand on the rail. "If I am in your picture as the other woman, be sure that for Dio it was only rebound under strain, and nothing on his mind was as major as finding you, and during all our week together he has been eating himself for injustices to you. I know that he isn't in love with me, and I—really don't think I'm in love with him, although I respect and cherish him. I—am no competition for you, Esther, and I don't intend to try to be."

It earned a smile from her, and she turned to meet my eyes. "I've been nearly eighty years alive, with a handful of bedfellows of my own; and I certainly don't plan to be squawky if you and my husband half my age had or will have affection and body-joy together." Then sober: "He isn't even my husband any more, although he doesn't know this —and don't tell him before I do; I divorced him unilaterally in nineteen fifty-seven, in a little principality that has such laws."

I said soberly, "From your note, he inferred that you would be in Paris and maybe at l'Odéon; from things omitted from your note that you would have been smart enough to include if you'd wanted, he inferred that you wished for him to come and get you. I think he'll have inferred your divorce from your present name Mme. d'Illyria."

Her head went down. She said softly, "Then he's up for grabs."

"I—don't think so. He came for you. He wants you. I was —comfort en route."

She looked at me oddly. "Then—you *really* aren't competition?"

I spread hands. "Here with both Dio and Rourke, I don't really know *what* I am. But as for competition with respect to Dio—with you here, if I wanted to be, how *could* I be?"

"Whatever else you two may have in common, you and Dio have this in common: both of you have regained your lost loves, but both of them have suddenly become a vast number of years older than yourselves, with decades of separate experiences. That's a great deal to have in common."

We thought about that.

I told the rail, "Whatever comes of all this, I want you to know that I like and respect you. I'll play it straight and open."

"Me too. Both."

My head came up, and I shook my hair. "To change the subject rather heavy-handedly—I wonder what the hell they're talking about. Somehow, I just don't think it's us."

Our reception in the ward room was most informally cordial. In our honor, the captain had ordered up a not-usual martini/manhattan buffet ahead of lunch, with chilled fruit juice for a few abstainers; and the petty officers had joined us. Fresh from their man-to-man conference, Rourke was contagiously ebullient, Dio cautiously easy-smiling: whatever it had been, it had come off all right. Once we'd served ourselves drinks, Rourke called for silence and introduced us three generally; whereafter we mingled informally, at first together, then more separately. When a half hour later the captain raised her voice to suggest that we grab another drink and be seated for lunch, I felt deliciously better about the whole thing, and Esther was smilingly easy; but Dio, from being facile and winning whenever he was talking with anybody, was perceptibly moody whenever he had a moment to himself.

We three newcomers and the commodore lunched at the captain's table: it was Rourke's ship, but Vanderkilt was master, and I learned that Rourke insisted on her protocol-precedence. It was therefore Captain Vanderkilt's prerogative to guide our luncheon talk; but rather soon, after chitchat, she turned pointedly to her boss: "Anything special on your mind this noon, Rourke?"

She was flanked at right by Rourke, at left by Dio; Rourke at right by me, Dio at left by Esther, no man between us visitor-women at this round table. Rourke responded with an appearance of lightness, mostly to the captain but generally to all of us: "Only a little metaphysical question, Clarice. How might the past be changed, do you suppose?"

She ate a bit before answering, and it occurs to me that I haven't described her: she was late-fortyish, tall and flat-chested thin, a heavy-lipped but skin-pale black with a mannish hairdo; and about her correct dress and sharp nose and deep mahogany eyes there was an austerity which however could, as Esther and I had just learned, melt into winning easy cordiality when the situation was right. I was beginning to suspect that some such combination of operational competency with genuine social ease was a necessary attribute of rank in Rourke's fleet. . . .

When she'd swallowed the bite, her return-look at Rourke was quizzical; I'd later surmise that she was remembering the Blois conclave and Ilya's report about Kali's past-changing for him. She remarked, "It just happens that I brought my music. Not long ago I read about such a theory in a science-fiction novel. If you don't want to hear that kind of theory, you'd better ask somebody else or change the question, because it's all I have to offer."

The Rourke-smile flashed open. "I *love* good science fiction! Who was the author?"

She smiled small. "I remember his theory; isn't that enough to ask?"

Unexpectedly Dio urged, "Go ahead, Clarice." They were on that basis already, after two martinis.

The captain went serious-thoughtful. "The idea was that everything happening in body including brain persists indefinitely and unchangeably in space and through time. The guy said that these little events make traces which stream out through space, and they may be cut through and experienced by later people on the revolving planets—"

Vividly it brought back our intensive speculation of last night (only last night?) about the reproduction of the Dio-fantasy in Rourke fifty years later; and I knew, and I'm sure Dio and Esther knew, that Rourke had raised the question as part of his decision-making process about a Kali-rendezvous in 1952. Now Dio incised, "Time-traces! What would cause them?"

Frowning down, the captain raised a finger. "The author expanded, although I'd say that his idea isn't proved or even provable. Here it is. Everything material consists of atoms which are alive and are interacting and through this interaction create all action including thought. . . . May I go on with it?"

"Go," softly said Rourke.

"All right. Within each atom, the interactive tension among nuclei and electrons is such that each particle, which is not hard but is live energy, is influenced by all other particles. The electrons are relatively large and possess little mass, while the nuclei are relatively small and possess most of the mass. So far we are within physical science. Now: the idea is, that as atoms perish in the course of action, the electrons dissipate into infinite magnitude and no mass, while the nuclei condense into no magnitude and infinite mass. Look, am I giving all of you headaches?"

"If I can follow it," Esther suggested, "Horse can follow it, and so can Mallory and Vogel. Don't stop."

With background-attention I caught Dio's appreciative glance at Esther as Vanderkilt pressed: "Well: the—I won't say infinitely small and massive, that's silly, but the undetectably small and unchangeably massive perished protons form time-chains one upon another, since all action is unbroken pulsating continuity. I'm trying to find an analogy—"

Eagerly I intervened: "Back in 1952, we recorded words and music electromagnetically on wires, and got the sounds back by playing the spooled wire through a transmitting machine. Like that, Captain?"

She nodded vigorously. "Later, Doctor, tape recordings replaced wire recordings, and now the tapes are being pushed out by microflakes; but your idea is the best analogy. The proton-strings would be like wire recordings preserving indestructibly all past events. And these recordings could be rerun, and the events reexperienced, by a mind that knew how to get at them."

All right: that maybe made physical sense for dream reproduction, or for dreams as reexperiencings of past real events; but Rourke couldn't take time to get into this aspect. He pressed, "So far so plausible—but the idea seems to make the past indestructible and therefore unchangeable. What in this theory allows for *changing* the past?"

I was experiencing a queer sort of chill, but its nature hadn't yet formulated itself. . . .

The captain responded: "I was coming to that, in the terms of this author. In the indestructible traces of the past are *if-nodes*: those are places where somebody has faced a choice and could have taken one direction but instead took another. The novelist used this idea to propose that each if-node was a pregnancy for novelty, that somebody could activate a past if-node and erect a parallel track—"

Rourke grabbed her wrist, and his face was very hard. "If a new parallel track is erected on an if-node—*what happened to the original track?*"

Vanderkilt stared at him; he released her wrist and gazed at the palm of his own hand. She murmured, "Why, Commodore! I didn't know you still cared—"

He said gently, "Clarice, I have *got* to know."

Again she took an eating-moment. Then she told her plate: "I am perfectly aware that you are command-serious for some reason. All right. This continues to assume, for the argument, that a novelist's idea makes physical sense. Well. When an alternate track is germinated on an if-node, remembering that this if-node and therefore the start of the alternate track occur in a bygone past, the author mentions two possibilities. One is, that the new alternate track might develop through time at the same rate as the original track had done, and therefore might be arrested and cease without ever breaking into germinal present, so that its existence would never be known or suspected. The second possibility is, that the alternate track might grow faster than the original track, might therefore break into germinality and contend with the original development until they would unify into a synthesis. But he did not mention a third possibility, which I see, and which is dismal. Shall I offer it?"

Dio said earnestly, "Pray do."

"My third possibility is, that the alternate track might cut off and replace the original track before either would attain present germinality. Then the original track, like a cut vine, might perish, while the alternate track would take over. In other words—to make a very plain and intimate analogy, Rourke Mallory: if your formation of RP in the fifties should be aborted by an alternate past-track in the fifties, it might mean that you never formed an RP fleet at all. And in that case, God only knows where you and I and all of us would be now."

Prolonged silence because of prolonged meditation by five people.

The meaning of my own chilliness a bit ago had now come clear, and I had to inject it. "Things have moved too fast for me to have thought of this before, and I'm not sure I can formulate it. I'll bypass Rourke and Esther for a moment, they're complicated cases, and I'll focus on Dio and me. Less than one day ago, he and I were operating in nineteen fifty-two, perfectly confident that as we moved along we were continually being and creating new events of our own fairly free volitions. Now abruptly we find ourselves alive in two thousand two, with all events in nineteen fifty-two— *even future* events in 1952—already predetermined be- cause they have already long ago happened. Are we there- fore now to imagine that all our prior lives in nineteen fifty-two were in fact fatalistically predetermined and voli- tionless? Have we just lost our meanings as individuals? Were we in fact programmed robots? And if we should return into nineteen fifty-two—*if Rourke and Dio and Esther and I should return into nineteen fifty-two for a rendezvous with Kali*—could our action there then possible be creative? Or is it in fact fatalistically predetermined at this very moment? And if the latter—*is this trip worth it?*"

And then I sat actually trembling.

Clarice Vanderkilt looked at me with iced-cucumber di- rectness. "To extrapolate from your question, Doctor—are we here in two thousand two living new lives? Or do we exist in the past of some already-accomplished future era? Well: if the first is true, we'd better think and operate; and if the second is true, what does it matter? And since we don't know, we'd better operate on the assumption that the first is true."

I saw the sense. It rather quieted me, although it left me with many unresolved questions. But I want to move on with the action. . . .

It was then Rourke said quietly, "Thank you, Clarice, I've made my decision. I can't consult this crew or my fleet on this one, it has to be my decision alone even though it may destroy all of us. Captain, please be good enough to activate surface-descent immediately for the *Ishtar* alone. To minimize Earth-alarm, we'll touch down about thirteen miles off Nantes and proceed on skimmer-drive to Blois. Do you agree that all things considered, five hours should do it?"

22.

————◆————

Spectacular indeed, for an earthling who hadn't yet seen the astronaut beginnings or even the detonation of the first hydrogen bomb, was our 2002 space approach to France. One of the dandy little things in 2002 was a restorative pill which contained no Benzedrine but blessed us with a sludging away of physical fatigue-poisons; our minds needed sleep, but our brains and bodies didn't know this, and so we could be alert until tonight when preclimactic sleep was scheduled.

As our approach neared, the daylit Earth surface streamed away from us on all sides until mostly one part of Earth lay below us. "France!" I uttered, map-knowing her north-western and western contours and her main rivers and her southern and eastern mountains. She seemed just below; yet still during minutes we came nearer, and her borders almost everywhere fell away into invisibility; and like a far-aloft special-effect shot in an imaginative film, the west coast of the French midriff including half the Loire moved languidly upward toward us. . . .

The ship's transparent overhead walnut-halfshells parted and receded into the hull, and skimmers hissed on, and the *Ishtar* settled into stability a meter above the ocean. Instantly cutting into full-power drive, she blew toward the Loire mouth at hair-tattering velocity.

That was when we went to Rourke's cabin for a maybe farewell talk with his fleet 50,000 kilometers off Earth.

Having asked his grave captains to activate the entire com system aboard every ship, the commodore conversationally told them:

"Regrettably this cannot be a conclave, it has to be a com-modore's monolog. I will inform you what I am doing, give you interim orders for fleet operations, and finally give you contingency orders in case I do not return.

"At this moment, as your recon screens will have told you, the *Ishtar* is proceeding up the Loire to Blois. This was my decision based on a new and personally disturbing theory about Kali. With my colleagues here—Inspector Horse, Dr. Vogel, and Mme. d'Illyria—I have reason to consider it unlikely that Kali will blow Earth before the present mission will have reached one or another conclusion.

"With respect to these three colleagues I must insert a plea to all of you, to every members of all our crews. None of you must imagine that Mallory has gone suddenly senile and has out-of-hand favored these three above any of you. All of you have long valued Esther as a peer-colleague. Esther once was married to Dio Horse, and his mental acuity, command ability, and tracking experience would be hard to measure. Lilith Vogel was my friend before many of you were born, indirectly she shares responsibility for the existence of this fleet, her psychologist's interest-areas are directly and peculiarly pertinent to the Kali-problem. In our consultations, your Blois-contributions about Kali were indispensable evidence; without them we could not have arrived at the theory on which I am now acting. Nevertheless, these three have had direct experiences with Kali far more intimate and revealing than any of your experiences—even yours, dear Chloris—and their lives like mine have become so tightly interbound with the Kali-problem that they have to be associated with me in immediacy. It remains that all of you are my beloved and incomparable comrades.

"Now:

"We four at Blois are going back together into nineteen fifty-two; this is a new-discovered ability that Horse and I have—you must have inferred it from the presence of Dio and Lilith from nineteen fifty-two. We will confront Kali at what we think was the moment of his birth, and we will do something about this. Afterward, as many of us as possible will return if we can. Further details will have to await the return of one or more of us; if none of us makes it, develop your own mythos and carry on."

As Rourke had moved through these several themes, the changing expressions on the captain-faces had been enthralling. Right now they were all in one or another condition of extreme disturbance; and I saw a few hands go tentatively up. . . .

"Please, no comments," Rourke almost begged. "Let me issue orders.

"First, the interim orders. Continue with your space maneuvers, and keep Captain Vanderkilt apprised of developments. Because she is most immediately in contact with me, she is interim fleet-commander. Should you lose contact with her, confer and decide and act. These orders prevail during forty-eight hours from this moment or until one of us four returns to contact you, whichever is sooner.

"Next, the contingency that neither Horse nor I returns, but either Mme. d'Illyria or Dr. Vogel returns. In this case, Captain Vanderkilt or another is to summon a conclave; and after Esther or Lilith has reported to all of you, elect an interim fleet-commander and carry on until you are ready to elect a permanent commander.

"Next, the contingency that Inspector Horse returns but I do not. Please be fully aware that the civilian police-rank of Horse is senior, he has army combat experience as a senior officer, his purview is vast, his insight is deep. He's also a damned good companion. In the contingency I mentioned, I urge him to take interim command of RP, and I urge you to accept his interim command; what may happen after that depends on the interdynamics among all of you.

"Finally, the contingency that none of us returns. Elect an interim commander, later a permanent commander; carry on; and think of me once in a while.

"In honesty, I must tell you one more thing. If I do return, it won't be for long. I have mosaic virus, apparently induced by Kali. My heir is Horse; please try him before you soberly decide to reject him.

"That's it, my belovèd companions. To understate it— thanks for everything."

He nodded to Vanderkilt for a com-cut; but she shook her head and gestured toward the multiple screens.

All captains were on their feet. Some men and women were weeping.

Snarled Chloris, "Oh, damn!" Beginning to weep, she cut visibility. Zeno, frowning hard, stated with definition, "Since you decided it, I'll buy it; even Horse, if it comes to that." Perpignan incised, "Acknowledged; agreed." Volpone affirmed with a silent nod. Teary Mengrovia throated, "Au revoir, tovarisch!" A few of them held stiff; most, in one way or another, affirmed.

Ilya wound it up with a comment of studied intelligence.

"Guru Kali can change the past, but he is selectively mischievous about it. I am confident, Rourke, that you too can
change the past, and that you will be judicious, and that you
will not be mischievous."

On that, Vanderkilt cut the com. I back-perceived an omission: Rourke hadn't mentioned that success on this mission
might back-cancel the very birth and existence of the RP
Fleet. I suspected that the omission had been deliberate and
that he felt deep guilt about his failure to confess honestly
his unilateral sentence of possible death upon the careers of
these his comrades. But when you thought about it, if their
careers were back-canceled, they would never know it, having
by retroaction never embarked upon those careers. It mattered profoundly to Rourke; but he must have decided that
their ignorance wouldn't in practice matter to any of the
others.

23.

We came to rest at a longshore pier just below the chateau;
we were not rope-tied to the pier but magnetically fastened
there. It was late afternoon, and the pier and the river were
languidly alive with homecoming sailors in much smaller
skimmer-craft and prop-craft and sail-craft. I became aware
that a number of crew people were informally assembling
on deck behind us, waiting in awkwardness; I turned to survey them: Captain Vanderkilt was there, and Lieutenant Wozniak, whom I'd met and appreciated, and a lot of others ranging from officers to deckhands. (Commander Duval stayed
below, electromagnetically caged.)

Rourke behind me: "I'll have to say goodbye to them."
I stepped away where I could alternately watch him and
them; so beyond him did Dio and Esther.

I won't linger over the farewells, because Rourke didn't.
There was a lot of nose-blowing, though; and it crossed my

mind that their outgoing concern for Rourke would have been just as unselfishly intent if all had realized that either his failure or his success might mean their own career demise, by tempostructure. Again the question became conscious for me, whether any time era was real, this or any other. And as Rourke walked silently among them, affectionately hugging the men and mouth-kissing the women from Vanderkilt down (with a most heaty buss for Wozniak, whose eyes were streaming), I consulted the eyes of Dio and Esther, and some telepathy told me with certainty that their wonder was like mine. . . .

Rourke had completed the goodbyes, not having missed a crew member; and now he was exchanging a final privacy with the captain; and I had turned from time-eeriness to savor a heartfilling personal world. My affection and admiration for this Rourke Mallory were boundless; and he cared for me, this was evident; and beyond any rational or intuitive doubt, Rourke was the future-not-real continuation of the Burk Halloran whom I had loved passionately and with compassion. But what I now felt or could feel for Rourke, and what he now felt or could feel for me, was not what Burk and I had felt. Far more than mere time had made the difference: his decades of making a splendid life, with me omitted from his assumptions, and his vast maturation, and perhaps my own somewhat-maturation—these had made the difference.

As of 1948, back there in the peony garden under a horned, beardless moon, *it was eternally true* for me and for Rourke that young Burk and young Lilith needed each other and with full bursting hearts were consummating that mutual need.

But this was 2002, or 1952, or whatever; and Rourke and I, perhaps a little like Rourke and Esther, had become old affectionate trusting friends, who thought together and felt together and could counsel each other and would always be comforted in each other's presence

if Rourke should survive.

Almighty Father, let *him survive in some way that will be good for himself and for your purposes.*

This is what time is: at any given moment, all the past coexisting and eternal, and all the future a truly indeterminate potential for creativity.

But what if the past is restless? What if the past can be changed?

I say that the events of the past, and their meanings for contemporary humans at the time when they were transpiring, can *not* be changed! There is no doubt, of course, that future people will change the past *as perceived*. And I now think it even probable—in view of my own experience which seems to say this—that at a given time an initiate can somehow *add* to the past, creating alternate time-tracks which may even in some cases affect the future. But such alternate tracks can *not* eradicate or even influence the *original* past: its events and feelings dwell as they were forever, and a human who remembers past events and wants to relive them can truly relive them in memory (to the extent that he can cut through brain-blur) as they were then and are always.

Part Seven

1952, AND SOME OTHER ERAS

24.

In his ship cabin, Rourke: "I brought you first by ship to two-thousand-two Blois in order to simplify the teletemportation problem for our amateur minds." He had us all join hands and concentrate; with closed eyes, quite easily now we jumpshifted ourselves to a Blois locale in 1952—so easily that I felt no transition and only later thought to tremble at this mystifying methodology which those two men were mastering and toward which we women were possibly contributing power. But then, with deep inward weird, I recognized that mere teletemportation was trivial beside the ultradimensionality that we would face.

Insofar as psychology is a science, it restricts itself to scientific method—which means, among other things, that it can use only evidence which is materially detectable, and that it can erect a theory only in terms of experimentally testable proposals which describe how anybody's creation of a given set of conditions will always bring about the same results. That's tough enough to do with minds which keep changing as they grow, which never seem to duplicate each other, and which start behaving extralogically as soon as they sense that they are being observed; and that's why psychology of the higher branches hasn't become bodaciously scientific. But we keep trying, as scientifically as we can —and this very self-restriction leaves oceans of possibilities untouchable. Many of those possibilities are termed "occult." It is unscientific to snort that occult phenomena are necessarily always faked or delusive; the scientific thing to say is, that occult phenomena will cease to be occult to the extent that science can get them under controlled study. But that isn't easy.

Kali was occult. His relationships with Rourke and with Dio were occult. In the manner of confrontation that we vaguely expected, without being able to make our expectations definite, Kali's existence would be called impossible—or, by an extracareful extra-imaginative scientist, absurdly improbable in terms of present knowledge.

And in this confrontation, which already transcended time between 1952 and 2002 and might (if the Cro-Magnon cave fresco meant anything) whirl us into time depths infinitely past, I now accepted as real the contingent possibility that not only the lives of Rourke and Dio, but even their souls, might perish.

Yet there was no hint of chill in the quiet merriment of Rourke and the hard grin on Dio as we four materialized on June 27, 1952, unromantically in the men's room of a hotel called Chênaie de Blois. "We'll hardly be noticed here," whispered Rourke; and indeed, only one of the two men at the urinals turned briefly to stare, whereafter he returned to his primary concerns. Faintly envying his shot-capability (Karen Horney would understand this), Esther and I followed our men out into the lobby; and just inside the lavatory door, I couldn't resist giving a franc to the guardian-woman who stared by turns indifferently at the *urinoirs* and the lobby and the wall.

Rourke at the desk obtained two communicating rooms, each with a double bed; and since now it was presupper drinking time, he led us to the tavern. After he had apologized for not putting us up in the chateau—"RP owns it in two thousand two but not in nineteen fifty-two"—we all fell into silence, pondering impossibilities.

After a bit of this, Rourke talked. He had dug back into his old logs and had established for certain that the yawl *Star of Boston*, which he and Randolph had co-owned in 1952, had been tied up here for several days centering on this date. Tomorrow morning Dio and Esther might pose as casual tourists and try getting access to the *Star;* they would probably meet Randolph, and they could take it from there; whereafter Rourke and I could follow them aboard, and Rourke would take it from *there*. . . .

Dio said hard, "But how about Halloran?"

He had fingered, of course, the time-paradox that all of us had carefully avoided fingering. And it set us into a deep wine-brood. For of course, Rourke Mallory *was* Halloran fifty years older, come back here into a time when Halloran had not yet changed his name and was present fifty years younger. And that would have to mean, not merely a Mallory-Kali confrontation, but with infinite additional difficulty, a Mallory-Halloran confrontation, and *their* confrontation with a Kali *who might still be part of Halloran.* . . .

Rourke, rallying, responded with a wry smile. "My answer to *that* horrible possibility is, everything about our presence in nineteen fifty-two is a time-paradox, affecting lives in a small way, from the w.c. guardian-woman to the desk clerk and the garçons in tavern and dining room and so on. And I haven't yet figured out how we can breathe here, when all the air molecules are fifty years dead. On the other hand, Dio and Lilith were thriving in this era a day or so ago. Maybe all eras, once they are born out of prior eras and have matured, are time-parallel and lose causal interrelationship, and people who know how can do a tourism back-and-forth among them. But if that's true, what are we doing here now? For a neutralization of Kali here-now would then have no causal effect on Kali in 2002. I *choose* to believe that we *are* here-now in nineteen fifty-two, and that what we do here-now has meaning for two thousand two and maybe for indefinite eras after that. Let's go in to supper."

Most of our eating was silent; we were looking for alternate topics.

One alternate topic occurred almost simultaneously to Esther and to me. We looked at each other and knew what we were thinking. We looked at the men: they looked at us, and they knew what we were thinking.

Esther broke it. Looking hard at Dio, she said, "During fifty years I've been dying because I thought you hadn't bothered to follow me. And now you're young and I'm old."

Rourke and I were watching them and each other. It came into me that his thoughts about me were the same as mine about him; and then for a few seconds we smiled at each other, and we knew how we wanted it to be tonight. Knowing this now with confidence, we turned to *them.* . . .

Staring at Esther, Dio: "I love you. Do you still love me?"

Her shoulders rose and fell. "No matter who was in bed with me, even my friend Rourke, whom I love—after Dio, there hasn't been anybody else since nineteen forty-five, if that's what you mean."

He incised, "That's—*exactly* what I mean when I say I love you. Sex or no sex, that's what I mean. For me there hasn't been anybody else, either." He turned to me, his eyes warm: "Not even you, my friend Lil whom I love."

I quick-smiled and quick-gripped his hand. Quickly withdrawing my hand, I looked at Esther. Ever since all of us had met, she and Dio had been avoiding this confrontation—just as Rourke and I, until now, had been avoiding this confrontation. . . .

Dio told her quietly, "You'd have to accept it that I am a career man, that isn't going to change. But I do it a hell of a lot better when you are around. I don't care how old you are, I'll never forget all our fire when we were young; I might just find a special interest in this new age difference, or I would settle for platonic love with you and pick up my nookie elsewhere if that were best. But I want you with me, always."

Gravely she dwelt upon him. "I don't care how young you are, I might just find a special interest in this new age difference, or I would settle for platonic love with you and pick up my horning elsewhere if that were best. But I want you coming home to me, always."

They mused with each other.

Radiantly smiling, Rourke said, "By the authority vested in me as commodore, I now pronounce you man and wife. I think they've just arranged the room assignments, my Lilith."

I want to dwell on this, and yet I don't want to dwell on this. How Rourke and I were with each other that night, it was the urgency and the caring of our peony-night enriched by our knowledge that now it was free, that neither of us *needed* the other, that in our affection and trust and my greater maturity and his *far* greater maturity we simply *wanted* each other now. The peony-night had been—well: for my part, a groping for meaning-in-Burk coupled with a strong sense of Eternal Mother role-playing; for his part, desperate need, semiconfidence merging into sudden confidence and explosive triumph, followed by subsidence into soul-relief in which I was his redeeming goddess. I will not fault this relationship: it was necessary and wonderful and good. But it could happen only once, and never again. Tonight, neither of us had any thought of trying to revivify that unique moment which is eternal in the past but only then; we remembered and savored and honored all the meanings of that moment, but now we embraced as mature old friends having with each other human-splendid pleasure-of-the-body blended with love, each honoring the other for his affectionate delight.

We lay there then, side by side, blessing it
                                        until he coughed. Badly.

I sat up alert. "Rourke—" Afterward I would find it interesting that I hadn't said "Burk."

He kept coughing, out of control. Death-alarmed but curiously not guilty at all, I tumbled out of bed and started for the door to find doctor-help. I heard him gasp, "Wait—" I turned. Sitting up in bed, he was fighting for self-discipline, and presently he got it enough to articulate, "Get Dio. That's top-urgent."

I was wholly governed by this command, I had no question. Hurrying to the communicating door, I rapped on it and called, "Dio! get in here with Rourke, fast, fast!" Then I listened unashamed, keeping an eye on Rourke, who was breathing hard but seemed to be settling, and I heard Esther say, "Get out of me and in there," and quickly the door opened and pajama-pantsed Dio was with us and pajamaed Esther not far behind.

Rourke, rigid: "Sit on my bedside, Dio."

He sat there, gazing at Rourke's eyes.

Rourke clutched Dio's shoulder and with a stupendous effort arrived at smiling wan and saying it light. "It comes fast, and suddenly it has come. I'd prefer taking my adventure-chances with the hereafter if any, but I can't duck Kali and Earth and the fleet. I'm hitting you with our agreement before lunch. Are you still willing?"

Earnestly Dio grasped a Rourke upper arm; and Esther and I knew that these men were in comprehensive intermind communion.

Suddenly, Rourke fell back dead.

I don't think you ever really know immediately what grief is. Painfully accepting the death, we women watched Dio.

After many seconds of sitting there gazing at dead Rourke, Dio slowly arose. Looking down at Rourke, absurdly he made as if to thrust hands into bathrobe pockets which weren't there; eventually he gave up the thrusting and let his hands hang.

He turned then to us. And we knew that everything of Burk Halloran and Rourke Mallory, from his birth on to 2002, was now in Diodoro Horse.

He said without emphasis, "Lilith, you be the one to close

his mouth and eyelids. Esther, you arrange his hands and feet. Kiss him then, or not if you prefer not, but then stand well back."

Esther and I required that we smile while we performed this duty. He was my Burk's good father, and yet my Burk too; he was Esther's profound friend. Together we bent to kiss his still-warm temples. Then we stepped back.

A full minute intervened before he vanished.

Dio filled and emptied his lungs, and told us, "His body is aboard the *Ishtar;* they knew from me just now that he was coming. You two go to sleep, if you like, in Esther's bed. I have to think, we can straighten out our tactics at breakfast."

His face went haggard. "Esther—I'm sorry—"

We women exchanged weary glances; then we went to flank Dio, who stared at the empty bed. Both of us at once hugged his hard waist, gazing at the bed; his arms clasped our waists and hugged us hard. Each of us kissed a Dio-cheek. We released him, and clasped hands, and went into the other room and closed the door. It was his to fight out.

Exhaustion came over us; we fell into bed and sleep.

25.

He awakened us at seven-thirty, and we wasted little time: before eight-thirty we were breakfasting, and our sober talk was purely tactical. We thought of Dio as Dio, but we knew that his mind was Dio/Rourke; during much of the night he had lain awake in labor while these friendly but new-acquainted and potently individuated minds now utilizing the same brain alternately discussed and fenced and probed and cajoled in their process of feeling toward mutual integration; eventually there had seemed to be general agreement that the Dio-mind must be in command with the Rourke-mind as highest-level staff, and the Dio-mind had

made some concessions to the Rourke-mind in order to facili-
tate this; and since they had now achieved the first major
step toward integration and ultimate mutual individuation,
both minds together had willed Dio to sleep so that the
process could advance through the night at subconscious
levels.

This morning, the process had reached a point where Dio
was the Dio-mind in unquestioned leadership with the
Rourke-mind everpresent urgently prompting. And the situation as between this man and us women was asexually
interhuman: Dio was in command, he had to be, we
wanted him to be—the issue didn't arise even mentally; simply we were his team.

By nine-thirty, we were down by the river. The chateau
overhung us; we ignored it, our concerns were with the
waterfront. We strolled it, trying to seem merry, exchanging greetings with docked fishermen and colliers, smelling
the Loire, keeping our eyes open for private yachts, of
which there were the usual several.

Not far down the line, we spotted a seventy-foot yawl
painted white. It meant *confrontation;* but I am going to
take you circumstantially with us through our somewhat
tortuous approach. . . .

I gripped Dio's biceps: "If Burk Halloran is here, he
shouldn't see me yet, it might mess up his future." We agreed
that Esther and I would hang back; and he designated a
signal, a simple wave, which would mean "All clear, move
in." Then Dio prowled forward while Esther and I stood
watching; with our minds attuned to his, we could see and
hear what he saw and heard. Esther murmured to me, "I'd
have given a pretty to have this ability during past years;
but now I'm glad I didn't, so forget it."

An American seaman was perched on a dock rail beside
the yawl. Dio did a friendly approach, hailing him in
American English, "Handsome yawl, friend!" The young
seaman grinned: "Hey, hello! you aren't a frog!" Restraining
a sarcasm, Dio came forward and halted just before him,
gazing at the yacht: "Nice to meet an American at riverside,
most of them are up touring the chateau. *Star of Boston.*
Who's your skipper?"

"Got two of 'em. No sweat, though: they get along."

"*Two* commanders?"

"Co-owners, Randolph and Halloran, both sweet joes, you

know, tough in a sweet way, easy to like if you work hard. I do."

"I'd like to go aboard," mused Dio, gazing upward. "Can you fix it?"

"Go on aboard, ask anybody for one of the captains. Where you from, friend?"

"Arizona originally, then New York City. And you?"

"Terre Haute. Hey, New York's a good city, too—"

Dio suffered a few minutes of interstate gossip, then consulted his wristwatch and jerked his head shipward: "Good luck, friend, but I gotta board that ship." And he mounted the gangplank, being careful not to wave at us—not yet.

Esther was cool-intent, but I was loaded with hypertensive symptoms. Loving and grieving for the Rourke-father who *had been* Burk, nevertheless I knew that this dread imminence *would be* Burk.

Once aboard, Dio knew with Rourke-nostalgia that he *had known* the *Star* as he had known Esther: inside and outside, hull and cabins and rigging, responses to fair weather and to stormy weather—although the body of the *Star* Dio had never boarded. And he knew with the certainty of memory where Halloran would be found. And he also knew the most probable location of Randolph, just as he knew Randolph. Troubled faintly by his foreknowledge that Randolph would be lost overboard in a 1954 squall, leaving everything to his Halloran-partner, whose name had changed late in 1952 to Rourke Mallory, Dio moved swiftly upward to the bridge.

Co-owner Randolph (sole owner until a year ago when Halloran had bought in) was a nervously affable ascetic in his early forties; Dio found him alternately admiring the chateau and absorbing the river and criticizing the deck work below. He turned, startled but not upset, when Dio appeared at the companionway-head and hailed him, "Mr. Randolph? I'm a visitor, name's Horse—" Randolph came instantly and stuck out his hand to help Dio up. "Good to see another American," Randolph commented in a thin tenor whose accent suggested Boston aristocracy with Harvard engrafted; and then, with a sharp look at Dio's complexion and features: "By the name and look of you, an Indian original."

Dio grinned. "Zuñi, but I've been naturalized. You don't mind a nosy tourist?"

(On the dock, Esther and I mindwatched and listened: I

needed no headphones now—Dio was unidirectionally transmitting to us his sensitives.)

Randolph, somewhat taller than Dio (what man isn't?), took a guest-arm and led Dio to a riveted-on table with four riveted-on swivel chairs and a clamped-down liquor stand firmly clasping several beverage bottles and a number of clean glasses. Dio begged off midmorning alcohol; Randolph approved in theory, but served two tomato juices with Tabasco dashes, his with and Dio's without vodka. "Wish my partner were here," said Randolph. "Tell me about yourself."

With restraint that Esther marveled at, Dio spread hands: "Just a tourist from Manhattan. Professional man off duty."

"Lawyer?"

"You could say that. I get a sense, Mr. Randolph, that you are the kind of guy I've always wanted to be: a freedom-millionaire with a yacht."

Randolph spread hands. "The life has its points. You like the *Star?*"

"Very much. She's free, easy, trim, a nifty lady with mean clean lines and impeccable rigging."

"You a sailor, Mr. Horse?"

"Landlubber," Dio half-lied, knowing with Rourke's memory that it was so no longer. "Love ships from a distance, read about 'em a lot. Get a thrill right down to here just being aboard."

"*Boy* would my partner like to meet you! Look, he should be back any time, he jumped ship last night. Hell, he may even have sneaked back aboard; but then he'd be in his cabin and wouldn't want to be disturbed, otherwise he'd have let me know—"

Dio decided to take a chance; and making a great show of peering at us ashore, he exclaimed, "Hey, what do you know! There's my wife with her niece!" And when Randolph instantly urged it, Dio waved at us; and aboard we came, listening all the way up to the bridge. . . .

Dio enthused, "They're going to *love* this! Hey—mind telling me what ports you like to make?"

Randolph leaned his head back on his hands to consult the sky. "Well, Halloran picks the places and times, really; we co-own the *Star*, but he's captain and I'm exec, actually, and I like it that way. That's why I never had all that fun until we teamed up: "I know ships and winds and currents and stars and such, but Halloran knows places and has ideas.

Like now for instance, we were in Lyons on some business that he was cooking up, and the notion arose that we should shift the business here to Blois, which is our headquarters; but Halloran got a sort of whimsy about that, and damned if we didn't come to Blois by way of the Suez Canal and Johannesburg! What do you think about *that*? Oh, wait—the ladies—"

Esther was Mrs. Horse, I was her niece Miss Vogel. After two or three minutes of Randolph-urbanity, Esther blurted, "Lil, take Horse below and seduce him or something—I want this Randolph!" Dio grinned merrily, knowing she'd half meant it; Randolph grinned fatuously proving Esther's late-middle-age charm, and offered drinks (we girls went the full Bloody Mary route); whereafter Randolph was burbling to conduct us everywhere aboard.

We three visitors managed to accept with delight. Soul-cold, we knew that we were accepting an invitation to confront the Hot Rind or the Gelid Core of Hell.

Toward the end of the tour, half an hour later, Randolph diffidently showed us a modest quarter-deck cabin, which he called "my digs—I don't really need much"; and then with flustered enthusiasm he bustled us onward to the adjacent door. "Halloran's cabin," respectfully he announced. (These guys were *partners*?) He knocked, observing, "Precaution—as I said, he just *might* have slipped back in."

We waited. He knocked again. We waited. Nothing.

Dio's mind said to us: "It was a chance I took, and now I feel him *deep* in there. Lilith, I'll need you with me for your psychology and because you knew him. Esther, I love you, but I'll be cuing you to decoy Randolph away; okay?"

Esther and I saw that it was here. Esther consulted my eyes, realizing that I was the emotional primary; I was wilting, but then I straightened and jerked my head at Dio: we must follow his lead. Esther's mind said to Dio, "Okay. Be careful. Come back."

Randolph opened the door a trifle, peered in, flung the door wide, ushered us in. "Halloran's command-suite. He didn't want all this, but I insisted—he's really the boss, and he owns sixty percent."

Maybe that was a *slight* relief. No, it was a trifle: continuing oppression . . .

We surveyed the cabin. It was a good deal less than an admiralty, but twice as spacious as Randolph's digs, and

furnished with plain elegance: commanded by a large desk
with leather-upholstered swivel chair, offering another easy
chair and a sofa for guests, and in one corner a well-mat-
tressed thirty-inch bunk and a washstand and a door labeled
HEAD and a roomy chest of drawers; nautical charts and a
globe and knickknacks in profusion. We stood appreciating,
not really daring to go deep in with Halloran absent.

Next to the door labeled HEAD was another door labeled
PRIVATE. Dio's alertness fastened upon this second door, he
seemed to freeze upon it; dismally I knew why, and so did
Esther.

Randolph's voice dropped to a secretive low. "I will say
that Halloran sometimes has—moods. Then he lets me know
that he will be in that room for a while; and we all know not
to disturb him, not even to bring him food." Awe crept in:
"You know how it is with great men—"

I was feeling a little sick. . . . Only, an unspoken Dio-com-
mand came into the minds of us women, and with it a soft-
ness for Esther: "I love you; stay in touch—I intend to win,
but you may not like the outcome, but I love you."

Esther looked at him briefly, and I felt her mind reach to
him: "I have never stopped loving you; and if you come out
of this distorted, I will figure out a way still to love you."

Mind-silence

then Dio's mental command: "Esther—*decoy*!"

Clutching Randolph's arm. Esther urgent-appealed, "For
God's sake, get me to a john, it's the curse—" And when
dull-startled he stared down at her: "I'm starting to *men-
struate*!" He gulped in a non-Harvard accent, "Oh Jesus!"
and he whipped her out of the room, ignoring the door
marked HEAD: in his mind, a ladies' john was a necessity.

I turned to Dio.

He was staring at the door marked PRIVATE. His mind
said: "Follow me in, Lilith. Halloran is in there, he won't
see us, but as to Kali, I don't quite know." And he stared at
the door; I had now a potent pro-sense that doors were forever challenges to Diodoro. . . .

Striding to the door, he opened it and barged through, leaving it open.

I followed him in and closed it and leaned back against it,
a little faint and most heartsick, watching what then was
happening to Burk Halloran.

26.

———◆———

The room was little more than a closet, maybe eight feet deep by six wide at the door wall; and this windowless room was a sanctuary illumined only by the two wavering candles on the altar against the far wall. Between the candles, centered on the altar were three brazen symbols candlelight-iridescent: in the middle, a cross; at left, an inverted cross with a circle atop it, like a female symbol—a distorted ankh; at right, and this hardened the lump in my throat, a star of David.

Before these symbols at the altar, bare to the waist with his forehead down on the altar and his arm-outspread hands clutching the ends of the altar, knelt mid-thirtyish Burk Halloran; there was no doubt of his identity even from behind. He was trembling, occasionally shuddering; and the soles of his bare feet were little more than a yard in front of me.

My mind was filled with the Burk-significance of this shrine: it was where he came to wrestle with himself when what he had rejected in himself was coming too powerfully back into him; and we were privileged or damned to be watching him at the climactic instant when what he had rejected was threatening to overwhelm him. . . .

He made no sound, but his shuddering was mighty, and his mind groaned out an ultimate command: *"To Hell with you. TO HELL WITH YOU, FREE ME. . . ."*

He collapsed, rolling onto his back with his feet a foot away from me, and lay shuddering, and quieted. His face and trance-unclosed eyes confirmed his figure and hair and mind: it was Burk. I started toward him to minister to him, but the Dio-mind restrained me; and I cowered back, watching a hideousness.

Out of the Burk-head issued a vapor; and gradually it

took form as a separate human figure, at first transparent, then translucent—and hung there, not solidly corporeal. It was a phantom twin of Burk Halloran; it sat naked beside him almost but not quite on the floor, cross-legged, head bowed, eyes closed. The face was totally Burk's, pending a view of the eyes; the flaming hair was Burk's; the torso and legs and feet were Burk-male; but the cross-legged posture revealed a virginal vulva where a phallus ought to have sprouted. . . .

All the little closet-cabin was pervaded with vicious evil. I will not say that I *saw* a shadow-figure behind the translucent doppelgänger of Burk, but something lurked, something was powering this

was that Dio hovering above the doppelgänger? Quickly I glanced right: no, Dio stood there, solidly watching; nevertheless, above Burk's phantom double now hovered a glare-eyed ghost of Dio that was murderously ferocious

and the Dio-ghost fused with the Burk-double

which instantly became solidly corporeal, only smallened now in stature, much smaller than inert Burk lying beside him

The head came up. The eyes came open; they were Burk Halloran blue. And the mind came hideously into my mind and into Dio's: *Good, I exist. Use me, Master.* . . .

The Halloran-double vanished; the pervasive miasma of evil dissipated.

Dio's voice: "Lilith—see to Burk Halloran."

There Burk lay. I ran to him and knelt concerned beside him. The large finger of my right hand touched his left cheek. He stirred, he smiled sleepily. . . .

Dio said harsh: "He's alive, thank God, he'll come around, he'll be Rourke Mallory and create the fleet, and the Rourke-aspect of me exists as it was when last night it came into me. Okay; very good; we've met the *first* Kali-rendezvous, we've seen him born, we know that he is primarily the bad from Rourke and secondarily the bad from me, and we know for sure who his master is. Lil—Lil, no chance; Burk mustn't awaken to us, you know that. Stand up, Lil: there's a lot of work to do. We have to confront mature Kali now at the *second* rendezvous: the cave at Mont Veillac, in two thousand two. And *that* takes me off the time-paradox hook: whatever happens, we won't be annihilating all the reality of RP!"

Without transition, again Dio and I sat with our backs against a cave wall in refrigerating darkness, holding hands lightly, balancing our breathing. . . .

He mentated: "Take it easy, Lil, we're here *again*, not *still*. It's two thousand two now, not nineteen fifty-two; the tube entrance isn't blocked, now, but nobody will interrupt us, I can tell. I don't know what made me imagine that there was to be only a single rendezvous; two were logical —one in nineteen fifty-two aboard the *Star*, to witness Kali's birth; another here in the Mont Veillac cave in June two thousand two, because Kali is poised here-now to trigger Earth's destruction—and *he doesn't want to do it.*"

Ducking silliness like "How do you know he's here?" I mind-queried, "Why doesn't he want to do it?"

"The dark side of Burk was enslaved to its impulses; once free of Burk, it was vulnerable to heavier evil. The dark side of me was enslaved to its impulses; once free of me, it was vulnerable to heavier evil. His dark side and my dark side fused in nineteen fifty-two, just as surely as Rourke and I freed of darkness have fused in two thousand two. The dark fusion named Kali was instantly mastered for dark purposes by the greatest of darknesses. But latent in Kali is a memory of something more long-range meaningful in Burk and in me; and in this semifinal instant Kali is obliquely crying to Rourke and me for rescue from whatever is compelling him. That's my analysis, Lilith; do you have any corrections to offer?"

My whole sense of his mentation was that the detective-inspector was at the threshold of solving his enigma, that confirmation would be soul-perilous, that because of the stakes he didn't care. Fiercely I thought at him: "No corrections, Dio, Rourke; what you have to do is what I have to do."

Instantly the little cell was flooded with ultraviolet light. On the far wall, the purple-haired violet-eyed predatory bird flared malevolent. . . .

Dio was on his feet, advancing on the bird, I immediately behind him. Dio outstretched his right arm slightly upward, index-finger stiff-extended; and the finger punched the violet eye of the sky-diving predator.

Demonic mind-laughter followed by a chortling mind-voice: *Bad guess, Dio-Rourke! Did you really think the bird's-eye masked a spring which would open the wall? No chance; the wall is solid rock, I'm far on the other side of it.*

You'll have to teleport yourself to me. Can *you teleport yourself?*

Dio-Rourke's mind-reply shocked me, but I guess it relieved me too. *No more so than Rourke or Dio ever could. Come off it, Kali, we've been on to you since before we spaced the fleet: you've monitored both of us all the way; when we wanted teleportation or teletemportation, you brought it off for us; when we needed telepathy, you gave it to us just as you are doing now. It's a fascinating reverse-chess game, Kali: instead of weaving in upon us, you've sucked us into weaving our way to you, and you plan to win if we checkmate you. Okay, right now you're in check, it's your move: are you going to sit there in check forever—or are you going to teleport us in?*

We dissolved through the cave wall. . . .

The background was another cavern cell brilliantly illumined, eye-stuffed with electronic apparatus and white-uniformed technicians, ear-filled with electronic hum. Against a far wall was a world map in polar projection, near whose center Alaska red-light-vibrated.

The foreground was flame-topped Kali, fully man-dressed in casuals, lounging in a wickerwork armchair with one leg on a wickerwork hamper while the other hung lazily swinging over the far arm. His right side was toward us, his face was turned away from us toward the works within.

We studied the frightening scene, comprehending what it threatened. Dio and I now were in perfect intercommunication, presumably as the cream of Kali's jest. Kali ignored us, until Dio's mind cold-challenged him: *Second rendezvous, Kali. Final rendezvous.*

Most deliberately the head swiveled around to us, the blue eyes penetrated us. There was no decay in this face: it was young Burk Halloran sublimated into ultimate charisma. The mind came compellingly into our minds: *Dio-Rourke, I begged you to unify me, but the unity is on my terms: there is never any other outcome to a compromise with me.*

He was smiling now, quite winningly, and his eyes were on me. *Dio-Rourke can wait while I captivate you again, Lilith, knowing you more intimately than Burk ever knew you.* . . .

Forgive me, Ben, I have to be sexually explicit about this if it is to have any meaning at all. His Burk-eyes began a leisurely inspection of all my body-skin; not merely did his eyes undress me, they *husked* me at leisure: fastened on my breasts, which grew restless; concentrated on my nipples, which repugnantly erected; inspected my navel, and my groin glowed. By now I was believing, in his case, the ancient idea that when we see, rays of *self* come out of our eyes and prowl the target: his eye-rays permeated, my under-the-clothes bare skin could feel their crawling-arousing tip-touch. They released my belly, dropped to my feet, sensuously caressed the crevices between my toes and the soles of my feet, liana-twined up ankles and calves and thighs: I was helplessly ready, past fighting. Flametop's purring mental mock poisoned my mind: *Lilith . . . Ishtar . . .* My mind was a peony garden in moonlight, but the peonies stank and the moon was ghastly

and his eye-rays penetrated target, charming wellsprings out of target, inhaling and tasting and probing target; orgasm began, and it was going to be obscenely sublime

but I prayed to God

and my eyes-and-mind comprehended in anomalous totality the male torso and the unseen virginal vulva, which was nonfunctional-dry: it was all mockery; and orgasm subsided before it exploded, leaving me a self-contained jangle of nerve endings. Can counter-cruelty in self-defense be forgiven? I required my eyes to hold focus on his untenanted crotch and my mouth to smile twistedly and my mind to formulate: *If you were clearly male or clearly female, or even both clearly, perhaps I would have surrendered. But you are neither, and not both, and therefore nothing that I want to surrender sexually to. And I won't mother you, because you are powerfully evil.*

I felt the eye-rays relax; then Kali gibed, almost petulantly: *Are you therefore some kind of sexual traditionalist, to require totally one or totally the other?*

But now I was beginning to be firm again. Nothing under the sun had ever owned an anatomy like Kali's anatomy; and nothing good beyond the sun would so have assaulted me; and therefore, Kali was evil.

Dio's icy mind said: *You lost with her, Kali. Now try me.*

With cosmic deliberation, Flametop turned his attention to Dio, captured the eyes of Dio.

Attack-weakened, I was sucked into Dio's Kali-experiencing, I *became* Dio, I became *Man* who was a male/female blend of Rourke and Dio and Esther and me. . . .

In the long process, I kept becoming Flametop and rejecting Flametop and losing Flametop and dying.

I was Australopithecus in jungles perfecting biological tools and venturing passional murder.

I was Pithecanthropus in jungles wit-and-strength-defeating Australopithecus and experimenting with stone tools and ritualizing murder.

I was Heidelberg in forests outmaneuvering Pithecanthropus and perfecting stone tools and snatching fire from lightning.

I was Neanderthal in forests and savannahs outwitting Heidelberg and proliferating more elaborate stone tools and stumbling upon the craft of driving wild herds over cliffs for weeks of rich, ripening meat.

I was Cro-Magnon at the feet of blue-frigid ice walls enslaving and running circles around dull-witted Neanderthal while elaborating totemism and ritual art and engraving on bones the beginnings of symbolical sign-communication and records and inventing new residential architecture with sticks and skins.

I was entirely human Man, still flirting with glaciers, in my so-called primitivism which was an early sophistication standing on the shoulders of all who preceded me, possibly a shade brighter than even brilliant Cro-Magnon, possibly the same species as Cro-Magnon with the same intelligence range: moving on into ultrafine hand-technologies and missile-hurling weapons, hunting selectively while propitiating the totem-ancestor of the animal I hunted, finding new kinds of food and inventing agriculture, elaborating my languages (growth-inherited from Australopithecus and prehuman forebears) with more and more abstract words, evolving my sign records into pictograms, deriving from my new agriculture the ideas of permanent clan-settlement and interclan warfare and clan-identity-and-pride, and somewhat inconsistently elaborating my concept of individuality; raising my animistic thinking to the abstraction level of spirits and demons and my ritualizations into propitiatory worship and launching upon the courageous-imaginative attempt to control uncontrollable nature that is called magic.

Kali was in each of my evolving identities. He was my flame whenever I was coming in with my newness. Whenever I had established my newness, my flame burned too hot, and I rejected it. Then my rejected flame became Kali: ensnaring Australopithecus in his passions until they fatally weakened him, immersing Heidelberg in his rituals until they fatally weakened him, pushing Neanderthal into more and bigger herd-slaughters until the scarcening of the herds fatally weakened him, enthralling Cro-Magnon and other full humans into their fatally weakening propitiatory complications. . . . Reject Kali, like a fire compulsively burning out all its forest-food, gleefully compelled each final self-destructive process until, at the end of it, with dismay Kali comprehended that he would die with the final destruction. Whereupon he joined the successor . . .

I was the Sumerians coming in to enslave more-primitive neolithic peoples in hot river-lush Mesopotamia and raising all previous ideas and achievements to the levels of gods, priestly hierarchies, pictography and then cuneiform writing, city-states, city walls, high architecture in stone and artificial materials like clay bricks culminating in temples, gracious human manners and living styles, canals for irrigation and transportation and flood control; high art for the gods and for its own sake in clay, stone, gold, copper, tin; weapons in copper and bronze; sailing ships; intercity hegemonies under kings. And I was their Hittite, Semitic, and Babylonian successors and improvers or debasers.

Kali was my flame when I was coming into my newness. When I had established my newness, I rejected my too-hot flame. Then Reject Kali drove warlord after warlord forward until the creativity of the cities was war-destroyed and each city was cowering in defensive weakness for easy overrunning by the Kali-powered outside-invader. And this continued until with dismay Kali comprehended that he would die with the final destruction. Whereupon he joined the successor. . . .

I was the Egyptian pharaohs and priest-nobles, particularly in the fourth, twelfth, eighteenth, and nineteenth dynasties, adapting almost all those Sumerian ideas and making them my own and moving far beyond them, substituting prescience for magic, paper for clay, light two-wheeled chariots for heavy four-wheeled carts, pyramid tombs for vault tombs (and then vault tombs again, but richer), people-inviting ground-level temples for aloft-aloof ziggurat-temples, higher education for lore teaching, highways for canals, tight-knit empire under nomarchs for loose intercity hegemonies; and, in place of fatalism and ultimate disaster, light and hope and resurrection under a transcendent God of gods.

In each of these dynasties, Kali was my flame when I was coming into my newness. When I had established my newness, I rejected my too-hot flame and settled down to consolidate my power in serenity. But each time, Kali maneuvered me into squatting as a self-satisfied totalitarian nabob while inflaming mob passions against my oppression. Each time, I fell into desuetude, to be toppled by internal insurrection or external invasion. But ultimately Kali comprehended that his manipulation of Egypt and his own vitality were about to die with Egypt. Whereupon he joined the successors. . . .

By then the massiveness of my civilizational maturity had reached high plateau; and in many contemporaneous and subsequent civilizations I proliferated into many diversified trends which played counterpoint with each other. I was the evolution of mythopoeic prescience into philosophy and science: nature-philosophy from Thales through Heraclitus and Democritus; idea-philosophy from Parmenides through Socrates, Plato, and Aristotle; mathematical and logical method from Pythagoras through Plato, Aristotle, Euclid; an accompanying diversification of other sciences and philosophies low and high, semiculminating in the theoretical-empirical structures of Copernicus, Galileo, Brahe, Kepler, Newton, Maxwell, Poincaré, Rutherford, Einstein, Russell, Whitehead, Eddington, and numerous contemporaries and successors; religious evolution from earth-mothers and serpent-gods-and-goddesses and storm-gods and bull-gods and sun-gods into I AM THAT I AM and then the Loving Heavenly Father and then the Son Personifying the Loving Heavenly Father, with subsequent amalgams of neo-Platonistic theism and Aristotelean deism and theocratic Puritanism and scientific naturalism, and with devoutly religious counter-attitudes of universal pantheism and agnosticism and atheism; the blessèd sunlight of one artistic renaissance after another in era after era, with accompanying humanism to earth-leaven religion's otherworldly austerity; following dynasty after dynasty and bureaucratic regime after regime of rule-by-whim, the enlightened concept of the Reign of Law mothering Representative Democracy. . . .

With respect to each of these my Hellenic-Western trends, Kali was my flame when I was coming in with my newness; and each time, never really learning, I rejected him when I found him too hot for my established serenity. And he operated with vicious glee as before. Nature-philosophy he vitiated by focusing on the Heraclitean emphasis on flux while suppressing the Heraclitean modification of eternal constancies. Idea-philosophy he perverted by converting changeless categories into everything and thing-flux into nothing. Mathematics he ruined by erecting the notion that whatever was mathematically proved was eternal verity while all else was illusion. Religion he made so involute-dogmentarian that it was counterattacked by religious relativity and ended by being laughed off. Art he polished off easily by convincing most critics that the artist is the sole judge of whether his art is art, with the result that the rhyming of "art" and "fart" often proved meaningful. As for Representative Democracy, the inflamed ambitions of the elected representatives interworked with the inflamed passions of the people until chaos allowed Kali to erect paranoid tyranny-cruelties like those of Hitler or Stalin or oligarchically unbendable cold-core social structurings like those of Mao and the U.S.S.R. Praesidium, or appetitive and undefeatable one-focus gigantisms like super-corporations. When manfully I tried to stitch it all together with devices like the League of Nations and the United Nations, Kali undermined the League with cowardice until it disintegrated, whereafter he utilized its own rules and principles to neutralize UN by the irresponsibility of its newly enfranchised underdeveloped nations. But as UN miserably and prolongedly died, and as therefore unilateral threats by great nuclear powers threatened to destroy Kali's food, which was Man on Earth, in desperation he joined the successors. . . .

The Kali-control of the Dio-mind ground on, continuing to entail Esther and Rourke and me with Dio as Man; but if previously my image-laden experiencing had been by turns inspiringly noble and diabolically vicious, for some time (as in a decaying dream-series) my images had been merely oppressive pseudo-images of concept-fragments without visual form or color or any emotive coloration, but only drear. Compulsively the semi-images continued and proliferated, as though Kali was making us feed on ourselves as he had fed on himself.

I was unable to free myself from a long thing about historical male-female relationships in the human species. Brute naked male had totally subjugated brute naked female, and when this had become ritual he was going into lethargy and his clan with him because Kali remorselessly compelled all his energies into eating what females brought him and then feeding on the females; but when Kali comprehended that his parasitized host the male would die with the clan, Kali joined the newcomers. Then flame-souled females instituted monogamous marriage, less for an equal sex-break than to destroy pluralistic manipulation by males and to gain some status as personalities; but once after innumerable generations the new regime was established in a well-balanced way, the females rejected Kali for serenity in the marriage bond, and the ultimate result was tolerable satisfaction entailing occasional bickering in the nineteenth-century double standard with its forms and proprieties of appearance. When again it seemed that males were growing irresponsible enough to imperil Kali along with his host-species, Kali joined the newcomers: flame-souled females introduced feminism and pressed for women's rights until by our time in 1952 females practically controlled marriage and children and joint property and could work for inferior wages; whereupon females dismissed Kali and settled serenely into it, while males yielded at home and oppressed females at work and in politics. But the home-yielding of males to females was now so seriously oppressing male initiative that males were lethargically settling in to corporation bureaucracy and the committee method and the money-status system and the satisfaction of power-need by self-interested subordinate bootlicking; whereupon an alarmed Kali realized that the whole system might collapse of its own self-satisfaction, leaving him nothing to feed on. So he joined several groups of newcomers; and in 1952 there was arising a whole new generation of flame-souled females who would eventually call themselves Women's Liberationists; and the new generation of babies, being the first generation in human history to grow up knowing that Man could destroy himself by inadvertently pushing a button, would go through a period of lethargy which would flame-flare in the sixties into open social-sexual-narcotic rebellion-retreat; and numerous intelligent young flame-souled blacks were to notice noisily and with increasingly frequent violence that blacks were still being kicked aside or eased over by the White Establishment now in the year preceding the hundredth anniversary of the Emancipation Proclamation. . . .

I was shocked out of the prolonged nightmare by a Dio-précis, mental and gentle and commanding. *Kali, you're caught in a reverberating circuit. Your problems and our resulting problems all come when you are rejected-out of an otherwise whole personality that fears to keep you in; the rejector for a while wins serenity, but he ought to know by now that eventually you will destroy him.*

The Kali-image, grown noticeably pale, hard-stared at Dio—who continued implacably: *And you ought to know by now that each of your capricious victories weakens your food supply, which is Man. And I think you are fearfully aware, Kali, that in two thousand two you are within a button push of achieving every parasite's ultimate objective: final destruction of his host, which is suicide for the parasite. But you aren't ready for suicide, are you, Kali? You like this hot life, creative or rebellious, n'est-ce pas? Unfortunately, there you are arrived at two thousand two, ready to push the button that will terminally destroy Earth AND THEREFORE YOURSELF—because you haven't yet located another human-level race on any planet of any other star, have you, Kali?*

It seemed to me that the runt-sized Kali was shriveling; I began to feel him as even smaller than Dio—who now drove *this* at him:

These are the large reasons why you have petitioned Rourke and me to unify you. Well, here we stand ready for that—but we dictate the terms. And we can dictate—because we know your small intimate personal reason for this game: you are weary of your master and finally nauseated by your own potent freakishness; you can be bargained into soul-subjection to us in order to win freedom from him. All right. Your move. Is it checkmate?

The Kali-mind was losing suave; it felt now almost like an anxiety-ridden patient clutching the jacket lapels of his doctor, about to flood him with a commingling of self-justification and appeal. *Look, this conversation is mortally dangerous; I am trying to jam the master with mental and electronic static, but he may penetrate. . . .*

Dio: *I too am mind-jamming. Get going with it, whatever it is.*

Kali: *Look, you see, you and Burk freed me, you can't comprehend the terror of total freedom; it is wanting everything without any power, without any ground for the uncertain feet. One came to me and corporealized me, and now through that one I have power for any action that I can think of in space or time or soul; and that is almost as terrible. . . .*

Sure of myself, calmly now I interjected: *So give him his due, Dio, he has done a great deal with his power: for example, he has turned a hundred million people from secularity to religious inwardness, he has granted a hundred million wishes. Why should you and I complain if the religious inwardness is self-centeredly shallow, or if he amuses himself by weaving bad practical jokes into his wish-granting? The big thing is, he has conquered time, and he is about to consummate his conquest of Earth by destroying Earth. Dio, don't you agree? Thou shalt not muzzle the ox that threadeth out the corn. . . .*

Of course I had precipitated soul-crisis. Kali was quivering, paranoid-fearful—which meant attack-ready or something else, there is never any sure telling. He brought himself under control, though; and modulating his mentation as though he had lowered his voice, Kali delivered the following upsetting response:

Dio-Rourke, Lilith, you are making one small mistake: you are thinking of me as The Enemy, but in fact I am only his high lieutenant in this era. And I am weary of this lieutenancy, it is a compulsive-wild servitude, there is no future in it except ultimate cosmic frustration and soul-killing boredom. I persuaded the master, if I may personify him, that it would be amusing to bring Mallory and Horse back to me, using a complicated game of indirection, and finally to capture both of them for the master's pleasures; but my private purpose was different; and this confession is soul-perilous, because we can't count on the effectiveness of our mind-jamming. Dio-Rourke, I propose this deal: take me back into you, inter-unify the three of us. I exact no price other than your tolerance of me again within you; I will even sacrifice my conscious identity.

Dio-Rourke cold-demanded: *And my incentive?*

It is double. You will be Kali in addition to being your-selves, you can pose as Kali and direct his forces and re-sources. And you will have within you the powers of Kali, to deploy at your own will.

I burst in: *But the powers of Kali are evil!*

Kali, still quietly: *Not so, Lilith. They are impersonal powers of the cosmos, usable equally for good or for evil: whether they are good or evil depends on the motives of the deployer. Dio-Rourke could not use them for anything but good.*

Dio-Rourke, implacable: *Yet I know without question that I will have to pay a price. Kali, what is the price?*

Kali, almost humble: *I gain nothing personally from your payment of this price. It is only that as soon as the master learns how he has been euchred, he will be hot on our soul-tail. You can hold him at bay with the powers that I bring you, and you can win; but you can also lose—it will be a question of your continual alert wit, with me unable to help intelligently because I will be forever subconscious within you.*

Delay. Then Dio-Rourke: *There must be a catch to this. But I don't seem to be finding it—*

Kali, nearly mind-inaudible: *I choose to be totally honest. The catch is, Dio and Rourke, that I was in each of you once, I practically ruined both of you, I could ruin you again. Even if I didn't want to ruin you, I could ruin you again.*

Dio-Rourke: *Do you want to ruin me?*

Kali: *Oh, God, no.*

Dio-Rourke: *Then come back with us.*

I, mind-screaming: *No, Dio! No, Rourke! Don't trust him! NO—*

I'm not sure what I then saw, not sure at all. It might have been Kali leaping upon Dio, arm-and-leg-clutching Dio. There may have been a struggle, I'm not sure.

Perhaps, at the terminus, Dio momentarily became transparent, then dissolved into Kali—maybe.

Kali became standing red granite. Beyond, unnoticing technicians continued busying themselves with humming technology.

I stood numb, contemplating final shipwreck. Only Kali, now: no Dio—and therefore, no Rourke—and consequently, no future whatsoever, unless planetary atomization could be called a future.

I hard-closed my eyes and inwardly screamed a prayer: *Let it all be a nightmare, return me to nineteen fifty-two, save Earth, save Man.* . . . I waited, prayerful, holding faith. But there was no sense of teletemportative queasiness, no through-the-window sounds of Manhattan traffic. . . .

Only the soft contralto-baritone of Kali addressing his people in the cavern: "Stay with it, good friends, but do not activate, I have meanwhile-errands elsewhere; await my message, be it a week or a month; I will return."

My shoulders went up and down in a slow shrug. Not all prayers are answered: He had let us have Egyptian and Babylonian and Roman and Islamic and Nazi captivities, to name a few; He had watched us through pogroms, including gas chambers; He had His inscrutable ways; blessèd be He.

Kali was watching me when I opened eyes; and his blue eyes were Burk's, but I resisted their compulsion. The machines and technicians had disappeared: Kali's backdrop was the predatory-bird mural ultraviolet-flooded from no evident source; in this light, the Kali-hair was purple. At first I thought his eyes were sardonic; then, an instant before the transition, they seemed thoughtful.

Part Eight

FRAGMENTATION
OF EARTH

27.

My next memory is Randolph pacing near the door of the
ladies' guest head; Kali must have spirited me to the 1952
yacht—and he wore now the seeming of Dio, which made
me hopeful until I revived enough to distrust. Dio's voice
called cheerily, "Hey, Esther, what's holding us up?" She
emerged prim, stood to one side while Kali-Dio pumped
Randolph's hand and thanked him effusively and pled a
luncheon date, suffered her arm to be clasped by Kali-Dio—
who, while clasping mine also led us ashore—and then, once
in an otherwise untenanted copse behind the chapel on the
chateau lawn at Blois, threw back her head and laughed
like a female satyr.

Unhappily I couldn't laugh with her. Kali-Dio, watching
her, allowed his Kali-appearance to reclaim him. When her
laughter had decayed into an occasional chuckle-blurp, he
ordered in the Kali-voice, "Open your eyes, Esther. I mean,
all the way."

She got a laughter-remnant stifled and looked at him. She
frowned at him. Up went her eyebrows, and her hands
flew to her mouth.

He waited.

She, so cold that I could feel it: "He lost, then. I could
wish for a different winner. Where is his body?"

"I've sent it indefinitely into the past; it will be rotted
out long before past archaeologists could have found it. His
mind I have kept, along with Rourke's. I am all of Dio and
Rourke that you will ever know in this world. And I want
you, Esther. I have given up on Lilith: she is intransigent."

Her hands hung by her thighs, now, as she stood in the
simple dignity of a great lady delivering an honor or a
reproof. "I too am intransigent, Kali. If Dio and Rourke are

in you, they are tainted by their new environment; and I prefer to remember their worth."

He shrugged, and his smile was twisted. "Nevertheless they are mine, and I am entitled to wear the body of either—"

Both of us women missed heartbeats as the Kali-image dissolved away into flame-topped Burk Halloran: the strong-whimsical blue-eyed midthirtyish face that Burk and Kali shared, atop the lithe tall flexible body of Burk-Rourke. He clasped our waists, and we rose out of 1952 as though we were twin inert Eurydice-victims being rescued aloft by a Hellish Hermes.

What immediately followed required astonishingly few hours, but hundreds of pages would be required for a semi-full account. I will summarize with merciless crisp, the more mercilessly crisp since I don't understand much of it.

28.

———◆———

In the commodore's cabin aboard the *Ishtar* in 2002 space —accompanied by Vanderkilt and Esther and me, all standing ironically beside the commodore's body and a small bronze wall-plate: ROURKE MALLORY, 1915–2002–1952, COMMODORE 1952–2002—Guru Kali in the guise of 1952-young Rourke hit the trivideo-assembled captains with the challenge which had reduced Vanderkilt to subjection: "Inspect me closely; do you know me?" After study, Zeno drawled, "I would have said Kali, but we're seeing you head to foot; why are you taller than those women?" Chloris blurted, "Zeno, no! he's Rourke, young again! Rourke, but you were dead—tell us what!"

While Esther strained in anguish and I fought vainly the Kali-spell which kept me from telling the truth, young Kali-Rourke grinned as he surveyed Rourke's elderly corpse, then dropped the grin and replied soberly, "To shorten it for now, it went like this. When I died, my mind entered Dio Horse, and together we confronted Kali and defeated him, but Dio was lost in the struggle while I was revived in youth—if thirty-seven is youth. It is a great mystery coupled with an enormous loss to all of us, but there it is. But we have a lot to do, and the detailed story must wait. Are all of you ready for any imaginable kind of action?"

That was when I witnessed something new for this fleet: they were all on their feet, *yelling* for Rourke; he had risen rejuvenated from the dead, victor over Satan, ready to lead them through another fifty years; the loss of Dio to them was a small price, they'd hardly known Dio. I was sickened, knowing that the seeming of Rourke *was* Satan, or his high lieutenant, about to lead us all into darkness; but I choked on my unvoiced protests while the Rourke-face stayed grave and the Kali-Rourke double charisma warmly flooded them and Dio was nowhere.

No mind-emanation could I catch from Kali: he had opaqued his mind to me and presumably also to Esther. I caught her inward lament: *Why does he keep us here? why doesn't he do away with us?* I mind-whispered back: *Jews know about crosses, Jesus was a nice Jewish boy. Maybe it is for the look of things; maybe it is Kali's dirty sense of humor; maybe God wants us to see this whatever the pain. Hold tight, Esther.* With closed eyes, she mind-replied: *I am holding.* Why had he left us with our telepathy?

Gradually my attention returned to the astonishing plan that Kali-Rourke was opening up to the captains. "We have conquered Kali," he told them, "but the evil which powered and sustained Kali is forever loose in the world, and the REM Device exists with no defense against it. The REM Treaty will be signed, but there is no trust. If we in RP now have one duty above all others—and we do—it is to find and construct the Ultimate Anti-REM.

"Toward this end, I want to fly an old notion of mine and see who salutes it. I've repeatedly dismissed this recurring fancy; but recently I've been giving it serious thought, and it is beginning to have the look of merit like the ugly old hag to the trapper after months in the wilderness. While you listen to it, backburner the judgment that it is impossible fantasy, and criticize its values and demerits assuming that it *might* be possible.

"Captains, this is such an Earth-portentous matter that I

require to discuss it before the entire fleet, all members of all crews, and obtain a weighted vote. Please activite two-way intercom among all crew members of every ship."

Long since, a seated Kali-Rourke had completed his presentation to the crews; and now he leaned back in his swivel chair, soberly listening to the babel of crew-discussions aboard eighty-nine ships. I was smashing my brain searching for the diabolically concealed catch: the notion, although technologically impossible even in 2002, seemed an enormous-energy possibility having persuasive merit despite its dismaying intercultural and psychosocial dangers; but coming from Kali . . .

They were all had, though: for them, it was coming from a Rourke who had slain Kali and regained youth in the process, and the persuasion was reinforced by subvert Kali-magnetism. As objections began to come in, they in fact were mere quibbles. For instance, the voice of Ilya Sarabin cut through the babel; by voting protocol, this transmission was unilateral from Sarabin to Mallory—no other ship could hear it until all voting was done; and Sarabin, reporting his weighted crew-judgment in which higher-ranking votes counted more but not dictatorially more, introduced only a proposed caution-procedure, apart from worrying about the technology.

One after another, the ships reported one or another variation of the Sarabin formula, except for three ships which flatly accepted the Kali-Rourke proposal and seven which flatly rejected it. Having inspected the computerized interpretation of the fleet vote, Kali-Rourke announced:

"Good: you tend to like the idea, but you aren't ready to say "go" pending three prior stages. First, get control of the technology; second, win the consent of the governments; third, if they generally agree, install the technology; finally, vote on the question of activation.

"All right. Captains, each of you be good enough to send me physically, from each of your ships, your best experts in matters pertinent to the technology: at least one from each ship. And I would suggest for your guidance that the pertinent disciplines will be: physics, astronomy, time theory, earth geology, massive space propulsion, electromagnetics, geopolitics.

"There is no time for your designates to converge here through space; the limited thrust of their minicapsules would

take as much as several hours. Be aware that I now have tele-
portative ability. Flag me when your people are ready, and
I will bring them here."

I was present on the "open" deck (transparently space-
closed) during several hours of the intricate discussion. Kali-
Rourke had excused Vanderkilt for other ship-duties; Esther,
after an hour of it, had whispered headache to me and had
retreated elsewhere.

What I understood of it was scarcely one bit of it. But
eventually it came clear that while these assembled experts
among them understood the *sort* of technology necessary to
bring off such a thing, this technology was simply not available in 2002.

Kali-Rourke said gently then, "Very well, ladies, gentle-
men. In my opinion, without what I propose, Earth won't
make it to any time much in the future, Kali or no Kali. But
we will have to assume that Earth will survive until we can
bring this off. Please stand by while I do a bit of mental
time-probing."

Leaning far back in his swivel chair, Kali in the Rourke-
body closed eyes and went into something resembling trance
while the others respectfully watched him. I gazed at him
quite disrespectfully, wondering whether now was the time
to expose him before these experts, deciding to save my
powder because nobody here would believe me.

After a bit of this, I sensed an alien stirring in my hintermind: the Kali-mind was inadvertently leaking to me. . . .

. . . *that you do see the point, Master; calm yourself, this
is the only way to do it if you are to survive and feed.
What delectable destructive grist, that Earth should blow because of her own endemic self-distrust! but on the other
hand, what sublime creative grist that the blow-off should be
followed, not by universal death with no other intelligent
planet available for your feeding, but instead by space-
disparate Earth-fragments writhing in their efforts to adapt
their old lore to semi-incommunicado space requirements,
with nothing to hold them in remote community but our
spacefleet commanded by your own lieutenants! It should
allow us many more centuries of sardonical fun, Master;
and when we are bored with it—poof! what is left for
rescue? and by then we may have found another intelligent
planet. . . .*

Repugnantly I felt a larger mind, driving, thrusting: *Bring it off fast, then!*

Kali in anguish: *No technology! For Hell's sake, no technology! Look, I've brought this to the crux, but we spoil the game if we introduce a miracle! Give me the technology in a human-believable way, even if it is only just human-believable. . . .*

Perhaps the strain of this exhausted me. I blanked.

Earth-Cluster, 2677:

"Commodore, we have an all-time-points Mayday from Earth two thousand two; it is crude but intelligible."

"Did you say two thousand two, Captain?"

"Exactly, Commodore: two thousand two A.D.—Our Year Zero."

"To understate it, fascinating! That was the year of the national coning and the blow-off; our archaeological records of the era are thin indeed, I didn't know they had tempomentation. What is the exact source?"

"The commodore of an international fleet—he calls it the RP Fleet."

"You aren't pulling my leg, sir?"

"Madam, I wouldn't dare—it is only early afternoon."

"Give me the gist."

"This commodore says that Earth is still a whole planet, but he anticipates an imminent blow-apart. He has assembled his scientists; he wants technology to cone the Earth nations—he knows how to do this time-retroactively if we will give him the technology."

"He—wants technology to—*cone the Earth-nations*? from *us*?"

"I know your thought, Madam, and he reinforces it. He warns that if we can't help him bring this off, tempo-retroaction may terminate our own existence—"

"Zerni, Zerni, I am feeling your mind and you aren't joking, and you are too thorough for me to doubt the reality. For the love of Czaluska, blessèd be She, red alert! red alert! Command all resources! Round up all experts in the fleet and every top expert on the subplanets. I will personally coordinate this. Zerni, we have *got* to force-feed two thousand two with all the technical assistance they can assimilate—"

29.

It was five hours later when I fully came to: nobody seemed to be noticing me, so perhaps I had seemed awake like a groggy but experienced fighter. Kali-Rourke still sat among his assembled technicians; and many of them wore mentation-headsets, presumably because these people had no inbuilt brain-devices. Kali was saying, "All right, you've heard all that, and among us we've wrestled out interpretations into contemporary terms. Do you now understand all the requisite technology, or don't you?"

A young man, possibly as old as thirty, concised, "In my opinion, the procedures from 2677 would be entirely adequate. But even armed with their knowledge, it would take us maybe a century to construct—"

Kali frowned: "Remember that they exist only because we *did* construct! I can have the necessary apparatus teletemported from 2677, and they've taught us how to tap into the magma-power. The big thing is that we now have the theory. Right now my most serious problem is the politics. If I were to start working on the Earth leaders a long time ago. . . . Stay put here, now; I'll need you again within the hour."

Again he went into trance, and I required myself to follow; and I heard his prayer: *Change it all, Master, so that Mallory has been working on them about this for a generation and has won. . . .*

During his trance, grotesquely they served us food. I don't know whether I ate.

He told the silence that greeted his self-revival: "All but seventeen small nations have agreed to the notion on my guarantees, after twenty-seven years of my retroactive lobbying just now. So we have completed Stages One and Two of the fleet vote.

"The most recent agreement that I assured was in nineteen hundred seventy-nine, so we can operate no earlier. I know that some of you were then occupied with the problem of rescuing Venice; but if now you go back into nineteen seventy-nine, you will be mere doppelgängers for your nineteen seventy-nine selves, and with care you won't come into contact. I have now the task of taking you all back into nineteen seventy-nine and sending you in various worldwide directions to make contact with the heads of governments and educate their experts and get the technology installed. This process has to be completed during twenty-three past years, between nineteen seventy-nine and two thousand two; whereafter we will all reconvene aboard the *Ishtar* in, say, three hours. If anybody has an urgent reason to duck this assignment, speak up now."

No demurrers. Whereupon Kali teleported them back to their ships for starters, and the long-short preparatory process began.

When they had reconvened, reporting completed installations in and around and beneath all nations of Earth during a twenty-three year period, including in some national constellations chunks of ocean or satellite-nations which either had agreed or were fearfully recalcitrant, Kali-Rourke convened the captains again. This conclave took longer than any of the others, each captain insisting on hearing the full report of every scientist and philosopher and technician.

At the end of it, wide-eyed Sarabin said, "The meaning of all this is spiritually changed by our own fleet-existence. Am I wrong, Commodore, or have you taken some evil Kali-idea and transmuted it into long-range Earth-good?"

Kali adroitly evaded, "This is what all of us have done together under my leadership." (Now why would the ultimate liar merely evade? Perhaps in his incorrigible delight with gamesmanship . . .) The commodore added, "All right: we have accomplished your first three stages; I now call for a captain-vote on the accomplishment of Stage Four—Activation."

The vote was eighty-four to three with two abstentions.

"Move unanimity!" tenored Volpone. And unanimity was voted, eighty-four to zero with five abstentions. After all, what were they risking? A potentially viable international space-cluster was better than a potential atom-cloud, and none of them intended to push the button. . . .

I stood on a hard ship's deck behind swivel-chair-seated Commodore Kali-Mallory, wondering whether it would be piously Jewish for me to strangle him, sensing that I shouldn't anyway until I knew where this was going, aware that it wasn't possible anyway because he would have paralyzed me before my fingers touched his throat.

Officers were coming and checking with Kali and going, and Kali was rotating slowly (with me staying behind him) to consider one-by-one hundreds of tri-d window-images like TV screens. Each window offered a sky-view of some different section of Earth-surface, but each surface-view was partially obscured by a complexity of 2677-imported apparatus floating above it near camera. The apparatus invariably sunlight- or moonlight-shone with metallic sheen, was thin and weirdly excresced; and from multiple points below the apparatus, an evanescent blue aurora flowed Earthward and disappeared into Earth. . . .

Captain Vanderkilt entered and pointed at an image where the aurora had ceased. "Sir, Captain Perpignan reports that she has completed the coning of France. As required, the convex face of the transparent but closed cone is situated an average of one thousand kilometers above Earth-surface; and the irregular conic volume angles downward-inward until it cuts the surface along the two-thousand-two borders of France, extended southward to the center line of the Mediterranean and westward to the center line of the Atlantic until it sweeps inward along the center line of La Manche to exclude the United Kingdom and Ireland. The volume continues to narrow downward-inward an average of fifty kilometers through the base of the crust, and there finally the cone is truncated to insulate it from the REM-created molten magma. This bottom shielding has been electromagnetically tested and is deemed adequately REM-resistant. Repulsors to drive and space-navigate France are installed and ready. Meanwhile more than a hundred top French officials and technicians have completed a five-year training course and are ready to mount operations instantly.

"Thank you," responded Kali-Rourke; "pray continue monitoring reports, notify me about every ten minutes or if something unexpected comes up." Vanderkilt departed; Kali recommenced his slow swiveling, and it was noticeable that on one screen after another the blue aurora was dying.

Absently Kali tossed a comment: "I considered making

the force-field cones space-*time* cones, insulating each 2002 nation not merely in space down into the mantle but also several billion years back, on the notion that this would endow each Earth-fragment with *all* its historical heritage. But we simply don't have good enough time-theory, not even in 2677; if we had done this, we might also have retroactively canceled the whole history and prehistory of animal and racial migration and evolutionary and cultural diffusion, wiping out in the process ourselves and the Earth we know—"

He cut it off, raising a warning finger. On various screens, the captains were beginning to report in from their various national insulation-coning assignments: Colette Perpignan confirming France, Chloris Doxidoras backed by Zeno Metropoulos for Greece and the Mediterranean/Aegean Isles and Cyprus and Crete and Rhodes and Turkey, Ladyrna Mengrovia for China and Indochina, Ilya Sarabin for Russia and Siberia, Joe Volpone for Italy-Sicily-Corsica, and so on. . . .

My eye-corner saw Esther stealing away. I stayed put; but I lost track of the reports after Volpone—presumably every quarter of Earth was covered. Kali-Rourke, working through the RP Fleet, and utilizing technology out of 2677, in 2002 had arrived at insulating Earth's nations against the REM Device.

Presently, unnoticed by the multiple-captain-preoccupied commodore, I stole bemused out of the cabin and went to look for Esther.

30.

———◆———

I found her at the forward apex of what would have been the main exterior deck had it not been for the *Ishtar*'s hull space-transparency. She leaned back against a rail, gazing above the opposite rail through that transparency at stars. Artificial deck-illumination was so dim as to be al-

most unnoticeable, and at first I didn't notice an interesting
new thing about Esther. Partly comforted to be in her
presence, silently I leaned back against the opposite rail two
meters in front of her and peered over her head at other
stars.

She said at length, "Tell me what has happened."

"Just now?"

"No. All of it. The meaning."

"Are you lost too?"

"Possibly more lost than you, Lil. Tell me."

Sick, I summarized: "It appears that Kali and his Master
have won their hellborn game with us four. They brought
us together through a combination of illusion and allure
and an ironical lending of their own powers to Rourke and
Dio. They killed off Rourke, but not until it was clear that
the admiration of these men for each other would assure
absorption of the Rourke-soul by the mind of Dio. I wish I
knew how much they influenced the Rourke-Dio decision
to confront Kali, with the men rashly depending on the
strength of their combined powers and wills: no direct challenge of Satan has ever been known to bring other than
sorrow, the best that people have ever been able to do is to
erect such mighty fortresses against him that he decides to
look elsewhere for his fun and games—"

"You believe in Satan, Lilith?"

"Serpentinely he seduced my divorced husband Adam
and my wife-successor Eve. . . . No, but seriously: I am
beginning to believe, a little—not necessarily in a personified
Satan, any more than I necessarily believe in a personified
God, but at least as a universal force-for-mischief which
can become personified in a human just as God can become
personified in a human."

"By that last, you don't maybe mean Jesus?"

"He got the best publicity; probably there have been
others. But I think he was genuine and admirable, within
human limits. I'm a Maimonides girl, myself—"

"But whatever God is, isn't he omnipotent Good? And if
Rourke and Dio were on the side of Good, how could Kali
defeat them and take command of Rourke's fleet?"

"To name one example, Jesus was on the side of Good,
but the Establishment defeated him and proceeded to take
over and corrupt his religion."

Silence. Then Esther, moody: "So then Kali gamed up
the confrontation, beefed up Dio's self-assurance that he and

Rourke together could defeat Kali *and indeed were* defeating Kali—and then, when they tangled, it was Kali who absorbed the Rourke-Dio soul and disposed of the Dio body. And all Kali gained was the RP Fleet, which would have become his anyway through the mosaic virus and Commander Duval. So the only purpose must have been the dandy game. Some game, if you can't lose!"

"Not the first in history, Esther."

"If I can accept all that, assuredly I have no difficulty in accepting also the facility of Kali at taking on the appearances of Dio and of Rourke: it might be hypnotism, but I could believe that it is psychophysical body-change. Only, how could Kali have materialized out of Rourke and Dio in the first place?"

"Maybe his Master produced alternate time-tracks out of nineteen fifty-two if-nodes, Esther—even though when I witnessed it, there was a deceptive appearance of ectoplasmic materialization like a wacky medium-séance. . . . Look, I love you, I know your hurt, but—can we skip technicalities for now?"

Silence. Then Esther, edgy: "Okay about that, but—what is he *doing* with it?"

Gripping the rail with both hands, I stared at space. I said, "Maybe this is no more unbelievable than any of it. He is slicing up Earth, to convert the planet into a mosquito cloud of subplanets inhabited by confused peoples howling for the lost past of their unity. And he is doing it to assure the existence of the future people who are helping him do it."

She wailed, *"I want Dio in 1952!"*

I muttered, "I want Burk in 1952." Then, grinning grim, I seized her wrist: "Esther—wouldn't we have been a hell of a foursome?"

She said low: 'When is it now, Lil—1952, or 2002, or 2677, or some other when? Wait, there's a lot more, it's a hopelessly complex question. If it is 2677, and all the past eras referent to 2677 are mutually simultaneous and therefore not causally interrelated any longer—then why can 2677 work back in time to help Kali and RP prevent Earth from disintegrating in 2002 and so make 2677 possible? And if either 2677 or 2002 is the present—why then, back in 1952 when you and Dio took off after me—well: if already you were operating in the past, were you really *operating,* or were you robots being retaken through already-accomplished motions and *imagining* that your wills were real?" Up came her head, and she faced me squarely: "That question could go on forever, and here I chop it. Any answers, Lil?"

Actually I thought I might have a lot of possible answers, even assuming the realities of all three eras and others. For instance: instead of starting from a concept of noncausal past and concluding that one's intuitions of will and choice while operating in that past are illusory and fallacious—why not go the other way, assuming the reality of one's choice and will while operating in the past, and from that assumption changing one's conceptions about past and future? Still again: what if in fact God has long since tracked out the general and individual patterns of all destiny, then infused souls into his robots in order to view how each soul responds to the surprises of its destiny, not realizing that it is destiny? What if free will applies only to soul-response, while all physical action is predestined? That might explain God's toleration of Kali and even of Satan. And so on . . . Only, there comes a point between girls when one girl wishes to stop appearing all-wise before the other girl, especially in an area where both girls and indeed all humans are ignorant.

And so I passed it with a half-grinning quip. "No answer ready. Look, Esther: there's a thing I've been whimsically puzzled about, aboard the *Star*. When Rourke brought us back into 1952, you were still seventy-eight looking about fifty—right?" She nodded. "But in your original 1952, you were twenty-eight—right?" She nodded. "Okay: when you pled the curse—*what*?"

Instead of amusing Esther, it troubled her. "Dammit, I don't have that much cockeyed wit. Dio mentally cued me to make a diversion—and instantly I *did* feel it coming on—now how could I remember that feeling? It must be like bicycle riding, you never forget. And it *did* come! And, Lilith—look at me now!"

I peered at her in deck-dimness, and with a new quality of weird I saw and comprehended. Late-seventies Esther, who had looked fifty, now looked thirty.

I squeezed my eyes shut. Considering the biochemical intricacies, this was more cosmic than Earth's fragmentation. . . .

Kali's Rourke-voice called cheerily, "Hey, girls, come back starboard-amidships; we're about to see Earth exploding. We think it will come off differently from the way we saw Contingency Omega—"

31.

Amidships, we gazed outward and downward at the Earth-agate.

Kali said conversationally, "We'll first test-launch Barbi-zet—that's a small uninhabited atoll which we've separately coned. Barbizet has grasses and trees; and we've fixed her up with test animals, including chimps, and with a number of test habitations ranging from a grass hut to a two-hundred-story high-rise, along with other acceleration-sensitive beings and structures.

"We had a compound problem: getting Barbizet airborne fast enough to avoid turbulence-damage from the ocean, yet slowly enough to avoid acceleration-damage to unprepared life and structures. We solved the problem with three more goodies from 2677. First, the repulsor engines are unlike today's rockets: they feed on space and therefore have unlimited fuel; and so we can loft Barbizet and even a continent in as gradual or as rapid a manner as we choose. Second, all cones have inertial shields which we can adjust up to a factor of 500, which means that creatures and structures within will feel only 1/500th of the actual thrust. And finally, when we cut all thrust after leaving Earth's gravitational field, we can substitute artificial gravity for the inertial shielding.

"Thus, we will start by blasting Barbizet upward at ten G acceleration, which is about ninety-eight meters per second per second. However, because of the inertial shielding, creatures and structures on Barbizet will *feel* initial thrust of only about one-fifth G, which is like accelerating sluggishly at about four and a half miles per hour every ten seconds. We expect that Barbizet, atmosphere and surface and all the underlying crust, will be clear of the ocean in thirty-two seconds after launch, which should minimize turbulence problems. Got it?"

Esther shuddered. I said flatly, "No."

"So be it for now," responded cheerfully Kali-Rourke. And he issued the order: "Activate Barbizet."

In some kind of Kali-illusion, Earth came very close to us, or us to it, with Barbizet viewed in oblique profile quite near us. The island rose up out of Earth smoothly, and the Pacific Ocean rushed turbulently in to fill, engendering monstrous clouds or Barbizet-shrouding steam out of the molten subcrust magma leaping up to meet the inpouring water.

Vanderkilt's voice: "H plus thirty-two seconds; Barbizet down to magma-shield is entirely clear of ocean surface; cutting back to one G for another four hundred seconds."

Kali, watching the lofted island, didn't answer; and I glanced at the second hand on my wrist-stopwatch (dandy for psychometric testing). Barbizet, now clearly airborne as she emerged from the steam shroud, appeared to be gathering upward speed; abruptly she seemed to be above us, and three blue-green glowings flared at her tail. . . .

Vanderkilt: "H plus four hundred seconds; altitude 1,306 kilometers; one G acceleration; all monitors indicate nominal launch, all systems go, life-support system intact, test structures intact, life forms responding well. Shall I continue the program?"

Kali: "Pray do."

Vanderkilt: "I have anticipated your affirmative; acceleration has been cut back to 1/100 G; inertial shield being progressively softened."

In an illusion-change, Earth receded swiftly, again it was a blue-white ball. "If you look sharp right down *there*," said Kali pointing, "you will see a sun-glare speck which is Barbizet coming upward toward us. We're cutting her acceleration back to minimum thrust until we slightly exceed orbital velocity; by that time she'll still be far below us, about twenty-five thousand kilometers above Earth-surface. We will then cut all thrust and let Barbizet coast into orbit just above us at fifty-two thousand kilometers. We'll meanwhile reduce the inertial shield to zero and then introduce artificial gravity as she clears Earth's gravity at six thousand, eight hundred kilometers. Life and structures on Earth are used to a steady one G drag; we don't want to reduce that very much.

"All this will take quite a while. To speed it for you, ladies, I am going to slow your subjective time by a factor of ten. Hold tight, everything will seem to rush around like an old Mack Sennett comedy with Donald Duck dialogue—"

"Rush around" understated it. Crew members blurred in, gabbled at the commodore, heard counter-gabble, blurred out; Vanderkilt's voice jabbered unintelligible reports, Kali's quacked back; the minute hand on my watch crawled visibly, eating up minutes like six-second intervals, while the second hand whirled manic; beside me, Esther convulsively jerked hands and feet and body, and my own hand-and-arm movements scared me with their snap; meanwhile the Barbizet glare-point grew large, resolved into Barbizet-shape, rushed upward past us at a distance which could not have exceeded twenty miles with repulsors no longer glowing. . . .

Abruptly all was normal again. Vanderkilt was reporting with perfect intelligibility: "Barbizet has been inserted into orbit 52,000 kilometers out, all systems go." I stopped my watch as she continued, "The appraisal is: launch successful, structures intact, life forms healthy, maintenance operating well, no malfunction anticipated at this time."

I had stopped my watch at one hour fifty-seven minutes after launch; and the sun had perceptibly changed position.

"Good," said Kali most quietly. "Go ahead and disintegrate Earth." And he added to us women, "I'm slowing your perception again for *all* of this final phase."

Earth exploded into hundreds of fragments dissipating from each other. Again a gabble of reporting and counter-ordering, this time involving all captains. . . .

Normalcy cut back in. I'd have guessed the elapsed time at ten minutes or so, fifteen at most; but my stopwatch insisted that it had been, again, a bit under two hours, and the sun agreed. One by one the captains reported in. Perpignan: "France orbited nominally." Mengrovia: "China-Indochina orbited nominally." Kirby: "United States and Alaska and Hawaii and the West Indies orbited nominally in colse contiguity." Sarabin: "Russia-Siberia orbited nominally." And so on until all the roll of nations had been called.

Where Earth had been, there remained a small ball of restless incandescence which darkened as we watched: the exposed and cooling molten magma around the hard mantle, with all the living crust, departed aloft.

Never at any other time in my life, except in my youth after desperate athletic effort, has my heart so labored.

Kali now turned from Earth's remnant, looking upward toward the bridge, and his Rourke-face was serene. "Captain Vanderkilt, please get the attention of all captains." Her radio transmission to them was amplified here on deck: "Now hear this all captains. Attention to the commodore. Respond. Over."

When Kali-Rourke spoke to them without benefit of microphone, his seriousness was impressive;

"Well done, all of you, it has gone as planned. As you know, the launch of Barbizet was real. As for the balance of Earth, it was a satisfactory test-similation: the intricate monitoring system which you have implanted assures us that an actual multicontinental launch would have every probability of working even under the most explosive conditions.

"Earth in reality is still intact except for Barbizet; but thanks to your competency and diligence, every nation is compartmentalized away from other nations in its own energy cone. As long as the planet remains intact, the peoples of Earth can intertrade and intercommunicate and even make war; but each national cone will perpetuate and propel itself separately in space if the REM Device should ever be activated. To cream the jest, every nation can now REM itself; so that if any nation should REM another nation imperiling the geological stability of Earth, every nation can activate its own survival take-off.

"This is the nearly perfect defense against the REM Device. This device can no longer destroy any nation; and by driving that nation off Earth, the aggressor will have imperiled himself and must depart Earth also.

"It is not, however, a perfect defense. The REM Device exists, nuclear weapons exist, and national paranoia exists. We cannot neutralize the REM Device, because even if all its apparatus were destroyed, the technology would still be known. Earth *can* be disintegrated; the controlled cataclysm which we have just tested *can* happen. All we have done is, to assure that such a cataclysm would not be Earthfatal.

"I now call on all of you to address your minds to a shortrange problem. Conceive that under our present arrangements, if any nation should consider nuclear attack imminent, it could either REM the enemy or REM itself or both without peril of self-destruction. How can we use this general leadership-knowledge adroitly to laugh nuclear warheads out of existence?

"After that, but also collateral with that, a pressing long-range problem. Address your minds to the possibility that the cataclysm of REM does happen. Maybe physical contiguity among the nations of Earth on a single tightening little planet has been creating and exacerbating many of our war-stresses. If this proposition is right, the nations may be collectively and individually better off if they become a system of little subplanetary spaceships each going its own way but all keeping in communion, with intervisitation privileges. An RP Fleet maintaining communication among such Earth fragments would be—serviceable, to understate it.

"What we have done is to *make possible* just such a fantasy if the necessity should arise. Our long-range duty as a fleet is to so operate among nations that the necessity will *not* arise. But out longer-range duty is to be ready for interspatial operations if the necessity *should* arise and the fact *should* transpire. Because Earth, even as a dispersed collection of space fragments, *needs* to continue being a community. As far as we now know—what else is there, anywhere?

"I therefore call upon all of you to make our operations under such fantasy-conditions a prime object of your realistic study. As long as you retain me in command. I will be frequently convoking you to discuss this problem; and I look for constructive input from everybody.

"The fleet condition is now Green. Captain Volpone, please carry out your preassigned mission of rescuing the Barbizet test animals. That is all."

Kali-Rourke finished and dropped his head, looking wan.

Inadvertently, he spotted Esther and me. He gazed at us, and he began to smile. Abruptly his face collapsed, and he bolted for his cabin.

We stared after him. . . .

A male lieutenant emerged from his cabin and came quickly to us. "Excuse me, ladies, I have a message from the commodore. He would like for you to join him for cocktails in his cabin in about thirty minutes, and he respectfully requests a reply."

Esther and I nodded at each other, and I said, "Thank

you, Lieutenant; tell him yes for both of us." When he had departed, though, both of us stood there, and my own thoughts grew dark, and I began to feel telepathic leakage of darkness from her.

I thought at her: *He is weakened now, he is vulnerable. If we have any chance to get him, it is now.*

Hesitant, she responded: *He is not only Kali. He is Rourke. He is Dio.*

He has swallowed Rourke and Dio. He is all, they are nothing.

How would we get him?

Pool our powers, Esther. Do it together. The powers are inherent in every human, they are in us, he is weakened, now is the only when.

We would probably lose. He would annihilate us. . . .

Esther—with Rourke and Dio nothing—relatively speaking, do you really care?

Mind-silence. Then: *Oh, God, no.*

32.

◆

Commodore Kali received us in Rourke's cabin with undemonstrative warmth; the casketed Rourke-corpse was gone, the bronze plaque remained. Kali served us drinks of our choice, and sat himself in Rourke's swivel chair with Rourke's desk behind him, facing us.

Full of our murderous project, well prepped in it, trying to mind-screen it, we sipped, studying Kali-Rourke. Burk Halloran to perfection. Moody as he watched us, but in no visible sense evil. I was marveling at this new illustration of the ways in which evil can dissemble good; I was persuading myself to be knowledgeably resistant. . . .

After maybe the third sip, Kali spoke—persuasibly Rourke, in Rourke's light baritone without even a hint of contralto. "Now I think I may have effectively screened off this cabin from the Master, but you never know for sure. Ladies, would you be good enough to reinforce the screening as well as you can? If you don't know how, an undercurrent of prayer might help."

It rather shook Esther and me: Kali proposing prayer to screen off Satan? We women interstared, not daring to intertelepath for fear of breaking our screen against Kali; but then it came into me that a screening off of his Master would leave Kali all the more vulnerable, and I nodded, and Esther nodded. I closed eyes and prayed in a way that I have learned, first filling my consciousness with the prayer and its all-immanent unvisualizable meaning-object, then allowing the prayer holding constant to recede into my hintermind so that my consciousness could attend to Kali while maintaining the prayer background-music potent. . . .

Kali and I, then Kali and Esther, interchanged gazing.

His mind opened to us. Our hearts and our prayers faltered.

Esther was the first to respond. *Then you won!*

He nodded slowly. We gazed entranced: there was absolutely no question—all his mind was open to us, with Dio/Rourke individuate-fused in complete dominance and Kali reduced to a subordinate glow of power and emotion with no selfness at all. . . .

His mind murmured: *Don't drop the prayer-screen. For a long time, maybe always, this will be precarious.*

Both of us nodded slowly, gazing, enfolding comprehension. That Dio/Rourke *had* absorbed the Enemy-weary Kali-mind, there in the cavern of Mont Veillac. That Dio/Rourke had resolved on the Enemy-deluding psychophysical masquerade as Kali which must perforce delude us women also because any mental leak would be perilous. That having established the delusion for an Enemy whose attention was diffuse except as it might be captured by particular people, Dio/Rourke, as part of an Enemy-ostensible Kali-plot, had assumed the young Rourke physical persona to resume command of the fleet and bring off a world-defensive coup while, down in the Mont Veillac cavern, the followers of Kali had sat idly by awaiting orders from Kali.

The orders would be, to drop the REM operation for now and return to worship in the worldwide Kali movement: since Kali had interested the Enemy in longer-range game, Alaska and the rest of Earth were reprieved for now. The Enemy would keep maliciously prodding the ambitious-

fearful leaders of the powers, while the Kali movement
(with Dio/Rourke occasionally appearing before them in the
Kali-persona and here and there granting an impossible wish
or two) would keep soothing the powers with the false security of the REM Treaty; meanwhile RP would maintain
world community, ready to move the same task into space
when in a week or a hundred years the inevitable blow-off
would come. . . .

We pondered it. I mused to him: *It is beautiful and devious, worthy of either of you and superbly of both of you.
I would only suggest that as long as you continue to present
the psychic face of Kali to the Enemy, you are a vulnerable double-agent, far more vulnerable to the Enemy than
other men are.*

Esther's quick correction: *The Enemy is no stranger to
Dio. And consequently perhaps Dio/Rourke is even less vulnerable than most men are.*

After that, for a while, our three minds—or was it four?
—blended in mutual love and support.

I was the first for whom it palled, my restless mind could
not hold it, my incorrigibly practical mind began introducing
ego-future concerns mingled with nostalgia. (But all the time,
my insulating prayer continued.)

He and she turned to me, worried. I felt their thought
entirely interfused: *We need you, Lilith—it will work itself
out. . . .*

I shook my head, biting my lip.

He leaned toward me, persuading: *When I was Burk, you
were my goddess. When I was Dio, you were my intimate
friend in my desperate need. Two nights ago, when I was
Rourke, you were my lover again. Now we are one man and
one mind using the power of subpersonal Kali for good
purposes which we formulate. We want you here with us,
Lilith—if you can come to terms with our psychic complexity and our protean body-manipulation. . . .*

I felt the warm endorsement of Esther: *I value you, Lilith,
and he values both of us; and even though I am young again,
I am much too old in experience to be jealous of those whom
I love and trust. We are a triad and a tetrad, sister; can't
we hold it this way?*

The unanswerable objection formulated itself. I confronted
him: *Burk-Rourke, Dio, each of you hear me individually*

*now. You want me, and I want you. But when you say you
need me—do you really* need *me?*

There was mental silence. I demanded: *Face it down.* Do
you?

Esther was sober, but a charming half-smile came onto
the Rourke-face.

My broad grin broke through, the humor was evident to
all of us: I loved them, but I didn't really need them either.
I spoke aloud with decision: "I continue to insist that I had
and will have free will in nineteen fifty-two—or as much
free will as any human any time, which is a great deal more
than lower animals have. And I think I was a damned good
psychologist then, with more and better years of it ahead.
And I also think I ought to look me up a nice Jewish boy—"

All images misted over, and I bit my lip hard to control
sobbing. . . .

My next external awareness was Burk Halloran standing behind me, his hand on my shoulder, telling me tenderly,
"I will squire you now back to nineteen fifty-two."

In front of me, only Dio sat with Esther. But they were
gazing at me, and their faces were wondrously loving.

33.

At Fishermen's Cove in 1952—on the dock, watching dark
water, and later in a small room which was not the penthouse room—Burk Halloran and I, rich with all our memories of fifty-four years, but he completely Burk divorced
for that while from Dio and Kali, attained soul-meaningful
realization of what had been promised in a peony garden.

Toward dawn, he reminded me: *You and I separately
have to go on. What do you need from me?*

I told him.

He put into me all his memories of all the Burk- and

Rourke- and Esther-encounters and conversations and dreams from 1948 onward.

Toward the end of it, which was here and now, I drifted into sleep. When I awoke, he was gone.

I returned to New York and went back to work, shorn of my telepathy, avoiding the police and the pother about lost Inspector Horse, eschewing liaisons, cultivating friendships. Three years later, I met and married a nice Jewish boy— you, Ben. And we've gone on pretty well from there, haven't we, Ben?

Only, Rabbi—pray for our kids. Pray for *all* kids.

EPILOG

Ben Glazer here again. It is 1994. All of you know about the existing world organization and international tension; and perhaps you will be aware of some related things. Rabbi Glazer has been immersed in psychotheology, and lamentably out of touch with ebbings and flowings in the sensory world.

I have never failed to pray for all kids.

Quite apart from the marvels in the Lilith-experience, one could do worse than ponder its meanings. There is, of course, one severe problem-meaning having to do with the reality of choice-and-decision in any present time when a future time already exists. So what do you think has motivated my self-immersion in psychotheology, other than Satan and this?

I have concluded that we must hew to a pair of observations in her memoir. *One:* Why don't we simply *assume* that we have decision-and-choice in our lives, and develop our time-metaphysics from that? *Two:* What if in fact God has . . . infused souls into his (predestined) robots in order to view how each soul responds to the surprises of its destiny, not realizing that it is destiny?" These two suggestions are mutually coherent, and neither conflicts with my conviction that God is creative and sympathetic and in-the-end good.

Lilith died in 1975; what then became of her mindsoul? She wasn't ready for eternal rest; and I refuse to believe that more of her than her delicious memory and abiding influence is inhabiting my mind. Even Moses Maimonides admitted the possibility of resurrection; but Lilith would have wanted it to be corporeal, this time around at least. And she had served her wonderful wife-time with me during twenty years, and it was a fine love that we had between us, and I hope eventually to dwell in love with her again.

May I speculate irresponsibly, feeling that I know what she would have wanted? Well: I think that Lilith would have wanted to rejoin the RP Fleet and swing creatively into its duties and delights. And I think that Dio/Rourke and Esther would want this. And I dare think that God would see mostly good in it.

They might even eventually find a place for me? I'm a fair psychotheologian but a lousy harpist.

B.G.

DAW ⍰sf BOOKS

☐ **ELRIC OF MELNIBONE by Michael Moorcock.** The first of the great sagas of the Eternal Champion—back in print in a new and corrected edition. (#UY1259—$1.25)

☐ **KIOGA OF THE WILDERNESS by William L. Chester.** Marooned in the lost land of the original American Indians —an adventure of Tarzan-like dimensions.
(#UW1253—$1.50)

☐ **PERILOUS DREAMS by Andre Norton.** The Norton-of-the-year book for DAW . . . an original of four dream worlds which were also real! (#UY1237—$1.25)

☐ **BROTHERS OF EARTH by C. J. Cherryh.** A brilliant sf novel of the clash of two cultures; selected by the Science Fiction Book Club. (#UW1257—$1.50)

☐ **THE BOOK OF FRITZ LEIBER by Fritz Leiber.** Introducing this Hugo-winning favorite with his own special selection. Back in print in a new edition. (#UY1269—$1.25)

☐ **THE SECOND BOOK OF FRITZ LEIBER by Fritz Leiber.** Winner of the August Derleth Award of the year for best short story collection. (#UY1195—$1.25)

DAW BOOKS are represented by the publishers of Signet and Mentor Books, **THE NEW AMERICAN LIBRARY, INC.**

THE NEW AMERICAN LIBRARY, INC.,
P.O. Box 999, Bergenfield, New Jersey 07621

Please send me the DAW BOOKS I have checked above. I am enclosing
$_____(check or money order—no currency or C.O.D.'s).
Please include the list price plus 35¢ a copy to cover mailing costs.

Name_____

Address_____

City_____State_____Zip Code_____
Please allow at least 4 weeks for delivery

DAW sf BOOKS

Presenting the international science fiction spectrum: